WATCHERS OF THE DEAD

WATCHERS OF
THE DEAD

Simon Beaufort

This first world edition published 2019
in Great Britain and the USA by
SEVERN HOUSE PUBLISHERS LTD of
Eardley House, 4 Uxbridge Street, London W8 7SY.
Trade paperback edition first published
in Great Britain and the USA 2019 by
SEVERN HOUSE PUBLISHERS LTD.

British Library Cataloguing in Publication Data
A CIP catalogue record for this title is available from the British Library.

ISBN-13: 978-0-7278-8891-4 (cased)
ISBN-13: 978-1-78029-595-4 (trade paper)
ISBN-13: 978-1-4483-0214-7 (e-book)

Typeset by Palimpsest Book Production Ltd.,
Falkirk, Stirlingshire, Scotland.

For Dusty, Henrietta, Florrie, Sybil, Olive, and Hulda

PROLOGUE

Roderick Maclean was going to kill the Queen. He had made his decision a week or two before but had confirmed it beyond all doubt the previous night, when he had been huddled in a tiny room with no fireplace, trying to stave off the chill. He had eaten virtually nothing for two days, and had been so cold that he could barely feel his hands and feet. He could not recall ever feeling so low and miserable. And all the while, the sounds of merriment came from Windsor Castle – of laughter, and people eating and drinking in warm, companionable luxury. It was hardly an equitable state of affairs.

Nor was his current poverty appropriate for a man who enjoyed a special relationship with God. Ever since infancy, the Almighty had read his thoughts and spoken to him personally about the mysteries of the universe. Because of this divine favour, jealous people had made his life a misery. They always wore the colour blue, which was an outrage, because God had created that particular hue for *him*, and no one else. They had committed him to asylums more than once, not to mention poisoning his relationship with his family – after all, there had to be some reason why his brothers declined to keep him in the lavish style he deserved, and only sent him a few measly shillings each week.

The Queen had joined the ranks of Maclean's enemies about five years earlier. He considered himself a poet and was sure Her Majesty would be honoured to hear from her most talented subject. He had sent her an ode about her love for Prince Albert, but she had not even deigned to read it. Instead, a Lady Biddulph had written, stating that the Queen 'never accepted manuscript poetry'. It was no way to treat God's chosen!

Now Maclean would send the ungrateful Queen – the woman he referred to as 'that old lady Mrs Vic who is an accursed robber in all senses' – to her Maker.

He reached inside his coat and felt the cold, hard metal of the revolver he had purchased in Portsea the week before for 5s. 9d – money raised by selling his beloved concertina and only scarf. He could have exchanged it for food or a bed for a few nights, but he had resisted the temptation. Once Mrs Vic was dead, he would not need a flea-infested cot in some shabby hostel, because he would be famous. Newspaper reporters from all over the world would want to buy his story.

Moments before, he had been happily settled in the first-class waiting room at the Great Western Railway Station, writing a letter to explain why he had killed the Queen. But the stationmaster had taken one look at his threadbare coat and grimy bowler hat and asked him to leave. Maclean ground his teeth in impotent anger at the insult.

He eased through the waiting crowd of people eager for a glimpse of the short, portly widow, monarch of the greatest empire that had ever existed. He stationed himself near a gateway that the royal cavalcade would have to pass through en route to the castle and looked around. Nearby were several photographers, one of whom might even catch the assassination with a camera. In his mind's eye, Maclean saw himself posing with the Queen's dead body, like the great hunters did in Africa when they felled a lion.

A hiss of steam and the squeal of wheels on rails signalled the arrival of the train. There was an anticipatory murmur from the crowd, and Maclean scowled at two Eton boys who jostled him as they pushed by. They regarded him haughtily, tall hats tipped back on their heads. He could tell they considered him beneath their contempt, and decided in that instant that they would die, too. Their kind – arrogant and entitled – brought nothing good to the world, and the country would be better off without them.

For several long minutes, nothing happened, and Maclean began to wonder if Mrs Vic had nodded off inside her carriage, and everyone would have to wait for hours until she stirred. He began to shiver – his thin coat was no protection against a bitter March evening, and he missed his scarf sorely.

Then came a bray of important voices. Princess Beatrice, the Queen's youngest daughter, alighted from the train and crossed the platform. Courtiers flowed at her heels, and there was a flurry of activity as the waiting carriages were readied. A door was opened and steps pulled out. Relaxed and confident, Beatrice turned to chat to the woman walking behind her – the Duchess of Roxburghe, Mistress of the Robes.

The two were joined by the Queen's Equerry, Colonel Sir John McNeill, and his friend, Colonel Sir Algernon Fleetwood-Pelham, one of Her Majesty's Grooms-in-Waiting, known for being something of a gossip. Maclean gripped the pistol harder. All four were intimates of Mrs Vic and might even have encouraged her to reject his beautiful poem. After the Queen and the Eton boys, they would pay the price. He had bullets enough for all of them.

Even as he imagined the shock on their haughty faces when he opened fire, the Queen waddled out. She was smiling, something she rarely did in public. Maclean knew she was taunting him, gloating because she was wearing a *blue* sash, the colour God had reserved for *him*. Rage surged inside him. She was handed into the carriage, and the cavalcade began to move, grey ponies straining at their traces. Maclean hauled out his gun and took aim.

The shot rang out and people screamed. Maclean prepared to fire again. But one of the photographers – a slight, sandy-haired fellow named James Burnside – acted without thought for his own safety. He seized Maclean's wrist and twisted the revolver from his hand.

Maclean tried to squirm free, but Burnside was too strong. Then a policeman – Superintendent Hayes of the Windsor Police – surged forward and grabbed Maclean's other arm. Moments later, the two Eton boys joined the melee, striking Maclean with their umbrellas. He cried out in pain and tried to explain about God, the colour blue, and his lovely poem, but no one would listen.

Except one man, who watched thoughtfully as Maclean was dragged away by the police, sure such lunacy could come in useful one day.

Reading, Wednesday 19 April 1882

The trial was a sensation. Everyone agreed that Roderick Maclean had indeed intended to shoot the Queen, and might have succeeded if Burnside and Superintendent Hayes had not intervened. They and the Eton boys were hailed as heroes, while the miserable Maclean was denounced as the devil incarnate. The trial lasted less than a day, and the jury took only five minutes to deliver the verdict: not guilty, but insane. It meant Maclean would spend the rest of his life in Broadmoor Criminal Lunatic Asylum.

Maclean did not really understand the implications of the sentence and was just glad he was not to be hanged. He had no idea why anyone should think him mad, but if it meant escaping the noose, then so be it. He settled his bowler hat on his head, squared his shoulders, and allowed himself to be marched away.

Because of their youth and prominent families, the Eton boys were singled out for special praise, and they revelled in it. Unfortunately, it was at the expense of Burnside, who was livid. After all, it had been *he* who had prevented Maclean from firing again, whereas the boys had only weighed in once Maclean had been subdued. He began to write increasingly angry letters to the Palace, demanding recognition for his services. His photographic business was struggling, and if he could snag just one royal commission, all his troubles would be over. But the Palace declined to assist him, turning him increasingly bitter. Indeed, there were occasions when he wished he had never stayed the assassin's hand.

London, Monday 4 December 1882

'This reminds me of the last time I stood in the cold, waiting for the Queen to appear,' muttered Burnside, shivering inside his fashionable but thin coat. 'I hope she won't need saving a second time, because my hands are blocks of ice.'

He was speaking to Alexander Lonsdale, a reporter for *The Pall Mall Gazette*. They were in the crowd that had gathered outside the new Royal Courts of Justice on the Strand, a glorious edifice, almost cathedral-like in its grandeur, which had taken some eight years to complete. Her Majesty was due to open it that day, and the two men were there to record the event – Lonsdale with words, Burnside with his camera.

It was a bitter afternoon, and a wicked wind scythed down from the north. The Queen was late, and they were chilled to the bone. Both seriously considered giving up and going home.

To take his mind off his discomfort, Burnside told Lonsdale how he had saved the Queen's life. Lonsdale had heard the tale several times already, but listened politely as it was trotted out again. Wryly, he noted that the roles Superintendent Hayes and the Eton boys had played grew less significant with every telling.

'Poor Maclean,' he said when the photographer had finished. 'Hunger and privation must've driven him to lose his wits.'

Burnside spat his disdain. 'He's a violent killer, and I risked death to disarm him. Of course, I got barely a nod of thanks for my pains. I should've been appointed Royal Photographer. Indeed, I wrote to the Palace suggesting it, but they haven't bothered to answer my last three letters. Maybe Maclean was right to take a shot at the old harridan.'

Lonsdale regarded him askance. 'The last *three*? How many have you sent?'

Burnside shrugged sheepishly. 'A fair number. But this is important, Lonsdale! Credit should go where it's deserved, not to a police officer who was just doing his job, and two boys who happen to come from wealthy families. Without me, the Queen would be dead.'

'Here she is at last,' said Lonsdale in relief – it meant the end of Burnside's tirade.

The royal carriage clattered to a standstill and important men hurried towards it. Once she had alighted, the Queen did not linger in the icy wind – she aimed for the massive porch at an impressive clip, glancing up as she passed through it in acknowledgement of its grandeur. Once inside, she made a short speech and unveiled a plaque, then indicated with a regal nod that she was ready for the guided tour she had been promised. Most reporters left at that point – the building was now officially open, so what more needed to be said? And it was far too cold to stand around outside.

Lonsdale longed to go too, but his sense of duty kept him rooted to the spot – he had been charged to report the event, and leaving while it was still going on was hardly professional. Burnside stayed too – he was so down on his luck that he had no choice but to follow every event to its bitter end in the hope of getting the picture that everyone else had missed. Their breath plumed in front of them as the temperature dropped even further.

'There's Alexander Haldane,' said Burnside, nodding to an elderly gentleman who was almost running in his haste to escape the wind. 'The famous barrister.'

'He owns *The Record*, too,' said Lonsdale, watching the man in question disappear through the Royal Courts of Justice's massive front door. 'The newspaper for Evangelical Christians. The assistant editor at *The PMG* reads it. It's quite influential in certain circles.'

But Burnside did not seem very interested in newspaper politics, so Lonsdale let the subject drop. They stood together in silence, watching the busy hubbub of the traffic clattering along the Strand. It grew ever colder as the short winter day faded into dusk. Smoke from tens of thousands of chimneys belched into the air, rendering it thick and choking, especially when a mist swirled up from the river. The evening was dull and gloomy, and the elegant spires and pinnacles of the Royal Courts of Justice were soon lost to sight. Burnside mumbled something about thawing his camera lenses, and loped away, unsteady on feet that were numb with the cold. Lonsdale considered following him, but professional pride kept him in his spot. That and his old-fashioned but warm woollen greatcoat.

After an hour, Burnside returned, his face pink and glowing. Lonsdale assumed he had been in a tavern, but there was no scent of alcohol on his breath. Then it occurred to him that the photographer might be so hard up that he had no money for drink, so had settled for a brisk walk to drive out the chill instead. He was about to suggest tea in the cafe opposite – his treat – when several solicitors emerged from the courts, talking in hushed, horrified whispers. Burnside stopped one and asked what had happened.

'Roderick Maclean,' replied the lawyer, and he shook his head worriedly, although his eyes were alight with excitement. 'The police have just released the news that he escaped from Broadmoor sometime this past month. Let's hope they catch him soon, as no one's safe with him on the loose.'

'Especially me,' said Burnside importantly. '*I'm* the one who stopped him from committing regicide. He may well want an accounting with *me*. I'll be ready, though.' He looked thoughtful. 'Or perhaps I should beg sanctuary in Buckingham Palace . . .'

At that moment, there was a ragged cheer from the hardy few who had waited for the Queen. She hurried down the steps and was inside her carriage long before Burnside could ready his camera. He swore softly to himself; he might as well have gone home.

'Someone must've told her about Maclean,' said the solicitor, watching the royal coach clatter away. 'And she decided she'd rather be safe at home until he's back under lock and key.'

As Lonsdale and Burnside turned to leave, there was a commotion inside the courts. As the Queen had gone, the building was open to the public, so they went in to see what was happening.

'They've just found Mr Haldane in the basement,' explained a clerk, who was sitting on a bench in the lobby, his face pale and his body shivering with shock. 'He's been murdered.'

'Haldane?' breathed Burnside, shocked. 'But we saw him a couple of hours ago.'

'How do you know he was murdered?' asked Lonsdale.

'Because I saw the body,' whispered the clerk, shaking his head in stunned disbelief. He looked up at them slowly. 'He'd been chopped to pieces.'

ONE

London, Friday 15 December 1882

Alexander Lonsdale should have been happy. He had recently been appointed full-time reporter at *The Pall Mall Gazette*, winning the honour against some serious competitors, meaning he was financially secure. He was also engaged to an accomplished young woman who loved him. Yet he could not escape the sense that life was carrying him along at a rate of knots to a place where he did not want to be.

He was not sure why he should be discontented – most anyone else would have been delighted to be in his place. He also knew he was being ungrateful, especially as there had been times that year when he was not sure he would escape alive, let alone be in a position where everything was going so well. But he could not escape the nagging sense that all was not right.

He had confided his concerns to his brother the previous night, but should have known better than to expect understanding from Jack, a barrister who dealt in facts, not feelings. Jack had dismissed his worries, claiming all would be well once the lunatic Maclean was behind bars once more. He had refused to listen to Lonsdale's startled assurances that he was not in the slightest bit concerned about Maclean.

Lonsdale knew the reason for his brother's failings as a confidant: Jack's fiancée, Emelia, whom he was scheduled to marry the next spring, absorbed his every waking thought. Personally, Lonsdale failed to understand what Jack saw in her, and considered her dull, narrow-minded and stupid, which was unfortunate, as he himself was engaged to Emelia's sister. This put him in Emelia's company more than he liked. Luckily, Anne shared none of her sister's flaws – she was intelligent, witty, and blessed with an independent spirit, although there had been a recent and rather worrying tendency for Anne to take her sister's point of view.

He increased his pace as he walked across Kensington Gardens from his home in Cleveland Square. It was just ten o'clock; the morning was overcast, though, and he suspected it would never be fully light that day. Christmas was in exactly ten days, and there was a sense of anticipation in the air that reminded him of happy family times in Northamptonshire. Being the son of a country vicar had its advantages, and an idyllic childhood had been one of them.

That year, though, he would spend the holiday in London with his prospective in-laws, which was not something that filled him with delight. It was rather too easy to offend the Humbages, and the only member of the family he liked, other than Anne, was Lady Humbage's mother. Lady Gertrude was an elderly woman with a wicked sense of humour and an interesting past that her stuffy son-in-law forbade her to mention.

Lonsdale pushed the disquiet from his mind and turned his attention to that day's assignment: the opening of the British Museum's new Natural History branch in South Kensington. The building had been designed by Alfred Waterhouse, who bucked the architectural trend of following the Gothic style and had created a Romanesque terracotta façade reminiscent of a cathedral, with round arches and a double entrance portal. The façade boasted carvings conveying the museum's purpose – the west or 'zoological side' was adorned with living creatures; the east or 'geological side' with extinct ones.

To Lonsdale, it was an expression of the age – grand, ornate, imposing and lavish. *The Times* called it 'a true Temple to Nature', not only because of its fabulous exterior, but also because of the attention to detail on the inside. Everywhere – on staircases, walls and floors – were sculptures and paintings of the living world, every one scientifically accurate. Best yet, access to the museum was free, so everyone could marvel at its treasures. It was an honour, he thought, to be asked to report on the opening of such a magnificent institution.

He glanced around as he neared the Albert Memorial, sure he was being followed. He was, and he grimaced when he recognized the oily presence of Henry Voules. Lonsdale and Voules had been rivals for *The Pall Mall Gazette* job, although both had been thwarted when the man they aimed to replace had decided not to retire after all. Lonsdale had decided to cut his losses and was on the verge of returning to the Colonial Service – much to the relief of his family and Anne, who had never approved of his love affair with journalism, which they considered an inappropriate occupation for a gentleman – when he received some astonishing news. The owner of *The Pall Mall Gazette* did not want to lose him, so had created a new full-time post in order to keep him on.

Voules had not been so fortunate, and had been told his services were no longer required. His wealthy father had found him a job at *The Echo*, a sensational rag that never allowed facts to interfere with a good story. As Voules was not very good at sniffing out the kind of lurid tale *The Echo*'s editor liked, he had taken to tailing Lonsdale in the hope that he would lead him to one – hopefully like the plot Lonsdale had exposed earlier that year, which had shaken the whole country. Lonsdale had no expectation of repeating the performance, but Voules was an almost constant shadow at his heels anyway. He did not like it, but Voules transpired to own an unexpected talent for following people, and was all but impossible to throw off.

Lonsdale heard the clock at the Church of All Saints strike the hour as he turned down Prince's Gate. He was early, which meant there was time to slip into the ABC tea shop for something to eat. It was one of his favourite places, mostly because no one else from *The Pall Mall Gazette* seemed to know about it, so it was somewhere he could sit quietly and think. Most ABC – Aerated Bread Company – cafes were at or near railway stations, but the one off Prince's Gate was new and offered breakfast at an affordable price. As Lonsdale had left home with only a cup of tea inside him, breakfast seemed a very good idea.

The ABC tea shop was clean, warm and heavy with the aroma of freshly baked bread. There was a buzz of lively conversation, and the decor was simple but tasteful, with bright white tablecloths and pale cream walls.

Lonsdale pushed open the door, then stopped dead in his tracks, so abruptly that Voules, following close on his heels, barrelled into the back of him. Voules mumbled an insincere apology and went to inspect the cakes.

The source of Lonsdale's surprise was his colleague, Hulda Friederichs. She occupied the best table in the window and looked very much at home. He grimaced his annoyance. Was there nowhere in the city he could enjoy a quiet cup of tea without his colleagues?

Hulda smiled triumphantly when she spotted him and indicated with an imperious flick of her fingers that he was to join her. He did so warily, wondering if she was there to announce that, as the assistant editor's favourite reporter, *she* was to cover the opening of the museum. It would not be the first time she had airily poached a good assignment, leaving him with something dull instead.

'What are *you* doing here?' he asked coolly.

'Waiting for you,' she replied. 'Do you want to sit while I tell you why, or will you hear it while you loom over me like a vulture with its prey?'

If there was anything Hulda was not, it was prey, thought Lonsdale. He sat, saying a silent goodbye to his peaceful breakfast, and bracing himself to be railed at by a woman who could make even the strongest men quake in their boots.

Hulda was Prussian, although her English was perfect. It had become even more so after W.T. Stead, *The Pall Mall Gazette*'s assistant editor, had suggested she make more use of the vernacular, so as to render her speech less 'foreign'. She had originally been hired as Stead's private secretary, but he had quickly recognized her talents and had made her a reporter. Moreover, he paid her the same salary as his male reporters – a first in the publishing world.

Lonsdale admired Hulda's intelligence and doggedness, but every time he started to like her, she infuriated or alienated him with her abrasive manners. He had all but given up trying to befriend her and had settled for a steely politeness that kept her at arm's length.

'Well?' he asked, irked that she should have anticipated his movements so accurately – not only that he would arrive early, but that he would visit the ABC tea shop. She had an uncanny ability to make him feel very staid and predictable, and he did not like it at all.

'Not that table, Voules,' she called, as *The Echo* man started to settle himself next to them. 'You'll be able to hear us talking, which I'm sure wasn't your intention, honourable fellow that you are. There's a spare spot over by the wall.' She smiled sweetly as she added under her breath, 'Near the lavatories.'

Voules blushed. 'Oh, Miss Friederichs! I didn't see you there. Would you like company? I'm a lot more fun than Lonsdale, who's a surly devil at the best of times.'

'He is,' agreed Hulda. 'But I have private business with him, so you must excuse us.'

Voules inclined his head and moved away. The table by the lavatories had just been taken, so he looked around for another. His eye lit on James Burnside, the photographer, who smiled a friendly greeting and indicated the empty chair next to him. When Voules sat, Burnside immediately began to gabble.

'We *can't*,' snapped Voules after a moment of it, firmly and rather loudly. 'It's too expensive and the technicalities are insurmountable.'

His response meant that Lonsdale knew exactly what Burnside had said, even though he had been unable to hear. Burnside was trying – yet again – to persuade a reporter that illustrating articles with photographs was the way of the future. Unfortunately for Burnside, most newspapers were unwilling to take the plunge. It was obvious from Voules's growing exasperation that it was not the first time Burnside had raised the subject with him.

Lonsdale watched the two men for a moment – one desperate enough to persist, even though it was obvious he was flogging a dead horse; the other more interested in reading the menu. Then he turned back to Hulda, noting that she had dressed unusually smartly that day, although her fair hair was scraped into a particularly austere bun. It boded ill for him – her assignment that week was overseeing the section of the paper called 'Occasional Notes', which entailed sitting at a desk and culling information from the morning papers. There should have been no need for her to make such an effort with her clothes, so he knew he should be suspicious of it.

'Stead learned something last night,' she said, leaning across the table and regarding Lonsdale with the intense blue stare he had come to know so well. 'The Natural History Museum has a great surprise for its visitors today.'

'A fabulous building designed by a talented architect who's done the nation proud?' he asked. 'I'll be less surprised than most – I was given a tour of it last week, by someone who works there.'

'Were you?' asked Hulda resentfully. 'You didn't tell me. I'd have joined you – to see the place before the hordes start screeching through it.'

'You weren't invited,' retorted Lonsdale, and winced. What was it about Hulda that brought out the worst in him? He was not naturally boorish, but there was something about her assumption that she should be informed about and included in everything that he found profoundly annoying.

She glared at him. 'But I would have been, had you thought to include me.'

'The offer was for me alone,' said Lonsdale, then struggled to sound less combative. 'It was a condition for my friend agreeing to it. He didn't want to let me in, because he's so busy with the opening, and it wasn't easy to persuade him to spare me an hour.'

Hulda continued to glare. 'And who is this "friend", exactly?'

'A man I met when I was the assistant to the Governor of the Gold Coast,' explained Lonsdale. 'His name's Tim Roth, and we spent two months together, conducting surveys of the southern reaches of the Black Volta River. He compiled some impressive zoological data, but the journey ruined his health, so now he's rather . . .'

He faltered, suspecting Hulda would not appreciate being informed that her bombastic presence might be too much for the now-fragile Tim Roth. There had been times towards the end of their survey when Lonsdale had thought Roth might die, although he had been robust enough at the outset. Roth had survived, but it had taken months for him to recover even a shred of his former vigour, forcing him to return to London. Six years later, Lonsdale also had left Africa, when he became disenchanted with the policies and actions of the British administrators in the Cape Colony and the Transvaal.

'So he's a sensitive soul,' mused Hulda thoughtfully. 'Don't worry – I'll treat him with goat gloves. When will we meet him?'

'Kid gloves,' corrected Lonsdale. 'And we won't meet him. We can't distract him from his duties today of all days – he'll be too busy.'

'But he might be able to give us inside information on the cannibals,' objected Hulda. 'And that's why I'm here.'

Lonsdale blinked his puzzlement. 'Cannibals?'

Hulda smiled superiorly. 'Real ones, brought from the interior of the Congo. They'll be on display in the Empire and Africa exhibition, and are sure to draw the crowds.'

Lonsdale frowned. 'Tim never mentioned cannibals, real or otherwise. Are you sure?'

Hulda smiled again. 'It's been a closely guarded secret, so as to maximize the impact. It'll create a sensation and attract even more visitors. So, your frail friend didn't confide in you, eh? Perhaps he doesn't hold you in as high regard as you believe.'

'Or he was sworn to secrecy and he's a man of his word,' Lonsdale flashed back. It was true that he and Roth had drifted apart since Roth had left Africa eight years before, but he was sure his old friend would never mislead him without good reason.

'You should've taken me on this tour, because *I* wouldn't have let him leave out the interesting bits,' declared Hulda. 'Besides, I've a particular interest in dinosaurs, and would've got a lot more out of a preview than you.'

Dinosaurs, thought Lonsdale sourly: dangerous reptiles that ate each other and fought all the time. Of course Hulda would like them! He made an effort to be pleasant. 'When I was in West Africa, I found a dinosaur claw. It's at home.'

'Then you should be ashamed of yourself,' scolded Hulda. 'First, much information is lost when fools take things from their original locations; and second, that claw should be in a museum, where everyone can appreciate it.'

It was Lonsdale's turn to be smug. 'I found it minutes before it would've been blown up by dynamite – it was in a mine, and had I left it there, it would've been lost for ever. Moreover, I've contacted the museum's director with a view to handing it over.'

'You mean Richard Owen, the fossil man?' asked Hulda keenly. 'I should like to meet him! I admire his work greatly. Of course, he's wrong to dismiss the theory of evolution. I'm sure God *didn't* put dinosaurs in the Garden of Eden, as that would have rendered it somewhat precarious for the other inhabitants.'

'Right,' said Lonsdale, not about to debate such a contentious subject in public – the tea room was crowded, and people were sensitive about matters touching on religion. 'I'll take the claw to him next week.'

'Then I'll go with you,' determined Hulda. 'I'll explain evolution in a way that will make it impossible for him to remain a creationist.'

'I see,' said Lonsdale, deciding to do whatever was necessary to keep them apart. 'But to return to the cannibals . . .'

'Stead sent me to find out exactly what the museum has in mind for them,' she explained. 'He hates the notion of "human zoos".'

It was not unusual for museums to use real native peoples in their exhibitions and, while Lonsdale appreciated that they added an air of authenticity, he also deplored taking folk from all that was comfortable and familiar to put them on show.

'Stead wants us to gather information about these cannibals,' Hulda went on, 'so he can write something that will prevent them from being paraded about like circus beasts. Other papers will trumpet about the sensation these cannibals create, but *The PMG* will take a more ethical stance.'

Stead was a great crusader for the downtrodden, and his sense of social justice was one of the things Lonsdale loved about *The Pall Mall Gazette* – that the paper often exposed social evils.

When the waitress appeared, he and Hulda each ordered tea and toast, and while they waited for it to arrive, Lonsdale wondered why Roth had not mentioned the cannibals. *Had* he been ordered to keep quiet, lest the press spoil the surprise? Or was it because Roth knew he would disapprove and might use *The PMG* to prevent it? Or was Roth in the dark, too? Cannibals *would* cause a sensation, and it was a clever way to attract more visitors, although the museum should not need such measures just yet, given the publicity surrounding its opening.

Their breakfast arrived, and Hulda regaled him with office news – editor John Morley was immersed in Irish affairs, as always; Stead was in trouble with his wife for ruining three good suits while investigating the lives of poultry farmers; and their fellow reporter Alfred Milner continued to help both develop their ideas dialectically, by playing devil's advocate over style, method and principle.

Then it was time to go.

'I'll speak to Tim,' said Lonsdale, beginning to rise, and aware of Voules doing the same. 'Thank you for letting me know.'

'Oh, no,' said Hulda, grabbing her coat. 'You're not getting rid of me that easily! I'm coming with you, and we'll assess these cannibals together.' Her eyes glinted mischievously. 'Besides, you may need me to protect you from them.'

The museum dominated Cromwell Road. For years, it had been nothing but a building site, swathed in scaffolding and tarpaulins. Now it could be seen in all its glory. No expense had been spared, and it was as impressive as any building in the Empire.

Inside was a great hall with a roof that allowed natural light to flood in. It boasted wide, sweeping stairways, and a space that Roth had said was large enough to hold the complete skeleton of a great whale. No whale was in evidence yet, although Roth thought it was only a matter of time before one was lifted into place. Off the main hall were more galleries, each remarkable in its own right.

Lonsdale waited while Hulda gazed around in wonder. He had seen it before, and secretly thought it had been more impressive when it had been empty. The noise that day was deafening, as adults clamoured their amazement, children squealed and shrieked, and shoes and boots clattered on the stone floors.

The Empire and Africa exhibition was on the ground floor, in one of the larger halls. As Lonsdale and Hulda headed towards it, they detected an air of excitement that was almost tangible. There was even an exotic scent, and they saw that small bowls of smouldering leaves had been placed along the passage. The effect was designed to make the visitor feel he really was travelling through a distant rainforest. The walls were hung with branches, and large plants stood in pots, lending the passage the aspect of a jungle. Lonsdale smiled – it was cleverly done.

The first gallery held maps and diagrams illustrating the development of knowledge about those parts of Africa under the sway of the British Empire. It had smaller sections on the areas under French, German and Portuguese control, as well as on independent regions such as Ethiopia and the Congo. Public interest in the Congo was increasing, as for several years the famed explorer Henry Morton Stanley, under the auspices of a Belgian organization, had been establishing treaties with local chiefs and setting up trading and scientific stations.

Beyond this was the explorers' section, which had photographs of the most famous travellers, missionaries, traders and hunters, as well as souvenirs of their journeys. Pride of place was held by Mungo Park's last journal, next to Livingstone's teaspoons and a slaver's whip that had once been exhibited in the House of Commons.

The lights in the next gallery were dimmed, so it was lit only by discreetly placed lamps behind tall foliage. In the middle was a mock explorers' camp set in the depths of what was called an 'African primeval forest'. On the columns were carved antelopes, buffaloes, warthogs, a rhinoceros, and other African mammals, and in the 'jungle' outside the camp were a stuffed baboon, four hippopotamus skins and an elephant skull.

The next gallery boasted tools, weapons, clothes and other

accoutrements from villages inhabited by cannibals. They included a selection of cooking pots and a fearsome array of knives, the purposes of which were illustrated by a series of graphic drawings. Hulda grimaced in distaste, although Lonsdale thought they owed more to the imagination of the artist than the truth. He had seen knives similar to the ones on display during his own travels on the Dark Continent but had never observed them used for preparing other humans for the pot.

The last room was dark and had a dais in the centre. It was scattered with leaves, and a statue of a lion stood in its middle. There was a strong smell of paint, and when Lonsdale reached out a surreptitious hand, he felt the statue sticky under his fingers.

'So where are the cannibals?' demanded Hulda, looking around with her hands on her hips. 'Clearly, the stage is for them, so where are they?'

'Perhaps they're being saved for later,' suggested Lonsdale. 'Or perhaps the curators decided that all these whooping and screeching visitors would frighten them, so they put the lion here instead.'

Hulda wrinkled her nose. 'I rather think that anyone brave enough to eat human flesh will be able to cope with a little noise and fluster.'

'Not necessarily,' countered Lonsdale. 'Some tribes do it as part of a grieving process – an act of compassion for the dead person's spirit. It's not all about victory over enemies.'

Hulda regarded him narrowly. 'You seem to know a lot about it, given that you had no idea cannibals would be here until I told you.'

'Tim and I came across it when we were on the Black Volta,' explained Lonsdale.

And they had been surprised to do so, because the resident Ashanti had sworn to abandon the practice in the Treaty of Fomena in 1874. Lonsdale had quickly learned that the issue was far from black and white, and that Western invaders – himself included – understood but a fraction of the cultural issues involved.

Hulda raised her eyebrows. 'You and Roth had an eventful time, it seems. But perhaps you're right, and the cannibals will appear after the initial frenzy. What time's the official opening ceremony?'

'There won't be one,' said Lonsdale. 'Owen decided just to open the doors and let people in. And why not? Opening ceremonies tend to be for the favoured few, but he wants his museum to be for everyone.'

'You sound like a follower of the Paris Commune! Personally, I like a little pomp and splendour. It must be the Prussian in me. Or do you think the Queen was asked but refused, lest someone shoot at her again. They still haven't caught Maclean, you know, even though the whole country's looking for him.' She glanced around quickly. 'Perhaps he's here.'

'Yes, if I were on the run, I'd certainly make time to visit a museum,' remarked Lonsdale caustically.

'A crowd is a good place to hide,' argued Hulda. 'Indeed, I can't even see your shadow Voules, although I doubt he's far away.'

'But Maclean's picture is on every street corner in the country,' pressed Lonsdale. 'It would be asking to be caught.'

'So where will your friend be?' asked Hulda, changing the subject because she had no rejoinder; it was something she did a lot, and was a habit Lonsdale found acutely annoying. 'We won't learn anything good out here, with the public. We need to go behind the scenes.'

'I'll ask if he can spare us a moment,' said Lonsdale. 'But please be discreet. We don't want anyone to think *he* spilled the beans if the cannibal exhibition was a secret.'

Hulda nodded assent. 'Send for him then. Tell him we'll be among the dinosaurs, which will be a lot more interesting than a painted lion and an empty stage.'

Lonsdale found a museum guard and asked him to deliver a message.

'Yes, I know Mr Roth,' said the guard. 'He's Professor Dickerson's assistant. I'll bring him to you at once.'

The dinosaur exhibition was even more popular than the Empire and Africa and was filled with whooping children and their parents. Its most precious items were the life-sized sculptures that palaeontologist Richard Owen had commissioned for the Great Exhibition some thirty years earlier. One was a very robust Iguanodon, which Hulda whispered was a mistake – Owen's colleagues had since worked out that the animal was far more gracile, although Owen stubbornly refused to agree.

'There he is!' she whispered in excitement, pointing to where a small, white-haired, baggy-eyed man was holding forth to a group that hung on his every word. 'Shall we go and hear what he has to say?'

Richard Owen had led the British Museum's Natural History Department for a quarter of a century, so it was no surprise when he had been appointed director of the new facility. He was a naturalist with an astonishing talent for interpreting fossils, and the museum's existence owed much to his campaign for his specimens to have a home of their own. He was, however, deeply unpopular with both his staff and his scientific contemporaries, who considered him spiteful, malicious, devious, arrogant and a plagiarist.

'Best not,' said Lonsdale, aware that some of the audience were courtiers and politicians – important people who would resent being joined by mere reporters.

Remarkably, Hulda did not argue, and only turned back to studying the Iguanodon. Lonsdale sought out the fiercer species and tried to deduce which one might have owned the claw he had at home. While he was staring at a Megalosaurus, he became aware of the familiar scent of old sweat and tobacco. He stifled a sigh.

'What do you want, Voules?' he asked without turning around. 'My opinion about whether Megalosaurus walked on two legs or four?'

'Oh, it was bipedal, without a doubt,' said Voules promptly. 'The discovery of Eustreptospondylus in Oxfordshire ten years ago resolved that issue, and Owen's interpretation of Megalosaurus is quite wrong.'

Lonsdale blinked his surprise that the slovenly, unintelligent Voules should have provided such an erudite response. 'How do you know?'

'I like dinosaurs,' shrugged Voules. 'They're fascinating creatures. But never mind that. Why are you loitering here? To see if Owen will deign to give you a quote for that rag *The Pall Mall Gazette*?'

Lonsdale blinked again, wondering how anyone who worked for *The Echo* could dare refer to the infinitely superior *Pall Mall Gazette* as 'a rag'.

'Was it you who wrote about Maclean's escape from Broadmoor?' he asked, recalling that *The Echo* had carried a particularly sensational account of the incident, along with the claim that no man, woman or child would be safe as long as the lunatic was at large, and that all slight, dark-haired men wearing bowler hats should be objects of suspicion.

'It was,' replied Voules proudly. 'My editor was pleased with it, although he added the bit about Maclean killing three guards before he jumped over the prison wall like an acrobat. It wasn't true, but he thought it added spice to the tale.'

'You didn't suggest he refrain from lying to his readers?' asked Lonsdale, amazed that any paper would knowingly print falsehoods.

Voules shrugged. 'Yes, but he said the article was more interesting with it in. He was right. Our account was much more exciting than the ones in other papers.'

'Because it was a pack of lies,' argued Lonsdale. 'No one was killed when Maclean vanished. Nor did he steal a gun from the medical superintendent, or leave a letter vowing to dispatch the Queen at the first opportunity.'

Voules grinned. 'Perhaps not, but it allowed me to use some lovely adjectives – terror, fear, frenzy, lunatic, murderer.'

'Those are nouns,' said Lonsdale, then supposed such niceties would not matter to a man who thought newspapers were to titillate, rather than educate.

Voules's small, pig-like eyes drifted across the gallery and the people who clustered and jostled around the exhibits. 'I see Miss Friederichs likes dinosaurs too.'

'She's waiting for Owen,' lied Lonsdale, aiming to have Voules out of the way before Roth arrived. 'He's promised her an audience in the insect gallery. He says they'll be able to talk privately there because it's quieter.'

Voules nodded briefly and moved away. Lonsdale watched him pretend to browse for a few moments, then aim for the door. He followed and was rewarded with the sight of the reporter scuttling towards the insects, clearly aiming to find himself a good place to eavesdrop. The man was so predictable!

Lonsdale returned to the Megalosaurus, where he saw someone else he knew. Burnside was struggling to take photographs of the fossil while, all around him, London's delighted public elbowed, pushed and cooed.

'This is like a foretaste of hell,' he muttered, grimacing when he pulled the cord on his camera just as a portly woman crossed in front of it. 'They should've let me come in early and take pictures when the place was empty. I asked, but they refused, even after I told them I was the man who saved the Queen.'

'What will you do with your pictures?' asked Lonsdale politely. 'Who'll buy them?'

'Newspapers would, if they had any vision,' replied Burnside gloomily. 'But they don't, so I'll sell them to folk in the provinces who can't come to see the real thing. There *is* a market for them, although it's distressingly small.'

Lonsdale left him to his work.

Not long after, the guard returned to report that Roth would join them shortly. Unfortunately, 'shortly' transpired to be more than an hour, at which point Hulda's temper was barely under control and Voules had come back to find out why she and Owen had not appeared in the insect section. Then Roth arrived, his fair hair in disarray and his thin cheeks flushed. He hurried forward to grasp Lonsdale's hand in an apologetic greeting. His grip was feeble and his hands were cold.

'Forgive me,' he murmured. 'Today wasn't a good time to visit. The doors opened before the mammal hall was ready, and I was still labelling the specimens when the first visitors poured in. I had to lock the cases and hope no one notices that half the labels are missing.'

'Then it's just as well entry's free,' remarked Hulda, 'or I'd want my money back. Such laxness is unforgivable.'

'May I present my colleague, Hulda Friederichs,' said Lonsdale. 'Don't look alarmed, Tim. She's jesting with you.'

'Oh,' said Roth, regarding her uneasily. 'I see. Very droll.'

'We understand you plan to display some cannibals today,' said Hulda before Lonsdale could introduce the subject in a more diplomatic manner. 'Is that true?'

Roth gaped at her. 'How did you . . . But that's a closely guarded secret!'

'We're the press,' said Hulda grandly, as Lonsdale eased her and Roth into a place where Voules would be less likely to hear what was being said. 'Nothing stays hidden from us for long. So what's your answer, Mr Roth? Is it true or not?'

Roth swallowed hard. 'No. That is to say, it *was* true, but now it's not.'

Hulda frowned. 'I don't follow.'

Roth looked uncomfortable. 'There *was* a plan to include some

real tribesmen in our Empire and Africa exhibit, but it's been abandoned for now, because they're not here.'

'Not here?' echoed Hulda, eyes narrowed. 'What do you mean?
That they've escaped?'

Lonsdale heard a sharp intake of breath, and saw that Voules had
oozed within earshot. Scowling, he shoved Hulda and Roth further
behind a case holding a reconstructed Compsognathus, and blocked
Voules from approaching again with the bulk of his own body,
heartily wishing the man would leave him alone and find his own
stories.

'Of course not,' retorted Roth coolly. '"Escaped" means they
were held against their will, but I can assure you that they were
here voluntarily, as paid employees of the museum. We had them
down in the basement, where it's nice and warm, but they . . .
left.'

'So, you've allowed a group of human-flesh-eating killers to
roam London?' demanded Hulda. 'What happens if they get
hungry?'

'They'll visit a chophouse,' replied Roth shortly. 'They aren't
savages, you know.'

'And what happens when they learn human meat isn't on the
menu?' pressed Hulda.

'They wouldn't touch it if it were,' answered Roth tartly. 'They'd
never eat anyone they'd never met in life – they'd consider it
unconscionably rude.'

Lonsdale glanced at Hulda. 'Now *he's* toying with *you*.'

'Very funny,' said Hulda sourly. 'But if you're not concerned
about Londoners' safety, then what about the cannibals themselves?
How will they fare in our winter weather?'

'They'll don hats and coats, just like you or I would. They've
been here since the end of summer, adjusting to the climate and
allowing us to show them our country. The plan was for them to
remain here until the new year, then take passage home.'

Hulda's eyes narrowed. 'Even if they're here willingly, you're
still running a human zoo – parading people around as though
they're exotic animals, to be cooed and poked at.'

'Not poked at!' Roth sounded shocked. 'And probably not cooed
at either. These are proud people, Miss Friederichs – they won't
stand for insults. Besides, you make it sound as though we kidnapped

them. They came of their own free will, and no one forced them to do anything. They're well paid for their services, and will return home wealthy.'

'So why did they run away then?' asked Hulda.

Roth winced. 'We don't know. They were looking forward to being the centre of attention, and I expected them to be back by this morning. But they've failed to appear.'

'You speak as though you know them well,' probed Lonsdale. 'Have you been involved in their care?'

Roth nodded. 'With Professor Dickerson, our chief zoological collector – he's my supervisor. He and I share two great interests – the comparative taxonomy of apes, and ethnography.'

'Ethnography?' probed Hulda.

'The study of different ethnic groups.' Roth smiled. 'That's why he and I were given permission to hire three native people for the Empire and Africa exhibit.'

'So who are these native people?' probed Hulda. 'Where do they hail from, exactly?'

'They're Kumu, from deep inside the Congo.'

'You say these Kumu have been here since the end of summer, and you've been showing them our country,' said Hulda. 'I assume you've taught them English? In other words, if they're lost, they can ask for directions. Yes?'

'They aren't what you'd call fluent, no,' hedged Roth.

'Then how do *you* communicate with them? Or do you speak Kumu?'

'Komo,' corrected Roth. 'Their language is *Komo*. And no, we don't. However, Professor Dickerson knows some Bantu dialects, so we manage with that, their smattering of English, and plenty of hand gestures. We like them very much. In fact, I thought we were friends, so it was a surprise to discover them gone.'

'You didn't mention them when I visited,' said Lonsdale. 'We went down to the basement, but they weren't there then. I would've noticed.'

'No,' acknowledged Roth. 'They vanished several days before you were here.'

'Several *days*?' echoed Hulda. 'You're telling us that cannibals have been loose in London for several *days*? How many is "several" anyway? Three? Ten? Fifty?'

'Eight,' replied Roth. 'They were gone before you came, Alec, so I saw no reason to mention them.'

'So where might they be?' asked Lonsdale. 'You must have some idea.'

'Well, I don't,' retorted Roth firmly. 'However, I suspect it won't be London. They found our city air very noxious. I imagine they've gone somewhere cleaner, perhaps by a river, where they can fish.'

'Is it possible they had second thoughts about being on display, so decided to make their own way home?' asked Lonsdale.

'Of course not,' said Roth impatiently. 'First, it's not as if there are lots of ships sailing for the Congo. And second, they *want* to do the exhibition. And they will, when they get back.'

'Could they have been abducted?' asked Hulda. 'Our assistant editor got wind of their presence here, so clearly, the "secret" isn't as well guarded as you think.'

'Clearly,' said Roth, giving her a cool look. 'But I don't believe they were taken against their will. For a start, they took their belongings – if they'd been dragged away by force, those would've been left behind. They'll turn up. We shouldn't worry—'

'Can we speak to Professor Dickerson?' interrupted Hulda. 'Perhaps he knows where to look for these hapless folk, given that you have no idea.'

'He's not here either,' said Roth shortly. 'He went to Devon, to retrieve some artefacts for the Empire and Africa exhibition. He promised to be back, but . . . well, he *is* absent-minded.'

'Maybe he and the cannibals are together,' suggested Hulda. 'Enjoying the fishing and the clean air.'

'He isn't *that* scatterbrained,' said Roth irritably. 'He knows the Kumu need to be here today, and wouldn't have kept them away. Besides, I saw him off on the train, and they weren't with him. I wish he *was* here, though – Owen is furious about their disappearance. Bringing them here was expensive, and he thought the money would've been better spent on more dinosaur statues.'

'I'm inclined to agree,' said Hulda. 'But does this mean that not everyone here thinks displaying cannibals was a good idea?'

'It does,' admitted Roth reluctantly. 'But Professor Dickerson is very persuasive, and he promised that the Kumu would be a sensation. By the way, I hope you won't put any of this in your newspaper, Alec. It would be a shocking betrayal of our friendship.'

'Of yours and his, perhaps,' said Hulda before Lonsdale could reply. 'But you and I have only just met. We don't have a friendship to betray. Of course, I might stay my pen if you let me see the basement and get me an interview with Mr Owen.'

'Done,' said Roth, extending a slender hand to seal the agreement.

The basement was a gloomy place used for storing specimens. It was kept cool to preserve them, but the Kumu had been housed near a steam boiler, in a room that was pleasantly warm. A flight of stairs led up to a tiny yard with a tree and some scrubby grass, which was both private and quiet. Roth said the staff used it for picnics in the summer, but as it was winter the Kumu had had it to themselves.

While Lonsdale and Hulda explored, Roth supplied them with more information about the tribesmen – he doggedly refused to refer to them as 'cannibals'. There were three of them – a young woman, her husband, and an older man. Roth remained adamant that all had been enjoying what they had considered to be a fine adventure. Everything had seemed rosy until he arrived one morning to find them gone.

'Bones,' said Hulda, poking some with her foot. 'Not human, I hope. Have any of your staff gone missing of late?'

'Those are from a horse,' said Roth stiffly. 'And the Kumu's last meal here was pork. It's their favourite meat, although I imagine they jest when they claim it tastes like human.'

Lonsdale was not so sure about that.

'I think I'll have fish for dinner tonight,' muttered Hulda.

'You'll keep your promise?' Roth asked her suddenly. 'Nothing of what you've learned here will appear in *The PMG*?'

'It won't,' Lonsdale assured him. 'Our assistant editor is a very ethical man, and he'd never publish anything that might result in your Kumu being put in danger – which they might be if word seeps out that cannibals are on the loose.'

'It's true – he wouldn't,' said Hulda, and glared at Roth. 'For which you should be grateful, because what you've done is irresponsible. You say the Kumu came of their own free will, but I doubt they had any real concept of what they were being asked to do.'

'You'll find they did,' countered Roth sharply. 'They aren't stupid. They leapt at the opportunity to live in London for a few weeks, especially when they learned how much we were willing to pay. Indeed, I rather think the real difficulty might come when it's time for them to go home.'

'Meaning what?' demanded Hulda.

'Meaning they like it here and will probably want to stay longer. All three are great fans of cricket, tea rooms, and Gilbert and Sullivan. We took them to see the first performance of *Iolanthe* last month, and they enjoyed it so much that we've been back to see it several times since.'

Lonsdale blinked, wondering if Roth was joking, but he could see from the earnest expression on his friend's face that he was not. Even so, cricket, tea and light opera seemed unlikely pleasures for folk who hailed from the Congo. He half listened while Hulda continued to ply Roth with questions, then began to wander through the basement on his own, looking for he knew not what.

As the museum was vast, so was the underground part of it. The Kumu had lived in the boiler room, but there were so many other nooks and crannies that he imagined it would be possible to hide there and not be discovered for weeks. It was full of cupboards, chests and cabinets, some of which were filled with curated treasures, and others that were still empty.

'This stuff was given to us by the explorer Joseph Thomson,' explained Roth, following Lonsdale into a particularly cluttered section. He spoke not so much as to provide information, as in the hope of escaping from Hulda's barrage of questions. 'He collected it from the region of Lake Tanganyika. I hope to start cataloguing it soon.'

'Why haven't you done it already?' asked Hulda. 'Isn't it scientifically important?'

'Very, and he'll be offended if he learns how little I've done so far, but opening a new museum is hard work. Besides, his collection's safe down here – it's the coldest part of the basement, so his materials are very well preserved.'

'When were you last in here?' asked Lonsdale from the darkest corner, where he crouched to inspect what he had thought was a pile of rags. His breath plumed as he spoke; it was indeed a chilly place.

'Probably not since October,' replied Roth. 'Why?'

'Because I've found a dead body,' replied Lonsdale softly, 'and I'm trying to assess how long it might have been here.'

Roth gaped at him, then inched forward to look for himself, reluctance in every step. His face was so white that Lonsdale stood to take his arm, afraid he might swoon. Hulda was made of sterner stuff, and strode forward confidently.

'It's Professor Dickerson!' cried Roth in horror.

'How can you tell?' asked Lonsdale. 'His face is under his arm.'

He did not mention that, below the arm, the head was so covered in blood that some serious rinsing would be required before any reliable identification could be made.

'I recognize his jacket,' gulped Roth unsteadily. 'That horrible old patch on the elbow, where he wore it through by leaning on his desk to write. How could this . . . why is he . . .?'

He reeled, so Lonsdale caught him and made him sit on the floor, some distance from the body. He told Hulda to fetch the police, but she lingered, wanting to hear more from Roth.

'When did you last see Dickerson?' asked Lonsdale, more to see if Roth was capable of speech than for information. He was no expert, but it was clear that the victim had been dead for days.

'When I saw him off on the Devon train,' replied Roth shakily. 'The nine twenty-five from Paddington Station.'

'Yes, but what *day*?' pressed Lonsdale.

'Last Thursday,' breathed Roth. 'Eight days ago. I remember, because I had an appointment with my doctor at eleven o'clock, and I treated myself to a bag of roasted chestnuts on the way. They were overly salted, and made me feel sick, so that my physician thought I might be in for another bout of my Black Volta trouble.'

The 'trouble' that had almost taken his life, thought Lonsdale. 'So you last saw Dickerson on the day that the Kumu went missing?'

'They didn't do this,' said Roth, seeing what he was thinking. 'They wouldn't. They liked him and he liked them.'

Lonsdale thought he would reserve judgement until he had more information – particularly information pertaining to whether any of Dickerson had been eaten.

'Presumably, you searched the basement very thoroughly when

you realized they'd gone,' he said. 'That means Dickerson must've been killed *after* the hunt was called off.'

'Not necessarily,' said Roth miserably. 'We were looking for three living souls, not a single, crumpled corpse, and I, for one, barely glanced in here. Besides, the Kumu don't use this bit, on account of it being so cold and cluttered. None of us examined it very closely.'

'And Dickerson definitely went to Devon last week?' asked Lonsdale. 'You saw the train leave with him on it?'

'I left when it was still in the station because of my appointment.' Roth swallowed hard. 'He *may* have got off – he's done it before. Owen told him to fetch these particular artefacts, but he didn't want to go – he wanted to stay here, because there was so much for him to do. He went under protest.'

'So he might've jumped off the train and returned here,' surmised Lonsdale, 'where he surprised the Kumu, who were expecting him to be away . . .' He turned to Hulda. 'Will you fetch the police, or shall I?'

'Please don't tell the authorities that the Kumu did this,' begged Roth. 'Once such a notion is in their heads, they'll see no other, and I'm certain they aren't to blame.'

'I'm afraid that's a conclusion they're likely to draw regardless of anything we tell them,' said Lonsdale soberly. 'It *is* the most obvious answer.'

'You wouldn't say that if you knew them,' said Roth wretchedly.

TWO

I t seemed an age before Hulda returned to say that a guard had been dispatched to summon the police and inform the relevant museum authorities about the grim discovery. In the interim, Lonsdale had given Roth his overcoat, afraid that shock and cold would rob his friend of what little health he had left. Hulda began to prowl, looking for clues as to what might have happened.

'Can you tell how he died?' asked Roth in a small voice, watching her.

'Not without moving the body,' she replied. 'Which we'd better not do before the police arrive. However, there's so much blood that foul play is a certainty, in my humble opinion.'

She sounded anything but humble, and Lonsdale supposed she considered herself an expert on such matters because of the murders they had solved earlier that year. She was about to add more, but there was a murmur of hushed, shocked voices, and the museum staff began to arrive, alerted by the guard before he had gone for the police. They came to stand in horrified huddles, but then a sharp voice cut through the babble of consternation.

'Don't stand in here gawping,' snapped Richard Owen; there was a burly guard at his heels to enforce his orders, should it be necessary. 'Not when our museum is crammed to the gills with visitors. Get about your duties, or I'll dismiss the lot of you. Go on, go!'

He clapped his hands, and most of the onlookers hurried away obediently. One remained, though – a man Lonsdale recognized as the talented anatomist-surgeon William Flower. Flower was widely tipped to be Owen's successor, despite the two being bitter rivals in a controversial debate about the nature of the human brain. He was a tall, patrician man, who appeared slim, elegant and refined next to the short and tatty Owen.

'It *is* Dickerson,' said Flower, crouching to inspect the body. 'His face is covered in dried blood, but I recognize his occipital bun – very distinctive. Poor Dickerson!'

'How dare he!' snarled Owen. 'Today, of all days.'

'How dare he what?' asked Flowers archly. 'Get himself killed?'

'Yes!' spat Owen. 'Now the papers will only write about his murder, rather than the opening of one of the greatest institutions London has ever known. I should never have let him bring cannibals to London. The public is far more interested in my dinosaurs. *Everyone* loves dinosaurs.'

'Yes,' acknowledged Flower. 'But everyone loved Dickerson, too. He was a good man, Owen, and I'm deeply saddened to see him thus. When will the police arrive?'

'Soon,' replied Hulda, bustling forward importantly. 'I sent for them myself.'

'And who are you, pray?' demanded Owen, regarding her with eyes that were unhealthily yellow, suggesting either a fondness for drink or some liver complaint.

'Hulda Friederichs, *The Pall Mall Gazette*,' replied Hulda briskly.

'I came to learn about your cannibals, but they seem to have vanished, leaving your professor dead in the basement where they've been staying.'

'I told you – the Kumu have nothing to do with this,' objected Roth in a low, strained voice. 'They'd never hurt the professor. They're his friends.'

'Out!' ordered Owen savagely, pointing a furious finger at Hulda. He turned to the guard. 'Driscoll? See this woman off the premises. And if she writes one bad word about my museum, I'll crush her.'

'He means metaphorically,' Flower assured Hulda hastily. 'But may I add my voice to his in begging that you think very carefully before you set pen to paper? Our future depends on good publicity, and we'll flounder if Londoners think it's dangerous to come.'

'On the contrary,' said Hulda wryly, 'it's likely to attract them in even greater numbers.' She turned back to Owen. 'And for your information, sir, I *always* think very carefully before setting pen to paper. I'm a professional reporter.'

'I don't care what you are,' snarled Owen. 'I've invested years of my life in this place, and I won't see it ruined by a newspaper.' He all but spat the last word.

'And it *is* a fabulous achievement,' said Hulda placatingly. 'Especially the exhibits of extinct species. Incidentally, I thought your monograph on the Little Archaeopteryx was nothing short of genius.'

'You can stay after all,' said Owen promptly. 'You're obviously a woman with a good mind, unlike most of my staff. However, not even that'll save you from my wrath if you write anything derogatory about my museum.'

'I won't,' promised Hulda. 'We *want* it to succeed. Indeed, Lonsdale here has a claw to give you – courtesy of *The Pall Mall Gazette*.'

'The West African claw?' asked Flowers, frowning. 'I thought that was the gift of a private citizen, not a donation from a newspaper. I'm not sure we'd have accepted it, had we known.'

'Oh, we'll accept it,' said Owen hastily. 'One can never have too many claws. It—'

He turned at a commotion by the door. Lonsdale expected it to be the police, but it was two courtiers, sent downstairs by a guard who knew Owen was in the basement. Lonsdale knew both by sight, from assignments that had taken him to Buckingham Palace. One was Sir Algernon Fleetwood-Pelham, a Groom-in-Waiting, whose official duties seemed to entail running errands for the Queen and supplying her with gossip. He was a curious-looking individual, in that the top half of his skull was far larger than the lower part, so that an enormous braincase and a huge handlebar moustache topped an almost non-existent chin. Lonsdale thought he might have been wise to add a beard to the moustache, to even things out, and wondered why no one had suggested it.

The second was Chichester Parkinson-Fortescue, Baron Carlingford. A career politician, Carlingford had served as a Member of Parliament for more than a quarter of a century before being elevated to the peerage. The previous year, he had been named Lord Privy Seal, a court sinecure that paid a handsome salary in return for very little work. He was short, slight and haughty – a small bundle of arrogance and bristling pride.

'We're here about the Queen,' began Fleetwood-Pelham, although he baulked when he saw the body. 'She intends to visit the museum later today, although I don't think we'll bring her down here, not if there's a corpse . . .'

Owen regarded him sourly. 'She should've accepted my invitation to open it. Then we wouldn't have had to resort to hiring cannibals to draw the crowds, and Professor Dickerson would still be alive.'

'The Kumu didn't kill Professor Dickerson,' said Roth again, although his voice was feeble compared to Owen's feisty bellow, and no one took any notice.

'Cannibals?' queried Carlingford, shocked. 'You have cannibals here?'

'That's Dickerson?' blurted Fleetwood-Pelham at the same time. 'You must be mistaken! He was a good man – and a good friend. *He* can't be dead!'

'Well, he is,' replied Owen shortly. 'And you'd better leave, because we can't accommodate the Queen today. Tell her to try again next week.'

Carlingford gaped at him. 'We can't tell her that!'

'Poor Dickerson!' breathed Fleetwood-Pelham, still staring at the body. 'What happened to him? Is that blood?'

'Yes,' replied Owen shortly. 'Now please leave. I—'

'I appreciate your distress, Owen,' interrupted Carlingford, 'but life goes on, and the Queen won't be denied. We must sit down and find a time suitable to accommodate her.'

'Not now,' snapped Owen. 'For God's sake, man, can't you see I'm busy?'

'We'll come back,' said Fleetwood-Pelham hastily, before Carlingford could argue. 'Dickerson must be their first priority, Carlingford. The Queen will understand.'

The expression on Carlingford's face suggested that she probably wouldn't.

When the police appeared, it was with all the paraphernalia the modern constabulary used to investigate serious crime. There was medical expertise, too, and Lonsdale and Hulda exchanged murmured greetings with the pathologist, Dr Robert Bradwell. A vigorous man with a ready smile, a head of black hair, and thick mutton-chop sideburns, he had been involved in the last case Lonsdale and Hulda had explored together.

Another familiar face was Inspector George Peters. He was slightly built with a droopy moustache that made him look mournful. Despite his unassuming appearance, he possessed a keen mind that had put many a criminal behind bars.

He was with one of the most celebrated policemen in London – Superintendent Hayes, famous not only for helping to save the Queen from being assassinated, but for his abilities as a detective. He was on secondment to the Metropolitan Police, charged with hunting down the escaped Maclean. Lonsdale did not envy him the task, especially as the gutter press was making a fuss about the time it was taking. Hayes's task was rendered no easier by the Metropolitan Police's Commissioner, Edmund Henderson, who kept using him to solve other major crimes, too.

The police went about their business with smooth efficiency, and the first thing they did was clear the basement of spectators. Everyone, even Owen, was herded into the staff room, where a team of experienced officers took names, addresses and preliminary statements. They spent longer with Lonsdale and Hulda, while poor Roth was bundled away to a private room to be questioned more closely.

'He's the professor's assistant, and, so far, he's the last one to see him alive,' explained Peters, when Lonsdale expressed his concern. 'Of course, we need to speak to him at greater length than anyone else.'

'I hope you won't accuse him of anything untoward,' said Lonsdale. 'His health is poor, and I'm not sure he'd have the strength to . . . How did Dickerson die, exactly?'

'We'll have to wait for Bradwell to tell us that,' said Peters, and turned as his superior approached. 'Superintendent Hayes, this is Alexander Lonsdale, who was so helpful to us earlier this year.'

Hayes's handshake was warm and firm, giving Lonsdale the impression of confidence and strength. 'You did good work. However, I recommend you leave Dickerson's murder to us. Bradwell says the attack was frenzied, and I shouldn't like to think of you in danger.'

His tone was avuncular, and Lonsdale was under the impression that his concern was genuine. Lonsdale nodded, although he would explore the matter if he wanted, especially if Roth was a suspect. The two of them might have grown apart since they had left Africa, but he knew that Roth was a gentle man, who would never hurt a soul.

'Wait for me in the dinosaur section, Lonsdale,' ordered Peters, when Hayes had gone. 'You too, Miss Friederichs. I may have more questions for you once I've spoken with Roth.'

Lonsdale nodded agreement and, with Hulda at his side, returned to the public part of the museum. Someone was waiting by the door.

'What's going on?' demanded Voules. 'I tried to get inside, but a policeman stopped me. Have *you* done something to precipitate all these official comings and goings?'

'Yes,' replied Hulda flippantly. 'We found a new dinosaur.'

'Really?' breathed Voules, reminding Lonsdale that he always had been credulous, especially where Hulda was concerned.

She began to elaborate. 'It was much newer than the others, leading Mr Owen to conclude that they still roam the plains of Argentina. They survive by scoffing cattle.'

Voules was agog, but Lonsdale was in no mood for jokes. He left them to it, and ascended the magnificent staircase, leaning his elbows on the rail at the top, to look down on the sea of heads in the main hall.

Here and there, reporters clustered around famous visitors, some of whom he recognized. One was Francis Galton, the eminent polymath, cousin to Darwin and one of the greatest thinkers of the age. Another was Clements Markham of the Royal Geographical Society, whose undercover mission to Peru was responsible for breaking the South American monopoly on malaria-preventing cinchona plants, and who had been the driving force behind Britain's polar expeditions. Then there was Thomas Henry Huxley, known as 'Darwin's Bulldog' for his support of the theory of evolution. And finally Samuel Baker, the African explorer, opponent of the slave trade, and ruthless slaughterer of big game on four different continents.

It appeared that Lord Carlingford was unwilling to return to the Palace empty-handed – he had cornered Owen, and was clamouring at him, fists clenched at his side. Fleetwood-Pelham was trying to stop him, although with scant success. All the while, Burnside hovered, tugging on the courtiers' sleeves whenever there was a lull in the conversation.

After a while, there was a shout, followed by a concerted move to the explorers' section, where Baker was to give a lecture on the elephants he had bagged. Carlingford and Owen did not follow the herd, nor did Burnside, who continued to linger in the hope of putting his case to a member of the Royal Household. Then someone joined Lonsdale at the railing. It was the courtier with the peculiarly shaped head – Fleetwood-Pelham.

'Burnside won't leave us alone,' he said, seeing where Lonsdale was looking. 'We're afraid to leave the Palace these days, because if he catches so much as a glimpse of a courtier, he's after us like a pack of hounds.'

'Because his business is failing and he's desperate,' said Lonsdale, sympathetic to a man down on his luck – he had been in that position himself before *The Pall Mall Gazette* had given him a job.

'I know, but there's something unsavoury about performing a heroic act and then expecting to be rewarded for it,' said Fleetwood-Pelham. 'We're grateful to him, but as far as the Queen is concerned, he did no more than his patriotic duty. She expects the same of all her subjects.'

'Owen said she refused to open the museum,' said Lonsdale, glancing at Fleetwood-Pelham. Close up, the courtier had kind eyes, and Lonsdale recalled that he had been popular with his troops when he had been in the army, although less so with his fellow officers, who disliked his flapping tongue. 'Is it because Maclean's on the loose, and she's afraid he might shoot at her again?'

'Not at all – she had a prior engagement with Monsieur Grévy, the French President; as Owen refused to change the day of the opening, she had no choice but to send her regrets. She was very disappointed, which is why we're here – to arrange for her to visit when Grévy leaves today.'

'Has Owen agreed to it yet?'

Fleetwood-Pelham smiled. 'No, but no one denies Carly for long. He'll have his way before we leave, and Her Majesty will have her tour today.'

Lonsdale was more interested in Maclean. 'I can't imagine he'll remain free much longer, not when the whole country is looking for him.'

Fleetwood-Pelham grimaced. 'I thought he'd have been caught already, and I'm amazed he's still at large. His escape beggars belief. Broadmoor is meant to be a secure facility. I said as much to my friend Archbishop Tait, not a month ago.'

'Tait was your friend? Then may I offer my condolences? I wrote his obituary in *The PMG* the day after he died.'

He did not add that it had been a difficult task, because the late archbishop had been a man of firm opinions, many of which had infuriated or alienated his colleagues. Lonsdale had not wanted to pen anything derogatory about a man who was not in a position to defend himself, but nor had he been willing to extol virtues that had not existed. In the end, the obituary had been what Stead had called a 'masterpiece of obfuscation'.

'He'll be missed,' said Fleetwood-Pelham sadly. 'Especially by his daughters. It's hard to lose a loved one so close to Christmas. But we've grown maudlin, so let's talk about something more pleasant. How will you spend the holidays?'

Lonsdale told him that he would be entertaining his future in-laws, which would give him a foretaste of what it would be like to be married. He experienced a lurch of the disquiet that had been dogging him ever since he had woken up – the uncomfortable sense that his life was no longer completely under his control.

'I'd have liked a wife,' confided Fleetwood-Pelham wistfully, 'but it was difficult to meet suitable ladies in the army. However, now I live in St James's Palace – all Grooms-in-Waiting have rooms there – I hope to encounter some lasses who might accept a lonely old warrior.'

Lonsdale was not sure his current position would provide better hunting grounds than the military, but Fleetwood-Pelham was rubbing his hands in happy anticipation, and Lonsdale did not like to disillusion him. Fortunately, he was spared from devising a tactful reply, because Carlingford began to yell at Owen, obliging Fleetwood-Pelham to hurry away before there was an unedifying scene.

Not long after, Bradwell emerged from the staff area. He was in a hurry, his battered medical bag under his arm, and his coattails flying behind him. Never a tidy man, he appeared even more dishevelled than usual in the bright light of the museum.

'I can't tell you more than you know already,' he said hastily, when he saw Lonsdale and Hulda. 'Which is that Professor Dickerson looks to have been dead for at least a week, although you'll appreciate that these things are never an exact science. However, there was an unused train ticket in his pocket, which suggests he never made the journey to Devon.'

'Roth said he might've jumped off before it left,' recalled Lonsdale. 'He'd done it before, apparently, and he didn't want to make the journey anyway.'

'The clothes on the body were the same as the ones he wore on Thursday, suggesting that he returned to the museum the same day,' Bradwell went on. 'Peters believes he was killed here, as it would've been difficult to lug a body inside without being seen.'

'How did he die?' asked Hulda.

'Multiple stab wounds.' Bradwell frowned. 'Surely you noticed? Neither of you are surgeons, but you still have an aptitude for anatomical matters.'

By that, thought Lonsdale wryly, he meant they did not swoon at the grisly things he did in the name of his so-called art.

'We didn't want to destroy evidence by poking about where we had no right to be,' explained Hulda virtuously. 'Can you tell us anything else?'

'Not yet,' replied Bradwell, 'because a dark basement is no place for a proper examination, so I didn't attempt one. I've asked for the body to be delivered to my domain, and I'll assess it tomorrow. You may watch if you like. Come at noon.'

'Thank you,' said Hulda, although Lonsdale could think of better things to do on a Saturday and had intended to decline. 'It will be our pleasure.'

Bradwell lowered his voice. 'It seems that the professor smuggled cannibals into the city, and they killed him. A glance at the wounds told me they might well have been caused by a weapon of the kind on display in the Empire and Africa exhibition, which these cannibals use at home. Of course, that's confidential information, so don't repeat it.'

It was then that Lonsdale became aware of a shadow behind one of the exhibit cases and cursed himself for a careless fool when he saw the distinctive shape of Voules. And *The Echo* man had clearly heard every word.

Time ticked past, and it was mid-afternoon by the time Peters emerged. He was with Hayes, who nodded an absent greeting to the reporters as he passed, then went to Owen to give a personal report of his findings. In his wake were uniformed policemen and plain-clothes detectives, all murmuring to each other in low voices.

'Do you have more questions for us?' Hulda asked the inspector. 'Or may we quiz you instead, beginning with who killed Dickerson?'

'Owen says the cannibals did,' replied Peters. 'Roth says they didn't, and Flower wants to keep an open mind.'

'But what do *you* think?' pressed Hulda.

Peters rubbed his chin thoughtfully. 'I'm generally of the opinion that the simplest explanation is usually the right one. In this case, the cannibals went missing on the day the victim was last seen alive – it transpires that no museum staff saw Dickerson after Roth left him on the Devon train.'

'Roth didn't see him either, once he left Dickerson at Paddington Station,' said Lonsdale quickly. 'He was shocked to see him dead in the basement. I could tell.'

Peters inclined his head. 'He's not a suspect at this stage of the investigation – we'll pursue the cannibals first. Of course, Bradwell doesn't think any of the victim has been eaten, but we'll know for certain tomorrow. Meanwhile, let's hope no one else finds out that we have cannibals on the loose. It would put the city in a dreadful panic.'

'Unfortunately, Voules overheard someone talking,' said Lonsdale, tactfully not mentioning that it had been Bradwell. 'He works for *The Echo* and won't stay his hand. Or his pen. You saw what he wrote about Maclean's escape, and he'll incite the same panic over the Kumu.'

Peters swore softly under his breath. 'Poor Dickerson! He'd have hated all this.'

Lonsdale frowned. 'You speak as if you knew him personally.'

Peters nodded. 'I met him once at the Albemarle Club. We conversed on topics as wide-ranging as botany, sport and music. He was very knowledgeable – kind and likeable, too.'

'Tim Roth never really recovered from the sickness that nearly killed him in West Africa,' said Lonsdale. 'He told me that Dickerson was very understanding of his limitations. The professor doesn't sound like the kind of man to excite a murderous attack.'

'Especially one as ferocious as this,' agreed Peters. 'Indeed, its sheer brutality makes me want to look no further than the Kumu, for the simple reason that they're fearsome warriors. At least, that's what Owen told me.'

'I doubt he knows,' said Lonsdale. 'His areas of expertise are zoology and palaeontology, and it sounded to me as if he didn't want the Kumu here in the first place. And now his reservations are borne out.'

'Should you decide to probe this matter yourselves,' said Peters, 'please be sensible. The culprit or culprits are extremely dangerous, no matter whom they transpire to be, so take the utmost care. And if you *do* uncover anything pertinent, tell me first – *before* publishing.'

'Of course,' said Hulda, offended that he should think otherwise; then she grinned mischievously. 'What do we get in return? You sharing information with us?'

Even the lugubrious Peters was unable to suppress a smile. 'I doubt Superintendent Hayes will agree to that. What you'll get, Miss Impertinent, is me looking the other way while you interfere with a police enquiry. Isn't that enough?'

'Not really,' replied Hulda audaciously. 'Who else is on your list of suspects, besides the Kumu?'

'No one – yet. However, Mr Roth informs me that the Kumu are devoted to Gilbert and Sullivan, and there's a performance of *Iolanthe* at the Savoy this evening. Perhaps you'll go and see if you can spot them. It shouldn't be difficult.'

Lonsdale regarded him sceptically. 'You don't really think they'll be there, but you feel obliged to follow what might be a lead, so you're sending us, rather than wasting your officers' time. Am I right?'

Peters laughed. 'I'm afraid so. But if you go, I'll be spared the ordeal myself – I've never forgiven Gilbert for his parody of the police in *The Pirates of Penzance*. You'd be doing me a favour.'

'And in return?' fished Hulda.

Peters laughed again. 'You never fail to astound me! All right, in return, I'll tell you something that you absolutely can't publish yet. Do I have your word that you'll treat the information with the utmost discretion?'

They nodded, and Peters took the precaution of ensuring that no one else was within earshot, especially Voules. Only when he was sure they were alone did he speak.

'Dickerson isn't the only prominent figure to be hacked to death this month. The Archbishop of Canterbury – Archibald Tait – didn't die a natural death either.'

Lonsdale stared at him. 'But the official bulletin said he died peacefully in his bed at Addington Palace. Are you claiming he was murdered and the fact hushed up?'

'Yes, I am.'

'Who was behind the cover-up?' asked Lonsdale. 'His family? The police? The Church?'

'Not his family – they want the matter explored. Not the police either, because my colleagues from W Division were very eager to investigate. I attended the scene of the crime with them, but we'd barely finished writing our preliminary reports before we were told that a "higher authority" had "deemed the situation resolved".'

'Meaning what, exactly?' asked Hulda.

'We assumed it meant that the culprit was a churchman who objected to some of Tait's more dramatic reforms. After all, Tait did upset a lot of vicars.'

'He did,' agreed Lonsdale, recalling the thin line he had trodden between truth and defamation in the man's obituary. Tait had not been a bad man – just one with intractable views, which had resulted in the Church suffering something of a battering under his command. Many clerics were relieved the post would now be in safer hands.

'Are you saying that Tait and Dickerson were killed by the same individual?' asked Hulda. 'This rogue churchman?'

'No one told us it was a churchman – it was a conclusion we drew with no evidence, although with hindsight, I rather think that was what this "higher authority" intended. And as to whether it's the same culprit – well, that's a question only Bradwell can answer, and we'll have to wait until tomorrow to find out.'

'But you're inclined to suspect it is?' pressed Lonsdale.

Peters nodded. 'I only hope I'm not barred from seeing justice served with Dickerson, too.'

'What made you go to the scene of Tait's death?' asked Lonsdale curiously. 'He died in Surrey, well outside your area of jurisdiction.'

'Superintendent Hayes took me – Commissioner Henderson wanted his best detective involved, given the identity of the victim. We were both astonished to learn that the murder was to be quietly forgotten.'

Lonsdale eyed him thoughtfully, aware of the anger beneath the unruffled exterior. Ignoring an unlawful killing went against everything Peters believed, and telling the reporters about it was the only way he could rebel. In other words, he aimed to encourage *The PMG* to do what he had been forbidden.

'We'll find the truth,' declared Hulda, eyes gleaming at the prospect of a challenge. 'Just leave it to us.'

A brief smile of satisfaction flashed across Peters's usually impassive features. 'Thank you. However, you must promise to be careful. I have a feeling that something very dark and dangerous is in play.'

'Almost certainly,' agreed Hulda airily. 'But nothing we can't manage.'

Lonsdale hoped she was right.

The D'Oyly Carte Opera Company was based in the new Savoy Theatre, off the Victoria Embankment. It was an imposing building of red brick and Portland stone, while the interior was all Renaissance style, with gold and pale yellow plasterwork, red boxes, and dark blue seats. The first public building in the world to be lit entirely by electricity, its 1,200 incandescent lamps were powered by a 120-horsepower generator. The electricity not only meant that the stage and seating areas were much cooler than they would be using gaslight, it also allowed new innovations in the performances; the most recent was electric wands for *Iolanthe*'s fairies, which had audiences gasping in amazement.

Lonsdale hurried home to change, then met Hulda outside the theatre. He felt his jaw drop when he saw her. Gone were her neatly practical skirts and jacket, and in their place was an evening dress of silk satin trimmed with tulle. The front was cream with pink trimming around the bodice and matching panels on the skirt. Her fair hair was released from its austere bun, and formed ringlets around her face. He was sharply reminded that she was very pretty when she had a mind to let it show.

'You look nice,' she said, looking him up and down appraisingly. 'Fashionable and smart. Who would have thought it of such an unsavoury rogue?'

'The same might be said of you,' he retorted, wondering why it was that every time he found himself admiring Hulda, she nipped the fondness in the bud with her sharp tongue.

He led the way inside and looked around for someone in authority. Eventually, he saw a young man with a massive moustache, who transpired to be George Edwardes, the theatre's managing director. Edwardes refused to answer questions at first, claiming he was too busy, but changed his mind when Hulda batted her eyelashes at him.

'We understand that the three Africans from the Congo came here recently,' Lonsdale began, 'with staff from the new Natural History Museum.'

'Yes,' replied Edwardes, addressing Hulda. 'An elderly professor, his assistant and three charming black companions. They attended several performances. The first time, the Africans listened in silence, but during the second, they began to sing along with the chorus. We had to ask them to stop.'

'Did they mind?' asked Lonsdale.

Edwardes continued to speak to Hulda. 'They were nonplussed, and clearly of the opinion that such joyous music *should* be bellowed from the stalls.'

'Describe them,' said Lonsdale.

'Two men and a woman,' Edwardes told Hulda. 'Handsome people – tall and strong, with beautiful white teeth. They were dressed plainly but fashionably and spoke no English – the elderly man interpreted for them.'

'You say they came several times?' asked Hulda.

Edwardes nodded. 'However, if you want to know more, I'll take you backstage later to meet Alice Barnett. She plays the Fairy Queen and talked to them more than anybody else here.' He winked at her. 'Your friend can stay out here and talk to the porters.'

'You're very generous,' said Hulda, 'but he's my secretary and I'll need him to take notes. Besides, an important man like you will be far too busy to waste time accompanying us. We'll make our own way backstage – with your permission.'

'Then here's a pass,' said Edwardes, handing her a card. 'But when you've finished with Alice, leave your secretary here and come to find me.' He leered meaningfully.

'It will be past my bedtime,' said Hulda smoothly. 'But perhaps I'll take you up on your offer tomorrow.'

She sashayed away, leaving him red-faced and ogling in her wake. Lonsdale trotted to keep up with her.

'Will you?' he asked. 'Come back tomorrow?'

'Don't be ridiculous, Lonsdale! Indeed, I don't want to be here tonight, so I suggest we find a chophouse, and come back when the show's over. I detest light opera, and I can't imagine what the Kumu found to enjoy in it. I've always assumed you had to be English to understand or appreciate it.'

'We promised Peters to look for the Kumu here,' Lonsdale pointed out. 'I doubt they'll appear, but if they do and we fail to raise the alarm, Peters will be disappointed in us.'

Hulda sighed. 'Very well. I suppose I can always sleep when the lights go down.'

Iolanthe was good-natured fun; although Hulda was bored, Lonsdale enjoyed it. Halfway through, he remembered that he had promised to take Anne to see it, but he had been too busy to set a date. He hoped she would never find out he had gone with Hulda instead, sure it would lead to ructions.

As he stood at the end of the final act, he felt he was being watched. He assumed it was Voules again, but then saw Emelia Humbage standing on the opposite side of the theatre, staring at him. Her parents were with her but, more to the point, so was Anne. She nudged Anne and whispered in her ear. Anne turned and her eyes met Lonsdale's.

He smiled and waved, mouthing 'work' but, even from that distance, he could see her looking rather hard at Hulda, who was facing the other way – in her evening dress, he was not surprised that Anne did not recognize her. Aiming to nip any misunderstanding in the bud, he abandoned Hulda to fend for herself and began to make his way to the foyer, but his side of the theatre was more crowded than Anne's, and by the time he reached it, she had gone.

'Are you looking for my daughter?' came a cool voice, and Lonsdale's heart sank when he recognized the haughty tones of Sir Gervais Humbage, his prospective father-in-law.

Humbage was a retired brigadier, and everything about him suggested he was used to being obeyed. He was pompous, narrow-minded and patriarchal, and was one of the reasons Lonsdale sometimes wondered if marrying Anne was a good idea. Humbage was clearly of the opinion that Lonsdale was not good enough for her and deplored the fact that he had given up a respectable career in the Colonial Service to follow the insalubrious profession of journalism.

'Yes – to tell her why I'm here,' explained Lonsdale politely. 'I'm working on a—'

'I don't want to hear it, and nor will she,' interrupted Humbage curtly. 'You promised to bring *her* to see this opera, but instead you come with another woman. She deserves better.'

Lonsdale bristled that Humbage should dare berate him. 'It wasn't a—'

'Lord Carlingford wouldn't countenance such behaviour,' interrupted Humbage sternly. '*He* has lofty standards, and I mean to emulate them. He's a great man, and a *very* good friend.'

Lonsdale stifled a sigh. Humbage had recently been introduced to one or two courtiers, and now claimed them as intimates, although they were no more than casual acquaintances. And Lonsdale was sure the brusque Carlingford would have scant time for such an ambitious social climber.

'I met Carlingford at the Natural History Museum today,' he said, more to change the subject than to win Humbage's approbation. 'He was there to arrange a royal visit.'

'And I suppose *you* were reporting,' said Humbage, managing to inject such scorn into the last word that Lonsdale bristled anew. 'Did you attempt to interview him? I can't see him having time to chat to the press.'

'We talked at length,' lied Lonsdale, sure Humbage would never know the truth. 'Although not as long as I talked to Fleetwood-Pelham.'

Humbage sniffed. 'Sir Algernon will natter to anyone – he's a dreadful rumour-monger. He never married, of course – it's a pity Anne is promised to you, because he's a much better catch.'

'He's also old enough to be her father.'

'All women need the guidance of older men,' declared Humbage. 'Indeed, it should be made law, and then we wouldn't have callow youths demanding the hands of our impressionable daughters and tainting them with inappropriate opinions. Indeed, Lord Carlingford said as much to me only last week, in the Athenaeum, where he invited me to dine.'

He began to brag about the occasion and held forth for several minutes before Lonsdale realized it had not been a cosy tête-à-tête, but an event with some sixty guests, at which Humbage had been a good distance from the host.

'Originally, I was seated next to a wealthy merchant from Birmingham,' Humbage hissed. 'That terrible place, which is a blot on England's green and pleasant land. But Sir Algernon saw my dismay and placed me betwixt two courtiers from St James's Palace. I'd have left if I'd been obliged to endure the merchant. He had an accent.'

He shuddered fastidiously, and Lonsdale felt his dislike of the man intensify. He made his excuses before they could quarrel and went to find Hulda.

'Pompous ass,' he muttered as he walked, wondering whether it would be Humbage or Emelia who would contrive to see him in the most trouble with Anne. Both would like nothing more than to see her marry someone else, and although Anne was strong-minded and intelligent, he knew she was finding it hard to ignore the two-pronged campaign to discredit him. He only hoped she would hold out until their wedding day, after which the Humbages would be stuck with him, whether they liked it or not.

Alice Barnett was the D'Oyley Carte's most popular performer. She was a portly contralto, who delighted audiences with her stout Fairy Queen, and it was said that Gilbert had written the role especially for her. When Lonsdale and Hulda reached her dressing room, she was busily removing the thick face-paints that transformed her from a plump, motherly woman into a rosy-cheeked sprite. The room was cluttered and not very clean; somewhere nearby, two men were arguing furiously.

'Mr Gilbert and Mr Sullivan,' explained Alice. 'They don't like each other very much, and it's astonishing that they continue to produce operettas that the nation loves.'

'*Does* the nation love them?' asked Hulda baldly. 'I thought audiences have been falling.'

Alice's smile was strained. '*Iolanthe* isn't their best work, but they're already working on another. *Princess Ida* will satirize women's education and the theories of Mr Charles Darwin.'

Hulda's expression hardened. 'What is wrong with women's education?'

Alice shrugged. 'Nothing, I suppose, if you've time for it. Personally, I think everyone would be better off learning about music. After all, angels sing – they don't sit around reading Greek plays or doing Latin declensions.'

'We wondered if you would tell us about the Kumu,' said Lonsdale, before she and Hulda could argue – it would be a pity if they lost important information because Hulda had a progressive attitude to women's education, and Alice was still in the land of the fairies.

Alice frowned. 'The what?'

'The foreign visitors who so loved your performances. Mr Edwardes said they wanted to sing along with the chorus.'

Alice smiled. 'Oh, them! They're Kumu, are they? I thought they were African.'

'They're cannibals,' put in Hulda mischievously.

'They're not,' countered Alice with conviction. 'When they came once, I ordered in some beef sandwiches, but they refused to eat them. They'd have gobbled them down if they'd been cannibals, wouldn't they?'

'Only if they were cows,' Hulda pointed out with impeccable logic.

'They were lovely people,' Alice went on. 'Polite and gentle. They only heard the music once, but they were able to sing it back to me almost word perfect. It was remarkable. Unfortunately, they only have one volume – loud.'

'How could they be word perfect?' asked Lonsdale, puzzled. 'They speak virtually no English.'

'That is what made it so impressive,' replied Alice. 'Astonishing folk!'

'When was the last time you saw them?'

Alice considered carefully. 'Two weeks ago today. They came with that nice Professor Dickerson and his assistant Mr Roth. The two of them were very solicitous of the Africans, and I remember thinking it was a joy to see people who had a genuine liking and respect for each other. Indeed, I was rather jealous of it.'

'Why is it that you can remember the day?' asked Hulda suspiciously.

'Because the Queen was here. She wanted to meet me, so the Kumu had to wait.' Alice dropped her voice as she leaned forward conspiratorially. 'Between you and me, I had more fun with the Kumu.'

THREE

The next morning, Saturday, it was drizzling heavily – the kind of rain that might last for days – and the sky was a monotonous iron grey. Lonsdale looked out of his window to see two bedraggled sparrows on the sill. He opened it and threw them some biscuit crumbs, but they flew away without taking them.

It had been very late by the time he had returned from the Savoy. He felt muddle-headed from lack of sleep, and even a wash in cool water and a hasty shave did nothing to invigorate him. He left his bedchamber and went downstairs, hoping to find a fresh pot of tea. Or better yet, coffee, although the cook had yet to learn how to make it properly. He wondered what would happen when Jack was married, as Emelia was not a lady to endure substandard beverages first thing in the morning. And what happened in Jack's household would affect Lonsdale, as the plan was for him – and Anne once she became his wife – to continue living there.

It had been Anne's idea. She pointed out that Jack's fine,

six-storeyed house in Cleveland Square, Bayswater, was too large for one couple. Ergo, Jack and Emelia would occupy the second-floor, she and Lonsdale the third, and they would share the reception rooms below. Her plan suited everyone. Anne and Emelia had always been close and were delighted that they would have each other for company when their husbands were out, while Jack was happy to have his spare rooms used, and Lonsdale would not have to rent somewhere less convenient. It was the perfect solution, and there was only one fly in the ointment as far as Lonsdale was concerned: Emelia. Lonsdale had finally admitted to himself that he disliked her intensely, and he knew she detested him.

He pushed her from his mind as he entered the morning room. Jack was already there and looked up from *The Times* with a smile. There could be no question that they were siblings. Jack was older and heavier, but they shared the same brown hair and open, friendly faces.

'You're in trouble, my lad,' said Jack. 'I sat with Emelia's grand-mother while the family went to the Savoy Theatre last night. When they got back, there was much discussion of the fact that you'd been there, too, with a beautiful woman. Anne is hurt and bewildered – you promised to go with her.'

Lonsdale groaned. 'It might have gone unnoticed if Emelia hadn't drawn everyone's attention to me.'

Jack raised his eyebrows. 'That's no defence! And don't blame my fiancée for your shabby antics. Who was this beautiful woman anyway? Do I know her?'

'Hulda,' replied Lonsdale glumly, slumping at the table and helping himself to lukewarm tea. He noticed that the tablecloth was badly in need of a wash, while there were ancient crumbs on the carpet. He wondered how long it would be before Emelia dismissed Jack's hopeless but likeable servants and hired others.

Jack laughed his disbelief. 'Emelia would never describe Hulda as beautiful!'

'Then shame on her, because Hulda is very pretty,' flashed Lonsdale, surprised by the anger that sparked at the notion of his colleague being insulted by Emelia.

'Well, no one will believe it was her they saw, so you'd better devise a more plausible lie before you next see them.'

'It's the truth.' Lonsdale went to the mantelpiece, where he fiddled with the dinosaur claw that sat there waiting to be delivered to the Natural History Museum. 'Ask Hulda – she'll tell you.'

'I'm sure she will,' said Jack. 'She thinks a lot of you.'

Lonsdale looked sharply at him. 'What's that supposed to mean?'

Jack shrugged. 'Just that she's fonder of you than she lets on, and will certainly lie for you, should it be required. Anne knows this, so I'd leave Hulda out of it, if I were you.'

'I'll visit Anne this morning and explain,' sighed Lonsdale, feeling he did not have time for such pettiness. He had to be at the mortuary at noon, and there was work to do first at *The PMG* offices in Northumberland Street.

'Then good luck. But be warned: she won't put up with this sort of thing once you're married.'

'What sort of thing?' objected Lonsdale. 'I haven't done anything!'

'Sir George Bowyer has died,' said Jack, changing the subject. 'He was a good man. And so soon on the heels of poor Haldane, who was killed in the Royal Courts of Justice two weeks ago. They'll be missed, and my profession is the poorer without them.'

'Bowyer was a barrister?' asked Lonsdale, leaning forward to read the back of the paper Jack was holding, even though he knew it was a habit his brother found annoying.

'A very influential one – he was the foreman of the grand jury that sent Maclean to trial for trying to shoot the Queen. He was once a Member of Parliament as well, although I forget which constituency.'

'He must've been pleased when Maclean was found "not guilty, but insane" and sent to Broadmoor,' said Lonsdale, most of his attention on an article about Egyptian dervishes.

'Actually, he wasn't. He felt the verdict should have been "*guilty*, but insane". So did Haldane. They were right: Maclean *did* shoot at the Queen, so how could he be not guilty? Bowyer and Haldane were two of several barristers who wanted the law amended.'

'I suppose it doesn't make much difference in the end,' shrugged Lonsdale. 'Maclean will spend the rest of his life in an asylum, regardless. Or he would have done, if he hadn't escaped.'

Jack suddenly became aware that Lonsdale was reading his paper. He snapped it down and shoved a different one across the table. It was *The Echo*, Voules's paper, which both brothers refused to buy.

'Read this instead. The housekeeper must've sent it up by mistake, and I imagine that as we speak she's deep in *The Daily Telegraph*'s analysis of the scientific value of the Transit of Venus, which will not occur again until the year two thousand and four.'

'No, thank you,' said Lonsdale in distaste, pushing it back at him.

'You should – it contains a piece claiming that Maclean is living in one of the better gentlemen's clubs, armed with the best weapons money can buy.'

'If the club is named, it means Voules applied to join and was rejected,' said Lonsdale.

'I can't get over the news about Bowyer,' sighed Jack after a moment. 'And Haldane. Moreover, I read today that Professor Dickerson is dead, too. It's a bad season for decent, kindly men.'

'You knew Dickerson?' asked Lonsdale, surprised.

'Only by reputation.'

'I don't suppose you ever met the Archbishop of Canterbury, did you? Archibald Tait?'

Jack fixed him with a beady eye. 'I don't move in those circles, Alec. That said, old Gillespie met him at the Athenaeum last year, and found him a most contrary individual. Tait had a good, ethical mind but was rather confrontational.'

'Do you know if Tait, Bowyer, Haldane and Dickerson were acquainted?' Lonsdale asked, suddenly assailed by the sense that the deaths of four prominent men could not be a coincidence – and he knew for a fact that Dickerson, Tait and Haldane had been murdered. He decided to find out how Bowyer had died, as a matter of urgency.

'I doubt Bowyer would've associated with the Archbishop of Canterbury, Alec – he was Roman Catholic. He was the one who paid for that lovely Church of St John of Jerusalem in Great Ormond Street. I have no idea who Dickerson knew, but Haldane and Bowyer were friends.'

Lonsdale picked up *The Echo* between his thumb and forefinger. 'The housekeeper buys this? You should tell her not to waste her money.'

'She doesn't buy it – it arrives each morning *gratis*. And, to be blunt, she'd rather read it than *The Times*. She has a taste for lurid lies.'

'Voules,' said Lonsdale in understanding. 'He delivers it! He wants me to know that he has more front-page articles than me and . . .'

He trailed off when he saw the leading piece in that day's edition. It brayed that dangerous cannibals were loose in London, and that they had already claimed one victim – an elderly man at the Natural History Museum.

'A fine example of how to weave a sensational tale out of a few half-understood facts,' he spat. 'Voules never lets the truth get in the way of a good story.'

'No one will believe it,' said Jack, and laughed. 'Cannibals? Really?'

'Unfortunately,' said Lonsdale, 'that bit *is* true.'

Outside, rain had turned the elegant white facade of Jack's Cleveland Square house dismal and dirty, with soot-filled runnels cascading down its front and dripping from its eaves. Lonsdale knew that lakes of filthy water would have pooled in the streets, so he hailed a hansom to take him to work, unwilling to arrive drenched in manure-impregnated spray.

He felt sorry for the driver, who was hunched into his coat, shivering. Even more, he pitied the horse, which, head down and mane dripping, plodded along the muddy streets. The wet seemed to accentuate London's familiar racket: the roar of iron wheels on cobbles, the clatter of hooves, the distinctive chorus of street vendors selling ribbons, greasy pies and pots, the slap of human footsteps, and the dull, distant rumble of heavy industry along the river.

The PMG occupied a tall, shabby building in a short, mean-looking thoroughfare that was more passageway than street. Its neighbours comprised a disused warehouse and offices for companies that sold cheap cloth, spare coach parts and cleaning products. Lonsdale stopped for a moment to stare at his place of work.

The basement housed the thundering Marinoni printing presses. The ground floor was a distribution area, and the next floor, reached by a dark, narrow stairway, had four rooms: the editor's, the assistant editor's, one shared by the sub-editors and city editor, and one for the reporters. The second floor was the domain of the business manager, his clerk and an advertising canvasser. And the top was where the compositors set in type the stories and editorials ready for printing.

'Did you read it?' came a voice behind Lonsdale, just as he was about to walk through the door. He turned to see Voules, who looked pleased with himself.

'Please don't deliver any more free copies,' said Lonsdale coolly. 'If we want them, we'll buy them ourselves.'

'But what did you think?' pressed Voules, grinning. 'All London will be talking about it, which is more than you can say about *The Pall Mall Gazette*'s leader yesterday. Who cares about boring old Forster's views on Britain's role in Egypt? He's no longer even in the Cabinet!'

Lonsdale glared at him. '"All London" will include the Natural History Museum and the police, who'll be furious with you. Moreover, what can be gained from frightening people?'

'Increased sales,' replied Voules promptly. 'Copies are flying off the presses. You were a fool not to publish last night. People don't care about Egypt – nor Morley's fascination with Ireland. He should accept his shortcomings as an editor and leave.'

'Mr Morley is one of the most talented and well-informed men in the city,' averred Lonsdale between gritted teeth. 'He's a close friend of Gladstone, and when he does finally take the plunge into politics, he'll play a major role in government.'

Voules sneered. 'Doing something tediously worthwhile for it, I suppose. However, I hope he goes soon, because *The PMG* will fare much better under Stead, who understands that people want to be entertained. There'll be no dull political analyses when *he's* in charge.'

Lonsdale drew breath to argue further, then decided not to bother. If Voules was incapable of understanding the concept that reporters had a moral obligation to print the truth, Lonsdale was not about to waste his time trying to explain it.

'Of course, leaving *The PMG* was the best thing I ever did,' Voules went on, although the resentful cant in his eyes told Lonsdale that he was lying. '*The Echo* is lively and exciting. Better yet, I don't have to work with any stupid women.'

Lonsdale's eyes narrowed. 'There are no stupid women in our—'

'Miss Friederichs,' spat Voules, his round, flabby face full of venom. 'Stead was wrong to appoint her. She's out of her depth. He should get rid of her and reappoint me instead, although I'm not sure I'd want to work here now. I like *The Echo* too much.'

Lonsdale laughed at the notion that Voules should consider

himself better than Hulda, then became serious. 'You also wrote the article about Maclean walking around London in his famous bowler hat – I recognize your style. Was he really seen, or did you make it up?'

The answer was clear in Voules's defensive sneer. 'That information is classified,' he hissed. 'Go and find your own sources.'

He was a fine one to talk, thought Lonsdale acidly, dogging the movements of another reporter in the hope of stealing a story. 'A word of warning: check your facts before going to press. Your piece on the cannibals contained so many errors it was embarrassing.'

'What errors?' demanded Voules indignantly.

'The cannibals are from where the Lualaba becomes the River Congo, not the "River Bonga". The dead man was Professor Dickerson, not Dr Richardson. And Owen never told anyone that dinosaurs are still rampant in Argentina.'

'That's your interpretation,' said Voules haughtily. 'Mine is different.'

'Very different,' muttered Lonsdale, turning on his heel and going inside.

The reporters' domain was a scruffy, homely place that always smelled of cigarette and pipe smoke, and the nasty La Jurista cigars that Hulda favoured. Lonsdale was one of only two non-smokers on the staff, and sometimes found it difficult to breathe, particularly when the wind was in the wrong direction, causing the chimney to smoke as well.

The office had ink-stained tables and wobbly chairs and was nearly always filled with an air of quietly excited industry. There was a plate of homemade lavender biscuits on one table, as Hulda, being made of sterner stuff than Lonsdale, had opted to spend the remainder of her night baking, rather than trying to sleep.

'It allowed me to think,' she said by means of explanation.

'Think about the murders?' he asked. 'Dickerson and Tait's?'

She nodded, and indicated the tall, pale, thin young man who sat near the window. Alfred Milner was Lonsdale's closest friend, and, like Morley, would not be a pressman for long. He had won four major Oxford University scholarships, been elected to a fellowship at New College, and been called to the bar at Inner Temple, but had stunned everyone who knew him by joining the staff of *The PMG*, where his remarkable abilities had quickly earned him Morley's unreserved respect.

'I told him about them,' said Hulda. 'And he has information to share.'

Lonsdale helped himself to a biscuit and turned to Milner.

'First of all,' Milner began, 'I can tell you that Dickerson and Tait visited the Broadmoor Criminal Lunatic Asylum not long before Maclean escaped.'

Lonsdale blinked. 'Surely you aren't suggesting that their deaths are connected to him! How do you know they visited it anyway?'

'Because Mr Morley sent me there last month, and I saw their names in the visitors' book. He wanted an article about its progressive treatment of criminal lunacy.' Milner withdrew a piece of paper from his pocket. 'I made a list of everyone who signed the book in the last year. You'll see that Tait and Dickerson are on it.'

Lonsdale blinked. 'Whatever made you do such a thing? I'm sure Mr Morley didn't ask you to do that!'

'The warders kept me waiting for an age, and I did it to pass the time. I thought I might compare Broadmoor's visitor numbers to those of a real prison – do its inmates have more or less contact with the outside world than those somewhere like Millbank? It was an idle notion that I've never followed up on, but one that's paid dividends for you.'

'And you just happened to remember the Archbishop of Canterbury and Dickerson?'

Milner smiled. 'Yes, because the guards put little red crosses by the names of any interesting or important people. There weren't many, so they stuck in my mind.'

Lonsdale took the list and scanned down it. It was not very long, considering the hospital had almost two hundred inmates, and only five or six names had been marked. Other than Tait and Dickerson, there were two politicians, Superintendent Hayes and Morley.

'*Mr Morley* went there?' he asked, glancing up at Milner in surprise.

'Gladstone wanted an independent report from a man he trusted,' explained Milner. 'Mr Morley was impressed. Last month he assigned me to write a piece extolling its virtues.'

'I understand why Hayes went,' said Lonsdale. 'It houses

criminals, so the police will obviously have dealings with those. Moreover, Hayes was the officer who arrested Maclean. But why would Tait and Dickerson enter such a place?'

'The guards were unable to say. However, look at the name below Dickerson's – "Timothy Roth, professor's assistant". Perhaps he will be able to answer your questions.'

Lonsdale decided to visit Roth that day. He felt he should go anyway, if for no other reason than to ask after his friend's health following the shock of finding his supervisor's body.

'There's another name of note,' he said, scanning the list more carefully. 'Voules.'

Hulda went to the window and peered out. 'He was lurking about outside earlier, but he's gone now. Pity. We could've asked him what he was doing there.'

'I'm sure he'll reappear soon,' said Lonsdale. 'He never strays very far from my heels these days.'

'Milner told me something else about the murders, too,' Hulda went on. 'Namely that we have *four* victims, not three. Besides Tait, Dickerson and Haldane, there's another who recently lost his life in a violent manner.'

'George Bowyer?' asked Lonsdale, and raised his hands in a shrug when Milner and Hulda regarded him in surprise. 'He played a role in Maclean's trial, and his death struck me as untimely when I read about it.'

'Well, it was,' said Hulda. 'And Milner thought the same. He knows Lady Bowyer, so he went to see her early this morning. She told him that Bowyer was stabbed outside their house.'

'Moreover,' put in Milner, taking up the tale, 'Bowyer had a connection to Maclean because he was the foreman on the grand jury that sent Maclean to trial.'

'So Bowyer was on the grand jury,' summarized Hulda. 'He and Haldane aimed to change the "not guilty, but insane" law, and Dickerson and Tait visited Broadmoor when Maclean was there.'

Lonsdale became businesslike. 'So, we need to find out why Tait and Dickerson went to Broadmoor. We also have to meet Bradwell at noon, and I want to check on Roth. Not to mention cornering Voules.'

'But first, we must see Mr Morley,' said Hulda. 'He told me to bring you to him the moment you arrived, so you'd better wipe

those crumbs off your face, Lonsdale, or he'll think you've been
sitting here devouring biscuits instead of following orders.'

Hulda and Lonsdale entered the editor's office respectfully – Morley
was a formidable presence; his intellect was unnerving and he rarely
smiled. He had once claimed to like drab men best, and his serious,
sedate sobriety ran through everything he did. In appearance, he
was nondescript, but such was the force of his personality that
Lonsdale invariably felt he was waiting on royalty when he was in
his presence.

He sat behind a table, which was lit by a pair of six-paned
windows, and to his left was a fireplace. He indicated that Lonsdale
and Hulda should take the two chairs opposite him. He wore a
single-breasted, navy-blue suit with a grey waistcoat and a crisp
white shirt. For a few days, he had sported a spotted necktie, but
had evidently decided this was too frivolous, and had soon reverted
to his usual grey one.

Other than Milner, with whom Morley shared a passion for 'great
affairs' – that is, Ireland and an unwavering opposition to state
intervention in social and economic matters – Morley always made
his reporters uncomfortable. This was in part because he had a
barely concealed scorn for popular journalism and was contemptuous
of the trivia that interested the general reader. His reporters, therefore, invariably ended up pretending that they had little interest in
'common' events either. He always listened to his staff with an air
of such gravity that Voules had once remarked that it was like having
an audience with God.

'Have you heard from Cook, sir?' asked Lonsdale, referring to
a fellow reporter who had been sent to Dublin, to follow the investigation into the infamous Phoenix Park murders. The fatal stabbings
of Lord Frederick Cavendish, the Chief Secretary for Ireland, and
his permanent undersecretary had been in May, but the killers had
not been caught. Morley published regular updates on the enquiry,
even when there was nothing much to say.

'Yes – there's still no news about the culprits,' replied Morley
grimly. 'But that's not why I summoned you. I understand you were
at the Natural History Museum yesterday, where there was a murder.
Stead aims to publish an account of it, but I want to know more
about it first. *The Pall Mall Gazette* doesn't print sensational tales.'

Seeing a chance to convince him of the story's significance, Hulda charged ahead in her inimitable fashion, telling him everything they had learned. Morley's eyes narrowed when he heard that Tait and Dickerson had visited Broadmoor in the period before Maclean's escape.

'They went to see him specifically?' he asked. 'Or just the asylum?'

'I can ask Roth what Dickerson did there,' replied Lonsdale.

'Good,' said Morley. 'However, I imagine Dickerson – and Tait, too – went to assure himself that conditions for the inmates are morally acceptable. I knew both men, and they were fine, upstanding individuals. They shared an interest in prison and law reform.'

'Broadmoor isn't a prison,' Lonsdale pointed out.

'No, but it still houses criminals,' countered Morley, 'and there are still high walls, locked gates, and cells. It would fall under their remit for scrutiny.'

He was silent, pondering. Lonsdale and Hulda knew better than to speak, and for a while the only sounds were the tick of the clock on the mantelpiece and the yells of the newspaper-sellers in the street below, urging the public to read the thrilling stories in their various papers. Voules was right, thought Lonsdale sourly: most Londoners *would* rather know about escaped cannibals than a politician's views about a country none of them was likely to see.

'So,' said Morley eventually. 'You have four influential men stabbed to death, all of whom had a connection in Maclean—'

'If visiting the asylum in which he was housed *is* a connection,' cautioned Lonsdale. 'Or, in Haldane's case, having an interest in the wording of Maclean's verdict.'

'You interrupted before I could finish,' said Morley sternly. 'Maclean isn't the only connection. There are two more. First, all four were friends, and second, all four were members of the Garraway Club on Exchange Alley.'

'The Garraway Club?' asked Lonsdale, frowning. 'I've never heard of it.'

'There's no reason to think you would – it doesn't bray about its existence. It was named after the coffee house that once stood on the same site, which was famous for intelligent political debate. The members of the current club honour that tradition, and most are Liberals, hoping to protect and enhance the freedom and liberty of the individual but doing so under the rule of law.'

'Are you a member?' asked Hulda.

'I was invited, but the demands on my time are substantial now that Mr Gladstone relies on me so heavily.'

'Do you know how many members it has?' Hulda asked.

'Two hundred or so, I believe, some of whom live outside London. You'll have to visit and see what you can learn, because the loss of these four men is a tragedy, not only for their friends and families, but for society as a whole.'

'I thought Tait was dogmatic, touchy and rude,' said Hulda baldly.

'He had a good heart,' countered Morley. 'So I want you to consider all four deaths as one case. You can go to Surrey to find out exactly what happened to Tait, then visit the London homes of Haldane, Dickerson and Bowyer.'

Lonsdale stood. 'We'll start as soon as we've heard what Bradwell can tell us.'

'See Stead first,' instructed Morley. 'He's more concerned with these missing cannibals than the murders. Then write something about the museum's opening for today's early edition – try to offset some of the damage done by that fool Voules.'

'We will,' promised Hulda.

'Oh, and you must have answers for me by Christmas Eve,' said Morley. 'I can't give you any longer.'

Lonsdale struggled not to gape at him. 'But that only gives us eight days! It'll take all of one to visit Broadmoor, all of another to visit the archbishop's family in Surrey—'

'Then you'd better make a start,' interrupted Morley, unmoved.

'Why the rush?' demanded Hulda, not bothering to hide her exasperation.

Morley looked down at his hands for a moment. 'I can't reveal much, but the Phoenix Park murders investigation will leap forward soon. Therefore, I'm sending Milner to join Cook in Ireland. That means Lonsdale will have to do Milner's work.'

Hulda frowned. 'But Milner does all the in-house editing duties and background research for our major stories. He rarely leaves the office and—'

'Quite,' interrupted Morley. 'Lonsdale won't have time to venture out after killers. Nor will you, because his new assignment means we'll be one reporter short.'

'But—' objected Hulda.

'This is not a debate, Miss Friederichs,' said Morley, giving her what his reporters referred to as his 'mean-eyed glare', which was reserved for those who annoyed him. 'You will do as I ask.'

Hulda inclined her head, and she and Lonsdale left.

Rather than speak to Stead immediately, Lonsdale took Hulda's arm and directed her back to the reporters' room, aiming to give her a few moments to master her temper. She had clearly annoyed Morley by questioning his orders, and Lonsdale did not want her to antagonize Stead as well.

'How stupid!' she fumed. 'We have to rush because Morley is obsessed with the Irish murders. Cook is perfectly capable of relaying what happens there, and it's quite unnecessary to send Milner to babysit.'

'He's the editor,' shrugged Lonsdale. 'It's his prerogative to make these decisions. So we'd better finish all our other work as quickly as possible, so we can concentrate on the murders. Yes?'

Hulda scowled. 'I suppose. Shall we go and see Stead then?'

'He's just gone out,' said Milner, glancing out of the window. 'To buy chestnuts for his chickens from the vendor on Villiers Street. Apparently the birds have developed a taste for those specifically, and he doesn't like to disappoint them by going anywhere else.'

While they waited for the assistant editor to return, Lonsdale dashed off his museum report, and Hulda wrote a review of *Iolanthe*. As the deadlines for the early edition were almost upon them, it was a frantic race against time.

Just as Lonsdale finished, and handed the completed piece to the waiting compositor's boy, Morley came to demand an article about Buckfast Abbey in Devon.

This had been suppressed during the Dissolution of the Monasteries under Henry VIII but, in October that year, six French Benedictine monks had arrived to start operations there again. Morley had just heard that their new church was to be dedicated the following day and wanted mention of it in the early edition. To him, allowing Catholic institutions to flourish again was a symbol of tolerance and reconciliation. To others, it was a dangerous precedent that threatened the Church of England.

While Hulda and Milner scrabbled through their reference books for facts, Lonsdale wrote. He shared Morley's opinion, and expressed the hope that the monks would have a peaceful existence in the rolling West Country hills. His hand burned from the speed at which the words flowed on to the paper, after which the compositor's boy snatched it away while the ink was still wet.

'There go the presses,' said Hulda, as a familiar rumble sounded in the basement. 'Let's hope you were in time, or Mr Morley is going to be vexed.'

She looked as though she thought that would serve him right for imposing unreasonable strictures on them over the murders.

While Morley's domain was neat and formal, Stead's was colourful and chaotic. There was a stuffed bear's head mounted on one wall. Its mouth was open, and one of the assistant editor's favourite pastimes was lobbing things into it. That day it was carrots, which he hurled like small javelins. Newspapers were scattered all over the floor, books lay everywhere, and there was a wheelbarrow in the middle of the room. It had been there a week, and no one had yet learned why. When Hulda and Lonsdale entered, Stead was lying in it, a bag of carrots in his lap.

'There you are,' he remarked coolly, legs hanging over one end and his arms over the sides. He looked irritable, although his semi-prone position was hardly one to inspire fear or respect. 'What kept you?'

'Buckfast Abbey, *Iolanthe* and the Natural History Museum,' replied Hulda. She liked Stead, and the feeling was mutual. 'But now we're ready for some *real* journalism.'

'The poor professor, I suppose,' said Stead. 'I'll pray for his soul, but I'm furious about his dealings with the cannibals. You know my feelings on the matter.'

Lonsdale and Hulda did, although that did not prevent Stead from repeating them.

'The exploitation of one human being by another is the greatest evil we face today,' he preached. 'We must do everything we can to stop it, whether it be northern mill workers abused by greedy industrialists, women turned to prostitution by unscrupulous men, or cannibals being paraded like animals.'

All the while he tossed carrots at the bear. When his bag was empty, he screwed it into a ball and threw that instead. It hit the nose and bounced off in such a way that it flew back at him. He flapped it away furiously, as though the stuffed animal had contrived to do it on purpose.

When the rant was over, Hulda told him what Morley had said about the four dead men. Stead listened intently and grimaced. 'These connections sound rather contrived to me, but you'd better do as Mr Morley asks,' he said. 'However, I want you to look for the cannibals at the same time. They're accused of killing one of your victims, thanks to Voules and *The Echo*, so you can tell him it's part of the same case.'

'I suppose it is,' said Lonsdale. 'But—'

'Besides, the police know their business and Peters is a good detective. He can find the killer without your help.'

'Not Tait's – he was told to forget about that,' said Hulda.

Stead sighed. 'Then see what you can do, although it can't be at the expense of the Kumu. Finding them must be your first priority, hopefully before they fall prey to some ignorant mob.'

'So you don't believe they killed Dickerson?' asked Lonsdale.

Stead spread his hands. 'Why would they? Your friend Roth says he treated them with kindness and respect – although he should've found them better lodgings than the museum basement – so they've no reason to kill him. I imagine they fled *because* he was struck down – they ran, to avoid being blamed or suffering the same fate.'

'It's possible,' hedged Lonsdale.

'Yes, it is.' Stead clapped his hands. 'So off you go. Keep me informed.'

Although it would make him late for Bradwell, Lonsdale decided to visit Anne first. Hulda offered to accompany him when she learned what he intended to do, but he did not think that would be a good idea, given what Jack had claimed at breakfast. He declined politely, settled her in the first hansom that happened past, then flagged down another.

The Humbages lived on Gordon Square in Bloomsbury. Their house was a fine, five-storey affair with grey walls, yellow shutters and twin marble columns flanking the front door. Humbage had recently spent a fortune renovating it, although Lonsdale thought the 'improvements' showed that the retired brigadier had more money than taste.

Lonsdale knocked on the door, and there was a moment when he thought Taylor, Humbage's butler, would refuse to let him in – the man regarded him with such contempt that Lonsdale was on the verge of pushing past before he finally stepped aside.

He entered the large, imposing hall, which was filled with so many paintings and sculptures that it verged on the vulgar. Rather like the Humbages themselves, thought Lonsdale. Other than Anne, of course. He could not imagine how such a sweet, intelligent lady could have been born into such a stuffy, narrow-minded family.

Before Lonsdale could ask to see Anne, her grandmother, Lady Gertrude, opened the sitting-room door and beckoned him towards her. Lonsdale liked the elderly lady, who delighted in exposing her son-in-law for the pompous fool he was. In response, Humbage kept her on a very short leash, and had instructed his family and the servants never to let her out alone, lest she said the wrong thing to people he wanted to impress.

'Look at this,' she whispered mischievously, and ushered him into a room that was being prepared for Christmas.

Lonsdale's jaw dropped. Humbage had ordered it decorated like the photographs of the great hall in Buckingham Palace. There was a tree so large that Lonsdale wondered how it had been carried inside, and it was smothered in candles, sweets, and impossibly gaudy baubles that had been purchased at Whiteley's on Westbourne Grove. There were five smaller trees dotted around the room, a giant wassail bowl that looked as if it could serve an army and still have drink to spare, and a spectacular Yule log sat in the fireplace.

'Gervais is nothing if not a follower of royal fashion,' chuckled Lady Gertrude. 'He's enormously proud of this, but I knew I could rely on you for an honest opinion. You think it's grotesque and didn't mind showing it.'

'It's horrible,' said Lonsdale with feeling. 'And he won't even be here at Christmas – you'll all be with us in Cleveland Square.'

'Not me,' said Lady Gertrude bitterly. 'Gervais informs me that I'm too frail to go out in the cold. I'm to stay here alone.'

'Then I'll fetch you in a hackney carriage myself,' determined Lonsdale, irked that Humbage should bully her so. 'One with plenty of blankets.'

'Brandy is better at driving the cold from elderly bones,' said Lady Gertrude, and patted his cheek affectionately. 'You can keep the blankets for Gervais – preferably to smother him with. Will you be having a decent whisky? Gervais hides his, you know.'

'I'll make sure you're well supplied,' promised Lonsdale.

She grinned, then turned her attention back to the room.

'I dislike all this Germanic nonsense,' she said, regarding the tree with a belligerent eye. 'I'd rather replicate the jubilant Christmases of my youth, but Gervais thinks that would make us look like pagans.'

'Why?' asked Lonsdale curiously. 'What did you do? Human sacrifices? Dancing naked around an oak tree with the local druids?'

She chortled. 'Not human sacrifices, although there was dancing – and nakedness, on occasion. The clergy were much more fun in those days. I said as much to the Prince.'

'Which Prince? Edward?'

She regarded him scornfully. 'That boy? No, I refer to Albert, the German himself. He was always keen to hear about English customs, and I'm sure he'd turn in his grave if he could see this room. And as for Christmas cards . . .'

'You don't approve of them?'

'In moderation, but Gervais sends hundreds. Archbishop Tait was very much against cards. He considered them irreligious, even though many have Jesus on the front.'

'You knew Tait?'

She grinned wickedly. 'I met him when he was a prim young curate in Marsh Baldon. He was a dour youth, and he grew into a dour adult, although you must remember that he lost five of his eight daughters in a little more than a month, then later his wife and only son. But he was a good man at heart. Honourable and steadfast.'

'I heard he didn't die a natural death.' Lonsdale dared not be too specific.

'It wouldn't surprise me – he was a man of strong, loud and inflexible opinions. But I admire that in a man. I can't abide the weak ones, who change their minds at the drop of a hat. Gervais is such a man, especially now he has friends at the Palace. He's so frantic to impress them that he'll say and do anything they ask, no matter how asinine.'

At that point, the door opened and Humbage himself walked in. He looked immaculate, and his soldierly bearing made him appear tall and strong. He looked down his nose at Lonsdale, his expression one of utter disdain.

'Were we expecting you?'

'I was,' put in Gertrude, before Lonsdale could invent an excuse for coming unannounced so early in the day. 'He brought me some German marzipan, because he knows I've loved it ever since the Prince gave me a piece.'

'That old story!' sneered Humbage. 'I doubt it's even true.'

'When were *you* last at the Palace, Gervais?' asked the old lady acidly. 'Or are you obliged to grovel to your new courtier friends elsewhere? Who are they again? Lord Curly-Tail and Fleetwood-Lighthouse?'

'Lord Carlingford and Sir Algernon Fleetwood-Pelham,' corrected Humbage irritably.

'Fleetwood-Lighthouse is a terrible blabbermouth,' Lady Gertrude went on. 'He leaked the tale about Lady Morningside's illegitimate child.'

'He wouldn't have been appointed a Groom-in-Waiting if that were true,' countered Humbage sharply. 'Courtiers need to be discreet.'

Lady Gertrude laughed. 'And soldiers need to be brave, politicians clever and bankers honest, but we have cowards, liars and numbskulls aplenty. Did I ever tell you that I knew Fleetwood-Lighthouse's mother? An interesting lady – she could juggle and catch sardines in her teeth from a distance of thirty yards.'

'Did you know Archbishop Tait?' Lonsdale asked of Humbage, more to change the subject before the man had an apoplectic fit than for information. 'Or Sir George Bowyer?'

'Yes,' replied Humbage shortly. 'But I decline to discuss them in present company. I wish you good day, and hope you'll send your calling card to warn us of your arrival the next time you visit.'

'What an ass,' muttered Lady Gertrude as her son-in-law stalked out. 'Calling card indeed! Who does he think he is? He spends so much time fawning over these courtiers – who aren't friends, but men who throw him the occasional nod – that I barely know him. He's grown bloated with ambition.'

Voices in the hallway heralded the arrival of other members of the Humbage household, and Anne walked in, followed by Emelia. To Lonsdale's alarm, they were holding hands, which meant that Emelia aimed to give her sister moral support against her errant fiancé.

'It was Hulda,' he began firmly. 'She scrubs up very nicely when she chooses, and we went to the theatre because we were looking for three Kumu. It was work, not pleasure. After the performance, we went backstage and interviewed Alice Barnett.'

'I might've known you'd have an excuse,' said Emelia sourly. 'However, it doesn't detract from the point that you promised to take Anne to that opera, and you elected to go with someone else.'

'It wasn't Hulda anyway,' said Anne tearfully. 'We know her.'

'It was,' insisted Lonsdale. 'And I think you should give me the benefit of the doubt. You know I'm not in the habit of lying to you.'

'If he says it was Hulda, it was Hulda,' interposed Lady Gertrude firmly. 'She has good bones, and I imagine she'd wear an evening dress with great panache. It's a pity you didn't take me to see *Iolanthe*, because I'd have recognized her, and you could've avoided all this silly weeping and wailing.'

'Why didn't they take you?' asked Lonsdale.

'Because Gervais thought Lord Curly-Tail might be there, and he didn't want me to meet him,' replied Lady Gertrude promptly. 'He's ashamed of me, even though I have more breeding in my little finger than all his ancestors put together.'

'Carlingford,' corrected Emelia. 'Lord *Carlingford*. Papa is his friend.'

'Pah!' spat Lady Gertrude. 'Gervais is like a dog on heat around him, and Curly-Tail will soon tire of it. Gervais thinks his sycophancy will win him a position at court, but it won't. He'd do better sucking up to me, because *I'm* the one who can put words in the right ears.'

'But you haven't, have you,' said Emelia archly, 'although you've had years to prove your so-called royal connections.'

'Em!' cried Anne, shocked. 'Grandmama isn't obliged to—'

'Because I chose not to inflict Gervais on people I like,' interrupted Lady Gertrude haughtily. 'And I'm glad of it, given that he kept me from seeing *Iolanthe*.'

'You were tired,' said Emelia, although Anne looked acutely uncomfortable, and Lonsdale was inclined to believe the old lady. 'You slept most of the afternoon.'

'Yes, so I wouldn't doze off during the performance,' snapped Lady Gertrude with asperity. 'I was looking forward to it. But, as it turns out, I had a very enjoyable evening with Jack instead. Indeed, I warrant I had a lot more fun than you did. Now, if you'll excuse me, all this foliage is making me want to sneeze.'

'I hope you haven't changed your mind about tomorrow,' said Lonsdale to Anne, wishing Emelia was not there. 'The Christmas cracker exhibition?'

Anne smiled, so he knew she had decided to take his side over her sister's. 'No, of course not. I'm looking forward to it.'

'Good,' said Lonsdale briskly. 'So am I.'

He bowed and took his leave before any more could be said, filled with a sense of exasperation and annoyance. Was this what married life would be like? A series of quarrels and misunderstandings, all brought about by Emelia's malice and Humbage's foolish pomposity?

FOUR

I t was difficult to remain morose for long when, all around, London was merrily preparing for Christmas. Lonsdale enjoyed the journey from Bloomsbury to Westminster, even though the volume of traffic made it torturous and long, because he liked to see the drab tones of winter enlivened by seasonal splashes of colour. All along Tottenham Court and Charing Cross roads were bright window displays, some very imaginative, while the scent of roasted chestnuts was on every corner. Then he saw Voules. He waited for *The Echo* man to catch up, thinking it was as good a time as any to question him.

'You went to Broadmoor,' he said without preamble. 'Why?'

'I never did!' declared Voules.

'Your name was in the visitors' book.'

'You think I'm the only Voules in the country? It's a very important name, and there are dozens of us. So, as it wasn't me, it must've been one of the others.'

Lonsdale shuddered at the notion of dozens of Vouleses scurrying around. He was about to ask more, but *The Echo* man strutted away, although only to duck into a shop in readiness for following Lonsdale again. Determined to lose him, Lonsdale jumped on and off horse trams and the new garden-seat omnibuses, zigzagged through alleys, and doubled back on himself. Voules was good, so it was with great satisfaction that Lonsdale finally threw him off his trail. He refused to acknowledge that it made no real difference, because Voules would probably guess where he was going anyway and would just make his own way there.

Eventually, Lonsdale left the bright shops and displays behind, and entered the shabby, impoverished area of narrow streets, dirty yards and crammed tenements on the border of Westminster and Pimlico, where Bradwell's domain was located.

The mortuary was the most unprepossessing building of all in a run-down neighbourhood dominated by the Millbank Penitentiary and the decaying Grey Coat Hospital. It was surrounded by brick walls topped with shards of glass – in such areas, corpses were considered fair game for thieves. Bradwell had suffered so many burglaries that he had despaired, so the Metropolitan Police, who employed him, had bought him a dog. Unfortunately, 'Ripper' was a gentle creature who loved visitors, regardless of whether their intentions were honest or otherwise.

Lonsdale hammered on the door, and was admitted by Bradwell's assistant, a dour man named Fox, who did not keep the place nearly as clean as his predecessor had done. The floors of both the long entrance hall and the autopsy room were stained and dirty, there were worrying things sticking to the walls, and blood had splattered on the ceilings. Lonsdale did not know how Bradwell could bear it. He said so, and the surgeon looked around in bemusement.

'But Fox gave the whole building a good scrub-down this morning, and now it's spotless. It has to be, or Ripper might feast on something she shouldn't.'

Lonsdale declined to dwell on that notion, and was glad when Hulda, who claimed irritably that she had been waiting there for at least an hour, changed the subject. She was perched on a table, legs swinging in a most unladylike fashion. Lonsdale tried to imagine Anne doing the same and failed.

'Your talents are wasted here, Bradwell,' she said. 'I don't know why you came back to the Metropolitan Police – they take advantage

of you. Why did you decline the post in the new City of London
Police mortuary?'

'My wife asks me the same question almost every night,' sighed
Bradwell. 'And the answer is that I enjoy what I do here. Moreover,
I have a lot more freedom than I would at the City of London, and
it allows me to continue my surgical work at Bart's.'

'I can't imagine Bart's pays very well,' said Hulda. 'Not with all
the charity cases they take on.'

'No,' agreed Bradwell, 'although the "charity cases" tend to be
a lot more interesting than the ingrown toenails and haemorrhoids
of the rich – not that I have the social connections to be let loose
on those, of course. But, luckily for me, money is irrelevant, because
my wife inherited a tidy little fortune in the summer. Thus, I can
do what I like.'

'So you're a kept man?' asked Hulda baldly.

Bradwell beamed. 'I am, and I'm happier than I can say. Well,
why not? I've no qualms about living off my wife, just as she had
none about living off me before she became wealthy. There's nothing
to say that it must be the man who provides.'

'I suppose not,' said Hulda. 'I wouldn't mind a husband who
stayed home to cook and clean while I earned the daily bread.'

Lonsdale tried to imagine Anne taking such a view, and nearly
laughed aloud. Anne was not lazy, but she had firm ideas about
what was socially acceptable, and a reversal of traditional roles
would be anathema to her. But time was passing, and he was cogni-
zant of the fact that he and Hulda could not sit chatting when they
had just eight days to discover why four prominent men had been
murdered.

'What have you learned from the professor's body?' he asked.

'Nothing, yet,' replied Bradwell. 'Because Superintendent Hayes
told me to wait for him before beginning my examination and . . .
hah! Here he is now, and Inspector Peters with him. Good. Now
we can start.'

The superintendent looked very dashing that morning, in a well-
cut suit with a sprig of ivy in the buttonhole. His grey hair was
perfectly groomed, and his bearing was erect and dignified. By
contrast, Peters's coat was too big, and his boots, although carefully
polished, were cheap. Hayes was not pleased to see Hulda and
Lonsdale.

'What're you doing here?' he asked, eyes narrowing.

'*I* invited them,' said Bradwell. 'They found the professor's body, and I shouldn't like *his* death to be brushed under the carpet, too.'

'Poor Archbishop Tait,' sighed Hayes. 'I was told you objected to the verdict of death by natural causes. It—'

'Damn right I objected,' interrupted Bradwell. 'He was murdered. There was nothing "natural" about it.'

'You can't say that with certainty,' cautioned Hayes. 'You never saw the body – it was his local doctor who issued the official report.'

'The "local doctor" was at medical school with me,' countered Bradwell. 'He told me about the wounds in the archbishop's body, and about the pressure put on him to lie in his report. Moreover, two more prominent men were killed in a violent manner, and it seems to me that nothing is being done about them either.'

'What two prominent men?' demanded Peters at once.

'Alexander Haldane and Sir George Bowyer,' replied Bradwell. 'I didn't see their bodies either, but I heard the rumours. Both suffered serious and distinctive wounds by an unknown assailant. Neither was "natural", and neither is being investigated.'

'I understand your frustrations, Bradwell,' said Hayes, while Peters was openly astonished by the news. 'Indeed, I share them. But, we were ordered by a higher authority that no further action is to be taken, so our hands are tied.'

'What higher authority?' demanded Bradwell. 'The Prime Minister? The Queen? God?'

'God, as far as I'm concerned,' replied Hayes wryly. 'Commissioner Henderson – the head of the Metropolitan Police and my superior officer. I'm duty-bound to follow his orders – and his order was to ask no more questions about Tait, because the case has been discreetly resolved.'

'Whatever that means,' muttered Peters under his breath.

'What about Haldane and Bowyer?' asked Lonsdale. 'Have their deaths been "discreetly resolved", too?'

'I wouldn't know,' replied Hayes. 'Those cases have been allocated to Inspector Wells.'

'Wells?' echoed Peters in disbelief. He explained to Bradwell, Lonsdale and Hulda: 'He's one of Henderson's favourite officers, although his record of solving crime is . . .'

'Unimpressive,' finished Hayes. 'I doubt he'll find many answers.'
'Perhaps the truth will come out anyway,' said Hulda.
'I hope so,' said Hayes flatly. 'I knew all four men. They had their flaws, but they deserve justice.'
'They do,' agreed Peters stiffly. 'Our commissioner must have a very strong reason for doing what he's done.'

Hulda and Lonsdale exchanged a glance, because Commissioner Henderson had a reputation for allowing himself to be manipulated – so eager to please his political masters that he willingly did whatever they required of him.

'I rather think the Church brought pressure to bear,' said Hayes. 'Tait's opinions didn't endear him to many of his more traditional colleagues, and it may well be that the matter was investigated by clerics who identified the culprit and dealt with him quietly.'

'But Haldane, Bowyer and Dickerson were killed in a similar way,' Lonsdale pointed out. 'Which may suggest the same culprit. I doubt *they* offended a murderous cleric, so either the Church released the culprit to kill again or the case hasn't yet been solved.'

'*I* don't believe the killer is a cleric,' said Peters. 'Lonsdale is right – it doesn't explain why Bowyer, Haldane and Dickerson were also attacked. We need to look for some "higher authority" other than the Church.'

Hayes considered for a moment, then came to a decision. 'Have you considered visiting Tait's daughter?' he asked the reporters. 'You didn't hear this from me, but she's still living in the Archbishop's Palace. I heard she was livid when the decision was made to investigate no further and she might have information or opinions to share.'

'We could speak to Commissioner Henderson as well,' said Lonsdale.

'You could,' said Hayes. 'But you won't learn much from him. He may be weak, but he'd never betray his political masters – whoever they happen to be.'

There was a lull in proceedings when a constable arrived with documents for Hayes to sign. Bradwell offered the superintendent the use of his tiny office, then went to begin preparing Dickerson for examination, leaving Lonsdale and Hulda with Peters.

'So you didn't know about Bowyer and Haldane,' stated Hulda, the moment the three of them were alone. 'I could tell by the expression on your face. Hayes did, though.'

Peters shook his head slowly. 'I imagine he's under orders not to discuss it. I like him – he's a diligent detective and a good man. If he lied by omission, it'll not have been his own choice. However, he feels the same way I do about Tait – that leaving his death unexplored is a travesty of justice. He'll be pleased if you can ruffle a few feathers.'

'We'll do more than ruffle them,' vowed Hulda. 'If there really is some sinister cover-up, we'll tear them out and expose whatever's hiding underneath.'

Peters regarded her sombrely. 'It's no mean feat to convince a Commissioner of Police to suspend a murder investigation. That means whoever did it is powerful and influential – and therefore dangerous. Please be careful.'

'Do you think our lives might be at risk?' asked Lonsdale, ready to sideline Hulda if they were. He felt oddly protective of her, although he realized she would be furious if she knew.

'Possibly – or you might be damaged in other ways, such as losing your jobs or your reputations. I dislike political games – they leave a sour taste in my mouth. Let's hope you find answers quickly.'

'Our editor has given us until Christmas Eve,' said Hulda.

Peters raised his eyebrows. 'Then you don't have a moment to lose. Hah! Here's Fox to tell us that Bradwell is waiting.'

Lonsdale was sorry to see Dickerson laid out on a slab, and even sorrier to watch Bradwell going to work on him. He glanced at Hulda. She was pale, but resolutely refused to look away. He could not imagine Anne showing such fortitude, then wondered why he kept comparing the two women, especially as Anne nearly always emerged unfavourably.

'Not stabbed,' said Bradwell eventually. 'But chopped with a wide-bladed weapon. A machete-type implement, perhaps. We should keep this discovery to ourselves, though, because I'll resign if the commissioner informs me that *this* was a natural death.'

'The attack on Tait wasn't quite so frenzied,' said Hayes thoughtfully. 'Just one or two wounds to his back. Trails of blood suggest he lived for some minutes after the assault and might even have survived if he'd been able to summon help.'

'Well, Dickerson wouldn't have lived,' averred Bradwell. 'One blow punctured a lung and another his femoral artery. He was beyond help, even if he had managed to call for some.'

'So *are* we looking at the same killer?' asked Peters. 'I know you never saw the bodies of the other three, but you did say you read your colleagues' reports.'

'Yes – the ones they wrote *before* they were forced to pretend that nothing untoward took place,' said Bradwell pointedly. 'But those injuries and these sound identical, which suggests the same weapon was used on all four.'

'Just because the weapon is the same, doesn't mean the killer is,' Hulda pointed out.

'No,' acknowledged Bradwell. 'But the weapon is distinctive – not some common blade, but something longer and broader.' He sketched what he thought it might look like on a scrap of paper, leaving bloody smears behind. 'I've heard them called "pangas" in the past.'

'It looks like something used in parts of Africa,' remarked Peters thoughtfully. 'The interior of the Congo, perhaps, where Dickerson's cannibals hail from.'

'Dickerson's assistant swears the Kumu are innocent,' said Hayes.

'They *are* innocent,' said Lonsdale, 'if that's what the weapon looks like. That's not from the Congo, but from East or Southern Africa.'

Everyone looked at him in surprise. 'How do you know?' asked Peters.

'From my time in the Colonial Service,' explained Lonsdale. 'That isn't a Kumu weapon.'

'Perhaps they took one from an exhibit,' suggested Bradwell. 'I saw plenty of them in the museum yesterday.'

'We checked yesterday,' said Hayes. 'None was missing, and I don't see the killer launching a ferocious attack, then calmly replacing the weapon in its showcase. Moreover, given that he used it three times – that we know of – before Dickerson, I suspect this is something he owns personally.'

'The cannibals *own* pangas,' persisted Peters. 'They were going to use them as visual aids in their performances, but when they ran away, they took the things with them.' He glanced at Lonsdale. 'I know you said a Kumu panga isn't the murder weapon, but perhaps they found one from another tribe in the basement. God knows, there's enough stuff down there to make that a possibility.'

'And Dickerson's body *was* found in the place where they'd been living,' put in Hulda. 'However, why would they also have dispatched the Archbishop of Canterbury and two lawyers they're very unlikely to have met?'

'Yet if they did, I understand why the government would want it kept quiet,' said Bradwell. 'If word slipped out that cannibals had murdered four prominent men, friendly relations with our colonies could suffer a serious blow. Perhaps Henderson is right to look the other way.'

'Is there any sign of cannibalism on Dickerson?' asked Lonsdale, glancing at the hollow shell that had once been a living, breathing person.

'None,' said Bradwell promptly. 'Perhaps he didn't look very appetizing.'

Peters turned his mournful gaze on Lonsdale and Hulda. 'Superintendent Hayes and I are barred from looking into the Tait murder, while Bowyer and Haldane have been given to the inept Inspector Wells. We'll do all we can with Dickerson, but I suspect it won't be long before we're told to desist . . .'

'Probably,' agreed Hayes. 'Although I aim to avoid Henderson for as long as I can – if I don't meet him, he can't give me orders.'

'So the only way we'll have answers is if you find them,' finished Peters. 'However, if you do decide to accept the challenge, will you keep us apprized of your progress?'

'Of course,' said Lonsdale.

It was late afternoon and growing dark by the time they emerged from the mortuary, the short winter day over almost before it had started. Hayes had a police coach waiting, and he and Peters rattled away into the gathering gloom. Bradwell lived in Hulda's direction and offered to share a hansom with her; she accepted happily. Lonsdale was the last to leave, waiting until Fox had locked the gate behind them. He walked slowly, head bowed in thought as he considered all he had learned.

He had just reached the end of the road when there was a sudden frenzy of angry barking from Ripper, who had done no more than wag her tail when everyone had left. Lonsdale glanced around and saw Fox hurrying back to see what had upset her. Ripper's din intensified, and Fox yelled in alarm as a shadow hurtled out of the mortuary yard and raced down the road, Ripper hot on its heels.

'Stop!' bellowed Fox, although neither dog nor shadow paid him any attention; then he spotted Lonsdale. 'After him, sir! I think he stole something from the professor! I'll stay here to make sure he doesn't double back.'

Lonsdale broke into a sprint, aware that his quarry already had a substantial lead. He was quicker, however, and began to catch up. The shadow was a man – slight, short, and wearing a bowler hat. Lonsdale could hear him breathing hard, suggesting he was unaccustomed to sudden spurts of speed. The man rounded a corner and almost fell as he skidded in a pile of horse muck. Something dropped from his coat as he flailed to regain his balance. He did not notice and raced on as soon as he was upright again. Lonsdale hesitated, not sure whether to pick up what had fallen or continue the chase.

He opted to continue the chase, but when they reached Victoria Street, an omnibus lumbered past. The man leapt on to the back of it, and Lonsdale saw him grip the handrail hard as he fought not to fall off. It was too dark to see his face, but Lonsdale thought he was more relieved by his escape than victorious. Lonsdale put every last ounce of his strength into catching the omnibus, legs and arms pumping furiously, but it gathered speed once it turned into Buckingham Palace Road, and he knew he was defeated. He staggered to a standstill, resting his hands on his knees as his labouring breath slowly returned to normal. By the time he looked up again, the vehicle was out of sight.

Once he had recovered, he trudged back the way he had come, and saw that what the man had dropped still lay where it had fallen. He bent to pick it up. It was a rolled-up copy of *The Echo*, in which were matches, kindling and a flask of oil. Lonsdale did not need to be told that their owner had intended to set a fire with them.

He whipped round at a sound behind him, ready to defend himself if the man had an accomplice, but it was only Fox, Ripper at his side.

'That's what he had in his hand,' said the mortuary assistant, stabbing his finger at the newspaper roll Lonsdale held. 'He was looming over Dickerson, so I assumed he was stealing it from him. What is it? Entrails?'

'His intention wasn't theft,' said Lonsdale soberly. 'It was arson – he'd have set your mortuary alight if Ripper hadn't raised the alarm.'

'No!'

'And if he was looming over Dickerson, then I imagine his aim was to destroy the body and any evidence relating to how he died.'

Fox frowned. 'He must've slipped inside while we were busy, and Ripper, bless her, didn't think there was anything amiss. The rogue heard me lock the door and went about his dark business, but Ripper knew that wasn't right, so raised the alarm. Thank God we were still close enough to hear her.'

'Thank God indeed,' murmured Lonsdale, following Fox back inside the building to see if the invader had left anything else behind.

The blanket covering Dickerson lay on the floor, but Fox declared nothing else was out of place. It seemed that Ripper had been in time to prevent a conflagration that would have destroyed not only what remained of the professor, but likely the entire building as well, including Bradwell's notes.

Lonsdale left in a thoughtful frame of mind. If he needed more evidence that someone wanted to keep the truth hidden, this was it. Perhaps the killer knew Commissioner Henderson was unlikely to pass off a fourth murder as natural, so had elected to take matters into his own hands. Regardless, it made Lonsdale all the more determined to find out what was going on.

He had only taken a few steps along Horseferry Road when he happened to glance behind him. He glimpsed a familiar figure, which ducked into a doorway when it saw him turn. It was Voules, who had indeed guessed he would visit the mortuary, and had staked it out after he had been given the slip. Lonsdale brightened: perhaps being stalked would have its advantages. He turned down Holland Street, pressed himself against the wall, then calmly reached out to grab Voules by the collar as *The Echo* man hurried past. Voules yelped his alarm.

'What're you doing?' he demanded, pulling away and brushing himself down. 'You frightened the life out of me – I thought I was about to be robbed. This is a shady area, you know, haunted by unsavoury characters.'

'I know,' agreed Lonsdale regarding him pointedly. 'Were you behind me when I came out of the mortuary?'

'Behind you?' echoed Voules, licking his lips nervously. 'I just happened to be passing when—'

'Enough!' snapped Lonsdale. 'We both know you've been glued to my side ever since I won the job over you. However, we might be able to help each other. So, were you outside the mortuary when I came out?'

Voules scowled. 'No – I got so cold loitering about that I went to a pub for a drink. I've only just come out.'

'So you didn't see me chase anyone?'

'No, why? Who was it?'

'Did you see anyone go in or come out of the mortuary, other than Bradwell and Fox?' pressed Lonsdale.

'Yes, I saw two police officers arrive. Then later there was a man in a bowler hat with a rolled-up *Echo* under his arm.' Voules preened. 'Today's edition, with my piece about the cannibals. Tomorrow's will reveal that they ate most of Dickerson. They—'

'What else can you tell me about Bowler Hat?' interrupted Lonsdale, not about to waste his time debating press ethics with the likes of Voules.

Unfortunately, Voules was not an observant man, so Lonsdale was not surprised when he shook his head. 'I think he had a moustache, but I can't be sure. Why? Is it important?'

Lonsdale nodded. 'And it's a pity you weren't more vigilant, because identifying him might have answered a lot of questions.'

Determined that Voules would not follow him again that day, Lonsdale hailed a hansom and jumped in, promising to pay the driver double if he hurried. He glanced through the back window as they rattled away, smiling when he saw Voules standing with his fists clenched in impotent fury. The hansom was moving too fast for him to follow on foot, and there was no sign of another. Lonsdale sat back and called the Natural History Museum's address to the driver.

It was a typical winter evening, with fog swirling up from the river, and an icy nip in the air. It trapped the smoke belching from thousands of chimneys, stinging eyes, staining clothes, and so thick that Lonsdale could feel particles of it cracking between his teeth. He was glad when they left the dinginess of the mortuary area behind and returned to the cheer of the shops along Cromwell Road.

Once at the museum, he was told that Roth had begged off work that day, and was at home, recovering from the shock of his supervisor's death. Lonsdale started to leave, only to meet Burnside, who was walking in with a camera over his shoulder. The photographer looked cold, tired and miserable.

'You aim to start work inside now?' asked Lonsdale, sure there would not be enough light.

'I've been in Hyde Park all day, taking pictures of visitors,' said Burnside, then, evidently feeling this was a demeaning activity for a man with designs on a royal appointment, added rather defiantly, 'Gladstone himself stopped to talk to me.'

Lonsdale sincerely doubted the Prime Minister would have deigned to exchange greetings with a lowly street trader but nodded politely. 'The rain didn't put people off?'

Burnside sighed unhappily. 'Let's just say that today wasn't one of the busiest ones. So I decided to take shots of the exhibits here instead. It's not so crowded in the evenings.'

He forced a smile, and Lonsdale was reminded of when he himself was struggling to make a living, not so long ago. On impulse, he invited him to The Brompton, which was not far, and served excellent *à la carte* chops. Lonsdale had a cup of tea and a light plum cake, while Burnside plunged into pork, peas, boiled potatoes and bread.

Once his hunger was sated, Burnside turned to his favourite subject – how the Queen had failed to show proper gratitude for him saving her life. It transpired that he was particularly angry at Fleetwood-Pelham, who had had the unenviable task of informing Burnside that he would not be rewarded with a contract to be the Royal Photographer, nor would the Queen supply his raw materials. Eventually, Lonsdale managed to turn the conversation to Christmas, hoping it would be less acerbic.

'I'm going to buy my father a pipe,' Burnside said, wiping the gravy from his plate with the last of his bread. 'From the Thurloe Square market. What are you getting for your fiancée?'

'Anne?' asked Lonsdale, as though there might be another. He shrugged. 'I haven't given it much thought.'

Burnside raised his eyebrows. 'Then you'd better start! Your life won't be worth living unless you produce the right present. Believe me, I know – my fiancée went off and married someone else when I came up short one Christmas.'

Lonsdale was about to remark that the engagement could not

have been a very loving one if his intended allowed something like that to change her mind, but then an image of Emelia came into his mind. She would certainly make a fuss if Jack failed in the gift department and would encourage Anne to do the same. Lonsdale saw he had better give the matter some serious consideration before it was too late.

'Come with me,' said Burnside, reading the consternation on his face. 'There'll be something suitable in the market, and you look as if you need guidance.'

Supposing Roth could wait, Lonsdale allowed himself to be led to Thurloe Square, a small garden surrounded by elegant houses. A Christmas market had set up there, with tiny wooden stalls selling all manner of exotic goods, from silks and spices to perfumes and gloves. It looked pretty with its swinging lanterns and coloured lights. They bought the pipe for Burnside's father, after which Lonsdale purchased a handsome set of pens for Hulda, wishing Anne was as easy to please.

'Is someone following you?' asked Burnside suddenly, stopping to peer back along the shops they had just walked past. 'I keep seeing the same man . . .'

'Voules!' exclaimed Lonsdale in irritation. 'How did he find me here?'

'It's not Voules,' said Burnside. 'It's a small, thin man with a moustache and a bowler hat.' He gripped Lonsdale's arm hard. 'You should be careful about poking your nose into that murder in the museum. It might be dangerous.'

'You mean because it may have been committed by cannibals?' asked Lonsdale, assuming Burnside had been reading *The Echo*. He peered into the gloom but could see no one who might be trailing him. 'I don't think they pose much of a—'

'Not them,' interrupted Burnside. 'Why would they attack the man who had looked after them all those weeks? I heard the museum staff whispering while I was photographing insects yesterday – they think someone else is responsible, because the cannibals seemed too nice for murder.'

'When we find them, we can ask,' said Lonsdale, and changed the subject, because he did not want to talk to Burnside about the investigation, sure Peters would never approve. 'Look at this silk waistcoat. My brother would like that.'

'What about Anne?' asked Burnside. 'She's why you're here, remember?'

But Lonsdale was uncertain about everything the photographer suggested, although he paused at a collection of sabres.

'Perhaps I should get one of these for Emelia. She'd enjoy disembowelling people with it.'

'From what you've told me, she won't need a sword for that,' quipped Burnside. 'She can use her teeth.'

Lonsdale took considerable care as he left Burnside and began to walk to Roth's lodgings, ducking into doorways and doubling back on himself. But he saw nothing suspicious and could only assume that Burnside had been mistaken about someone following him.

The clocks were chiming seven by the time he reached Roth's small but pleasant rooms on Shawfield Street. He had been there several times before, but that day he noticed a peculiar smell on the landing outside, which intensified as Roth opened the door. Roth was even paler than usual and looked as though he had been crying.

'Alec,' he said, manfully trying to summon a smile. 'It's good of you to come.'

Lonsdale followed him inside, and almost tripped over a box that had been inconveniently placed. He put out a hand to steady himself, but in so doing knocked over a pile of wooden spears that had been leaning against the wall. These slid sideways and clattered into a shield that was covered in antelope hide. He was about to ask where they had all come from – they had not been there the last time he had visited, nor had the three large crates in the middle of the room – when he saw Roth was not alone.

'Mr Lonsdale,' said Fleetwood-Pelham, standing politely as the reporter entered the sitting room. Again, Lonsdale was struck by the odd shape of the man's head – the great dome above, and the small chin below the huge handlebar moustache. 'I had no idea when we spoke yesterday that you're with *The Pall Mall Gazette*. I have the honour of counting your editor, John Morley, among my closest friends.'

'The professor admired Mr Morley, too,' said Roth miserably. 'I still can't believe he . . . If only I'd stayed to make sure the train left with him on it! Then he might still be alive.'

'You can't know that,' said Fleetwood-Pelham kindly. 'And

blaming yourself will accomplish nothing. The best thing is you can do what *he* would want: return to the museum and continue the work he loved.'

'Yes,' sniffed Roth. 'He would want that. It's just that it won't be the same without him, and I'm not sure I can do it.'

'You'll feel differently in a few days,' Fleetwood-Pelham assured him gently. 'Now, I've told you how to contact me at St James's Palace, should you need anything, so I'll leave you in the capable hands of your friend.'

He took his leave, donning an unusually large hat to accommodate his princely dome. Roth saw him out, then slumped down on a chair before explaining why the courtier had visited.

'He knew the professor and wanted to say how sorry he is,' Roth grimaced. 'He's rather a gossip, actually, so I suspect his real mission was to see what he could find out.'

'I hardly think a courtier would go to that sort of length for a bit of tittle-tattle.'

Roth's expression suggested he thought otherwise. 'He told me the Queen is worried about what impact the murder might have on the museum – that people won't come if they think folk are dispatched down in its cellars. I hope her concerns are groundless. The professor would have hated the thought of his death harming the museum.'

'The public have short memories,' said Lonsdale. 'It won't matter in a week or two.'

'Fleetwood-Pelham also quizzed me about the Kumu,' Roth went on, 'no doubt thinking cannibals will make for more interesting chatter for Her Majesty than the usual gamut of unwanted pregnancies and scandalous affairs.'

'Depends who's having the affairs and pregnancies, I imagine,' muttered Lonsdale.

'And yet South African subjects killing British citizens might cause a diplomatic furore,' Roth went on, ignoring him. 'So perhaps *that* was his real concern.'

'Perhaps,' said Lonsdale. 'But the Kumu come from *Central* Africa, so I wouldn't think so.'

'I meant to say Central Africa.' Roth rubbed his eyes tiredly before gesturing around him at the crates. 'Most of this originates in West and Central Africa, and I've been immersed in it.'

'It smells of something familiar, although I can't place it. But where did you get it? It wasn't here last week.'

'A solicitor visited this morning, to tell me that I've inherited the professor's whole ethnographic collection,' said Roth, his eyes filling with tears. 'Lord only knows where I'll put it – he'd been collecting all his life, and this is just a fraction of what he had.'

'He left it *all* to you?' asked Lonsdale, astonished. 'Nothing to the museum?'

'I'm to catalogue it, then pass the most valuable items to the museum. The rest I can keep for myself.'

'That doesn't sound like much of a legacy! The museum gets the cream, while you're left with the milk.'

'It belonged to him, which means I'll cherish it,' said Roth, a tear rolling down his cheek. 'Of course, I'll drown in pangas, shields, spears and beads. He also charged me to look after the Kumu, although that'll be difficult when I don't know where they are.'

'You've no idea at all?' fished Lonsdale.

'I wish I did. They love our tradition of tea and cakes, so perhaps I'll trawl some cafes tomorrow, to see if they've fetched up in one.'

'I hope they haven't,' said Lonsdale. 'All London is looking for three dangerous Africans, and if they waltz into the Ritz demanding scones, they'll likely be lynched.'

'The Kumu did *not* kill the professor,' snapped Roth. 'How many more times must I say it? They liked each other – he was like a father to them, as he was to me. They would never have hurt him.'

'I believe you,' said Lonsdale soothingly. 'Although it's a pity they vanished the same day that he was last seen alive. It looks suspicious, to say the least.'

'It does,' acknowledged Roth. 'But that doesn't mean they're guilty.'

Lonsdale was thoughtful. 'Then maybe they abandoned the museum *before* he died. Or they went to Paddington Station to snatch a word with him before the train left for Devon, which would explain why he got off. Perhaps a member of his family might know more.'

'He had no family,' said Roth, 'which is why going to Devon was such a chore for him. The ancestral home offered no friendship, and was little more than a storage facility. But his London lodgings are on Selwood Terrace, only a fifteen-minute walk from here. I tried to make myself go today, to see if he'd left any clues about what happened, but I couldn't go in.' He brightened. 'Will you do it? I can give you the key.'

'It would be better if we went together.'

Roth shook his head. 'I can't. Please, Alec – go tomorrow. We must prove the Kumu innocent, because I'll never forgive myself if they're hanged for a crime they didn't commit. Nor will you.'

'Very well,' agreed Lonsdale, although he was not sure how he would keep his promise when he had arranged to take Anne to the Christmas cracker exhibition with Jack and Emelia. He wondered if they might help him search Dickerson's house, but dismissed that notion at once. Anne would be game, but Emelia would object and would certainly report it to her stuffy parents. 'However, you should be aware that Dickerson was killed by a panga. I told the police it wasn't a Kumu-style weapon, but I'm not sure they believed me.'

He took pen and paper and sketched from memory the one Bradwell had drawn.

'The Kumu would never use anything like that,' declared Roth confidently. 'They prefer ones with longer, thinner blades.'

Lonsdale stood to leave, then paused. 'Just one more question: why did you and Dickerson visit the Broadmoor Criminal Lunatic Asylum?'

'To see the chaplain, Thomas Ashe, who had some Ashanti artefacts that he wanted to donate. Ashe didn't have time to come to London, so we went to Broadmoor, as the professor hoped he'd have something we could use in the Empire and Africa exhibition.' Roth shuddered. 'He didn't, and I still have nightmares about that place.'

'Why?' asked Lonsdale. 'Is it so terrible?'

'It stank of cabbage, dirty feet and despair,' said Roth. 'And there was a nasty, reverberating echo every time a door was slammed shut. It was horrible.'

It was nearing nine o'clock when Lonsdale finally arrived home, tired, cold and grubby from the soot-impregnated fog. He left his hat and coat in the hall, then heard voices emanating from the drawing room. For a moment, he thought it was Emelia and Jack, but then recognized Hulda's distinctive tones. Puzzled as to why she should be visiting at such an hour, he pushed open the door and went inside.

'There you are at last,' said Hulda, speaking from his favourite hearthside chair, where she was settled very comfortably with a glass of Jack's best brandy – brandy that had been forbidden to Lonsdale on the grounds that he would not appreciate it. 'Where have you been?'

Lonsdale told her, including the news that someone had been so determined to muddy the waters around Dickerson's murder that he had tried to burn down the mortuary.

'So you were within grabbing distance of the killer, but you let him go?' she asked incredulously.

'If he was within grabbing distance, he'd be behind bars,' retorted Lonsdale tartly, sitting on the chaise longue, which was not nearly as comfortable as his chair. 'But he had too great a lead. Why are *you* here?'

Hulda waved a sheaf of papers. 'Because Bradwell asked his medical friends for copies of their reports on Haldane, Tait and Bowyer, and he sent a set to me. Obviously, these are the notes they made *before* the three deaths were designated "natural" by the police.'

Lonsdale leafed through them. 'So all three were killed with what each surgeon thought – independently – to be some kind of machete-type weapon. Dickerson's makes four identical murders.'

'Bradwell asked to examine the other bodies, to compare wounds, but permission was denied by Commissioner Henderson himself, who informed him that all three died of natural causes. Besides, Tait and Haldane have already been buried.'

'This is nasty,' said Jack, looking from one to the other in distaste. 'I thought you'd have had your fill of violent death, and yet here you are, meddling again. Are you insane? It could be dangerous – like it was the last time you tried to show the police how to do their jobs.'

'He's right, you know,' said Lonsdale, after suggesting that Jack might sleep easier if he listened to no more of the conversation; Jack went with alacrity. 'Burnside thought someone was following me at the Thurloe Square market. Not Voules, but someone slight, dark and bowler-hatted. Four murders and an attempted arson . . . we aren't dealing with angels here.'

Hulda was sombre. 'Peters came to the office to say that while he was glad we were ready to swim in waters that have been forbidden to him, he won't condone us putting ourselves at risk.

He wants us to be extremely careful, and if there's any hint of danger, we're to desist immediately.'

'Why didn't he say that in the mortuary?'

'Because he didn't know then that *I* was followed as well – by a short, thin man with a moustache and a bowler hat, who sounds remarkably similar to the person Burnside saw trailing you. Peters went on to remark that Maclean is small, slender, moustachioed, and favours bowlers.'

Lonsdale blinked. 'Maclean and half of London! Peters can't possibly think that Maclean is following us based on that sort of description.'

'Well, my account was more detailed than Burnside's,' said Hulda. 'Personally, though, I'm inclined to believe that Maclean has more pressing matters to concern him than a pair of reporters.'

Lonsdale was not sure what to think. 'Commissioner Henderson is a weakling, who bends with the political wind. He won't have decided to cover up these murders on his own, so who's been talking to him?'

'The Church?' asked Hulda. 'Although Peters didn't think so, and religion seems to have played no major role in the lives of the other three.'

'On the contrary, Haldane ran a newspaper for Evangelicals, Bowyer was a Catholic who paid for a church in Great Ormond Street, and Dickerson was a committed High Anglican. Ergo, religion was important to all four, although as Bowyer was a Catholic and Haldane a non-conformist, I'm not sure we can blame the Church of England.'

'Then what about the government?' asked Hulda.

'If so, then the person I chased must've been a hireling. I didn't see him clearly, but there was nothing in his demeanour that suggested high political office.'

'A hireling who could've led us to his master,' said Hulda pointedly.

Lonsdale rubbed his chin. 'His master won't be Maclean. I don't care what Peters or *The Echo* says – Maclean isn't some cunning genius who can manipulate high-ranking police officers into over-looking his crimes. If Maclean has been following us, then he'll have been hired, too.'

'You may be right. We'll find out on Monday.'

'Monday? Why not tomorrow?'

'Because I'm going to archery practice, and you're booked to entertain your prickly wife-to-be and her fearsome sister.'

Lonsdale was sorely tempted to point out that Hulda was more fearsome than Emelia could ever be. 'The Christmas cracker exhibition at the South Kensington Museum.' He brightened. 'That's not far from Selwood Terrace, where Dickerson lived. I wonder . . .'

'You're thinking of leaving them to powder their pretty noses for an hour, while you see what might be learned from the professor's humble abode,' mused Hulda. 'I suppose I could join you there. My targets won't object.'

'Then we'll do it,' determined Lonsdale. 'We won't solve the case by Christmas Eve unless we make some sacrifices.'

'True,' said Hulda. 'I'll meet you at Selwood Terrace at ten o'clock.'

'Two o'clock,' countered Lonsdale. 'Some of us have to go to church in the morning. The Humbages have taken to worshipping at Christ Church of Lancaster Gate with Jack and me, and my absence would be noted. I don't want Humbage and Emelia condemning me as a godless heathen, on top of all my other flaws.'

Hulda regarded him oddly. 'You shouldn't let them bully you, Alec. They aren't better than you, no matter what they think.'

Lonsdale was taken aback, not only by the vague compliment – she was not in the habit of dispensing those – but by her use of his first name. It happened so rarely that he was inclined to take note when it did.

'Perhaps I *should* stand up to them,' he acknowledged.

Hulda went to collect her hat. 'Until two o'clock then. And if you need an excuse to satisfy your ladies, tell them you're going to collect their Christmas presents. That'll shut them up.'

FIVE

Although Lonsdale was not especially devout, going to church was something he had always done – his father was a vicar, and Sunday services had been the highlight of the week in the Lonsdale household. Christ Church of Lancaster Gate lay just across Bayswater from Kensington Gardens, so was a convenient place to attend. Its vicar was also noted for his concise sermons, which was another point in its favour. The church was a handsome Gothic affair with a needle spire and was once known as 'the thousand pound church', because of the huge sums the wealthy Bayswater congregation put into the collection plate each week.

It was another grey day, but at least it was not raining. Lonsdale and Jack were slightly late because Lonsdale had overslept, while Jack had been unable to find the cufflinks Emelia had given him, which she had asked him to wear that day. As they hurried along, Jack talked about Haldane and Bowyer.

'Good men,' he said, 'although Sir George had a sharp tongue and Haldane never paid for anything if he could help it. They were both devoted to the law, and how it must ensure fairness for all, regardless of social status. They'll be missed.'

'What was that?' said Lonsdale, turning suddenly at a movement that flickered at the corner of his eye. He thought he saw a small figure dart away, but when he looked harder, he only saw the portly silhouette of Voules.

'Him!' said Jack, wrinkling his nose in disgust. 'Still, at least there's no Sunday edition of *The Echo*, so we don't have to worry about the servants sending it up while we're entertaining the Humbages. I can't see Sir Gervais being impressed with that.'

'We'd better hurry,' said Lonsdale as the clock struck ten. 'We're late.'

They arrived to find the whole Humbage family – with the exception of Lady Gertrude, who had recently declared herself an agnostic as an excuse to stay in bed – waiting outside the church with barely concealed irritation. Humbage and his wife Agatha muttered crossly to each other, while Emelia's face was as black as thunder. The only one to smile was Anne.

'We were beginning to think you weren't coming,' said Emelia pointedly. 'The service is already starting.'

'Of course we were coming – there are no religious sceptics in *our* family,' retorted Lonsdale, unable to help himself. He offered his arm to Anne and led her inside before Emelia could think of a rejoinder.

The others followed, Emelia speaking in a furiously hissing voice to her mother, no doubt about Lonsdale's surly rejoinder. Meanwhile,

Humbage was regaling Jack with what he and his dear friend Lord Carlingford thought of cannibals rampaging around London, not to mention dangerous lunatics absconding from Broadmoor. Lonsdale smothered a smile when Jack guilelessly remarked that Carlingford had told *him* that he had no opinion one way or the other about either.

'There should be an enquiry into both, though,' said Humbage, floundering for a way to save face. 'It would be a better use of public funds than poking about in the private affairs of prominent people. I refer, of course, to Superintendent Hayes's irritating insistence on exploring what happened to Haldane in the Royal Courts of Justice.'

'Of course he should insist,' said Jack, startled. 'Haldane was chopped to pieces, and as a conscientious officer, he's naturally keen to catch the person who did it.'

'It was suicide,' came Humbage's astonishing response. 'He was a bankrupt, which is why he never paid for anything. He killed himself because he couldn't bear the shame.'

Lonsdale stopped walking and turned to Jack. 'Is it true? Haldane was in debt?'

Jack raised his hands in a shrug. 'It's the first I've heard of it.'

'My friend Sir Algernon told me,' said Humbage smugly. 'So of course it's true.'

'Fleetwood-Pelham is a notorious tattle-mouth,' said Jack curtly. 'And you can never trust a gossip to tell the truth.'

'Sir Algernon *is* a gossip, but I trust anything he tells *me*,' returned Humbage sharply. 'Haldane's death was self-murder. Ask Commissioner Henderson if you don't believe me.'

There was no time for further debate, as the choir was already processing into the chancel, signalling the start of the service. Lonsdale would have sat at the back to conceal the fact that they were late, but Humbage marched to 'his' pew at the front, his entourage trailing at his heels. Lonsdale winced as Humbage bulled his way through the last of the choristers in order to get there, and a whole verse of 'Lo! He comes with clouds descending' was without its basses.

The church looked pretty, decked out with holly ready for Christmas, and the third of the four Advent candles was already lit. There was an atmosphere of joyous anticipation among the congregation, and Lonsdale enjoyed singing the carols he remembered so well from his happy youth. He tried not to dwell on the murders, or the fact that he had very little time to solve them and would waste a day with Emelia and Anne. Then it occurred to him that if he thought spending a day with his betrothed was 'wasting' it, perhaps he should not be engaged at all.

After the service, everyone was in a better mood, and there were no snipes or arguments until they arrived at Jack's house, where Emelia sniffed the scent of the cooking dinner and angrily declared that Jack should have remembered how she hated lamb.

'It's beef,' said Jack. 'At least, that's what the cook told me.'

'It's lamb,' declared Emelia sulkily. 'And your cook would be better employed brewing up vats of broth in a workhouse. I won't have her here when we're married.'

'You will,' said Jack firmly. 'She's been with me for years, and I won't oust her.' He smiled to take the sting from his words. 'We can always eat out a lot – you like that. But let's talk about this afternoon. Are you looking forward to the exhibition?'

'Not really,' said Emelia petulantly. 'Who cares about Christmas crackers?'

'Perhaps you should stay home then,' suggested Lonsdale at once, thinking how much more pleasant the excursion would be without her.

She glared at him. 'Anne can't go without a chaperone. It would be improper.'

Lonsdale thought of all the times he and Hulda had been alone together. Why was it acceptable for one woman, but not another? Or did Emelia feel Hulda was not worthy of the same degree of consideration as Anne? The notion made Lonsdale dislike her even more.

'I don't think Anne's reputation will suffer an irredeemable stain by being seen with me at a public exhibition,' he said. 'You and Jack can do something else if you like.'

'No!' said Emelia quickly, when Anne started to agree. 'I must come; it's my duty.'

When they sat at the table, Emelia declared that two of her forks were filthy and must be replaced, then complained about a hole in the tablecloth. Desperate to discuss something other than his domestic shortcomings, Jack rashly mentioned that Lonsdale would be looking into the murder of Professor Dickerson. Lonsdale shot him an irritable glance.

'You should've refused,' said Humbage immediately. 'Morley declines to dabble in such low matters, and you should strive to emulate him. I deplore your fascination with the dangerous and disreputable.'

'So do I,' put in Emelia haughtily. 'It should be beneath your dignity, and you should leave it to the police. Besides, I can't imagine his bereaved family will want the gutter press prying into their private lives.'

Lonsdale bristled. '*The Pall Mall Gazette* is *not* the gutter press!'

'Morley isn't,' acknowledged Humbage. 'But Stead is a different kettle of fish. If you're to be my son-in-law, I'd sooner you stopped working for him.'

There was silence around the table, as everyone waited to see how Lonsdale would react to being told to abandon his chosen career. Jack held his breath, Anne looked stricken, while Emelia and her mother's expressions were gloating. Lonsdale struggled to control his temper, not about to give Emelia the satisfaction of letting her father have a piece of his mind for such pompous presumption.

'I'll bear your concerns in mind,' he managed to say mildly. 'But shall we send for pudding? The cook's made Jack's favourite – semolina. He once told me that he'd never marry any woman who didn't share his passion for semolina.'

It was wholly untrue, as Jack didn't much like it, but Lonsdale had the satisfaction of watching Emelia force down her helping of the glutinous mass – which he ensured was a large one – in an effort to win her future husband's approbation.

The exchanges with Humbage and Emelia had left Lonsdale more irritated than they should have done, and he spent much of the journey to the South Kensington Museum quietly fuming. He was conscious that Emelia was gratified to have annoyed him, and she chatted merrily to Anne, who kept glancing at Lonsdale, trying to gauge his mood.

Eventually, he realized he was ruining his afternoon with the woman who would be his wife, and made an effort to snap out of his funk. He forced a smile as he, Jack, Emelia and Anne alighted from the carriage, and was politely solicitous when Emelia misjudged the distance to the kerb and stumbled in a puddle. Anne instantly endeared herself to him by bursting into laughter. Emelia snatched her arm away from Lonsdale and stalked inside.

'She means no harm, Alec,' Anne whispered as she and Lonsdale followed. 'She's only trying to do what's expected of a proper Victorian lady. Don't let it bother you.'

The clocks were just striking two o'clock as they entered the South Kensington Museum, which meant that Lonsdale would be late for his meeting with Hulda. He tried to recall what shops were nearby, which might have a suitable present. He remembered a fishmonger, although that was hardly helpful. Then he recalled Garrard in Albemarle Street. It was a good twenty minutes' walk, which would explain why he needed an hour to run his errand.

Feeling it would be suspicious – and rude – to disappear imme-diately, he fussed about buying tickets, escorting the ladies to the cloakroom to divest themselves of their winter coats, and then strolling around the main exhibition room.

Christmas crackers had been introduced to the country some thirty years earlier, and were twists of paper containing sweets. They had grown increasingly popular and elaborate, and some now cost a fortune, as they were filled with jewellery or were painted with gold leaf. Lonsdale gaped his disbelief at some, wondering who would spend such vast sums of money on something so utterly frivolous.

The exhibition was not particularly busy, despite its seasonal nature, and Lonsdale supposed most of the crowds had gone to the Natural History Museum, where they could see dinosaurs. Thus it was easy to spot a familiar figure among the browsers.

'For heaven's sake, Voules,' he snapped. 'Can't you even let me have a Sunday without dogging my every move?'

'Lonsdale!' exclaimed Voules in unconvincing surprise. 'Fancy seeing you here! I adore crackers, and this is the third time I've been to look around. Lovely things, crackers.'

'Then who designed the first one?' demanded Lonsdale, who had read the answer on the ticket, where it had been presented as a fact that anyone remotely intelligent should already know.

'Tom Smith of Finsbury Square,' replied Voules promptly. 'Although the paper hats, little gifts and pretty designs were innova-tions introduced by his son Walter.'

Lonsdale blinked, sure Voules could not have known such details unless he really had been there before. Just then, Anne, Jack and Emelia approached. Polite greetings were exchanged, then Lonsdale told Anne he was going to collect her Christmas gift. She was gratifyingly dismayed to lose his company but smiled sweetly anyway.

'But Mr Voules is an authority on crackers,' he added airily. 'I'm sure he'll be delighted to answer any questions you might have.'

'I will,' said Voules graciously, and Lonsdale was under the impression that he meant it; he smiled at the ladies. 'I aim to write a piece about crackers for *The Echo* tomorrow. The editor never puts a paper to bed without a contribution from me, so the presses won't start up until I oblige him.'

'Then how about a story on the Natural History Museum?' asked Lonsdale wickedly. 'And the fact that Richard Owen is going to use electricity on his fossils, which will bring them to life. Forget the escaped cannibals – resurrected dinosaurs will be much more terrifying.'

'They would,' agreed Voules, his eyes so bright with interest that Lonsdale experienced a twinge of conscience. It was like stealing sweets from a baby – easy but hardly fair.

'Just a moment,' said Emelia, raising her hand when Lonsdale began to back away. 'It's Sunday. No shops are open, so how can you collect a parcel?'

'By special arrangement,' replied Lonsdale loftily, daring her to challenge him further and experiencing a flash of unreasonable annoyance at Hulda for devising an excuse that was so glaringly flawed.

'With Garrard, the official Crown jewellers?' persisted Emelia in brazen disbelief. 'They will open on the Sabbath for *you*?'

Lonsdale realized he had dug himself into a terrible hole – now he would *have* to buy something from Garrard because Emelia would know if his gift to Anne came from elsewhere. It would cost a fortune – money he would far rather spend on something more practical.

'Of course,' he replied, trying to sound nonchalant. 'And I'll be late unless I leave now.'

'Then go,' said Anne with a fond smile that made him feel guilty. 'I can't wait for Christmas now! A gift from Garrard. I wonder what Jack has bought for you, Em.'

Jack's panicky expression revealed it was nothing so exotic, so that Lonsdale experienced another twinge of guilt as he took his leave.

It was only a short way to Selwood Terrace, and the house the professor had bought for its proximity to the Natural History Museum. Even so, Lonsdale was half an hour late. He stopped outside, breathing hard from running the whole way, and saw a pretty, two-storey terraced house built of earth-coloured brick. The door was black, and so was Hulda's mood. She glared at him as she rose from where she had been sitting on the garden wall.

'I could've been shooting,' she said icily, 'but instead I've been here, twiddling my thumbs. Being late for an appointment is rude!'

'Yes,' acknowledged Lonsdale. 'It is, and I apologize without reservation. Unfortunately, escaping from Anne and Emelia is easier said than done, and it took longer than I anticipated. In the end, I left them with Voules, who just happened to be there.'

'With Voules?' echoed Hulda, and her face broke into a grin of delight. 'I can't imagine that'll please them. No one wants to spend Sunday with a slug.'

Lonsdale laughed, and turned to the front door. The key slipped into the lock easily, and then he and Hulda were in a hallway in which hung a collection of African shields, weapons, masks and beaded clothing. The main room contained more of the same, along with a bookcase stuffed full of academic tomes on ethnography. Hulda quickly moved to a desk, through which she began to rifle. Lonsdale began to search through a bureau.

'Here's a letter from Medical Superintendent Orange at Broadmoor,' she announced after a moment. 'He thanks Dickerson for his helpful remarks and promises to look into them. It's dated two days *after* Dickerson and Roth signed the visitors' book that Milner saw. Roth was lying.'

Lonsdale took it. 'I'm not sure—'

'Roth said he and Dickerson went to speak to Chaplain Ashe about donating Ashanti spears to the museum, but instead, they met this Orange and made some sort of commentary that Orange has promised to review. We'd better have another word with your friend.'

Lonsdale wanted to argue, but she was right: the letter from Orange did indeed suggest that more business had been conducted at Broadmoor that day than speaking to the chaplain. He made no reply, and for a while they worked in silence.

'There are lots of receipts and ticket stubs,' he said eventually. 'For tea rooms, restaurants, operas and concerts.'

Hulda indicated the desk. 'And here's evidence that they enjoyed a few cricket matches shortly after they arrived. Of course, we already knew that the Kumu like those things.'

'But we didn't appreciate quite how much time the professor spent with them,' mused Lonsdale, 'or how much money – probably his own – he spent. Moreover, nearly all these tickets are in blocks of six: Dickerson, the three Kumu, Roth and . . . who else?'

Hulda held up a letter. 'Perhaps William Ingram, owner of *The Illustrated London News* – the paper his father founded.'

Lonsdale took it from her. It was a brief note thanking the professor for his hospitality and the opportunity to meet the Kumu at *Iolanthe* the previous evening and expressing the hope that there would be many more such occasions in the future.

'Roth didn't mention him,' said Lonsdale.

'No, said Hulda pointedly. 'He didn't. How very interesting. But we've done all we can here, so I suggest we visit Mr Ingram immediately.'

'No,' said Lonsdale firmly. 'First, Ingram lives in Boston, his parliamentary constituency. And second, I can't abandon my fiancée to race to Lincolnshire with you.'

Hulda smiled superiorly. 'But Ingram is in London, which I know as I read *The Illustrated London News* to remind myself why our paper is such a superior vehicle. He's retired from politics and is in the city because his sister Ada is married to a monkey.'

'Monkey Hornby!' exclaimed Lonsdale. 'Of course! Earlier this year Hornby became the only man ever to captain both our national rugby and cricket teams. Even you should be aware of this, Friederichs – he's the best-known sportsman in the country. *The Illustrated London News* has pushed the connection strongly because everyone loves sport.'

'Not everyone,' said Hulda pointedly. 'Other than archery, shooting and cycling, of course. Regardless, Ingram's in London, so we'll visit him and ask how often he was the sixth member of this social party. He may even know where the Kumu are hiding.'

'We can go this evening, after I've taken Anne and Emelia home.

We can go to see Roth as well – ask why he didn't mention meeting Orange at Broadmoor.'

'And here's something else,' said Hulda, holding out another letter. 'This reminds Dickerson about a meeting he was to attend back in November – a meeting of a group styling itself "the Watchers".'

Lonsdale took it. 'It's signed "Grim Death". It must be a joke.'

'I don't believe it is,' said Hulda. 'Read the message, Lonsdale – there's nothing amusing or light-hearted in its tone. I would say it was deadly serious.'

Lonsdale scanned it quickly and was inclined to agree.

> *My dear Dickerson,*
> *All proceeds apace for our meeting of this month. All London will see what the Watchers are capable of on Christmas Eve. It will be an event to catch the city's entire attention but will be nothing compared to the unspeakable Happening for the following day. Then, we shall give our minds, bodies and souls to our Great Lord, and he will reward us with the blood of life. We shall make a sacrifice and gain untold riches in return. We are the chosen, to do his bidding, and London will never be the same once we have made His will known.*
> *Your faithful servant,*
> *Grim Death*

'Have you heard of the Watchers?' he asked Hulda.

'No, but it sounds sinister, and I think we should see what we can find out about it. Here's another letter from "Grim Death", this one calling a meeting on the fourth of December, to discuss "the demise of our much-loved brother".'

'That's the day after Archbishop Tait died,' said Lonsdale. 'Do you think it refers to him? That he was also a member of these Watchers?'

'It would make sense, given the other connections between Dickerson and Tait,' said Hulda. 'But look at the end of the second letter, Lonsdale. It again mentions the great event planned for Christmas Eve, when all Watchers will stand united for one "supreme sacrifice".'

Lonsdale regarded the letter uneasily. 'We need to find out more about this sect and its intentions.'

'A "happening to change the world" is mentioned in this letter, too,' said Hulda, handing him a third missive, although the handwriting was different and it was unsigned. 'It also says that on Christmas Eve some two hundred people will learn exactly what the Watchers are capable of, and London will never forget it.'

'This letter definitely makes it sound as if the "happening" entails something very sinister,' said Lonsdale, taking it from her and reading it quickly. 'Listen: "And all Watchers will make a sacrifice of their very souls to the Great Lord in return for drinking their fill of the sacred blood of ultimate sacrifice."' He looked up at Hulda. 'What Great Lord do they mean . . . God?'

'That does not sound like a holy "Great Lord" to me,' averred Hulda worriedly. 'Not if it involves blood and sacrifices. It sounds more . . . frightening, Satanic even.'

'Could it be the "higher authority" that prevented Superintendent Henderson from exploring the murder of Tait?'

'That makes sense,' nodded Hulda. 'After all, the language and imagery of these letters make it clear that the Watchers aim to do something terrible. Why else would they talk about "what the Watchers are capable of"? You can tell from the tone that Londoners won't like whatever they intend to do. Not on Christmas Eve *or* Christmas Day.'

Lonsdale agreed. 'Which means we have to stop them.'

Hulda regarded him with eyes that were huge in her pale face. 'Then there's not a moment to lose!'

In an agitated, anxious frame of mind, Lonsdale returned to the South Kensington Museum to discover that Emelia and Anne had tired of Voules's company and were impatient to go home. Lonsdale had taken longer than the promised hour, which Emelia made sure no one forgot for the rest of the day. Worse, Anne begged to look at the parcel he had collected, and he was obliged to tell another lie about it not being ready. Thankfully, she believed him; Jack did not.

'You do realize you'll have to provide something really special now,' he murmured as they waited to hire a brougham. 'It's that or be exposed as a dissembler. Let me know how much money you want to borrow, because Garrard is expensive.'

'I don't suppose you'd get me something, would you?' Lonsdale muttered back. 'I won't have time, not now this group – the Watchers

– is planning something we must stop. I need to spend every waking moment on it.'

'If I do, Emelia is sure to find out, and then you'll really be in trouble. You must buy it yourself, no matter how busy you are. Anne's going to be your *wife*, Alec. If you can't find time to do something that'll please her, then perhaps you shouldn't get married at all.'

Lonsdale was not sure how to respond, although he found himself more concerned with his enquiries than a future that seemed distant and somewhat unreal. He was engrossed in his thoughts all the way home. Fortunately, Anne and Emelia were more interested in denigrating Voules, so did not notice.

They arrived at the Humbage home in Gordon Square, where Lonsdale broke the news that he would be unable to linger.

'But I expected you to stay for dinner,' cried Anne, disappointed, 'after which we'll have music around the piano.'

Lonsdale was grateful to be spared the ordeal, as none of the Humbages were in the slightest bit musical, and their efforts tended to be painful. Moreover, he had no desire to spend time with Humbage. He could hear the man from the hallway, braying to Jack about something else his 'good friends' at the Palace had confided.

'Is he bragging about his association with Lord Curly-Tail and Fleetwood-Lighthouse again?' muttered Lady Gertrude, who held a very large glass of sherry. 'Fool! They'll never give *him* a job at the Palace – they have real friends they'd rather promote.'

'His obsession with winning a court appointment is partly your fault, Grandmama,' said Anne quietly. 'You talk about your old connections, and it makes him feel inferior because he doesn't have any. So he aims to acquire some of his own.'

Lady Gertrude cackled. 'You don't just go out and "acquire" them, girl! They have to be earned, and poor Gervais doesn't have the knack. If he has any sense, he'll desist before he makes a total ass of himself.'

She hobbled away to top up her glass, leaving Lonsdale and Anne to spend a few minutes on their own, free from chaperones and escorts. By the time he left, Lonsdale remembered why he had fallen in love with Anne and was more at peace with his decision to marry.

It was a filthy evening, not only bitterly cold, but sleeting as well, and there was an unpleasant wind scything in from the north.

Lonsdale was aware of Voules trailing after him as he left Gordon Square, but by the time he reached Tottenham Court Road and hailed a hansom, *The Echo* reporter had disappeared. Lonsdale was not surprised – it was no night to be out.

He arrived at Roth's lodgings, then had a chilly half-hour while he waited for Hulda. He considered going in without her, but she had made it clear earlier that she would be vexed if he did, and Hulda vexed was not something he wanted. Moreover, he was sure her tardiness was revenge for him keeping her waiting at Dickerson's home that afternoon.

He stamped his feet and blew on his fingers, trying to stay warm. He wished he was at home and had a sudden image of himself lounging in front of a fire with the papers and a bag of toffee. There was a woman opposite, and Lonsdale was somewhat surprised when it transpired to be Hulda rather than Anne.

She appeared eventually, looking warm and toasty inside a greatcoat with a fur collar. He glanced down at her legs, and thought she might be wearing trousers, although it was difficult to tell in the dark. Anne would never don male attire, and Lonsdale found it rather refreshing that Hulda was willing to buck convention – Anne talked about independence of spirit but would rather admire it in others than express it herself. He thought she might, when they had first met, but since becoming engaged she had fallen happily into the role of the traditional Victorian lady and all that entailed.

'Are you ready for this?' Hulda asked. 'It occurs to me that your friend might be the killer – that he murdered his mentor and arranged for the Kumu to be blamed by making them disappear. The Kumu may not even still be alive.'

Lonsdale blinked. 'That's a wild conclusion to draw from virtually no evidence! Besides, we've agreed that whoever killed Dickerson also dispatched Tait, Haldane and Bowyer. Tim Roth has no reason to harm any of those.'

'No reason that we know of,' corrected Hulda. 'Yet he lied about his visit to Broadmoor – it wasn't to collect artefacts, but to discuss something with the medical superintendent. He also failed to disclose that he, Dickerson and the Kumu were joined by a sixth person on their little outings.'

'But we never asked him about the outings,' objected Lonsdale, 'so it's hardly fair to expect him to have volunteered information about it.'

'Perhaps he's a Watcher, too, like his mentor Dickerson,' persisted Hulda. 'And he is also involved in this "unspeakable" event that is planned for Christmas.'

Lonsdale was sure she was wrong, and there followed an intense argument, after which he found himself thinking that Hulda was the last person he would want sitting opposite him at the hearth, to read and share his toffee.

They were still annoyed with each other when Lonsdale knocked on Roth's door. Roth answered wearing a baggy jacket and felt slippers and started to say he was too tired for visitors, but Hulda ignored him and stalked inside. In the sitting room, the central table was covered in old books and African gold jewellery; again, Lonsdale was aware of the odour he had noticed the last time he had been there.

'We have some questions,' began Hulda without preamble. 'Starting with Broadmoor, where we know you went to talk to Medical Superintendent Orange, not Chaplain Ashe.'

Roth stared at her. 'What makes you think that?'

'Never you mind. Just tell us the truth this time.'

'I told you the truth last time,' objected Roth. 'We went to speak to Ashe about spears. I hated the place, and had to leave when the noise of the doors slamming—'

'Did the professor leave with you?' asked Lonsdale.

Roth shook his head. 'He stayed to finish his business with Ashe.'

'So he might have gone to talk to Orange when you weren't there to see?' pressed Hulda.

'He might, I suppose, although I can't imagine what the head of a lunatic asylum and the professor had to say to each other.'

'When we searched Dickerson's house – on your recommendation – we discovered a letter indicating that Dickerson gave Orange some suggestions.'

Roth looked blank. 'Suggestions about what?'

'We don't know – yet.'

Roth shrugged. 'I know nothing about any suggestions. However, if you aim to visit Broadmoor to find out, be warned that it houses a lot of very dangerous criminals. If I were you, I'd have nothing to do with it. Now, is there anything else, or may I go to bed? I'm very tired.'

'We also found evidence that Dickerson spent a lot of money fêting the Kumu,' Hulda forged on. 'And that you were a member of his party.'

The second part was pure conjecture, but Roth nodded. 'I was, and he *did* spend a fortune. I offered to pay my own way, but he refused, on the grounds that I was his employee.'

'*He* hired you?' asked Lonsdale, surprised. 'I thought the museum paid your wages.'

He shot Hulda a triumphant glance: Roth would not kill the source of his income.

Roth nodded. 'I thought I might have to find another job when he died, but the solicitor came again today. Not only did the professor leave me his collections, but also a large sum of money. He asked that I use it to catalogue his artefacts, but it isn't binding – the choice of whether to do it is mine.'

It was Hulda's turn for the victorious look. 'He wanted you to give the best bits to the museum, but if you never curate the collection . . . well, you can keep it all, and no one will be any the wiser. *And* you have a handsome legacy into the bargain.'

'Yes,' acknowledged Roth. 'But he trusted me to carry out his wishes, and I shall.'

'Were you aware of this bequest before today?' asked Lonsdale, more for Hulda's benefit than his own.

Roth shook his head. 'It was a pleasant shock.'

'The tickets in Dickerson's house reveal that he paid for *six* people to go out and about,' said Hulda. 'Him, you, the three Kumu and who else?'

'William Ingram, owner of *The Illustrated London News*,' replied Roth. 'He didn't come all the time, though. He was writing a piece about the Kumu, although I can't imagine he'll publish it now they're accused of murder.'

'I imagine he will,' countered Hulda. 'Pictures of cannibals at play will sell like hot cakes.'

'He's not that kind of man,' said Roth earnestly. 'He believes they're innocent, just like I do. But why not ask him? I expect he'll be at his club tonight.'

'Which club?' demanded Hulda.

'The Garraway,' replied Roth. 'It's on Exchange Alley. Do you know it?'

Lonsdale frowned as he recalled what Morley had told him about that particular establishment. 'Tait, Haldane, Bowyer and Dickerson were all members of the Garraway.'

'Dickerson certainly was,' nodded Roth. 'So are two hundred others, including Ingram. It's how he and the professor met. They put me up for membership – I was formally admitted a few weeks ago. It was good of them, because it's a nice club.'

'Are the fees not too expensive?' asked Hulda, looking pointedly at the cramped lodgings.

'They have "commoners" – men who want to contribute to the life of the place, but who can't afford to join. The fees are waived in return for certain basic services, like acting as wine steward or serving food. Thus the money that would've been paid to servants goes on our membership instead.'

Hulda looked deeply suspicious of such a benevolent arrangement. 'So did you meet Tait, Bowyer and Haldane at this progressive establishment?'

'Not to my knowledge,' replied Roth. 'But I wouldn't have recognized any of them, so perhaps they were there when I was, but perhaps they weren't. I can't say, I'm afraid.'

'And the cannibals?' asked Hulda, frustration turning her caustic. 'Did the professor offer to make them "commoners", too?'

Roth smiled. 'I hardly think the Khoikhoi would appreciate that! They wouldn't understand or enjoy the ethos of a club, no matter how pleasant.'

'Khoikhoi?' asked Lonsdale. 'You mean Kumu.'

Roth blew out his cheeks in a sigh, and pointed to the table, with its books and jewellery. 'Forgive me. I've been working on the professor's Khoikhoi collection today – he loved all African culture, but Southern Africans were his real speciality – so they're in my mind. A slip of the tongue from a weary man in indifferent health.'

'But not too weary to start going through Dickerson's belongings,' said Hulda pointedly, 'especially the gold ones.'

'He *asked* me to do the gold ones first,' said Roth crossly. 'In his will.'

'Right,' said Hulda, and moved to another subject. 'Have you heard of a group called the Watchers?'

Roth blinked his bemusement. 'Not offhand.'

'Professor Dickerson was a member of it.'

'Was he?' asked Roth, looking bewildered. 'He never mentioned it to me, but we did not have the kind of relationship that entailed sharing—'

'What about Grim Death?' interrupted Hulda briskly.

Roth's mystification intensified. 'What about it?'

'I refer to a person calling himself that,' said Hulda. 'A person who corresponded with the professor, and who signed several letters with that name.'

Roth spoke sharply, to prevent her from cutting off his explanation a second time. 'I was his *assistant*, Miss Friederichs. Our relationship, while affectionate, was professional. We rarely discussed our private lives, so I've no idea if he knew a "Grim Death" or was a member of this Watchers Club.'

'Then how can we find out?' persisted Hulda. 'By going to Devon? He had a house there, did he not? That's where he was going when you saw him off at Paddington – to collect materials for the Empire and Africa exhibition.'

'You'd be wasting your time if you did,' said Roth. 'He spent all his time here. He had no family in Devon, and his only friends, as far as I know, were at the Garraway or the museum. And I've met no one in either of those called Grim Death.'

Hulda regarded him with a stern eye. 'Your mentor and employer – a man you profess to love and admire – was brutally murdered, Mr Roth. Are you sure you know nothing that will allow his killer to be brought to justice?'

'If I did, Miss Friederichs,' retorted Roth curtly, 'I'd have told the police.'

Outside in the street, Lonsdale and Hulda began to argue again. He was sure Roth was far too gentle – and physically feeble – to launch the kind of frenzied attack that had deprived Dickerson of his life, while she thought Roth had lied throughout the entire interrogation, and not a word he uttered should be believed.

'He has a motive,' she said, as they left the quiet, residential streets and aimed for the more brightly lit Fulham Road. 'He benefited hugely from Dickerson's will. No one will monitor what he does with the professor's collections, so he can give the museum the rubbish and keep the best for himself.'

'Dickerson trusted him to be honest,' argued Lonsdale. 'Besides, it's clear to me that Roth had no idea about the professor's bequest. As far as he was concerned, Dickerson's death meant the loss of his livelihood and the work he loved.'

'Of course he knew,' scoffed Hulda. 'They would've discussed it, so Dickerson could tell him what he wanted done. The moment Roth found out that Dickerson dead was worth more than Dickerson alive, he dispatched him.'

'Very well, let's assume that Roth killed Dickerson for money,' said Lonsdale. 'Tell me why he murdered the other three? Bradwell believes all four victims were claimed by the same hand, so why did Roth attack them? He just told us that he wouldn't have recognized any of them.'

'How do you know he was telling the truth? Besides, just because we don't know his motive doesn't mean he's innocent.'

Lonsdale shook his head in exasperation. 'You're wrong, Friederichs. He's lost more than he gained by Dickerson's death – regular and fulfilling employment, an introduction to a club, free trips to tea rooms, operas and cricket matches . . .'

'Cricket is dull and incomprehensible; English cakes are stodgy and tasteless, and as for light opera . . .' Hulda sniffed. 'Well, *I* might kill to escape being dragged to all that nonsense. Perhaps *that*'s why the Kumu vanished – to escape Dickerson's awful outings.'

'He took them because they wanted to go,' argued Lonsdale, although he realized he only had Roth's word about that.

'Is that Voules behind us?' asked Hulda, as she glanced behind in readiness for crossing the road. 'No, it's too small. Lord! It looks uncannily like Maclean!'

Lonsdale peered into the misty darkness and saw the familiar short, bowler-hatted figure. 'Or the person who tried to set the mortuary on fire. Stay here.'

He broke into a run, but so did the man. Then the fog thickened suddenly. Lonsdale skidded to a halt and listened intently, hoping for footsteps to reveal where his quarry might have gone, but there was nothing, and he was forced to concede defeat and return to Hulda.

'I could have told you he was too far away to catch,' she scoffed. 'We should've separated – one to act as a decoy, and the other to sneak up and grab him from behind. I'd have suggested it if you hadn't hared off like a rabbit.'

'It's nine o'clock,' Lonsdale said, as a nearby church clock began to chime the hour. 'Not too late to go to the Garraway Club and see what its surviving members have to tell us about the deaths of four of their own.'

'I'll go with you,' averred Hulda, and risked life and limb by stepping into the road to hail a hansom. She ignored the driver's angry tirade as he was obliged to swerve.

'You won't be allowed in,' warned Lonsdale. 'Clubs are for men.'

'We'll see about that,' determined Hulda, and climbed in the carriage. 'So, to recap. Four members of the Garraway have been murdered, and we need to ask what its other members can tell us about it, especially Ingram, who accompanied Dickerson on some of his outings . . .'

'We also need to find out if any member is named – or, more likely, nicknamed – Grim Death, and see if we can learn more about these worrisome Watchers and their nasty sacrifices. And while we're there, we should see if anyone will tell us what "unspeakable happening" is being planned for Christmas Eve.'

'I don't like the sound of these Watchers at all, Lonsdale,' said Hulda unhappily. 'Events to change the world; minds, bodies and souls sacrificed to some Great Lord; drinking sacred blood and sacrifices; wanting to show everyone what they're capable of . . .'

Lonsdale agreed. 'I just wish we had longer than a week to prevent them from doing something terrible.'

Gentlemen's clubs were members-only establishments that had become popular in the early decades of the century. They were places where men could relax away from the stresses of work and home, and usually boasted a dining hall and rooms where its members could play billiards or cards, smoke, chat, read or doze off. Most were discreet on the outside, with a porter to exclude gatecrashers. Lonsdale's own club was the Oxford and Cambridge on Pall Mall, a handsome building with palatial facilities within.

There were dozens of them in the city for men in the upper and middle classes. Some catered to specific professions or religious denominations, others revolved around sport. Others still were established for men with specific political leanings – the Garraway was for Liberals and those interested in social welfare.

It was located on Exchange Alley, a curiously dog-legged lane in the City, its layout a relic from an age when buildings and thoroughfares had been smaller. The club occupied a fine, marble-faced edifice, identifiable because lights burned inside it – all the others were business premises, and so closed on Sunday evenings. Lonsdale and Hulda stepped into a handsomely appointed vestibule, where a porter immediately asked them to leave. Hulda argued, but in vain, and Lonsdale was about to suggest doing as they were told when help came from an unexpected source.

'Lonsdale!' exclaimed Burnside. 'What are you doing here?'

'What are you?' countered Lonsdale, surprised to see the photographer there.

'I'm a member,' explained Burnside. 'Or a commoner, to be precise. Obviously, I can't afford the fees for such a place, but they have a scheme whereby talented men are admitted in exchange for certain duties. I'm about to take on the role of night porter, relieving Bird here.'

Bird had already donned his hat and cloak and was halfway out the door, more than happy to leave awkward visitors for someone else to sort out. He nodded a farewell to Burnside and was gone.

'So, what do you want, Lonsdale?' asked Burnside. 'You know you can't come in – especially with a lady. They're not allowed.'

'Why not?' demanded Hulda fiercely. 'Do you think I might discuss petticoats and embarrass you all?'

'I don't think you'd need to discuss petticoats to do that,' muttered Burnside; he cleared his throat. 'Club rules, ma'am. I didn't make them – I only enforce them.'

Lonsdale took her arm and pulled her towards the door. 'Go home. They won't let you in and arguing is futile. I'll see what I can find out and tell you tomorrow.'

He thought she would argue, but she gave a brisk nod and swept out. In the street, he saw her scowl at Bird before climbing into the hansom he had flagged down for himself.

'So,' said Burnside. 'Tell me what I can do for you – consider it payment for the chops you bought me yesterday.'

Lonsdale told him why he was there. Burnside had known the four dead members but was able to say nothing that Lonsdale did not already know – that they were good Christian men, but with flaws of character that made them human. Tait was tactless, Bowyer had an offensive tongue, Haldane was miserly, and Dickerson a bore.

'Were these flaws serious enough to warrant them being murdered?'

'Of course not!' replied Burnside, startled. 'And they weren't murdered anyway – they died of natural causes. The police came and told us so today. Between you and me, I was surprised to hear it about Dickerson and Haldane, because I was to hand when their bodies were found, and the rumour then was that both had been hacked to pieces.'

'Who told you that Dickerson's death was natural? Superintendent Hayes?'

'An Inspector Wells,' replied Burnside. 'But it was official – he had a letter signed by the Commissioner of Police. Incidentally, your editor, John Morley, was invited to join the Garraway, but he said he was too busy.'

Lonsdale was glad Morley had refused, given what was happening there. He moved to another matter. 'Have you ever met Grim Death?'

'On a daily basis, when I take pictures of corpses for their grieving families. It's not an enjoyable aspect of my work, but it has one advantage: the subjects stay still and don't spoil the exposure.'

'I mean a person called Grim Death. He may be a club member.'

Burnside raised his eyebrows. 'There's certainly no one of that name on our books, although I suppose it could be a nickname. However, if it is, I can't tell you for whom.'

'Then have you heard of a group named the Watchers?'

Burnside shook his head. 'No, why? Who are they?'

'That's what I'm trying to find out. I don't suppose you know anything about an event for Christmas, do you? Something "unspeakable" and dangerous?'

'Well, a few of us will be feeding the poor,' said Burnside wryly. 'That's dangerous, because you get between them and their food at your peril.'

Lonsdale saw he was wasting his time. As a commoner, Burnside was too lowly to know anything important. 'I need to speak to William Ingram,' he said. 'Will you let me in for ten minutes?'

Burnside glanced this way and that to make sure no one was within earshot. 'Go on then, but if anyone asks, you slunk in through the back door.'

No one took any notice of Lonsdale as he walked through a series of pleasantly appointed rooms looking for Ingram. As the Garraway boasted more than two hundred members, unfamiliar faces were nothing unusual.

Eventually, he reached the smoking room, which was similar to the one in the Oxford and Cambridge Club – lots of armchairs filled with dozing ancients, a large fire and a sideboard with an array of beverages and glasses. Over the fire was the usual picture of the Queen, and to one side was a painting depicting an angel standing on top of St Paul's Cathedral, its wings furled. Its face was hauntingly beautiful, and Lonsdale thought it was a much better work of art than the royal portrait, which made Her Majesty look fat.

Before he could spot Ingram, he saw Humbage's 'friends' Lord Carlingford and Fleetwood-Pelham. Carlingford looked through him blankly, but Fleetwood-Pelham recognized him and smiled a friendly greeting.

'Lonsdale! Are you here as a guest of Gervais Humbage? He told me that you're to marry one of his daughters.'

Lonsdale just managed to stop himself from gaping his astonishment to learn that Humbage was a member of the Garraway. He made a noncommittal gesture, to ensure Humbage could never accuse him of using their relationship to sneak inside.

'Humbage,' mused Carlingford. 'Which one's he? The short, fat one with the eye-glass?'

So much for Humbage's claims to intimacy, thought Lonsdale.

'Lady Gertrude's son-in-law,' said Fleetwood-Pelham, eyes agleam. 'You must remember her, Carly. She once did an impression of Prince Albert's older brother after he was diagnosed with the French pox.'

Carlingford chuckled. 'Then I *do* remember her! A wonderful lady – excellent sense of humour. Her son-in-law . . . no, can't place him at all.'

At that point, Fleetwood-Pelham noticed an elderly member struggling to carry his overly full glass of brandy, so went to help him. Lonsdale took the opportunity to ask Carlingford a few questions about the murdered men. Fortunately, the surly lord seemed willing to talk.

'I knew Tait well,' he said. 'Bowyer, Haldane and the museum man less so. Their deaths are a tragedy, but grim death comes to us all in the end, and all we can do is pray for their eternal souls.'

'Grim death?' pounced Lonsdale.

Carlingford regarded him shrewdly. 'It's what'll happen to you if you invade other men's clubs and pretend you were invited. I've spent a lifetime among politicians and courtiers – I know when a man is lying.'

'I *was* admitted by a member,' said Lonsdale truthfully, and changed the subject before Carlingford could ask whom. 'How will the Garraway celebrate Christmas? With something special?'

'Oh, yes,' said Carlingford, smiling at last. 'We shall all go to church to celebrate the birth of our Lord Jesus Christ, then have a nice big dinner with crackers and plenty to drink.'

Lonsdale could gauge nothing from his expression and, before he could ask more, Carlingford excused himself and went to exchange greetings with a short, fat man who boasted an enormous moustache and jet-black hair that shone with oil. Carlingford addressed him as Señor d'Atte, leading Lonsdale to surmise that he was Italian. He was about to resume his hunt for Ingram when Fleetwood-Pelham returned.

'That's Viscount Sherbrooke, the former Chancellor of the Exchequer,' he said, nodding to where the old man he had helped was already asleep in a chair, the brandy glass empty at his side. He lowered his voice to a gossipy whisper. 'Drinks too much, you know.'

'This seems like a nice club,' said Lonsdale, although it had gone down in his estimation once he had learned that Humbage was a member.

Fleetwood-Pelham smiled. 'Are you thinking of joining?'

'I might,' lied Lonsdale. 'It's more conveniently located than my current one. However, I'm also considering membership of the Watchers, and I can't do both. I'll have to make a choice.'

Fleetwood-Pelham frowned. 'The Watchers Club? I've not heard of that one. Where is it?'

'It's more a sect than a club,' elaborated Lonsdale. 'It's based around here somewhere.'

'I see,' said Fleetwood-Pelham, although his mystified expression revealed that the explanation had done little to enlighten him. 'So what do these Watchers watch exactly?'

'I'm not sure,' admitted Lonsdale.

Fleetwood-Pelham raised his eyebrows. 'Then I wouldn't think you had any choice to make – a genteel establishment like this one, which enrols courtiers, churchmen, lawyers, scientists, and military men, or an organization that "watches" something, but you don't know what and you are uncertain where. Has it occurred to you that it might be something distasteful?'

'Yes,' said Lonsdale. 'It may be something to change the world.'

Fleetwood-Pelham's eyebrows shot up in alarm. 'Then I sincerely hope you will keep your distance! Claims of that sort of outcome are rarely for the good and you'll likely find yourself embroiled in something unpleasant. Personally, I think you should warn the police. If it is innocent, no harm will be done, but if it is not . . .'

'I will,' promised Lonsdale. 'Of course, the Garraway's reputation isn't pristine either – four of its members are dead in mysterious circumstances.'

Fleetwood-Pelham regarded him coolly. 'Not so! We were informed officially today that they all died of natural causes.'

'But *you* know Dickerson didn't,' said Lonsdale. 'You saw his body.'

'There did seem to be rather a lot of blood for a natural death,' conceded Fleetwood-Pelham. He glanced around to make sure no one else was listening, then spoke in a low voice. 'I won't lie to you, Lonsdale. The consensus at the Palace is that he, Tait, Bowyer and Haldane were involved in something untoward. But let the police handle it: they'll get to the truth.'

'How will they, if the deaths have been deemed natural?' asked Lonsdale. 'The truth will be buried along with the victims.'

'What the police say and what they do aren't always the same,' cautioned Fleetwood-Pelham. 'Remember: we're talking about the Archbishop of Canterbury, two prominent lawyers, and an esteemed man of science, so the police *will* investigate, you can be sure of that. But they'll do it discreetly.'

'Superintendent Hayes is their best detective,' argued Lonsdale. 'But he wasn't given the Bowyer or Haldane cases.'

'Of course not,' said Fleetwood-Pelham. 'He's so well known that a discreet enquiry by him will be impossible. I imagine Henderson has appointed a man who can move without being recognized by the press – perhaps someone who is investigating all four murders without his colleagues even knowing.'

But Lonsdale did not believe that Henderson would commission a secret enquiry and remained certain that some dark force was at work to ensure the murders were never properly explored.

'Speaking of members of the press, is William Ingram here?'

he asked, changing the subject because Fleetwood-Pelham seemed like a decent man, and he had no desire to tell him that his faith in Henderson was recklessly naïve.

Fleetwood-Pelham smiled. 'He'll be in the reading room. Follow me.'

The reading room was more of a dozing room, because every man who occupied a chair was fast asleep, and the air rang with snores and heavy breathing. Fleetwood-Pelham left Lonsdale to it, and went to talk to Señor d'Atte, who wanted to discuss some music the club was organizing for the Christmas period.

Lonsdale had met Ingram several times through Morley, who knew him well. He was a dark-haired, bustling man in his thirties. He had a copy of his own newspaper folded across his paunch, as if advertising it to fellow members. Lonsdale sat opposite him, and when Ingram did not stir from his slumbers, he contrived to poke the fire noisily enough to wake him up.

'Lord!' muttered Ingram, blinking stupidly as he came to. 'What's the time? I promised to be home by ten o'clock. My sister Ada will be worried about me. But dropping off after dinner is what happens when one has too many late nights and spends too much time racing across the city like a hansom driver.'

'Doing what?' asked Lonsdale curiously.

'Oh, this and that,' replied Ingram, scrubbing at his face to render himself more alert. 'I didn't know you were a member, Lonsdale. I invited Morley to join, but he said he was too busy.'

'He *is* busy,' said Lonsdale. 'Which is why he sent me here on his behalf. He's concerned about the four members who died in mysterious circumstances.'

'Then you can tell him that there's nothing to worry about. There were rumours of foul play, but the police say those are false. I'm not surprised – they were decent men, not the kind to attract murderous attention. Especially Dickerson. I knew him well, and a gentler, kinder man never existed.'

'And generous,' said Lonsdale. 'He treated his Kumu to cricket matches, tea and light operas.'

'Did he?' asked Ingram, suddenly furtive.

'He did, and you went with him.' Lonsdale raised his hand before Ingram could deny it. 'Tim Roth told me.'

'The young fool!' snapped Ingram angrily. 'Why couldn't he have kept his mouth shut?'

'Are you writing a story about the Kumu?'

For a moment, Lonsdale thought he would deny it, but then Ingram sighed resignedly. 'I thought our readers might be interested in how visitors from another culture see our great city. But then they disappeared, so I decided to abandon the project.'

'Or did you abandon it because you can hardly publish the opinions of people who might be murderers?'

'The Kumu didn't kill Dickerson,' said Ingram firmly. 'No one did – ask the police. He died of natural causes.'

'I saw his body,' persisted Lonsdale. 'It was hacked with a machete-like weapon – a panga, perhaps.' He showed Ingram the sketch he had made. 'His death was most certainly *not* from natural causes.'

'Even if you're right, the Kumu aren't responsible,' said Ingram. 'First, Dickerson was like a father to them and they adored him. Second, if they had killed him, they'd have sampled his flesh as a mark of respect, but the pathologist saw no evidence of cannibalism whatsoever. And third, they wouldn't have used that style of panga.'

'Roth agrees with you,' acknowledged Lonsdale. 'But do you know where they are? If so, please tell me. They're in danger as long as they're out and unprotected. They need the police—'

'The police believe them guilty,' interrupted Ingram harshly. 'So they're a lot safer in hiding than trusting in the criminal justice system. However, I've no idea where they went. Nor do I want to know. All I can say is good luck to them.'

He stood to leave, but before he reached the door there was a sudden commotion in the hallway outside – a lot of shouting and shocked gasps. Lonsdale inched forward in an attempt to find out what was going on.

'Samuel Gurney!' Señor d'Atte was shrieking in dismay; his English was heavily accented. 'He is dead! *Dead!* Another of us snatched away before his time.'

'Who's Samuel Gurney?' asked Lonsdale of Ingram.

'A banker,' replied Ingram, shocked. 'A nice chap. Liked to attend All Saints, Margaret Street, because it's so High Church as to be almost Roman Catholic, but I never held that against him.'

'What is happening?' wailed d'Atte at no one in particular. 'Police *say* the other deaths were natural, but this makes *five* men dead. It cannot be mere happenstance. It just can not!'

Lonsdale was sure of it.

SIX

L onsdale woke the next day with an uncomfortable sinking feeling in his stomach. He felt time was running out, and he had no clear notion of how to solve the mystery surrounding the deaths of the four – or perhaps now five – members of the Garraway Club. There were six days until Christmas Eve, after which he would become office-bound and the entire investigation would grind to a halt. He would have failed Morley and Peters, who wanted the killer caught, and Stead, who wanted him to find and protect the Kumu.

It was still dark, and would be for at least another two hours, given that it was nearly the shortest day of the year. Dawn also arrived later in smoky, fog-bound London than the rest of the country, and there were some days when it was barely light at all.

He washed in lukewarm water – another nasty failing in the servants that Emelia had vowed to correct when she was mistress of the house – and rasped a razor over his stubble. He walked downstairs, where he found it was too early for the morning papers, so all that was available was the weekly *Illustrated London News* – Ingram's paper – now two days old. As he had had no time to read it over the weekend, he took it to the breakfast table, and leafed through it while he waited for the maid to bring him some tea.

Jack appeared a few moments later. He wrinkled his nose when he saw what Lonsdale was reading.

'It's full of pictures of Archbishop Tait's funeral and the aftermath of that terrible fire at the Alhambra Theatre,' he said disapprovingly. 'Printing such images is in poor taste.'

'You should tell Ingram,' said Lonsdale. 'Still, at least he believes the Kumu are innocent, which is something in his favour.'

'So is the fact that his sister's married to Monkey Hornby,' said Jack, smiling suddenly. 'The greatest sportsman of our age. But I can't imagine why people would want to see pictures of a funeral – unless someone hopes to spot himself among the mourners.'

'Humbage might,' said Lonsdale. 'He'd cut it out and keep it, to prove he was once in company with the highest-ranking churchman in the country, even if Tait was dead at the time.'

'I'm beginning to wish Em had a different family,' sighed Jack. 'Other than Grandmama Gertrude, who's a gem. Humbage has grown pompous now he has friends at the Palace.'

'Friends who have to be reminded who he is,' muttered Lonsdale, and told Jack about his visit to the Garraway Club. 'He despises me for being a reporter, but that's more respectable than fawning over people who barely know he exists.'

'He *has* become obsessed by appearance and convention. Last week, he forbade me to accept *pro bono* cases, lest they bring me in contact with criminals and he becomes tainted by association. He's terrified of what *your* work will embroil him in.'

'Then he shouldn't have agreed to me marrying Anne.'

'He wishes he hadn't! Apparently Gertrude contrived to get him tipsy before Anne begged his permission – if he'd been sober, he'd never have allowed it. Em did her best to stop it, but she was no match for Gertrude. I'm sorry Em's taken against you. I wish you could be friends.'

Lonsdale did not think that would ever happen and was sadder than he could say that his favourite brother would marry a woman who would sour their relationship with her insidiously poisonous tongue.

'Did you know Samuel Gurney?' he asked, to change the subject from one that was so profoundly painful.

'Only by reputation. He's honest, upright, and as dull as ditch-water. Why?'

'He was a member of the Garraway, like Tait, Haldane, Bowyer and Dickerson. And news arrived last night that he's dead. I don't know how – yet.'

Jack regarded him in alarm. 'Another suspicious death? This is becoming dangerous, Alec! I urge you to step away. And think of Anne – she hates you risking yourself for a story.'

'It's not for a story,' objected Lonsdale. 'It's because something wicked is unfolding, and the truth needs to be discovered.'

Jack remained concerned. 'Then don't let Humbage know what

you're doing. He'll force Anne to break off the engagement if you're drawn into anything unsavoury.'

'Then I'll sue him for breach of contract,' said Lonsdale hotly. 'Let's see how being the defendant in a lawsuit sits with his lofty opinion of himself.'

'Well, don't ask me to represent you,' said Jack. 'But to return to these Garraway deaths, do you think it has anything to do with the case you solved earlier this year – that someone has decided to resume the dubious research that you exposed?'

Lonsdale shook his head. 'These attacks are frenzied – angry – using an unusual weapon. I suspect the motive is rage, rather than dispassionate execution. Yet none of the victims were men to excite that sort of reaction. Everyone who knows them describes them as decent.'

'With one or two annoying habits that prevent them from being saints,' mused Jack. 'Such as Tait's fanatical religious opinions, Haldane's meanness and Bowyer's cruel tongue. So what are your plans for today?'

Lonsdale rubbed his eyes. 'The office first, to report to Stead and Mr Morley. Then Bradwell, to see what he can tell me about Gurney. Then I'll visit the families of Haldane and Bowyer, to ask if they know why the police declared the deaths natural – and what they think about it. Tomorrow, I'll travel to Surrey to talk to Tait's daughter . . .'

'That should keep you busy.'

'I should visit Broadmoor as well,' Lonsdale went on, 'to find out what suggestions Dickerson made to the medical superintendent. I also want to ask about Voules – he denies visiting Broadmoor, and I've no idea if he's telling the truth.'

'He won't be,' predicted Jack. 'You say he's been following you around – that's not the action of an innocent man. He may well be involved in this affair.'

'I'm not entirely sure Ingram was telling the truth either. He knows more about the cannibals than he's willing to admit – and perhaps more about Dickerson, too.'

'Speaking of cannibals, here's Voules's latest offering,' said Jack in distaste, as Sybil, the maid, finally brought the morning papers. They included *The Echo* – despite Lonsdale having asked her to keep it downstairs. 'They're still at large, a danger to honest Londoners.'

'So are dinosaurs,' said Lonsdale, leaning over his shoulder and laughing. 'Brought to life by electricity. I can't believe the editor let Voules publish this!'

'Why not?' shrugged Jack. 'It makes for an amazing tale, even if there's not so much as a shred of truth in it. There's a paragraph on Maclean as well.'

'And the whole thing ends with a question,' said Lonsdale, and read it aloud. *What is most deadly to the innocent Englishman: marauding cannibals, rampaging dinosaurs or escaped lunatics?* Lord, Jack! How can anyone take this seriously?'

'Alarmingly, people do,' said Jack soberly.

It was raining as Lonsdale hurried to Northumberland Street. *The Pall Mall Gazette* building appeared gloomy and unprepossessing in the semi-darkness, the outside only partially illuminated by the street's gas lamps. There was a pile of soggy leaves near the door, and Lonsdale jumped in alarm when it shifted, thinking it was a person. He forced himself to relax. Being followed by Voules and Bowler Hat – who might be Maclean – was getting to him.

Inside, the building was brightly lit and busy, as the paper's employees went about the frenetic process of writing, typesetting and printing sixteen pages of news, reviews, and advertisements. There was a hum of concentrated activity that never failed to stimulate him, and he found himself thinking how fortunate he was to be a part of it.

He walked up the stairs, and learned that Morley had been there all night, because of major developments in the hunt for the Phoenix Park assassins. Two men had been arrested, which would mark the beginning of the resolution of the horrible affair.

Needless to say, he had no time for Lonsdale, but Stead, who had arrived early, called him in as he passed. The wheelbarrow was now upside down, being used as a rack to dry the assistant editor's wet shoes. The room reeked of wet feet, soggy leather and the hurled carrots that were quietly decomposing in and around the bear's head.

Stead was eating what appeared to be raw Brussels sprouts, taking them from a paper bag and tossing them into his mouth like sweets. Lonsdale politely declined a handful, feeling they were considerably nicer cooked. Stead listened intently while Lonsdale outlined all he had learned since they had last met.

'I suppose you'd better continue exploring these murders and this Watcher business,' he said unhappily, 'although we can't talk to Mr Morley about it, because he's immersed in this Irish business. I daren't interrupt. However, you mustn't forget the cannibals. I want them found and brought here, where they'll be safe.'

'You want to house cannibals *here*?' blurted Lonsdale, startled.

'Why not?' shrugged Stead, chewing a sprout. 'They lived in the Natural History Museum all those weeks. At least here they can look out of the windows.'

Lonsdale glanced out of Stead's. The view was that of a dirty, disused warehouse, and did nothing to raise the spirits.

'We can protect them,' Stead went on, popping another sprout into his mouth, then lobbing the next one at the bear's head. '*We* won't allow them to be arrested for a crime they didn't commit.'

'Perhaps that's what Ingram's doing,' suggested Lonsdale. 'There was definitely something he wasn't telling me last night.'

'No, he'll be using them for a story, which is unethical and must be stopped – it's exploiting vulnerable human beings for monetary gain. Besides, where would he put them? Not in his Lincolnshire home – his wife would never allow it – and they won't be in his London residence, because his sister and her husband Monkey Hornby are living there.'

'*The Illustrated London News* office?' suggested Lonsdale. 'It's quite large – bigger than our building.'

Stead's eyes blazed. 'Then you'll have to search it and rescue them.'

Lonsdale laughed. 'And how do I do that? Ingram's unlikely to let me in.'

'The resourceful Miss Friederichs will find a way,' averred Stead. 'And, while she does, I suppose you can interview the families of these dead men.'

Lonsdale eyed him thoughtfully. 'You're not happy about us exploring the murders, are you?'

'I don't think it's as pressing as saving the Kumu,' replied Stead. 'Yet the business *is* worrisome. You *saw* Dickerson's mutilated body, and it's common knowledge that Haldane suffered a grisly end in the Royal Courts of Justice. Not even a Commissioner of Police should pass those off as natural.'

'Do you think Henderson is trying to lull the killer into a false sense of security?' asked Lonsdale. 'Fleetwood-Pelham thinks a little-known detective will be appointed, one who can investigate quietly, without fuss.'

'It's possible, although it sounds too clever an idea to have come from Henderson. But let's consider what we know of the victims. First, Archbishop Tait – an attack on the Church. Next Haldane – an attack on the legal system and publishing, as he owned a newspaper. Next Dickerson – an assault on a national museum. Then Bowyer – the legal system again. And last Gurney – an attack on a financial institution.'

'I don't think the murders have anything to do with what the victims did in life. The connection is the Garraway Club – and the fact that all five knew each other.'

'There's also a connection with Maclean,' mused Stead, sprouts forgotten as he turned his sharp mind to the case in hand. 'Tait and Dickerson visited Broadmoor, where he was incarcerated; Haldane and Bowyer were members of the courts that saw him convicted; and Gurney's bank pays the Crown's barristers.'

'I'm not sure Maclean is capable of working all that out,' said Lonsdale doubtfully. 'The man is damaged – his mind doesn't work properly.'

'But you've said that he's been following you,' argued Stead. 'And possibly tried to burn down the mortuary. I rather think you might be underestimating him.'

Lonsdale was not sure what to think. 'The man I saw *could've* been him, but it was too dark to be sure. However, I still don't think he's the killer. His attempt on the Queen was clumsy and open, whereas these other deaths are sly and brutal. And I doubt he would kill with a panga.'

'He might,' countered Stead, 'given that no one is likely to sell him a gun. However, that isn't the point I wanted to make. The pattern *I* see is that all these murders do one thing: attack our great British institutions. The Church, the law, the banks, an educational facility and the press . . . and the Crown, too, if Maclean *is* involved and we can include the attempt on the Queen. Perhaps *that* is the nature of the Watchers' "unspeakable happening" – the destruction of the pillars that hold our society together.'

'It's possible, I suppose,' conceded Lonsdale, albeit reluctantly. 'Although I think a more fruitful avenue of enquiry would be to probe the Garraway Club.'

'Then do it,' said Stead. 'I want you to write something insightful on the recent Austro-German alliance this morning, then you're free from all other assignments until Christmas. Concentrate on finding the Kumu and identifying the killer, because you'll have no time for anything else once you take over Milner's duties.'

On his way out, Lonsdale stopped to talk to Hulda, and cautiously repeated Stead's order that she was to search the premises of *The Illustrated London News* for the missing cannibals. He expected her to be irked, but she smiled with considerable enthusiasm.

'You don't mind?' he asked, surprised.

'On the contrary, it'll be an enjoyable challenge.' Her eyes gleamed. 'However, you should talk to Bradwell before doing anything else. He might be able to tell you more about Gurney – whether we really do have five victims.'

'Already planned,' said Lonsdale.

'Don't go to the mortuary, though,' Hulda went on, as if he had not spoken. 'He's always at St Bartholomew's Hospital on Monday mornings. But first, tell me what happened at the Garraway last night – other than learning about Gurney's death. Incidentally, I was taken aback to see Burnside at the Garraway. He seems to be every-where these days.'

'He's a photographer, who makes a living by taking images of important events. Of course he's everywhere.'

'But there haven't been any "important events" at the Garraway – well, other than the untimely deaths of five of its members. Perhaps it's not Maclean who's been following us at all, but Burnside.'

Lonsdale regarded her askance. 'Why would Burnside follow us? Besides, the man I saw was slight and dark haired. Burnside has sandy hair.'

'Hair can be darkened with soot. It's called donning a disguise, Lonsdale.' Hulda raised her hands in a shrug. 'Perhaps his appear-ances here, there and everywhere are innocent, but there's something about him that makes me acutely uneasy. Him and Roth – two men whose association with the case bears careful scrutiny.'

'Not by me,' said Lonsdale firmly, thinking her imagination was running away with her. 'But we only have six more days to come up with answers, so we'd better get on with it.'

Hulda nodded. 'We'll slip out through the back door. You probably didn't notice, but Voules is hanging around the front.'

St Bartholomew's Hospital was an ancient foundation in Smithfield.
It was large and imposing, and could accommodate nearly seven
hundred patients at any one time. Some were the wealthy clients of
the city's top surgeons, who occupied handsomely appointed private
rooms, while others were paupers who were seen free of charge
and housed in large wards.

Although the hospital was progressive, especially in its attitude
towards and treatment of consumption, it still smelled of death, sweat,
fear and dirt. The noise was colossal, too, with voices echoing around
in marble halls and feet clattering. Lonsdale had visited Bradwell
there before, but the pathologist had since been offered a surgical
fellowship, and his haunts in the massive complex had changed.

After wandering hopelessly for a while, Lonsdale was directed
to Bradwell's new domain – one of the newer wings, which had
pastoral murals on the walls and elaborately decorated ceilings,
presumably so the sick would have something to stare at as they
lay in their beds. A number of fashionably dressed men moved
around the wards – medics monitoring their charges.

Lonsdale could not see Bradwell and was about to leave when
one came to intercept him. He gaped. Bradwell wore a smart black
suit, a crisp white coat, and his unruly hair was neatly brushed. He
looked like a successful and affluent surgeon, rather than the harried
and underpaid pathologist who examined the dead for the
Metropolitan Police.

'I have to dress well here,' Bradwell explained, seeing his reaction. 'Patients like their *medicus* to look the part and I don't want
any of them to die, just for want of a trip to the tailor. But at the
mortuary . . . well, the dead aren't fussy.'

'So why persist with them?' asked Lonsdale. 'I imagine the pay's
better here.'

'It is, and most of my patients thank me for my efforts, which
the dead never do. But corpses teach surgeons a great deal, and I
do find pathology fascinating.'

'I'm here about Samuel Gurney,' said Lonsdale. 'Have you seen
his body?'

'Briefly,' replied Bradwell. 'I had a feeling someone would come and take it away from me before I'd finished with it, so I hastened to examine it at once.'

'And did someone take it away?'

Bradwell nodded. 'No more than ten minutes after it arrived, Inspector Wells appeared with an order to return it to the man's family – an order endorsed by Commissioner Henderson, so I had no choice but to comply. However, ten minutes is a long time for a surgeon.'

'What did you find out?'

'That Gurney was killed in the exact same way as Dickerson and the others. Indeed, the culprit must have dropped his weapon at one point, because its bloody imprint was on the victim's shirt. It was exactly how I drew it for you when we looked at Dickerson.'

'The same weapon and the same *modus operandi* suggest the same killer.'

'That would be the logical conclusion. And I found this.'

Bradwell reached into his pocket and withdrew a paper bag. Inside it was a long piece of grass, which he held up for Lonsdale to see. It was a pretty plant, with long, slender leaves and a head of feathery pink seeds. Lonsdale regarded it in mystification.

'Found it where? And what's its significance?'

'Its significance is that I found an identical piece on Dickerson. I assumed it had fallen into his clothes by accident. But when I saw this on Gurney . . . well, it can't be coincidence.'

'Two victims, two pieces of grass,' mused Lonsdale.

'*Five* victims, *four* pieces of grass,' corrected Bradwell triumphantly. 'As you know, I have copies of the initial reports on Bowyer, Haldane and Tait – the ones my colleagues wrote *before* they were told to change their verdicts. There was mention of grass with the bodies of Bowyer and Haldane, too.'

'But not Tait?'

'No grass was *recorded* on Tait,' said Bradwell. 'Which means the doctor may have found some, but didn't think it was worth noting. I've written to him, to ask.'

'Do you think the killer put them there?'

Bradwell nodded vehemently. 'I do – it must be some sort of ritual. A calling card, if you will. He assumed that every victim would be examined by a different doctor, so the relevance of it would be missed. But he reckoned without me.'

'And without Inspector Wells arriving ten minutes too late to stop you from examining another of his victims.' Lonsdale took the grass and studied it carefully. 'Is it rare or unusual?'

'What I know about grasses can be written on the back of a Penny Lilac postage stamp. You should visit Kew Gardens. I'm sure someone there can help you.'

But Lonsdale had a better idea. The eminent gentleman-scientist Francis Galton, whom he had met on his previous case, was an acknowledged expert on grasses. It would be quicker to ask him. Eager to have answers as soon as possible, he hired one of the hospital porters to take his card to Galton's house on Rutland Gate, with a request to call on him that evening as a matter of some urgency. Galton was old-fashioned – one did not simply arrive on his doorstep and expect to be received.

'If it does transpire to be rare, it may lead us to the culprit,' he said to Bradwell, 'which begs the question as to why he left it behind. Surely, it's an unnecessary risk?'

'I rather think he considers us too stupid to work it out,' replied Bradwell. 'He has powerful connections – enough to ensure that his crimes are brushed under the carpet by no less a man than the Commissioner of Police – and his arrogance knows no bounds. I suspect this is his way of thumbing his nose at us, daring us to challenge him.'

'Then challenge him we will,' said Lonsdale grimly. 'He won't get away with this.'

Bradwell smiled. 'Good. Will you take this grass to Peters and tell him what I've told you? To *Peters* – I don't trust anyone else, not even Hayes.'

Although it was hardly Lonsdale's job to run errands for Bradwell, the grass was too important to entrust to anyone else. He flagged down a hackney carriage, his thoughts racing as it rattled along the Strand and down towards 4 Whitehall Place, where the Metropolitan Police headquarters was located.

The building was not large enough for everyone who worked there, and Peters had been allocated a room so tiny that it was almost a cupboard. He shared it with four other inspectors although, as they worked different hours, there tended to be no more than two of them in it at any one time. Even so, Peters beckoned Lonsdale outside, his stony expression warning him to say nothing until they were alone. They took a tortuous route through the building, which included going through several locked doors. Finally, they emerged on to a back lane called Great Scotland Yard, which had given the place its popular name.

'What was that about?' asked Lonsdale, as they walked towards the Victoria Embankment.

'Precautions,' replied Peters shortly. 'Now, what do you want to tell me?'

Lonsdale outlined what he had learned about the murders – and the Watchers – since they had last met, then handed over the grass. Peters examined it, then passed it back.

'I daren't take it,' he said. 'If I do, it'll go in an evidence locker, and it won't be safe.'

Lonsdale stared at him. 'You have a thief in the station?'

'The killer has considerable power and influence. If he can get Superintendent Hayes and me reassigned, and the commissioner to declare his victims dead of natural causes, he can make a piece of grass disappear.'

'So what do you want me to do with it?'

'Leave it with Galton. From what you say, his house is stuffed full of exotic grasses, so where better to hide this one? But for God's sake, don't let him lose it.'

They walked a little further, and Lonsdale turned suddenly at a flicker of movement out of the corner of his eye. But there was nothing to see.

'Maclean again?' asked Peters, who had turned with him. He was braced, and Lonsdale was under the impression that if he said yes, the inspector would hare off in pursuit.

'It's more likely to be Voules, who clings to me like glue. Or perhaps the man who tried to burn down the mortuary – who may be Maclean, although I don't really think so. Why would Maclean want to burn Dickerson when Bradwell had already examined him?'

'Maclean is insane,' said Peters. 'You can't expect to understand the way he thinks. And he's definitely in London – we've had confirmed reports of several sightings, although we're nowhere close to catching him.'

'He can't remain at large for much longer,' said Lonsdale. 'Not with *The Echo* printing sketches of him every day.'

'Let's hope you're right,' said Peters gloomily. 'So, what's your next move? You'll ask Galton about the grass, but what else?'

'Visit the victims' families – assuming they'll talk to me. They may refuse. If they do, I'll have to tell them that five dead men in one club is suspicious, and that too many people saw Dickerson for his death to be anything but murder. Not even Commissioner Henderson can deny that.'

Peters's smile was bitter. 'No, he couldn't suppress that crime as he did the others. He had no choice but to assign an officer to explore what happened to Dickerson.'

'You and Hayes,' said Lonsdale. 'You attended the post-mortem and made initial enquiries.'

Peters's expression was carefully blank again. 'I've been ordered to investigate the theft of lead from churches, while Hayes is to protect the Houses of Parliament. He's beside himself with frustration.'

'So who is investigating Dickerson's murder?'

'Inspector Wells.'

'The officer who was allocated Bowyer and Haldane,' mused Lonsdale, 'and who arrived at the mortuary ten minutes after Gurney and stopped Bradwell from examining him by presenting an order signed by Henderson.'

'The very same,' said Peters. 'A man who stands about as much chance of finding a killer as that pigeon over there.'

'You told me before that he's one of Henderson's favourites.'

'His lickspittle,' said Peters, with uncharacteristic venom. 'I know for a fact that innocent people are in gaol because he's drawn conclusions without sufficient evidence. He's a disgrace! So, Lonsdale, the only way these five dead men will get justice is if you and Miss Friederichs provide it for them.'

'Is Wells dangerous?' asked Lonsdale, and shrugged when Peters turned to regard him in surprise. 'If Hulda and I are to meddle, it would be good to know how seriously he'll object.'

'He wouldn't notice anything amiss if you came up and accused *him* of being the killer,' replied Peters. 'However, that's not to say you should be complacent. Someone arranged for the Metropolitan Police's least competent detective to be appointed, and that person *is* dangerous.'

'And you can't help us at all?' pressed Lonsdale.

'I'm being closely monitored,' replied Peters, 'which is why we didn't leave through the front door. I don't want to be seen with you but, equally importantly, I don't want you seen with me. If we meet again, remember that.'

SEVEN

The rest of Lonsdale's day was not very productive, even though he spent a fortune on hansom cabs to zigzag him across the city, feeling that walking would take too much time.

First, he went to Gurney's home in Finsbury Square. He was surprised that a wealthy banker should choose to live in an area that, while pleasant, was not the equal of his own lodgings in Cleveland Square. That said, Gurney's home was by far the most extravagant in the street. Lonsdale arrived to find it in an uproar, as the bereaved family struggled to accept a steady stream of well-wishers. Lonsdale joined the end of a party of congregants from All Saints Church, walking in behind them as though he had every right to be there.

He was not entirely comfortable with what he was doing, but he need not have been concerned. Benjamin Gurney seemed interested only in explaining why his father had elected to live on Finsbury Square – because he planned to buy every house on it, renovate them to a high standard so that 'people of quality' would want to live there, and thus make large sums of money.

'For his little projects,' sneered Benjamin disapprovingly. 'Such as a retirement home for horses and schools for workhouse girls.'

By the time Lonsdale was able to escape, he had learned that Gurney had been both deeply religious and a resourceful entrepreneur, but that his son was an overindulged scion riding on the father's coattails. Lonsdale asked questions about the Garraway Club, the Watchers and Maclean, but it quickly became clear that Benjamin knew nothing of them.

Next, Lonsdale went to the Bank of England on Threadneedle Street, where Gurney had worked. The dead man's secretary agreed to an interview, and he was taken to a handsomely appointed office that reeked powerfully of dog. The secretary was a well-dressed, middle-aged man who exuded a sense of brisk efficiency. He introduced himself as Mr Salathiel Olive.

'Sit, Dusty!' he snapped at the animal that came to investigate Lonsdale's legs, wagging its tail. Dusty made no effort to comply.

'Nice dog,' remarked Lonsdale, when they were settled on opposite sides of the desk with Dusty lying between them. 'Yours?'

'Mr Gurney's,' replied Olive. 'Although I suppose she'll be mine now, as his son won't want her. He says she stinks, although I've never noticed any odour. Nor did Mr Gurney. Can you?'

'Er . . . perhaps a little,' replied Lonsdale, thinking he had never encountered a smellier beast. 'Did Gurney like animals then?'

Olive smiled fondly as he nodded, and went on to depict a kinder, more gentle picture of the banker than the son had done, although there was no question that Gurney had been an astute businessman with an eye for a profit. His worthy causes included his church, prison reform and animal welfare. Lonsdale listened patiently and carefully but learned nothing to tell him why the banker had been killed. He stood to leave, thanking Olive for his time.

'He *loved* animals,' sniffed Olive, as he walked Lonsdale to the door. He glanced at the dog, which wound around their legs, feathery tail swaying. 'If Dusty had been allowed to go home with him, he'd still be alive. She'd have seen those monsters off.'

'Monsters?' asked Lonsdale, hoping he was not about to be told the Kumu were responsible.

'The ones who killed his friends from the Garraway Club as well – four of them, all dead before their time. The police claim they're natural, but Mr Gurney didn't believe it. He said they were murdered because of their good works.'

'The others were involved in charitable causes, too?'

Olive nodded. 'They invested time and money in matters they considered important. Of course, not everyone appreciated where they chose to spend it. For example, there's a man at the Garraway – James Burnside – who became angry with Mr Gurney for donating money to the horse sanctuary. He thought the funds should've gone to him instead.'

Lonsdale frowned. 'What grounds did Burnside have for making such a claim?'

'That charity should begin at home – his business is failing, and he felt his wealthy friends should help him out. But if there was one thing Mr Gurney couldn't abide, it was beggars. He hated being asked for money, and if anyone did, they were always given short shrift. Burnside was dismissed with a flea in his ear.'

'Did Gurney ever mention a Garraway Club member who calls himself Grim Death?'

Olive raised his eyebrows. 'Not to me.'

'Then what about a group called the Watchers?'

'Oh yes, Mr Gurney was a Watcher,' replied Olive. 'He was proud of the fact.'

Lonsdale's pulse quickened. 'Can you tell me anything about it?'

'Only that the society was exclusive, and that membership was by invitation only. I know Professor Dickerson was admitted, and I believe Archbishop Tait was, too. I don't know about the other two – Sir George Bowyer and Mr Haldane. The only other thing I can tell you is that they have something very special planned for Christmas.'

Lonsdale wanted to grab his shoulder and shake it, to emphasize the importance of his next question. '*What* was planned, Mr Olive?'

'Mr Gurney said it was something that would change the way Londoners look at things. I asked what he meant, but he refused to elaborate.'

'Were you under the impression that it was something good or something bad?'

'I expected something good, being as it's the season to be jolly, but Mr Gurney was angry about it. When he spoke, there was a flash in his eyes – the same kind of flash that came when his son disappointed him. Ergo, I rather think it might be something bad.'

Unable to flag down a hansom, Lonsdale trotted briskly to Haldane's chambers at King's Bench Walk in the Inner Temple. His hurried pace made it easy to see that someone was following him again. He pretended not to notice, aware that the person was small and light on his feet, although he kept his distance. Lonsdale ducked into a haberdasher's shop and hid behind one of the displays. Moments later, Burnside strode in.

'Looking for me?' Lonsdale asked, watching the photographer jump in alarm.

'Lord, Lonsdale!' Burnside exclaimed, putting his hand over his heart. 'You frightened the life out of me! And no, I'm not looking for you, I'm looking for buttons.'

'You just happened by moments after I spotted someone following me?'

Burnside's eyebrows shot up into his sandy hair. 'I wasn't following you! I've just come from Temple Station. Look – here's my ticket, with the time and date stamped on it by the conductor. And I always buy buttons here, because they're cheaper than anywhere else.'

Presented with hard evidence, Lonsdale could only suppose it really was a coincidence that Burnside had materialized. 'I've just been talking to Gurney's secretary. He told me that you and Gurney quarrelled before he died.'

'About horses,' nodded Burnside. 'He thought they were more important than people, and I told him he was wrong. It was arrogant of me, and I apologized afterwards.'

They talked a while longer, then Lonsdale left him to his shopping. Out on the street, Lonsdale looked around very carefully, but there was no sign of anyone else taking a particular interest in him, and he wondered if he had let his imagination run away with him.

Space was at a premium in the Inner Temple, so Haldane's son had been contacted and politely asked how soon he could clear out his father's rooms. The younger Haldane had hurried to London to oblige. He had given up the legal profession to join the Church and was now Dean of the Diocese of Argyll and The Isles, so it had been a journey of some considerable duration. Lonsdale arrived to find he was being visited by Lady Bowyer – two people united by loss.

Both were happy to talk to Lonsdale, although neither had heard of the Watchers, Grim Death, or a significant event planned for Christmas. The dean thought his father would have spent Christmas Day at prayer, while the Bowyer household had a tradition of church, then games and music. The dean then went on to say that while his father *had* experienced a recent financial setback, it was nowhere near as serious as Humbage had claimed so gloatingly.

'People accused him of being miserly,' he said, 'but the truth is that he gave a lot of money away. For example, when I was a curate at Calne in Wiltshire, he paid for nearly all the pews when he learned my congregation couldn't afford them.'

'The same people accuse my husband of having a cutting tongue,' put in Lady Bowyer. 'He could be sharp, but only to those who deserved it – like that dreadful Gervais Humbage. And *he* was quietly generous, too – he helped the families of the criminals he sent to prison. How many barristers can claim that?'

'Not many,' agreed Lonsdale.

'They were both murdered, you know,' Lady Bowyer went on unsteadily. 'I don't care what the police claim now. I saw my husband's body, and he did *not* die a natural death. Anyone who says otherwise is a liar.'

'Inspector Wells,' put in Dean Haldane. '*He's* the liar. Superintendent Hayes was assigned to both cases at first, and he promised us answers. I believe we'd have got them.'

'But Commissioner Henderson saw fit to replace him with that blundering buffoon Wells,' said Lady Bowyer bitterly.

'Wells came to see me yesterday, but all he did was drink tea and eat cakes,' said the dean. 'You've asked me about Grim Death, Watchers and Christmas, but he asked *nothing* and he told me less.'

'I think that Garraway Club has something to do with their murders,' put in Lady Bowyer. 'My husband sometimes stayed there very late, but when he did, he never came back rosy-cheeked with drink as he did when he went to the Savile Club. I asked him what he did there that entailed him lingering until the early hours, then rolling home stone-cold sober, but he always refused to say.'

'Talking, probably,' said the dean darkly. 'Because it was the same with my father. I had the sense that he'd been in some sort of meeting.'

A Watchers' meeting, Lonsdale thought, but did not say.

'Break in to the place,' suggested the dean, and his eyes gleamed. 'That's the only way you'll get answers. I'll help. I've never committed burglary before, but if it'll catch my father's killer . . .'

'Count me in, too,' declared Lady Bowyer, who was well into her seventies and stout.

'It's a kind offer,' said Lonsdale hastily. 'But let's stick with more conventional methods first. I promise to keep you informed.'

He stood to leave, and saw the dean was using copies of *The Echo* in which to wrap his father's valuables. He supposed the porters had supplied them, as he was sure the dean had loftier tastes. On the front of one was a drawing of Maclean, which made him look vaguely like a bowler-hatted rodent.

'A sly face,' remarked the dean, seeing where he was looking. 'But one I'm sure I've seen since I arrived in London.'

'You've probably seen *him*,' said Lady Bowyer, pointing through the window to where a man stood on the pavement opposite. The hat hid most of his face, but Lonsdale was sure it was the man who had been following him – and who had tried to incinerate the mortuary.

He did not wait to hear more. Blurting his apologies, he left the chambers at a run, tearing into the street so fast that a passing hansom struck him a glancing blow on the shoulder. He staggered, trying to regain his balance, as Bowler Hat took to his heels. The hansom driver swore, and there was an unpleasant crunch as his vehicle collided with one coming the other way. Lonsdale jigged around the resulting melee, but Bowler Hat had gone. Lonsdale raced to the end of the road, but there were too many directions his quarry could have taken, and he was forced to concede defeat.

He rubbed his shoulder as he went to apologize to the hansom driver. *Had* the figure been Maclean? He was sure it was not when the possibility had first been mooted, but now he was less certain. The man could well be the would-be regicide – small, slightly built and nondescript – although Lonsdale failed to understand why Maclean would follow him. Was it because *The Pall Mall Gazette* was exploring the five murders? But if Maclean *was* the culprit, what powerful and influential person was contriving to cover it up by dismissing competent detectives, hiring lazy ones, and ordering pathologists to alter their reports? It made no sense.

Feeling guilty over the collision, although there was luckily no damage to vehicles or horses, Lonsdale hired the hansom driver to take him the short distance to the Royal Courts of Justice, where Haldane had worked and died. He learned nothing of note, and it was mid-afternoon and beginning to rain by the time he emerged. Bowyer's offices were in Kensington, so he hurried there next, but although the man's colleagues were eager to help, they knew nothing of relevance.

As he was close, he decided to visit Roth, and arrived to find his friend working on more artefacts from Dickerson's collection. This time, it was an exquisite selection of beads, some of which were silver.

'These are pretty,' he said, picking one up. 'Are they valuable?'

'Probably,' said Roth. 'Although I like them for the artwork. Of course, they're not as nice as Khoikhoi beadwork. The public would've had a rare treat if our Khoikhoi had put on the display we'd organized. The professor was right about that.'

'*Kumu*,' corrected Lonsdale. 'That's the second time you've got their name wrong, Tim, and you can't blame work this time, because these beads aren't from West *or* Southern Africa.'

'No – they're Kikuyu,' said Roth, scrubbing tiredly at his face. '*East* Africa. It's hard to keep track of them all.'

'That's not something a professional ethnographer should admit,' chided Lonsdale jocularly, 'especially the one who's been given the task of curating the Dickerson Collection.'

Roth smiled wanly. 'No, it's not, so let's not tell anyone, shall we?'

They chatted desultorily for a while, then Lonsdale broached the subject of the Garraway.

'I met Gurney there once,' said Roth. 'He smelled of dog.'

'Your rooms smell of something.' Lonsdale sniffed the air, trying to place an aroma that was instantly familiar. 'It reminds me of Africa.'

Roth waved a thin hand at the piles of crates. 'It's coming from these. It's nice, isn't it? Puts me in mind of happier times, when I still had my health and my life seemed full of promise.'

'It's full of promise now,' said Lonsdale. 'You're financially secure and you have interesting work to keep you busy for years.'

'But I also have the police accusing my cannibals of murdering the professor, and your Miss Friederichs convinced that *I* did it. Tell her to back off, will you, Alec?'

Lonsdale nearly laughed at the notion of telling Hulda what to do. He plied Roth with more questions about the club and the Watchers, but his friend could tell him no more, so he took his leave.

Outside in the street, Lonsdale hesitated, wondering what to do next. There was no sign of Bowler Hat, although he thought he saw Voules slithering out of sight. He sighed irritably. He had to show the grass to Francis Galton that evening, and he could not have Voules trailing him there – Galton would never forgive him if a reporter from *The Echo* rolled up and started asking impertinent questions. Then he remembered Turkish Ma.

Ma, who was not Turkish at all, was the owner of a small 'gentlemen's parlour' that catered to middle-class men with time on their hands in the middle of the day – she closed at six o'clock prompt, on the grounds that she had better things to do with her evenings than work. She and Lonsdale had been friends ever since he had helped her after a road accident several years before.

Making sure Voules kept him in sight, Lonsdale walked the short distance to Ma's domain and pretended to look around furtively before stepping inside. Ma was at the front desk and broke into a beam of welcome when she saw him.

'There's a man following me,' he said, slipping her ten shillings. 'I need to lose him. Will you help?'

Ma grinned and indicated two pretty young women who had draped themselves over a nearby couch. 'Henrietta and Florence will distract him for you. He won't even remember you exist after ten minutes. They're very good.'

While the two ladies readied themselves for what Lonsdale thought would be a very distasteful session, Ma led him to the back of her house, where she unlocked the door to a small yard. He emerged in a dank lane, but it was only a few steps before he was back on Cromwell Road. He took a hansom home, where Sybil the maid handed him a note from Galton, inviting him to dine that evening.

Lonsdale groaned. He had hoped to learn what he needed to know in half an hour, whereas dinner with Galton – an eccentric who loved to talk – might last all night. He groaned a second time when he saw the postscript at the end of the message, saying how delighted Galton would be if Lonsdale would bring his colleague, Hulda Friederichs, who had written 'the brilliantly biting review of that nonsense *Iolanthe* today'.

He dashed off a message to Hulda, telling her she would be expected, and was about to change when a carriage arrived outside. His heart sank when he saw it was Humbage.

'I'm not here to see you, Lonsdale,' said Humbage rudely, pushing his way past Sybil the moment she opened the door. 'I want your brother. My friend Lord Carlingford has a question about the law, and I offered to answer it for him.'

'Jack's at work,' said Lonsdale. 'He always is on weekday afternoons.'

'But you're here lounging around, I see,' sneered Humbage.

'Changing for an appointment with Francis Galton,' said Lonsdale, aiming to shut him up with his own bit of name-dropping. It failed.

'Galton isn't even a knight of the realm,' said Humbage in disdain. 'You should nurture more important connections than *that* if you want to make something of yourself.'

'I understand you're a member of the Garraway Club,' said Lonsdale, going on an offensive of his own. 'A place where five members have been murdered.'

'Not according to the police,' said Humbage between gritted teeth. 'You should get your nose out of *The Echo* and read a respectable paper, then you'd know the truth. Besides, I only joined because Lord Carlingford recommended it, but he rarely goes there, so neither do I.'

'He was there on Sunday,' retorted Lonsdale. 'With Fleetwood-Pelham and several of his other close friends.'

Humbage could not hide his dismay. 'But he told me he was going to White's.'

Although it would have been deeply satisfying to suggest that Carlingford had lied in order to escape from him, Lonsdale could not bring himself to be cruel. Instead, he asked if Humbage had met anyone nicknamed Grim Death.

'No, but if I did, I'd tell him such an appellation was in bad taste and suggest he change it.'

'Then have you heard of some event involving Garraway Club members at Christmas?'

'No, but do you know if Lord Carlingford is going?' asked Humbage eagerly, and for the first time, Lonsdale felt he was more to be pitied than disliked. 'Because if he is, I'll have to cancel my engagement here and go with him instead. He'd want me at his side on such an auspicious day.'

'Why is it auspicious?' asked Lonsdale, wondering if Humbage had heard something in the club, but had not realized its importance.

'Because it celebrates the birth of our Saviour Jesus Christ,' replied Humbage haughtily. 'Why else?'

Lonsdale had asked Hulda to meet him at Hyde Park Corner at seven o'clock. It was an hour before they were due at Galton's house, but he wanted time to discuss the case with her first. He specified the centre column of Decimus Burton's Ionic Screen – originally built as part of the grand approach to Buckingham Palace – which was always well lit and had benches where they could sit and talk.

He was surprised when she arrived with Fleetwood-Pelham, who had agreed to be interviewed about the Queen's Christmas travel plans, as long as she asked her questions while he shopped for presents at Liberty and Harrods. To save her taking notes, he had offered to lend her his copy of the itinerary, and as St James's Palace was not far from Galton's home, he had suggested she collect it that evening. So much for our discussion time, thought Lonsdale resignedly.

'Perhaps I should write about how Richard Owen refuses to set a date for Her Majesty's visit to his museum,' said Hulda, as the three of them set off across Green Park together.

'He says he's too busy for the commotion it will entail,' said Fleetwood-Pelham, and grinned rather slyly. 'She'll be furious when I tell her.'

'Then perhaps you shouldn't,' suggested Lonsdale, although if the courtier heard, he gave no sign of it, suggesting he rather relished the prospect of setting the cat among the pigeons.

'Isn't it treason or something?' asked Hulda. 'To deny the Queen?'

Fleetwood-Pelham chuckled, revealing small, even teeth in his curiously minuscule lower jaw. 'If only it were! I wouldn't mind putting Owen's head on the chopping block, as I've never met a more odious individual. He told me he was glad the cannibals had killed poor Dickerson, because he'd never wanted that exhibition in the first place.'

'The cannibals didn't kill him,' said Lonsdale. 'The more I learn about the case, the more I'm sure of it. He was murdered by someone else. And he *was* murdered, no matter what the police claim.'

'So you said at the club last night,' mused Fleetwood-Pelham, before recounting an amusing anecdote involving the Queen's favourite horse. They were all laughing as they arrived at the Palace, where they were admitted by soldiers of the Grenadier Guards.

It was the first time Lonsdale had been inside St James's Palace, which was the official residence of the Queen's Equerries and Grooms-in-Waiting, as well as the site of various formal ceremonies. It was an ancient building, smaller and more modest than Buckingham Palace, but beautifully appointed and with an atmosphere of hushed refinement.

Fleetwood-Pelham had been allocated a pleasant suite of rooms on the ground floor, which opened on to a private garden in the back. They were a curious combination of British comfort and colonial exotic, mixing delicate Regency furniture with a selection of items from his travels across the Empire, particularly India and Hong Kong, where he had served in the 80th Regiment of Foot. There were also several watercolours, including one of Gangkhar Puensum, the highest mountain in Bhutan, and Mount Korbu, the tallest peak in the Malayan state of Perak.

'These are attractive,' said Lonsdale. 'Who's the artist?'

Fleetwood-Pelham turned from his desk, where he was rummaging for the itinerary. 'Me – I like to dabble.'

He was overly modest, because they were skilfully executed by someone with considerable talent. Meanwhile, Hulda went to the window and peered out, trying to see the garden, although it was dark and the lights spilling from the room only illuminated the first few feet. 'Is that a glasshouse in your courtyard?'

'Just a small one, and there's nothing in it at the moment,' replied Fleetwood-Pelham. He smiled. 'I aim to spend many happy hours there in the summer, as I've promised to fill the Queen's chambers with orchids and African violets.' He brushed past Hulda to close the curtains. 'To keep out the winter chill. Now, where is that list . . .'

'It looks as if you've travelled a great deal,' said Lonsdale, looking at a display of gourds, all decorated with tiny coloured stones. 'Where are these from?'

'China, mostly. I plan to give them to the Natural History Museum. Roth assures me that they'll be well-cared-for.'

'Just don't leave them to him in your will,' muttered Hulda, and went to look into a purpose-built case containing combs. 'These are lovely. I especially like the red and white one.'

Fleetwood-Pelham opened the lid and took it out. It was carved from bone and studded with beads. 'Please take it – it'll suit your complexion perfectly.'

Hulda demurred, embarrassed, but Fleetwood-Pelham placed it in her hair, and Lonsdale found himself thinking that it looked a lot nicer on her than it would on Anne. He blinked, shocked by such disloyal thinking to the woman who would be his wife.

'I can't,' objected Hulda, although she allowed Fleetwood-Pelham to guide her to a mirror so she could see herself. 'It must be worth a fortune.'

'I'm afraid you picked a very unremarkable piece. It cost me the equivalent of a penny when I bought it after the Battle of Ulundi. Had you picked one of the ivory pieces from Singapore, I wouldn't have been so generous.'

'Then thank you,' said Hulda, turning this way and that.

'It suits you much better than Lady Morganton, who borrowed it for a ball. Do you know her? She's the one who married her butler.'

Neither Hulda nor Lonsdale knew what to say to this piece of gossip but, taking their silence for interest, Fleetwood-Pelham elaborated, eyes gleaming as he related the more scandalous details. Only when the subject had been exhausted did he hand Hulda the itinerary, and ring for a servant to escort them out. While they waited, Lonsdale turned the conversation to the Garraway, more to prevent another scurrilous dialogue than for information, as he was sure the courtier had told them all he knew already. Fleetwood-Pelham was happy to chatter.

'My duties keep me here or at Windsor most of the time, so I don't visit the club as often as I'd like. I knew Dickerson, of course, but of the five I liked Archbishop Tait best. People will tell you he was a fanatic, but I always found him charming company.'

'I learned that Dickerson and Gurney were Watchers,' said Lonsdale. 'Are you sure you've never heard of the group?'

'Quite sure,' replied the courtier. 'Although you did tell me that *you* were thinking of joining it, so perhaps you should reconsider, given that it sounds so dangerous. Would you like me to put out a few feelers the next time I go to the Garraway? Perhaps Señor d'Atte will know something – he spends half his life at the club.'

'Best not,' said Lonsdale hastily, sure that the killer would not appreciate such an inveterate gossip probing his business, and not wanting a sixth victim claimed. 'At least, not until we know more about it.'

'As you wish,' shrugged Fleetwood-Pelham. 'But let me know if you change your mind. Morley is a good friend, and if I can help his paper, you only need say the word.'

'Thank you,' said Lonsdale, hoping it would not be necessary, and that he would find answers without sending Fleetwood-Pelham into the fray.

Lonsdale and Hulda took a hansom to Galton's house, which allowed them a few minutes to exchange news. Lonsdale went first, then Hulda.

'I searched the offices of *The Illustrated London News* from top to bottom,' she said, 'including broom cupboards and boiler rooms. The cannibals aren't there.'

'How did you manage that?' asked Lonsdale, startled and impressed.

'I told Ingram that *The Echo* had hidden a spy inside. He was so appalled that he even lent me some printers to help me roust the culprit out. When we finished, I suggested we search his house, too. Both were Kumu-free.'

'Lord!' breathed Lonsdale. 'What happens when Ingram next meets the editor of *The Echo*, and accuses him of espionage?'

'He'll deny it and Ingram will assume he's lying,' replied Hulda briskly. 'But speaking of *The Echo*, have you seen Voules today?'

Lonsdale grinned. 'Yes, but he won't be trailing us to Galton's house. Turkish Ma has taken care of that.'

Hulda pulled a face. 'Turkish Ma? She sounds like a prostitute!'

'Funny you should say that . . .'

Francis Galton and his wife Louisa lived in a bright white, five-storey house in a corner of Rutland Gate, just to the south of Hyde Park. The great man was protected from unwanted visitors by a heavy-set, self-important butler, who tended to admit guests only if he liked the look of them. He did not like the look of Lonsdale and Hulda, but had been told they were coming, so had no choice but to let them past. He took them to an empty sitting room, which was fire-less and unwelcoming, then disappeared without a word.

'Odd behaviour,' remarked Hulda, bemused. 'Did we arrive too
early?'

Lonsdale nodded to the clock on the mantelpiece. 'Not according
to that.'

The door opened, and the butler indicated with a surly flap of
his hand that they were to follow him to the dining room. They
obliged, entering just as Galton was straightening the tablecloth and
Louisa was setting out the last fork.

'We're suffering a domestic crisis,' explained Galton by way of
greeting. 'The cook was sick all over the croquettes of leveret and
has retired to bed to await the physician. Unfortunately, most of the
rest of the staff have followed her example—'

'Other than the butler, the footman and the scullery maid,' said
Louisa. 'And, as the men can't cook, we have to rely on Ethel to
provide tonight's victuals.'

'So sit down and let's see what she has made for us,' said Galton,
rubbing his hands together enthusiastically. 'She has promised us a
meal fit for a queen.'

Lonsdale and Hulda sat, but there was a long delay before the
first course appeared. Galton refused to do business until he had
eaten, 'entertaining' his guests with a rambling monologue on how
his experiments growing sweet peas contributed to his development
of the idea of regression to the mean. All the while, Louisa gossiped
about the servants, interjecting her remarks at random points during
her husband's discourse, so it was clear that neither of them was
paying the slightest attention to the other.

'Eugenics is the only way to solve society's problems,' preached
Galton, launching into another of his favourite topics. 'We can't
have everyone breeding as and when they please, and there must
be regulations.'

'The footman is a homosexual,' announced Louisa, seemingly
oblivious of the fact that the man in question had just arrived
with the *hors d'oeuvres*. 'I have no objection to those, generally
speaking.'

'I am glad to hear it,' Hulda managed to say before Galton cut
across her.

'Weavers, for example. We should teach them *not* to procreate,
because their skills are redundant now we have mills. If none of
them breed, we'll not have their hungry mouths to feed. Miners, on

the other hand, are much in demand, so we should reward them for producing fodder for the mines.'

He droned on, blithely unaware that his guests found his remarks outrageously offensive. Lonsdale decided it was best not to listen and concentrated on the food instead. The first course was garlic mushrooms, and comprised one small piece of fungus apiece, smothered in uncooked garlic cloves. Galton and Louisa did not seem to notice the pungent flavour as they cleared their plates, although Lonsdale only managed half of his, while Hulda just ate the mushroom.

'The butler won't be kissing the chambermaid if he devours any of this!' Louisa sniggered, as the man reached to take away the plate. 'She'll be able to smell his breath from Cheapside.'

Hulda released an unladylike snort into her wine glass, and Lonsdale saw she was struggling not to laugh. She need not have worried about displays of unmannerly mirth, he thought acidly, because Galton and his wife were too engrossed in themselves to notice anything she might say or do. Then the next course arrived.

'Beef and oyster pie,' intoned the butler gravely.

It looked delicious, with a layer of flaky golden pastry across the top, but when the butler sliced into it, it was to reveal four very rare steaks stacked on top of each other, surrounded by oysters still in their shells.

'I told Ethel to use her imagination,' said Galton, by means of explanation, and launched into a harangue about universal suffrage.

'Ethel has one *serious* flaw among her many minor ones,' said Louisa, sawing her meat with considerable vigour. 'She's a dreadful gossip.'

This time, Hulda's snort was much louder, and when Lonsdale nudged her foot under the table, he thought she might choke with her efforts to retain her composure. Her face turned red and her eyes watered.

'Of course, that's why the rest of them are pretending to be ill,' continued Louisa. 'They see it as an opportunity to have a night off for some malicious chatter.'

The last course was a 'sweet tart', which was an apposite description, as it was a topless pie and it was sweet. Indeed, it seemed to comprise pure sugar, and Lonsdale did not think he had ever eaten anything so sickly. Galton gobbled his slice at a furious

rate of knots while holding forth about the current state of the
navy, and Louisa mused that Ethel's mind had probably been on
the boot boy while she had been cooking, because she aimed to
bed him.

When the plates had been cleared away, Galton declared it was
time for the men and Hulda to retire to the drawing room for port
and cigars. Louisa, the only one excluded from the invitation, took
the hint and left.

Galton's drawing room was large, old-fashioned and dark. It was
full of the treasures he had collected from his travels in Egypt, the
Ottoman Empire and Southern Africa, and smelled unpleasantly of
the potions he used to preserve them. He indicated that Lonsdale
and Hulda were to sit, poured them some port, and set a box of El
Diamante cigars on the table. His eyebrows shot up in astonishment
when Hulda took one and lit it with the panache of an experienced
tobacco connoisseur.

'To business, then,' he said, as Hulda proceeded to fill the room
with thick, reeking smoke. 'I understand you require my expert
opinion on a matter of some importance.'

'Of *great* importance,' said Lonsdale. He produced the grass and
explained it had been found on a killer's fifth victim. 'Can you
identify it?'

'It's African,' replied Galton, then his eyes narrowed. 'I hope you
didn't take this to Henry Morton Stanley before consulting me. That
man is an ignorant braggart.'

'We didn't—' began Lonsdale, but Galton was on a roll.

'He's just come back from the Congo because he says he's
"exhausted". What does he think African travel is – a holiday? He's
an upstart, who knows nothing about exploration except hacking
through jungles and letting native porters do all the work. He has no
intellectual refinement or scientific knowledge, and shouldn't be
allowed on the Isle of Wight, let alone the Dark Continent.'

Lonsdale had considered Stanley's journeys remarkable. 'I
think—'

'He's Welsh, you know,' said Galton in a hiss, as if it were a
disease.

'So is my mother,' Lonsdale managed to interject. He smiled
rather challengingly. 'Which makes me half Welsh.'

Galton changed tack. 'And illegitimate. He grew up in a workhouse.'

'Then how impressive that he rose above it and achieved so much – all on his own merit,' said Hulda pointedly. '*He* had no rich and famous family to set him on his feet.'

Rather than acknowledge her point, Galton altered course again. 'Let me get my magnifying glass to look at this grass. Lord! Is that *blood* on the stem?'

'Yes, sir,' replied Lonsdale. 'Samuel Gurney the banker's.'

'I've never liked bankers,' remarked Galton absently. 'They have the effrontery to think they know more than I do about money.'

'How presumptuous,' said Hulda, with such a straight face that Lonsdale nearly choked on his port.

'Hah!' exclaimed the great man, eyes gleaming as he peered at the grass through a huge magnifying glass. 'I *do* know this little beauty. It's one of a group that grows in the southern reaches of Africa. Its Latin name will mean nothing to you. However, as it has a tendency to favour high, barren areas that are good for nothing except burials, one local name for it translates as the Watchers of the Dead.'

Lonsdale stared at him, levity forgotten. 'Are you sure?'

Galton regarded him coolly. 'If I hadn't been certain, young man, I wouldn't have said it. Of course I'm sure. I encountered it when I was in Africa.'

'Does it grow anywhere near the Congo?' asked Hulda.

Galton wagged a finger at her. 'You want to know if those escaped cannibals left it on their victims. Well, they might have done, but I can tell you for a fact that this isn't a plant they'd have at home. Of course, they should never have been ripped from their villages and transplanted here in the first place. It was a wicked thing to do.'

'Yes,' agreed Hulda soberly. 'It was.'

'There are many different sub-species of watcher-grass,' Galton went on. 'The differences all lie in the shape of the seeds. I may even be able to give you a precise location for this fellow, given time.'

Lonsdale rather thought Galton had given them enough by saying the plant was not native to the Congo, as it seemed to exonerate the Kumu, but he accepted the offer of further investigation with a murmur of thanks.

'I don't suppose you're a member of the Garraway Club, are you?' asked Hulda, to see what else Galton might be able to tell them.

'Certainly not! I prefer *not* to hobnob with churchmen, lawyers and bankers, if it can be avoided. I prefer the Athenaeum or the Oxford and Cambridge, where Lonsdale and I first met.'

'Then have you heard of a group who call themselves the Watchers? We know that at least two of the dead men belonged to it, and all were members of the Garraway.' Hulda nodded at the grass. 'Perhaps that's their emblem.'

'In the Bible, Watchers are fallen angels, who keep an eye on people,' said Galton. 'Some are said to have taught us how to use weapons or read the weather. It's a lot of twaddle, of course, but I can see why the name might appeal to people with delusions of grandeur. However, I've not heard of such a society.'

'The painting!' exclaimed Lonsdale. 'There's a painting in the Garraway of an angel sitting on St Paul's Cathedral, looking down across London.'

'Well, there you are then,' said Galton. 'The Garraway must be the place where this organization gathers. Did this angel have an evil visage or an amiable one? That might give you a clue as to what manner of activities your Watchers promote.'

Lonsdale considered. 'Its face was hauntingly beautiful, but neither evil nor amiable. It was just watching.'

'Then I suggest you tread very carefully,' said Galton. 'Once men start thinking they're akin to celestial beings, they tend to consider themselves free from the rules that bind the rest of us, and that makes them extremely dangerous.'

EIGHT

Despite being bone weary after his day of traipsing around the city in search of answers, Lonsdale did not sleep well that night. It had been nearly midnight by the time he had taken leave of the Galtons, seen Hulda safely home, and returned to Cleveland Square. Then he had sat in the drawing room for an hour, sipping a brandy and thinking about what Galton had said.

Dickerson and Gurney – and perhaps the other victims, too – had been Watchers, and the grass left on the bodies was known as the Watchers of the Dead. Did that mean a fellow Watcher was dispatching them? Or someone who disapproved of whatever the society did? And what about the Watchers' plans for Christmas Eve – the sacrifices that would 'show what the Watchers were capable of'? Was the killer aiming to prevent it; in which case, was he actually dispatching people who aimed to commit some dreadful atrocity?

Lonsdale went to bed, only to toss and turn for an age, plagued by questions and worries. He fell into a deep drowse about an hour before Sybil woke him by raking out the fire in the room below. He groaned, wondering how she could contrive to make such an ungodly racket armed only with a poker and a brush. He sat up, blinking blearily, and began to plan his day.

It was Tuesday, which meant that in five days it would be Christmas Eve, when the Watchers' 'unspeakable' plan would swing into action. He *had* to prevent it, knowing he would never forgive himself if lives were lost. Moreover, any number of people had expectations of him: Morley had ordered him to solve the murders by then; Dean Haldane and Lady Bowyer were desperate for answers about their lost loved ones, and Stead wanted the Kumu found and taken to a place of safety. Lonsdale had no idea how to do any of it.

He rubbed his eyes, took a deep breath, and tried to concentrate. Most immediately pressing were the murders, especially as the Kumu seemed to be doing a perfectly good job of keeping themselves hidden. He had spoken to the families of Bowyer, Haldane and Gurney, and had quizzed Roth about Dickerson. Now he needed to speak to Tait's daughter, still at the Archbishop's Palace, to see if she had answers the others had failed to provide.

He decided to catch the first available train to Surrey that morning. When he came home, he would visit the Garraway Club again, to ask about the painting of the angel, and if he was denied access, he would break in and see what he could learn by stealth.

Feeling a little more optimistic with a plan in place, he dressed quickly and hurried downstairs, where he asked the cook for eggs – it was going to be a long day, and he was not sure when, or if, there would be another opportunity to eat. The morning papers were stacked on the sideboard, and he scowled when he saw *The Echo* among them. He discovered why it kept finding its way upstairs when he happened to glance out of the window and saw Sybil deep in conversation with Voules. They were laughing together, and he supposed Voules had either bribed or charmed her into making sure it reached the brothers.

'You should dismiss her,' he said to Jack, who arrived shortly afterwards dressed for a day in court. 'If you don't, Emelia will – she won't want a maid who flirts with the likes of Voules.'

'She won't want a maid who flirts with anyone,' averred Jack. 'But I'm not getting rid of Sybil. She is the only maid I've ever known who can make a decent cup of tea.'

Unable to help himself, Lonsdale opened *The Echo*. He recognized Voules's distinctive style in the article about dinosaurs being bred in the Natural History Museum, but the cannibals and Maclean's escape had been parcelled out to other reporters, all of whom seemed determined to create as much fear and suspicion as possible. When Lonsdale's eggs arrived, he turned to *The Standard*, and read of several unprovoked assaults on black people, almost certainly a result of the rubbish published by the gutter press.

'I don't like the foreign news,' remarked Jack, who had *The Daily Telegraph*. 'The French have forced the Chinese to abandon Tonkin, and now control a large swathe of the Far East, while Bismarck's son is visiting Austria, which is an indication of a stronger German-Austrian alliance. It bodes ill for the future.'

While he ate, hurrying so as to leave for Surrey as soon as possible, Lonsdale told Jack what more he had learned about the murders, including what he and Hulda had gleaned from Galton the previous evening. Jack's eyes widened in alarm when he saw his brother was being drawn into some very dark waters but, before he could speak, there was a knock on the door. They regarded each other in surprise – it was far too early for visitors. Their surprise turned to astonishment when Anne walked in, her maid in tow as a chaperone.

'Is something wrong?' asked Jack in alarm. 'Emelia? Is she ill?'

'All is well,' replied Anne soothingly. 'I just wanted to see my fiancé, and before dawn is the only time I can be sure of catching him. I came at ten o'clock last night, thinking he was sure to be home, but there was no sign of either of you.'

Lonsdale smiled, but inside was cursing himself for wanting breakfast. If he had gone to the station as soon as he was dressed, he would have been on his way to Surrey, whereas now he would be delayed indefinitely. Then he berated himself sharply. What was he thinking? This was the woman he loved, and if he thought being with her was not the best use of his time, there was something seriously amiss.

'Would you like some tea?' he asked, forcing himself to not fiddle with the silverware to betray his agitation.

She accepted and began to chat about a meeting she had attended on women's suffrage, while Lonsdale watched the minute hand of the clock on the mantelpiece. He stopped listening, his mind on the murders again. Absently, his gaze fell on the dinosaur claw that he had promised to take to the Natural History Museum. He had intended to do it that week, although he doubted he would have time now. His attention snapped back to Anne when one sentence permeated his consciousness.

'Papa wanted to make sure you aren't still pursuing these nasty murders. He's worried that such an unsavoury matter may drag the Humbage name through the mud by association.'

Lonsdale frowned, ignoring Jack's warning kick under the table. 'He sent you here to tell me to flout my editor's orders?'

Anne shook her head impatiently. 'He didn't *send* me, Alec – I chose to come. But he's right. Murder *is* sordid, not to mention dangerous, and I don't want you embroiled in it.'

Lonsdale took one of her hands in his; it was icy cold. 'It's my job. Besides, the victims of this lunatic deserve justice, and *The PMG* has always prided itself on—'

Anne jerked her hand away. 'But I don't *want* you to do it. What if something happens to you? It would break my heart.'

'Nothing will happen,' Lonsdale assured her. 'I can look after myself.'

'That's not very comforting,' said Anne wretchedly. 'It means you know how to brawl, which is hardly laudable.'

'Nor is looking the other way at injustice,' argued Lonsdale. 'That's why I like working for *The Pall Mall Gazette*. Our articles make a difference by drawing the public's attention to—'

'No!' interrupted Anne, raising her hand to stop him. 'That's a lot of self-righteous twaddle, designed to make you feel better about something you know you shouldn't be doing. You can't pull the wool over my eyes – I *know* you.'

But Lonsdale stood his ground, and within minutes, the disagreement had escalated into a full-scale row. It reached a climax when he pointed out that they used to think alike, but ever since their engagement, she seemed to have lost her capacity for independent thought and listened too much to the repressive views of her father and sister. Eyes flashing furiously, Anne jumped to her feet and swept out, the maid scurrying at her heels. Lonsdale should have been appalled to see his betrothed leave him in such a manner, but all he could think was that it meant he could still make the nine o'clock train.

'Your marriage is going to be a stormy one,' remarked Jack, who had pretended to read the paper throughout in the hope that he would not be drawn into the spat.

'I'm not sure there *will* be a marriage,' said Lonsdale stiffly. 'I can't have a wife who denigrates my chosen profession. No man can.'

'Do you love her?' asked Jack quietly.

'Yes,' said Lonsdale, then reconsidered. 'Or perhaps I love the *idea* of her. She's pretty, intelligent, and we have much in common. However, I'm learning that there are rather a lot of things we disagree about, and I have a feeling those will be the ones that will matter.'

Jack looked out of the window. 'When I first met Em, I thought about her all the time – I could barely work for longing to be with her. She meant everything to me. I was besotted.'

'And now?' asked Lonsdale, surprised by the confession.

'And now I feel as though I'm married already. She berates my servants, criticizes my choice of clothes, and reports all my confidences to her father. I'll still marry her, but I rather feel the shine has gone.'

Lonsdale was sorry to hear it.

Before leaving for Surrey, Lonsdale needed to get rid of Voules – *The Echo* reporter abandoned Sybil mid-giggle and began to follow him the moment he left the house, sticking to him like glue as he set off for Charing Cross. Lonsdale ducked down an alley, then stepped out in front of Voules when he followed a moment later.

'I'm going to West Wickham,' he informed him curtly. 'Shall we sit on the train together or would you rather continue this pretence of going my way by chance?'

Voules grinned, unabashed. 'Just doing my job, Lonsdale. It's because of you that I got the scoops on the cannibals and the dinosaurs, so it's well worth the effort. And you're involved in Maclean's escape, so it's in my interests to keep you in my sights. Did you like my editorial today? It—'

'Maclean?' interrupted Lonsdale. 'What are you talking about? I know nothing about him or his escape.'

Voules nodded off down the road. 'Then why's he following you?'

Lonsdale looked to where he indicated and saw the now-familiar bowler-hatted figure.

'That's Maclean?' he demanded. 'Then why haven't *you* made a citizen's arrest? You've been braying for all "loyal Londoners" to lay hold of him and take him to the police, so why not follow your own trumpet call?'

'Because he might be armed,' replied Voules, not unreasonably.

Lonsdale grabbed his arm and hauled him into someone's back garden, where they lurked behind a dripping buddleia tree until Bowler Hat hurried past. Lonsdale leapt out and seized him by the scruff of the neck, eliciting a yelp of alarm. But once he had him, Lonsdale could see that he had snagged the wrong man. His captive was not the person who had been following him, but an innocent clerk going about his business. He let him go with profuse apologies, while Voules chortled.

'Don't blame me,' he shrugged when Lonsdale rounded angrily on him. 'You just pounced on the first man with a bowler who happened past. You should have checked it was the right one before flying into action.'

Lonsdale stalked away, glad when Voules made no attempt to follow. On the main road, there was no sign of 'Maclean', or anyone else with a bowler hat.

Unfortunately, the episode with Voules was just the first in a catalogue of mishaps that characterized the rest of Lonsdale's day. It, and his argument with Anne, meant he missed the nine o'clock train, forcing him to wait for the next one. It was late, then proceeded to sit for half an hour at the platform before finally chuffing away. He changed at London Bridge for the North Kent Railway, but the only available seat was in a very ancient coach that stank of soot, grease and the goat that had been brought aboard by the passenger opposite.

The train groaned and rattled its way to Lewisham, where he changed again, this time to a Mid-Kent Line train for New Beckenham. There he missed his connection, obliging him to sit for two hours in the middle of nowhere, growing increasingly agitated as the porters kept assuring him that the next train would 'arrive at any moment'. It appeared eventually, and took him to West Wickham, where he found his woes were not yet over.

It was pouring with rain, but there was no trap or carriage in sight. He asked for directions and was horrified to learn that Addington Palace was two and a half miles away, and the only way to reach it was on foot. Having come so far, he was not about to go home empty-handed, so he turned up the collar of his coat, tightened his belt to keep his trousers from dragging in the mud, and set off.

It was a miserable hike, with the wind driving in his face the whole way, so by the time the Archbishop's Palace – a sprawling, rather ugly eighteenth-century mansion – came into sight, he was soaked to the skin, muddy, and very cold. He knocked on the door, where a manservant looked him up and down in distaste, and it was fortunate that Tait's daughter happened to be walking her dogs at that moment, or he was sure he would have been turned away.

Lucy Tait was a tall, mannish woman, whose clothes were covered in horse hairs. The horses were her primary concern, because there were a lot of them, she loved them dearly, and she had not yet found a new home that could comfortably accommodate them all. And she knew she was running out of time, because her father's successor would be named in the next day or two and would want to move in to his new official residence as soon as possible.

She did not invite Lonsdale inside, perfectly warm and comfortable in her thick riding coat and waterproof boots, so the entire interview was conducted in the teeming rain. Lonsdale shivered almost uncontrollably, but she failed to notice his discomfort, although at least she was willing to answer his questions, especially when he told her that her father's death was not the only one he was exploring.

'He was a difficult man,' she began, 'but I adored him, and no one had the right to steal his life. He deserved better, and I'm glad you aim to see he gets it, especially as the police have suddenly decided that violent stabbings equate with "natural causes".'

'They were told that the matter had been settled by a "higher authority", and the investigating officers ordered to take it no further.'

Lucy raised her eyebrows. 'God is the only higher authority my father would have recognized, and I don't think *He* undertakes murder enquiries, not when He'll recognize the culprit by the stinking blackness of his soul.'

'The police think someone in the Church has asked for discretion.'

'Oh, I'm sure someone did, but "discretion" isn't the same as "sweeping under the carpet", which seems to have happened to my father's death. The Church will go a long way to avoid a scandal, but it would never conceal the callous murder of its leader.'

'Not even if the culprit is another clergyman?'

'You refer to the fact that my father's policies made him enemies,' mused Lucy. 'And you are right to ask, because he did rub people up the wrong way. However, not even the most vitriolic of his clerical critics would resort to murder. At least, not in so brutal a fashion. Did you hear how he was killed?'

Lonsdale nodded. 'The other four victims suffered similar attacks.'

Lucy winced. 'Before you came along, I had no idea there *were* other victims. I'm sure Superintendent Hayes and Inspector Peters would have told me, as they seem honest and competent men, but once Inspector Wells took over, all communication stopped. He hasn't been to see me once, despite my daily letters demanding news of his progress.'

'Wells has been assigned to the other murders, too.'

Lucy regarded him astutely. 'Yet I have the sense that his refusal to contact me has nothing to do with five murders being a lot for one man to handle, and more to do with this "higher authority" not wanting the case solved. The authority must be Commissioner Henderson, because it was he who wrote telling me that Wells had been appointed.'

Lonsdale struggled not to wince as icy water began to run down the back of his neck. 'I suspect Henderson was acting on the orders of someone higher still. I think it might be something to do with a group called the Watchers. Have you heard of it?'

'Oh, yes. My father was a Watcher, and was very proud of the fact, although he wasn't a vain man. I'm not sure what they did, but I do know they met at the Garraway Club.'

'Is there anything in your father's belongings that might tell us what being a Watcher entailed?' asked Lonsdale, not averse to spending an hour indoors, where he might be able to set his wet clothes by a fire to dry before the homeward journey.

'I had a look after he died,' replied Lucy. 'But then the Church Commissioners came along and boxed everything up for their archives. I was thorough, though, because I was desperate to know if he had anything that might explain why he was murdered. There was nothing. And I'm *still* desperate, which is why I'm standing out here with you, getting soaked to the skin.'

'We could go inside,' suggested Lonsdale hopefully.

'We could, but then you'd miss the last train back to London, and I don't think you'd enjoy a night on the station bench. But to return to the Watchers, do you think my father was killed because of them?'

'Dickerson and Gurney were Watchers, and they're dead. I don't know about Bowyer and Haldane – yet. However, it seems likely. Are you sure you can't tell me more about them?'

'It was a *secret* society – its members never discussed what they did or said. However, my father wouldn't have countenanced anything untoward.'

'Two more questions,' said Lonsdale quickly, aware that he was in the process of being dismissed. 'Who discovered your father's body?'

'I did. He'd been killed in his study, probably with some kind of axe or sword.'

'I don't suppose you noticed a piece of grass on or near him?'

Lucy frowned. 'It's funny you should ask, because there *was* one. I assumed it had blown in through the window, which the killer left open as he made his escape. I threw it away, but I can tell you that it was long with pinkish seeds.'

'It's from Africa, where one name for it is Watchers of the Dead because it grows near burial sites. Did your father have any African connections?'

'He never mentioned any to me, but going through his papers, I discovered that he donated large sums of his own money to a hospital in Natal. I wish he'd told me – I could have said it made me proud. He was a *good* man, Mr Lonsdale, in ways that matter. He didn't brag about his charity, but kept it between him and God.'

'Did he ever talk about the Garraway Club?' asked Lonsdale, trying to stand firm as she began to ease him towards the gate.

'Only when he wanted to tell me about that wretched Grim Death.'

Lonsdale's pulse quickened. 'Grim Death?'

'Better known as Grimaldi d'Atte from Italy. Professor Dickerson started calling him Grim Death, and it amused my father, so he did it, too. Señor d'Atte is the Watcher who convened the meetings, and he always signed himself Grim Death. I found several of his letters in my father's study. I burned them, lest the Church Commissioners got the wrong idea.'

'Why "that wretched" Grim Death?'

'Because he can't sing to save his life, although he considers himself a serious rival to Edward Lloyd, who has the voice of an angel. He's always applying for leading roles with the best opera companies, and my father loved to tell me of his antics, because he knew they would send me apoplectic with disbelief.'

'Your father enjoyed taunting you?'

'*Teasing* me. It was something special we shared.' Her eyes filled with tears. 'And the killer ripped that away. I hope you track down the bastard, Mr Lonsdale. And when you do, land a good punch from me.'

The journey home was even worse than the outward one. The train from West Wickham was late and the waiting room was closed, which meant Lonsdale had to stand outside. It had stopped raining, but he was still wet and quickly grew chilled. Then he arrived at New Beckenham to discover that a cow on the tracks had delayed all northbound trains.

There was another long wait at Lewisham because of flooding, so by the time he alighted at Charing Cross, it was nearly nine o'clock. He almost wished Voules and Bowler Hat *had* been on his tail all day, because it would have been satisfying to see them share his misery.

And yet the day had brought its rewards, in that he now had an identity for Grim Death, not to mention confirming that Tait had been a Watcher and the killer had left a piece of grass with the body. He also had more evidence that Commissioner Henderson was complicit in ensuring that the murders were never solved.

He was exhausted but decided to visit the Garraway and demand an interview with Señor d'Atte that night anyway. The club seemed to lie at the heart of the mystery, after all. He wondered if Burnside would let him explore it when all the members had gone home – the photographer was short of money, so might well agree to look the other way for a price. And the following day, he would go to Scotland Yard and demand to speak to Commissioner Henderson – to see if he could find out who had ordered Hayes and Peters to be dismissed in favour of the inept Wells.

As he was wet and muddy, he went home to change first, knowing he would not be allowed in any club looking like a vagrant. He arrived to hear voices coming from the dining room. He assumed Jack was entertaining Emelia, and braced himself accordingly, but when he went in, it was to see Hulda. She had dressed for dinner, and her new comb looked pretty in her fair hair.

'What're you doing here?' he blurted.

'Waiting for you,' she replied. 'I thought you'd be home hours ago.'

'So did I,' said Lonsdale, slumping on a chair and helping himself to a boiled potato, which was all that was left of what had evidently been a very hearty dinner, judging by the remains on their plates.

He told her and Jack all he had learned, then listened to Hulda explain how she had concentrated on finding the Kumu. She had spoken to Owen and the other museum staff first, then had gone to Roth's lodgings, where she claimed to have interviewed him with great gentleness and tact. However, as she thought he had responded 'shiftily' to her questions, she had spent the remainder of her day monitoring him.

'But he knew I was there and escaped through the back door,' she finished resentfully. 'I spent all afternoon watching an empty house, which I only realized when it became dark and no lights went on. However, his slippery antics suggest we should certainly visit him again tomorrow. Perhaps *you* can prise the truth from him.'

Lonsdale did not think there was anything to prise, but nodded agreement. Then Jack spoke.

'I went to speak to Anne for you,' he said, and with a guilty pang Lonsdale realized he had not given his fiancée a single thought since their quarrel that morning. 'I think I've smoothed things over, although you'd better give her a spectacular gift for Christmas.'

'Lord!' groaned Lonsdale. 'I've spent rather a lot on hansoms and trains these last few days, so I hope Garrard has something relatively inexpensive.'

'I'll lend you some money,' said Jack. 'I dislike the sight of blood – and yours will be spilled unless you do what's expected of you on Monday.'

'I should change,' said Lonsdale, his mind already back on the investigation. 'I want to speak to Grim Death tonight.'

'You'll be too late,' predicted Jack. 'By the time you get there, the club will be empty. Or do you know where he lives?'

'No,' admitted Lonsdale. 'But perhaps Burnside will be on duty and will let me in to search the place. D'Atte's address is sure to be recorded somewhere.'

'And if Burnside isn't there?'

'I'll break in,' replied Lonsdale, aware of a sense of growing excitement as he felt answers within his grasp at last.

'I'll come with you,' said Hulda, and raised a hand to quell his objections. 'You aim to enter on the sly, so what difference will it make if you do it alone or with a woman? Now go and change, because I don't want to commit burglary with a drowned rat.'

It was nearly eleven o'clock when Lonsdale and Hulda walked up Exchange Alley. They took up residence in a doorway opposite and studied the Garraway carefully. Most of its lights were out, although lamps were still lit in the hallway and the dining room. Voices emanated from within, laughing and joking. Moments later, the door opened, and several men emerged. They called amiable goodnights to each other, then walked away in different directions.

'I can see the night porter,' whispered Hulda. 'It's not Burnside.'

Lights began to go out, and Lonsdale saw Jack had been right to predict that it was too late for Grim Death to be available for questions. They went to the back of the premises, where Hulda deftly picked the lock on the door that led to the kitchen – a skill Lonsdale could never imagine Anne acquiring. There was a smell of roasted meat, and the leftovers in the pantry suggested that members of the Garraway enjoyed fine food to go with the luxurious surroundings of the dining room.

The ground floor was for servants – or rather, for commoners like Burnside and Roth – as, beyond the elegant entrance hall, there was a shabby but comfortable sitting room for them, along with beds for those whose duties kept them late at night. There was a cellar that held an impressive collection of good wine, while the formal dining service was hand-painted in gold. Curiously, there were several crates of old plates stacked in the hallways, while four huge casks of beer formed an inconvenient obstacle in the scullery.

There was a nasty moment when a snort came from the darkness, and Hulda and Lonsdale froze in alarm, but the commoner sleeping there did not wake, so on they went. They climbed a flight of wooden stairs, alert for any indication that they were discovered, and found themselves on the main floor.

'Lord!' muttered Lonsdale, as they peered around the dining-room door and saw the Christmas decorations that had been erected since his last visit. There was a huge tree, paper chains, red candles, and so many silver balls that the room seemed to sparkle. Long tables had been set out. 'It looks as if they intend to entertain a lot of guests – you could seat two hundred people in here!'

'And they'll do it on Christmas Eve,' whispered Hulda, pointing to a printed schedule pinned to a door, which stated the dining room would host a private event the following Sunday afternoon – Christmas Eve. All club members were politely requested to stay away until the following Tuesday.

'A "private event",' mused Lonsdale, 'on the day that the Watchers aim to do something that involves blood and sacrifice and will prove what they're capable of. If they do it when this hall is full of people, the number of casualties could be horrifying!'

The library and reading rooms were empty, but voices could be heard in the smoking room. They crept towards it and saw Roth with Burnside. The photographer was emptying ashtrays and collecting old papers, while Roth trailed after him, muttering.

'So, Roth came *here* when he gave me the slip so slyly,' breathed Hulda. 'Can you hear what he's saying?'

Roth was speaking in a very low voice, but Lonsdale thought he heard the word 'Khoikhoi' because, if pronounced properly, it had a click at the beginning. It was the third time Roth had mentioned that particular people – although the first two had allegedly been slips of the tongue. Lonsdale was bemused by it, especially when it was clear that Roth was agitated, unsettled and fearful.

'We should confront him,' whispered Hulda. 'Demand to know why he contrived to escape from me. Look at him! Have you ever seen a more furtive demeanour?'

Lonsdale had, but not often. 'We can't do it here. He'll want to know how we got in, and I refuse to admit that we picked the lock on—'

He broke off and pulled Hulda into a broom cupboard when he heard footsteps in the hall behind them. They had only just stepped out of sight when Lord Carlingford stamped past, Fleetwood-Pelham scurrying at his heels. Carlingford was shaking with fury.

'It's outrageous!' he snarled, stalking into the smoking room. Seeing his angry face, Roth and Burnside nodded polite greetings and made a tactful retreat to the commoners' quarters, clearly unwilling to be in the firing line when the testy baron was in a temper. 'How *dare* they charge us extra after a price was agreed! I'm going to *kill* him!'

'Easy!' cautioned Fleetwood-Pelham. 'It's not as if we can't afford it.'

'That's not the point,' raged Carlingford. 'I can't abide men who go back on their word. I'm going to blast out his meagre brains!'

'Please don't,' said Fleetwood-Pelham tiredly. 'The police have enough murders to explore with Tait and the rest. They don't need another.'

Carlingford was about to argue further when his eye lit on the painting of the angel. He stalked towards it, and then there was another outburst.

'Look at this! Some light-fingered bastard has stolen the name-plate off the bottom of this picture! God save us! Is nothing sacred?'

Fleetwood-Pelham peered at the empty spot in dismay. 'Who could've done such a thing?'

'Those bloody commoners!' spat Carlingford. 'They are thieves to a man. If they can't pay the fees, then we shouldn't let them in. It's a stupid scheme, and Gurney should never have introduced it. I'd rather pay for servants.'

Fleetwood-Pelham glanced around to make sure no one was listening, then lowered his voice to a gossipy whisper. 'Burnside's down on his luck, and bitter about the way he thinks he's been treated by the Queen. I wouldn't put it past *him* to steal.'

'Where is the rogue? I'll chop off his thieving fingers,' railed Carlingford, and stalked back the way he had come, Fleetwood-Pelham hurrying after him.

Lonsdale heaved a sigh of relief, not liking to imagine what Carlingford would have done to him and Hulda, had they been caught. He peered around the door to make sure they had gone and saw a piece of paper lying on the floor. It had not been there before, so he assumed the courtiers had dropped it.

'So someone's cheated them,' mused Hulda, watching Lonsdale pick it up. 'I wonder if the culprit will be the next victim.'

'It's a baker,' said Lonsdale, showing her the paper. 'Here's a bill for a thousand mince pies – God only knows why the club needs that many – with an original price and a much higher revised one. I don't blame Carlingford for being irked – he'll never get another baker to fill such a large order at this late stage.'

They heard Carlingford and Fleetwood-Pelham talking in the library shortly afterwards, at which point the commoners began dousing more lamps. Hulda and Lonsdale waited until they had finished and the club was quiet, then began to explore, eventually finding an office where the club's records were kept. Lonsdale closed the curtains and laid a rug across the bottom of the door to hide the light, while Hulda lit a candle.

It was not long before they realized they were wasting their time. There was nothing about the Watchers, and nearly every file pertained to purchases of the basics that kept the club running – food, wine, fuel, books, snuff and tobacco. They exchanged a resigned, disappointed glance, and prepared to leave the way they had come, via the back door.

All was well until they reached the hall, at which point they met Roth, who released a shrill howl of alarm. Lonsdale grabbed Hulda's hand and hauled her towards the front door instead, glad it was dark and Roth had not seen their faces. The yell alerted others. Burnside hurtled up from the basement, and Carlingford and Fleetwood-Pelham emerged from the library.

'Stop!' bellowed Carlingford when he saw the shadowy figures running away. 'Or I'll shoot.'

Before Lonsdale and Hulda could oblige, there was a colossal bang, and the doorframe next to Lonsdale's head flew into splinters. He and Hulda ducked in alarm, and began wrestling frantically with the bolts, praying they could slip them before they were gunned down.

'Carlingford, no!' cried Fleetwood-Pelham. 'You can't shoot people in—'

There was another shot, and the glass in the door shattered. Lonsdale glanced behind him to see Fleetwood-Pelham frantically trying to wrest the gun from Carlingford's hand, simultaneously yelling for Roth and Burnside to lay hold of the thieves, although neither commoner would oblige as long as Carlingford was waving his gun in that direction. Then Lonsdale noticed that Carlingford was not the only one who was armed: so was Roth.

Hulda's bolt shot back, so Lonsdale hauled open the door. A third shot followed, although Carlingford's aim was spoiled by Fleetwood-Pelham struggling to disarm him. With the baron's scream of rage ringing in their ears, they raced into the night and allowed the darkness to swallow them up.

NINE

Neither Lonsdale nor Hulda felt like going home after their narrow escape, so they took a hansom to Northumberland Street. They made the journey in silence, both shocked by the ferocity of Carlingford's reaction to intruders. It was not unusual for burglars to be shot, but the police took a dim view of it, especially when the culprits were unarmed and leaving empty-handed.

'He wanted to kill us,' Hulda whispered, when they were in the reporters' room with steaming cups of tea. Her face was ashen. 'Gun us down where we stood, with Fleetwood-Pelham, Roth and Burnside looking on.'

'Fleetwood-Pelham tried to stop him,' said Lonsdale.

'The other two didn't,' said Hulda. 'Roth is a coward, even though he had a gun, too, while Burnside probably remembers what happened the last time he played the hero – his efforts barely acknowledged.'

'We'd better not tell anyone else about this,' said Lonsdale, sipping the tea, 'or Mr Morley will take us off the case. I'm not sure we'll have answers by Christmas Eve, but we made some progress tonight, and I don't want to give up now.'

'What progress? We learned nothing about the Watchers.'

'On the contrary, we knew they had something "unspeakable" planned for Christmas, and now we can surmise that it will happen in the Garraway – the preparations we saw indicate that a large number of guests are expected. That information might allow us to thwart them.'

'True. Do you think Carlingford is our murderer? He was very free with his pistol tonight, and he threatened to kill the baker. He's a violent man with an uncontrollable temper, and Bradwell did say the five victims were killed in *frenzied* attacks.'

'It's possible. What about Fleetwood-Pelham as a suspect?'

'He is such a chatter-head that he'd betray himself by dint of wanting to gossip about it. Besides, he knows we're exploring the case, but hasn't tried to stop us. On the contrary, he's offered information and advice. However, the same can't be said for Roth and Burnside.'

'Roth isn't a killer,' stated Lonsdale firmly. 'And it can't be Burnside, because he was with me when Haldane was murdered – we saw Haldane enter the Royal Courts of Justice together, and he was still with me when the news came about his death.'

'He was with you the whole time?' asked Hulda, growing sleepy as the fright of their close call began to recede, leaving exhaustion in its wake.

'Yes, he . . .' But Lonsdale trailed off, because Burnside *had* disappeared – for about an hour, returning pink-faced and warm, although it had been a cold day. The photographer could easily have entered the building, killed Haldane, and come out again.

Yet Burnside did not seem like a murderer any more than Roth did. Lonsdale glanced at Hulda and saw she was asleep. She had not heard his hesitation, so he decided to keep his concerns to himself. He would share them with her if they became relevant but, until then, there was nothing to be gained by pointing the finger at a man who was almost certainly innocent.

'Come on,' he said, shaking her shoulder gently to wake her. 'We should both go home. We have a busy day tomorrow.'

Again, Lonsdale woke feeling lethargic and thick-headed from lack of sleep, jolted from a deep slumber by the racket Sybil made laying the fire in the room below. He sat up, aware of a sick, uneasy sensation in the pit of his stomach. It intensified when he remembered that he had just four days left, and he and Hulda had a lot to do if he aimed to catch a killer, save the Kumu, and thwart the Watchers.

He planned what needed to be done that day. Most urgent was cornering Grim Death and demanding information about the Watchers, given that the Italian was in charge of convening their gatherings. Then he should visit the office to update Morley and Stead on his progress. Next, he would speak to Roth and Burnside, to see if they could tell him what was brewing at the Garraway and, after that, contrive a meeting with Fleetwood-Pelham. Hulda was right to say he was a gossip, so perhaps he could be persuaded to chat about Carlingford, and where the baron was when five men were brutally murdered.

He washed, shaved and dressed, then hurried downstairs, pausing to warn Sybil that if she continued to flirt with Voules, she could look for another job.

She regarded him sullenly. 'You have a visitor,' she said. Then added with a smirk, 'He's in a filthy mood.'

It was Humbage, who was standing at the window with his hands clenched into angry fists behind his back. It was unsociably early for visiting, and Lonsdale was tempted to say so.

'I understand you've failed to heed my orders,' he said before Lonsdale could open his mouth. 'You've continued to meddle in unsavoury business. Worse, you committed burglary last night – that's a *criminal* offence.'

'Burglary?' blustered Lonsdale, supposing he had been recognized after all. Regardless, Humbage had no authority to 'order' him to do anything, and Lonsdale resented the presumption.

'My friend Lord Carlingford wrote me a most irate note about it,' Humbage went on with barely concealed fury, and held up the comb that Fleetwood-Pelham had given Hulda. 'This was found on the street outside his club after two intruders raided it.'

'It's not mine,' said Lonsdale flippantly. 'It would clash with my eyes.'

'Don't play the fool with me, Lonsdale,' snarled Humbage. 'It proves you and that woman were somewhere you had no right to be – inside a *gentlemen's* club.'

Lonsdale regarded him coldly. 'It "proves" nothing. You say it was found outside, so if the comb does belong to Miss Friederichs – and it does look like the one Fleetwood-Pelham gave her when he took us to the Palace – the chances are that she lost it earlier in the day.'

'Sir Algernon took *you* to the Palace?' blurted Humbage, envy in his voice.

'To his rooms,' elaborated Lonsdale. 'Have you been there?'

Knowing he was being baited, Humbage resumed his attack. 'And the woman just happened to "lose" it outside the Garraway, the very same day that two people matching your descriptions were up to no good inside?'

'Miss Friederichs had the building under surveillance,' replied Lonsdale coolly, 'because it's connected to some very unsavoury activities.'

Humbage bristled. 'I'll have you know that the Garraway is a respectable establishment, patronized by important and influential men.'

'Men like Grimaldi d'Atte?' asked Lonsdale archly, 'who convenes meetings of a sly and sinister society calling itself the Watchers?'

'The Watchers?' echoed Humbage, and Lonsdale knew him well enough to read genuine mystification; he was not a member of that exclusive sect. 'Never heard of it! However, I admit that d'Atte is below the Garraway's usual standards. Indeed, I was delighted when I heard he'd taken himself off to Glasgow to sing opera to the barbarous hordes.'

'When will he be back?' asked Lonsdale, trying to conceal his dismay that a promising line of enquiry might have been cut short.

'Not for months,' replied Humbage. 'He left his lodgings and had all his belongings put into storage. But I'm not here to provide you with tittle-tattle – I'm here to demand an explanation for your actions last night.'

'You can demand all you like,' said Lonsdale. 'But I don't answer to you.'

'You do if you aim to marry my daughter. I specifically asked you not to involve yourself in a scandal, and you promptly go out and commit a crime. I won't have my good name sullied by an association with a common felon. Do it again, and I shall forbid the match.'

'You can try,' said Lonsdale, sure Anne would not permit it. 'Now, if there's nothing else, I have work to do.'

When Lonsdale left the house, he saw Voules standing with Sybil, and supposed she felt free to ignore his ultimatum, because she knew Jack liked how she made the tea. He approached them, and saw her expression was wary but defiant. He addressed Voules.

'Sir Gervais Humbage,' he said in a low voice. 'You might want to follow him today, because then you'll be sure of a good story.'

'What good story?' demanded Voules suspiciously.

Lonsdale declined to elaborate, and only gave him a conspiratorial wink as he left. However, when he glanced behind him a few moments later, he saw *The Echo* man hurrying in the direction Humbage had taken. Good, he thought. At least he would have one day without being followed – as far as he could tell, there was no sign of Bowler Hat either.

It was still early – dawn was only just shedding its cold grey light across the city – but Lonsdale decided to visit Roth before going to the office. This time, he vowed, he would have the truth about whatever secrets the Garraway harboured – ones that compelled Roth to arm himself – and he would not leave until he had them. However, he arrived to find the door to Roth's rooms open, and a team of cleaners within.

'He moved out,' explained the landlady who watched the workmen with an eagle eye. 'Paid what he owed and bade me farewell. All he left behind are some bits of broken wood and that peculiar stink. I'm not sure I'll ever get rid of it.'

It was the smell that Roth said came from the professor's collections. Lonsdale still could not identify it, but knew it was familiar. It was a spice or some sort of scented wood . . .

In one corner was a broken headrest of the kind favoured by natives of the Cape Colony. He picked it up. The break looked recent, and he wondered if Roth had been using it to sleep, to remind himself of happier times – before his health was shattered and he still had a future full of excitement.

'Did he tell you where he was going?' asked Lonsdale.

The woman shook her head. 'Which was peculiar, because what happens if letters come for him? How do I forward them?'

'How indeed?' murmured Lonsdale, perturbed that Roth should have left the morning after the trouble at the Garraway. Moreover, the fact that Roth had a gun meant he anticipated the kind of situation where one might be needed. He had not shot at the 'intruders' himself, but Lonsdale had not been happy with the sight of it in his friend's hand.

Reluctantly, although he remained convinced that Roth was not a killer, he conceded that he was certainly involved in something untoward.

The reporters' room felt like Lonsdale looked – dull, shabby and tired. There was a December moth fluttering against the window, and the day outside was so dreary that Lonsdale thought the creature must imagine it was night. Hulda was there, so he told her his thoughts on Roth being armed and leaving his lodgings so precipitously.

'Which means he must be embroiled in something questionable,' he finished. 'Although it's difficult to believe, as he's a gentle, honourable man. I can't imagine how he let himself become drawn into . . . whatever's happening at the Garraway.'

'*Murder* is happening at the Garraway,' said Hulda harshly. 'And *I've* never had a problem with Roth as a suspect. He's obviously short of money, so the prospect of a legacy from his mentor must've proved irresistible.'

'That would suggest his affection for the professor wasn't as deep as he claimed, but I'm sure he was telling the truth. Moreover, it's a motive for dispatching Dickerson, but what about the others?'

'They were all members of the Garraway, and who knows what goes on behind the closed doors of "gentlemen's" clubs? Besides, people change, Lonsdale. You knew Roth a long time ago. Perhaps poverty and poor health turned a once-good man bad.'

Lonsdale knew they would never agree, so changed the subject. 'Did you realize you dropped your comb outside the Garraway last night? Humbage waved it at me this morning, while accusing me of burglary, which means our part in last night's escapade is common knowledge. It may even be why Roth fled – he knows we're coming closer to the truth.'

'I knew I'd lost it, but I didn't know where. Did you get it back for me?'

Before Lonsdale could tell her it had been the last thing on his mind, Stead walked in. The assistant editor was wearing a smart suit, but there was a large ceramic lizard poking from one pocket in lieu of the more usual handkerchief. Stead offered no explanation for this peculiar fashion statement, and Hulda and Lonsdale declined to ask.

'You must go to Broadmoor,' he said without preamble. 'I have intelligence that suggests the answers to all your questions lie there.'

'What intelligence?' asked Lonsdale.

'That the escaped Maclean is the killer you've been hunting. He's been seen at the sites of all five murders – returning to the scenes of his triumphs. And if we can show he's the culprit, *The Echo* will have to apologize to the Kumu for all the disgusting, bigoted, unwarranted vitriol they've published over the last few days.'

'Who told you what Maclean has been doing?' asked Hulda warily.

'The urchins I pay for such information: five boys who've never met, so don't say they concocted a tale together. Maclean is the killer, and you'll go to Broadmoor to prove it – and quickly, because a mob gathered outside the Natural History Museum last night, blaming Owen for "importing flesh-eating monsters". You *must* end this nonsense before an innocent is hurt.'

'What will a trip to Broadmoor tell us?' asked Lonsdale, sure it would be a waste of time, as it was clear to him that the real solution lay at the Garraway.

'Maclean's medical records,' replied Stead promptly, 'which may explain why he's taken against those specific victims. If you can predict who might be next, you can help the police trap him, and see him returned to a place where he can do no more harm.'

'A man who looks like Maclean has been following us,' said Hulda. 'A slim person in a bowler hat.'

'Then you must hurry,' said Stead, alarmed by the notion of a killer in Hulda's vicinity. 'How long will it take you to get to Broadmoor?'

Lonsdale glanced at the clock on the wall. 'Too long – unless we leave right away. It'll be more efficient to go first thing in the morning, because then we can speak to Burnside, Fleetwood-Pelham and Carlingford today, and try to gain an understanding of what they're up to and how – if – it relates to Maclean.'

'That's not a good idea,' said Hulda in alarm. 'Not if they know it was us who broke in last night. Even if the three of them are innocent of murder, they'll be angry about what we did, and will refuse to answer our questions.'

'Broke in?' echoed Stead in horror. 'I hope you haven't done anything illegal. *The PMG* won't countenance crime.'

'Not even to save the Kumu?' asked Hulda slyly.

'Perhaps we should just question Burnside,' said Lonsdale before Stead could press her for an explanation. 'I'm sure I can convince him to cooperate.'

Nevertheless, a warning bell sounded at the back of his mind when he recalled the photographer's timely disappearance outside the Royal Courts of Justice when Haldane was killed.

'He's a liar,' declared Hulda uncompromisingly. 'On the day the mortuary was nearly burned down, he told you that he was busy taking pictures of visitors in Hyde Park and that Gladstone stopped to greet him. But Gladstone wasn't in London that day – he was giving a speech in Bristol for his Corrupt and Illegal Practices Prevention Act.'

'We *must* find the Kumu and keep them safe,' said Stead, returning to the issue that concerned him most. He opened his mouth to add more, but the moth flew into it. He snapped his jaws closed, stood utterly still for a few seconds, then opened his mouth again. Out flapped the moth unharmed, and he continued as if nothing had happened. 'Very well – you may explore other leads today. But tomorrow, you'll visit Broadmoor.'

'If you insist,' said Lonsdale, still sure it would be a fool's errand. 'Although while that may take us to Maclean, it won't help us find the Kumu. I'm not sure how we'll do that.'

Stead pondered for a moment. 'Go to see Henry Morton Stanley. He's been to the Kumu's bit of the Lualaba River – the first European ever to do so – and may be able to tell you what sort of environments they favour. Kew, among the tropical plants, the forests of Hampshire . . .'

Lonsdale was sure that would be even less useful than Broadmoor. 'It won't—'

Stead cut across him. 'See him this morning. He won't turn away two of my best reporters, no matter how busy he claims to be.'

'He's not well,' said Lonsdale, sure he and Hulda would get nowhere near him and loath to waste time trying. 'He's still recovering from the haematuric fever he caught in the Congo.'

'He was well enough to enjoy a public spat with Francis Galton last week,' argued Stead. 'But go, go! It's Wednesday today, so you only have four days to catch Maclean, find evidence that he committed those murders, thwart the Watchers, and rescue the Kumu. Hurry!'

Knowing from experience that they would be turned away if they appeared unannounced at the home of so eminent a person, Lonsdale sent a boy with his card and a request to visit Stanley as soon as possible. While they waited for the reply, Hulda dashed off an article on that morning's announcement from Canterbury – that the Bishop of Truro, Edward White Benson, would be the next Archbishop.

Lonsdale, meanwhile, said he wanted some air, but the moment he was outside, he took a hansom to Burnside's home, suspecting the photographer would be more willing to talk to him on his own. It was a risk, given that Burnside would know that Lonsdale had broken into the Garraway, but time was short and Lonsdale was desperate for answers.

The photographer and his landlady were both out, but Lonsdale peered through the windows and saw his rooms were still occupied – unlike Roth, Burnside had not made a run for it. He hesitated. Should he visit St James's Palace in the hope that Fleetwood-Pelham would be willing to talk to him? Hulda was right to recommend staying away from Carlingford, as he would more likely shoot than answer questions, especially ones that might incriminate him. Moreover, it would be better to let her speak to Fleetwood-Pelham – he liked her enough to give her a comb, so she was more likely to be successful at prising answers from him. Lonsdale jumped into a hansom and asked the driver to take him to Exchange Alley, where he stood opposite the Garraway, peering up at its shuttered windows.

Nothing moved inside, and eventually he conceded that staring at it was an exercise in futility.

He hurried back to the office, only to find Voules waiting outside.

'I thought you were monitoring Humbage,' he said, struggling to mask his annoyance that *The Echo* man was back to being his shadow again.

'I was, but he gave me the slip – he's better at losing me than you are.' Voules spoke without rancour, clearly believing that being slyly ditched was par for the course.

Yet Lonsdale was surprised to hear the blustering, pompous Humbage was capable of a stealth that exceeded his own. It was suspicious, so perhaps he *was* right to suggest Voules should follow him. He flailed around for a way to convince Voules to go after him again.

'So some other paper will have the story,' he said, feigning regret. 'Sorry, Voules. I did my best to pass it to you once Stead deemed it too sensational for us.'

'I trailed him to St James's Palace,' said Voules, eyes gleaming. 'Is the scandal something to do with royalty? Unfortunately, while we were both hanging around the door – him to be let in and me waiting to see what would happen – he spotted me. Then, when the guard refused him admittance, he stalked off and made sure he lost me in the park.'

'He was barred from going in?' asked Lonsdale, intrigued.

'Very firmly – he argued, but the guard insisted that Lord Carlingford isn't taking unwanted callers today. It was an insult, but he didn't seem to take offence.'

'Because his "friend" Carlingford can do no wrong,' muttered Lonsdale. 'Try looking for Humbage at the Garraway Club. I imagine he'll go there at some point today, in the hope of meeting the man he aims to make a crony.'

'I snagged a boy earlier, who said you're off to meet Stanley the explorer,' said Voules. 'Can I come? Stanley refuses to see anyone from *The Echo*, but if he thinks I'm with you . . .'

'No!' blurted Lonsdale, astounded by the audacity. He thought fast. 'We're going to see his bead collection, so unless you think *Echo* readers are interested in those . . .'

'They prefer killers and cannibals. And man-eating dinosaurs of course – my editor was delighted with the scoop on those. As it

came from Miss Friederichs, I owe her a tip in return, which is why
I'm here, but she won't come out to get it.'

'Tell me instead,' said Lonsdale.

Voules rubbed his chin, then nodded. 'Just make sure you tell
her it came from me, so she knows we're even – no claiming you
found this out for yourself. It's about the Garraway Club – your
maid Sybil overheard that you think Señor d'Atte might know
something about the murders.'

'She eavesdropped on me?' demanded Lonsdale indignantly.

'Not deliberately,' lied Voules. 'However, it's a good thing she
did, because she told me, and I can save you a lot of trouble.
D'Atte fancies himself a singer and was warbling in the chorus
of *Iolanthe* when Tait, Bowyer and Gurney were killed.'

Lonsdale stared at him. 'How do you know?'

Voules held out a crumpled programme. 'Because here's his name
in black and white, and he lives for opera, so you can be sure he
was there. You can check with the rest of the cast, but you'll find
I'm right – he has alibis for three of the murders. You should believe
what you read in *The Echo*, Lonsdale. The *cannibals* are the culprits.'

It was only a mile or so to the rooms that Stanley rented at
30 Sackville Street in Piccadilly, so Lonsdale and Hulda walked
there. It was in a three-storey terraced house of brown brick with a
slate roof. Lonsdale knocked on a shiny black door that stood impos-
ingly between a pair of Doric pilasters and was surprised when
Stanley himself opened it. The world-famous explorer looked
more distinguished in life than in his promotional photographs, his
closely cropped, greying hair offsetting his lined, deeply tanned
face.

While it was an honour to meet him, Lonsdale was wary. The
explorer had a reputation for surliness, and he and Hulda would not
be the first reporters to be sent away with insults ringing in their
ears. But he need not have worried, as Stanley was gracious, polite
and helpful.

'I thought he'd be wearing a pith helmet,' whispered Hulda, as
they followed him into a pleasantly appointed sitting room that
contained not a single item from his travels and looked more like
the domain of an elderly maiden aunt than a man in his prime.

'I understand you want information about the Congo,' said

Stanley, once they were settled in chintz chairs with cups of tea so delicate that Lonsdale was almost afraid to pick his up.

'The Kumu,' said Hulda. 'The people who—'

'I hope you haven't solicited Francis Galton's opinion,' interrupted Stanley haughtily, 'because that man is an ass. He thinks he knows more about central Africa than Livingstone or me, even though he's never been near the source of the Nile *or* the headwaters of the Lualaba. His theories are wild, absurd, and childish. I can't *abide* the fellow.'

'He *is* an acquired taste,' agreed Hulda, while Lonsdale recalled that Galton had said much the same about Stanley. 'And his book *The Art of Travel*—'

'Is rubbish!' spat Stanley. 'Drivel, penned by a man who never ventures farther than the armchair at his club.'

'Speaking of clubs,' said Lonsdale, 'are you a member of the Garraway Club or a society named the Watchers?'

Stanley sniffed. 'I don't have time for clubs, no matter how much they beg me to join. Besides, I was friends with Robert Barkley Shaw, who explored the Pamirs and Chinese Turkestan. *He* joined the Watchers and look what happened to him.'

Hulda and Lonsdale exchanged an alarmed glance. 'What?'

'He was murdered in Whitechapel a month or so ago,' replied Stanley. 'It was blamed on robbers, but I know a panga wound when I see one, and I can tell you that Shaw wasn't killed by some common criminal.'

'Was he a member of the Garraway?' asked Lonsdale keenly.

'I believe so. However, he was certainly a Watcher. But why do you ask? Is there a connection between the two?'

Hulda nodded. 'It seems that all Watchers are members of the Garraway, but not all members of the Garraway are Watchers – the Watchers comprise a select few. Unfortunately, we have no idea what this society does or why specific people join it.'

'Shaw told me that Watchers are dedicated to making the world a better place, but without self-serving fanfares. Their number includes politicians, lawyers, churchmen, bankers, explorers, publishers, writers, and the landed gentry, all with one common goal.'

'To do good?' asked Hulda.

Stanley nodded. 'Which is why they call themselves the

Watchers – they see themselves as the fallen angels, who mind the affairs of men with loving eyes.'

'And yet they aim to do something terrible on Christmas Eve,' said Hulda, 'which doesn't sound very angelic to me.'

Stanley shrugged. 'It wouldn't be the first time something good turned to something bad because fanatics or lunatics have become involved. However, Shaw was a decent fellow. He was determined to expose the desperate plight of London's poor, and he asked me to join the Watchers because he thought I could help the natives in the Congo.'

'But you declined his invitation?' asked Hulda.

'The people of the Congo don't need my help, because King Leopold of the Belgians has vowed to keep them under his beneficent eye. He promises they'll be much better off once he's opened up their country to commerce.'

'Right,' said Lonsdale, not sure they would, although Leopold would certainly grow fat on the proceeds. 'Have you ever visited the Garraway?'

'Once – I went there to be photographed by that sly dog James Burnside. I wore the clothes I used for crossing Africa, and looked very handsome, but he refused to let me have the picture until I paid him. What kind of gentleman demands payment on delivery? I told him I'd send the remittance in due course, but he declined to believe me.'

'Why was Shaw in Whitechapel?' asked Hulda, changing the topic. 'Did he live there?'

Stanley laughed. 'Of course not! It's one of the meanest, roughest areas of London – more dangerous than the deepest Congo. He was there to research poverty. The police said he was killed during a robbery, but I was called to identify his body, and I saw the panga wounds.'

'Did you tell the police?'

'Of course, but they didn't believe me. Some incompetent oaf named Wells had the effrontery to pat my arm and advise me to spend less time in the sun.'

Lonsdale and Hulda exchanged another glance. So, the cover-up in which Wells was instrumental had started before Haldane was killed, and the death toll – that they knew of – was now six. They quizzed Stanley more about Shaw, but he could not tell them if a piece of grass had been found with the body, and only recommended that they ask the police.

'The Kumu,' said Lonsdale, eventually recalling why Stead had sent them in the first place. 'They were brought to London to appear in a display at the Natural History Museum.'

'Yes, I've been reading about your concerns for them in *The Pall Mall Gazette*. You should've come to me earlier, because I can tell you a lot about the Kumu.'

'Such as where they might be hiding?' asked Hulda eagerly.

'No, but I can say that no Kumu would have dispatched Dickerson and left him uneaten. They would have been afraid his angry spirit would return to haunt them. If he was intact, then the Kumu are innocent.'

'Have you mentioned this to anyone else?'

'Inspector Wells, but, again, he declined to listen.'

'So you're sure the Kumu didn't kill Dickerson,' pressed Lonsdale, to be certain.

'Completely,' replied Stanley firmly. 'However, that doesn't exonerate the natives who were in Dickerson's care – the ones who went missing after his murder. I refer to the people who *claim* to be Kumu, but who are nothing of the kind.'

'What?' asked Lonsdale warily. 'How do you—'

'Dickerson visited me several times and pumped me for information,' explained Stanley. 'Information that would have been easily obtained from his guests, if they were who they purported to be. However, his questions made it obvious that he'd never met a real Kumu.'

'So who did he have in the museum's basement?' asked Lonsdale.

Stanley shrugged. 'Some other African tribal people, I imagine.'

Suddenly, Lonsdale had a vivid memory of Roth saying *Khoikhoi* when he had meant Kumu. *Had* it been an innocent slip of the tongue, because he had been going through the Khoikhoi part of the professor's collection? Or had the slip come because Stanley was right, and Dickerson's 'Kumu' were nothing of the kind?

'Could he have hired some Khoikhoi instead?' he asked.

Stanley nodded. 'They'd certainly be easier to recruit than any Congolese, who are difficult to reach and suspicious of foreigners.'

'So he may have been staging a massive hoax?' asked Lonsdale, shocked. 'Do you think Owen and the other museum officials knew?'

'I doubt it. Of course, most visitors wouldn't know the difference between a Kumu and a Khoikhoi anyway, so I suppose it doesn't really matter.'

But Lonsdale rather thought it did. 'Can you think of anything that may help us find them? Even if they aren't Kumu, they're still in danger.'

'I can't, I'm afraid, but try William Ingram of *The Illustrated London News*. He was with Dickerson on several of his visits here. He was going to write something about the Kumu and their Congo home. Perhaps he can suggest a way forward.'

'I've already spoken to him,' said Lonsdale glumly. 'He says he can't.'

'Then press him harder,' advised Stanley, 'because I was under the impression that he knows a lot more about the Kumu than your average fellow.'

Lonsdale stood to leave, filled with the sense that a solution – or part of one at least – might be to hand at last. So Stead had been right to send him and Hulda to interview the explorer. Who would have thought it?

It was raining as Lonsdale and Hulda hurried down the street to Piccadilly, where they hoped to flag down a carriage to take them to the offices of *The Illustrated London News* on the Strand. Lonsdale walked fast, his energies renewed with the prospect of answers.

'We learned a lot from him,' panted Hulda, struggling to keep up in her elegantly heeled boots.

'Most important of which is that there's yet another victim,' said Lonsdale. 'How odd that no one else has mentioned Shaw – a member of the Garraway *and* a Watcher. We should ask Peters how many other sudden deaths have been allocated to Wells, because there may be a lot more than six murdered men.'

'I don't like the fact that Wells ignored what Stanley told him about the Kumu,' said Hulda.

'Him or his paymaster,' said Lonsdale. 'We know from Peters that Wells is Commissioner Henderson's creature, but I rather think this conspiracy of inactivity goes higher.' He looked around for a free hansom, but the rain meant every one was occupied. 'It'll be quicker to walk than wait – we can do it in a quarter of an hour. Come on.'

He set off before Hulda could point out that a mile in his sturdy shoes and sensible overcoat was not the same as one in her fashionable boots and non-waterproof wrap.

'So, Dickerson's Kumu are likely not Kumu at all,' he said as they went. 'Does that mean they *did* kill him and then fled the scene of their crime?'

'It might, but that leaves the question of why they dispatched the other victims,' replied Hulda. 'Personally, I suspect their only crime is one of dishonesty, committed in cahoots with Dickerson and your friend Roth. It would certainly explain why he's been so furtive.'

Lonsdale agreed. 'He might have gone along with the deception because Dickerson asked him. There was genuine affection between them – like a father and son – and men do things for friendship . . .'

'So what do we know about the false Kumu? *Are* they cannibals or just some random tribesmen rounded up because they were available?'

'We won't know until we ask them. However, we have been told that they enjoy three very English activities – tea rooms, cricket and light opera.'

Hulda sniffed. 'I've lived here for years, and I don't understand cricket or light opera. The formality of tea rooms is also something that we foreigners find curious.'

Lonsdale stared at her. 'You're right! Cricket *is* complicated, and I don't see anyone acquiring an instant taste for it, especially as our false Kumu arrived in late summer – which Roth told us they did.'

Hulda frowned. 'What does that matter?'

'Cricket is a summer game. They can't have seen many matches before the season ended. And you're right about Gilbert and Sullivan, too – it's peculiarly British, and strangers don't suddenly gain an understanding of it.'

'Meaning?' demanded Hulda.

'Meaning that our false Kumu have probably lived in a British culture for some time, perhaps even their whole lives. And there are the beef sandwiches to consider.'

'What about them?'

'Alice Barnett provided some when they visited her at the Savoy Theatre, but they refused to eat them, and I was under the impression that they considered them taboo. There's no avoidance of beef in most African societies, but some Cape Colony people honour their livestock – cattle, sheep and goats – and only eat them on ritual occasions.'

'Go on,' said Hulda, when he paused, collecting his thoughts.

'In some of these tribal groups, cattle are called "God with a wet nose", and classified not as animals but as a spiritual bridge between an individual and his ancestors. So a beef sandwich would be both offensive and forbidden.'

'You and Stanley mentioned Khoikhoi . . .'

'You may have heard them called Hottentots, but they call themselves Khoikhoi. Although they're traditionally nomadic, they've interacted extensively with British settlers in Southern Africa – where cricket is played, tea enjoyed, and Gilbert and Sullivan performed.'

'So Dickerson's Kumu from the Congo are actually Khoikhoi from Southern Africa?'

Lonsdale nodded slowly. 'It's beginning to make sense at last! If they were imposters, it explains why he kept them in the basement – to prevent other ethnographers from talking to them and seeing through the deception.'

'I did think it was an odd place to house people,' mused Hulda. 'Roth said it was because it was warm, but some parts were actually very cold.'

'Dickerson escorted them on all their excursions to prevent the ruse being exposed, and he doubtless aimed to be on hand at the exhibition to field awkward questions. And there's their English, of course.'

'Explain.'

'I asked Roth if they spoke it, and he said no. Neither he nor Professor Dickerson knew Komo, so how would they have communicated the intricacies of Gilbert and Sullivan, let alone cricket?'

'But English is spoken in the Cape Colony?'

'Precisely! And Roth did let slip at one point that Dickerson's main speciality was Southern Africa. Moreover, I saw a broken Cape Colony headrest in Roth's room, left when he fled. I wondered if he'd been using it to remind him of happier times, but it wasn't him – it was the Khoikhoi. They'd been sharing his rooms! They were almost certainly there when we visited the first time. No wonder he was edgy!'

Lonsdale and Hulda reached the Strand, which was unusually busy with pedestrians, and he was aware of men pressing in on him and Hulda from both sides. His mind was so full of Roth's antics that by the time he realized something was amiss, it was nearly too late. The men – five of them – began to crowd him and Hulda towards the edge of the pavement. Then he saw a hand stretch towards her, ready to push her into the path of an oncoming omnibus. He reacted fast, knocking it down and swinging a punch at the culprit's jaw.

The man howled, which had the effect of encouraging his friends to speed up their murderous assault. Lonsdale was pushed so hard that he stumbled off the kerb, where a cart missed him by the merest fraction. It might have ended badly, but Hulda pulled out a gun and levelled it at the man nearest to her.

'Christ!' he gulped and took to his heels.

His companions backed away as Hulda whipped around with the weapon, then turned and ran. Lonsdale set off after them, aiming to catch one and demand answers. The would-be assassins jigged across the Strand, darting in front of a horse-drawn tram with reckless disregard for their safety. Lonsdale was forced to wait for it to lumber past, by which time they had disappeared down an alley. Lonsdale raced down it, but there was no sign of them. Defeated, he returned to Hulda, who had replaced the gun inside her coat, and was waiting none too patiently for him.

'Who were they?' she demanded.

'Hirelings, probably,' replied Lonsdale. 'And I'm not sure they could've told us anything even if I had managed to catch one. They weren't very competent – not like the killer himself. Still, we must have him worried, or he wouldn't have bothered.'

'At least he didn't arm them with pangas,' she remarked, but her voice shook, so he put his arm around her. He expected her to pull away, but she seemed glad of the contact, so they stood there for a moment.

'We need to take extra care from now on,' he said eventually. 'Watch out for each other. Will you move into Cleveland Square until we've caught him?'

'I can't live in your house!' she exclaimed, pulling away in shock. 'I have my reputation to consider. Besides, what would Humbage – or Anne – say about such an arrangement?'

'I really don't care,' said Lonsdale. 'Your life's worth more to me than their opinions.'

Hulda flushed and made no more objections.

TEN

Both Lonsdale and Hulda glanced around uneasily as they reached the offices of *The Illustrated London News*, half expecting another assault. Lonsdale was about to enter when it occurred to him that they needed some sort of strategy if they aimed to accuse the owner-editor of a prestigious publishing house of being complicit in a crime. He was about to say so, when Hulda grabbed his arm and hauled him behind the hansom that had just pulled up – idly, Lonsdale noticed a large box on its floor.

'Look – Ingram and his brother-in-law, the monkey,' she hissed, as two men emerged from the building. Ingram was tall and distinguished, Hornby slight and agile, characteristics that had earned him his nickname. 'Look at the way they're glancing around as they walk! I don't think I've ever seen a more furtive pair.'

'No,' agreed Lonsdale. 'Shall we follow them, and see where they go?'

Ingram and Hornby began a series of zigzags that were clearly designed to throw off anyone who happened to be watching. It did not work, because Lonsdale had learned a lot about shadowing people from his experiences with Voules and Bowler Hat. The pair crossed roads, turned back on themselves, and ducked into doorways, but Lonsdale was able to keep him and Hulda out of sight until their quarry returned to the Strand and clambered into the waiting hansom – the one with the box inside it.

'Now what?' asked Hulda, watching it clatter away.

'We do the same,' said Lonsdale, risking life and limb by darting out into the road to hail another. He helped Hulda in, and offered the driver double the fare if he could follow Ingram without being seen.

The driver was delighted by the challenge – and the reward – and set about it with alacrity.

'As soon as we know where they're going, you need to come back and contact the police,' said Lonsdale to Hulda, glad Ingram's carriage was not moving very fast, as he was sure their driver would have loved nothing better than a high-speed chase along London's crowded thoroughfares. 'I'll keep them under surveillance until help arrives.'

'And what exactly am I supposed to tell them?' demanded Hulda. 'That a rich man and his monkey are acting suspiciously? We need more than that to call in the cavalry!'

'Not the cavalry,' said Lonsdale. 'Peters. He's the only one we can trust. Tell him that Ingram is involved in something untoward. We don't know what, but the chances are that it involves the "cannibals" – the people who may know something about Dickerson's murder.'

'But you said we were going to watch out for each other,' objected Hulda. 'How can we do that if we separate?'

'We've no choice. Besides, Ingram might react badly if he sees you – you got a full guided tour of *The Illustrated London News* premises under false pretences.'

The two hansoms clattered up Charing Cross Road and then turned west into Oxford Street. What not long before had been mostly residential was now full of shops, with drapers, furniture-sellers, jewellers, and haberdasheries being joined by new stores such as John Lewis. Street vendors still did a roaring trade outside them, although Hulda and Lonsdale barely noticed the glittery Christmas theme of the wares, so intent were they on the vehicle in front. Ingram's carriage turned right at Marble Arch and began heading up Edgware Road.

'They could be going to Paddington,' said Hulda. 'To catch a train, perhaps.'

But Ingram passed Praed Street and Harrow Road and continued on.

'Lord's Cricket Ground!' exclaimed Lonsdale suddenly. 'Of course! Hornby was one of Lancashire's stars this year, and *The Illustrated London News* ran a number of stories about his victories, one of which was by nine wickets over Middlesex – at Lord's.'

Hulda regarded him askance. 'You think they're going to watch a cricket match?'

'It's winter – Lord's will be closed. But any groundskeeper

minding the place won't mind Hornby popping in and out. Lord's will be safe, comfortable and deserted – the perfect place to secure the Khoikhoi.'

Hulda was disgusted with herself. 'If I'd remembered that cricket is a summer sport, I might have worked all this out days ago!'

When they reached the corner of St John's Wood Road and Hamilton Terrace, Lonsdale asked the driver to stop. He clambered out, paid double what he had promised, and asked him to take Hulda to Scotland Yard as fast as possible.

'I'm not happy with this,' said Hulda, while the gleeful driver counted his money. 'It might've been Ingram who hired the thugs who tried to push us into the moving traffic. We should send the driver for the police and go inside the cricket ground together.'

'But we need *Peters*,' argued Lonsdale. 'Only you can make sure *he* comes and not Wells. Because if Wells turns up, we'll be in trouble for certain.'

'And what if Peters can't get away?' she snapped angrily. 'He's being watched, too.'

'Don't underestimate him,' said Lonsdale. 'He'll find a way. Now, lend me your gun.'

Hulda reached for it, then scrabbled about in consternation. 'It's gone! My pocket is ripped – those ruffians must've torn it when they manhandled me and the gun fell out. Damn! I was fond of that weapon!'

And Lonsdale was fond of his life, which might have been better protected with a firearm to hand, especially as he knew Roth had one.

Eager to please, the hansom driver raced away as fast as his horse could run, leaving Lonsdale hoping Hulda would arrive at Scotland Yard in one piece. When they were out of sight, he hurried down St John's Wood Road, where he peered around the corner. Ingram and Hornby had alighted and were removing the box from the floor of their hansom. Hornby staggered as he took its weight.

Ingram looked around carefully, then took a key from his pocket and opened a door in the wall that ran around the perimeter. He held it open for Hornby, then glanced around again before following him through and closing it behind them.

Lonsdale inched forward but was not surprised to discover the door had been relocked. He looked up at the wall, which was too high to scale, especially in broad daylight, when he would be seen. He began to trot along it, looking for weaknesses, and found it in an area of wooden fencing at the back. There was a small hole in the bottom, which he suspected had been made by boys who wanted to see their heroes play but could not afford the entrance fee.

It was a tight squeeze, and he ripped his coat on a jagged piece of wood, but he was through eventually. He stood and looked around him.

He was in a scrubby area of dead ground, which was obviously designated for development at some point in the future. Ahead lay the pitch in all its glory, the wicket swathed in tarpaulins to protect it from the winter weather. Beyond that was the pavilion, an ornate building with iron pillars and balustrades. It had two floors, the upper of which was covered by canvas tenting. The lower part contained facilities for the cricketers and their wealthier supporters – changing rooms, dining hall, bars and so forth. In front of the pavilion was permanent seating in the form of benches.

Feeling horribly exposed, Lonsdale padded around the ground, expecting at any moment to hear the yell that would tell him he had been spotted. But no shout came, and he reached the pavilion breathing hard, heart pounding. He saw the door at the front had been left ajar, so he eased towards it, wincing when the wooden steps creaked under his weight. He pushed it open and peered inside.

It was more than twelve years since he had last been to the home of the Middlesex County Cricket Club – he had been playing for Cambridge University at the time. It had changed in the interim and boasted a handsome hallway with a glass case to exhibit the trophies and honours Middlesex had won. Also displayed were the historic memorabilia of the Marylebone Cricket Club, the owners of Lord's, who were responsible for the Laws of Cricket.

In another case were relics highlighting the University Match, first held there in 1827. He experienced a pang of nostalgia as he saw the ball his teammate Frank Cobden had used in 1870. With Oxford needing only three runs to win, Cobden had taken a hat-trick: in three balls one of the Oxford batters had been caught out and the last two bowled, giving Cambridge the win.

He was jerked out of his reverie by voices. They were coming from a small side room, which – fortunately for him – overlooked the back rather than the field side, or he would have been seen when he was outside. Then he detected a smell – the same one as at Roth's home. The door was ajar, and he looked through it to see a comfortably furnished dining room.

Ingram had his back to the door, while Hornby had deposited the chest on the floor and was busy unfastening it. Watching him was Roth, looking even more fraught than when Lonsdale had last seen him, and three Africans – two men and a woman. The Africans wore bulky woollen coats, although the woman had a beaded band around her head that Lonsdale recognized as a type favoured by migrant pastoralists in the Cape Colony. He allowed himself a small smile of satisfaction. Lord's in the winter was indeed the perfect place to hide fugitives.

'Bush tea,' declared Hornby, brandishing a packet. 'Not easy to buy here, but one advantage of being a sporting hero is that people like to please me. An old Boer friend had a stash, and happily gave me some when I expressed a fondness for it.'

'It stinks,' said Ingram, wrinkling his nose as the Africans greeted Hornby's gift with cries of delight. 'And how did the Kumu acquire a taste for Southern African tea anyway?'

Lonsdale grimaced. Of course! He should have recognized the smell of bush tea at once and was disgusted that he had allowed himself to believe it came from Dickerson's collections. If he had taken the time to analyse the clues that were right under his nose, he might have had answers a lot sooner. He wondered how long it would take Hulda to fetch Peters – a round journey of about six miles – and hoped Ingram would enjoy a lengthy session with the people he had hidden so slyly. The best scenario would be for Peters to arrive when all six were there together, so Ingram could not deny his involvement. In the interim, all Lonsdale could do was eavesdrop on what was being said.

'Thank you for the supplies,' Roth was saying to Ingram. 'But we won't detain you.'

Ingram sat, much to Roth's obvious consternation. 'Give us a moment to breathe, will you? We came all the way out here with your victuals, so the least you can do is give us a few minutes of your time.' He turned to the Africans. 'Or rather, of theirs.'

'They're tired,' said Roth quickly. 'They don't want to talk today. Besides, my Komo isn't good enough to translate for you yet. Give me another week, and I'll be much better.'

Lonsdale listened with interest. Roth was presenting the Africans as hailing from the Congo. Did that mean Ingram was an unwitting foil in the deception?

Ingram was exasperated. '*Another* week? I can't keep these people here at my expense indefinitely. It's time to show a little good faith by letting me ask them a few questions. I'm tired of you taking my help but giving me nothing in return.'

'It's becoming urgent, you see,' Hornby explained, more kindly. 'If he doesn't publish soon, Stead will pre-empt him, and *The Pall Mall Gazette* will be credited with exposing the evils of human zoos. We know for a fact that Stead sent his best reporters to hunt the Kumu down, because Voules told us – we hired him to spy on them for us.'

So that was why *The Echo* man had been so annoyingly persistent, mused Lonsdale. It was not just the prospect of stories to steal, but because he was being paid to do it. It also explained why Ingram had been so alarmed when Hulda told him *The Echo* had planted a spy on *his* premises – he knew such things happened, because he did it himself. Absently, Lonsdale wondered what *The Echo*'s editor would think of Voules accepting money from a rival paper, and was sure he would be dismissed if it ever came to light.

Roth was looking panicky. 'But the professor wanted . . . he told me to . . .' He trailed off, then spoke in a miserable wail. 'Oh, God! I don't know what to do! I wish Dickerson was still here to tell me. I should never have moved them from the museum!'

Lonsdale congratulated himself on being right about one thing: Roth was not the killer, because Dickerson's death had landed him in an awkward predicament.

'Calm down!' ordered Ingram sternly. 'You did the right thing. When Dickerson went to Devon, and left you to care for these cannibals alone, you were wise to take them home – a place safe from the unwanted attentions of other scientists.'

'Owen and Flower,' whispered Roth. 'One frightened them with his bristling hostility, while the other kept asking them about the Congo. The professor could repel them, but I . . .'

'Taking them home saved them from being arrested for murder,' put in Hornby comfortingly. 'Everyone thinks they killed the professor. We're the only ones who know they didn't.'

'No, they didn't,' averred Roth. 'They left the basement before he was killed, and they haven't been back since. Yet I can't stop thinking that if they *had* been there, he'd still be alive – I'm sure he went down there looking for them, and I keep thinking how worried he must've been when he found them gone.'

'Don't dwell on it,' advised Hornby gently. 'It'll do no good.'

'But who came to your rescue?' asked Ingram haughtily. 'Me! When people began to visit your home, and you were all living in terror, I brought you here.'

'Yes,' acknowledged Roth tiredly. 'You did.'

'So it's payback time,' Ingram went on. 'My blistering exposé of human zoos is ready. All I need is an interview with some real victims and it can go in the next edition.'

'Can't you do it without them?' asked Roth, glancing at the Africans, who were following the discussion more closely than their alleged lack of English should have allowed. 'They don't want to be famous.'

'They're already famous,' retorted Ingram. '*The Echo* saw to that. And no, I can't do it without them, as I need the personal touch that only they can provide – I want my readers to see them as real people with names, hopes, and fears.'

'He aims to create such a stir that the issue of human zoos will be raised in Parliament,' elaborated Hornby. 'It could save hundreds of people from being paraded about like animals. This is *important*, Roth.'

'I know,' said Roth wretchedly. 'And I will help, but not today – Khade isn't well. If she's better tomorrow, we'll do it then.'

The woman obligingly put her hand to her stomach.

'Do I have your word?' asked Ingram, clearly displeased but sensing that was the best he was likely to get. 'My paper has a much bigger circulation than Stead's, and if he publishes first, not only will he get all the credit, but it will weaken the impact of my work. It *must* go in the next edition.'

'Come tomorrow,' said Roth miserably. 'Khade should feel better by then.'

'We brought all her favourites,' said Hornby, nodding towards the box. 'Fresh scones, strawberry jam, poacher's relish and Cornish fairings. They should help.'

Business completed, he and Ingram aimed for the door, Ingram full of exasperated disappointment. Lonsdale wondered what to do. Prevent them from leaving, so all six would be there when Peters arrived? Or let them go, as neither would be difficult to find later? Common sense prevailed. Lonsdale was alone, and it was arrogant to think he could prevail against five men and a woman, four of whom he was about to expose as fraudsters. Besides, it was now clear that Ingram's only 'crimes' were to help four frightened people and to compete with Stead.

He ducked behind a cabinet full of memorabilia and let Ingram and Hornby hurry past unchallenged.

Minutes ticked past. Ingram and Hornby had gone, locking the door behind them. The African men began to unpack the chest, while Roth slumped in a chair with his head in his hands. Khade stood next to him, talking in a low voice. Lonsdale slipped out of his hiding place and went to eavesdrop again.

'It's time for us all to leave,' she was saying in perfect but accented English. 'You've done your best, but once the professor was murdered – well, the game was up. We should've come clean immediately, rather than try to wriggle out of the mess we made for ourselves.'

'Leave and go where?' croaked Roth in despair. 'Half the country is looking for you, convinced that you're killers. At least here you're safe.'

'But only until tomorrow,' said Khade. 'Without the professor, we'll be exposed as frauds in moments. Mr Ingram knows a lot about the Kumu – we know next to nothing.'

Lonsdale felt he had heard enough. He sensed the Africans were not violent people, and while he knew Roth had a gun, he trusted his friend would not shoot him. He pushed open the door and stepped inside. All four people gaped at him in horror, then Roth leapt to his feet and fumbled for his firearm. He pulled it out and held it in a hand that shook so badly he was in serious danger of shooting someone by accident.

'Put it down,' ordered Lonsdale. 'I know you won't—'

The sound of the weapon discharging was shockingly loud. Lonsdale and the Africans flinched, then stared at Roth in astonishment.

'I'm sorry, Alec,' whispered Roth unsteadily, 'but I can't let you turn us in. The professor would haunt me forever. It was the last thing he said to me – to look after his friends.'

'I know they didn't kill him.' Lonsdale raised his hands to show he meant no harm. 'I heard what was said just now – that you took them from the museum before he died—'

'I begged him not to go to Devon,' interrupted Roth bitterly; Lonsdale winced as the gun wobbled precariously. 'I was terrified that Owen would find out what we . . . so I took Khade and the others home. It was only supposed to be for one or two days . . .'

'But Dickerson failed to reappear,' prompted Lonsdale. 'And you were stuck.'

Roth nodded miserably. 'I kept thinking he'd come back, but he never did. Then Owen and Flowers realized they'd gone and ordered a search.'

'Which you conducted, but not very carefully, because you knew they weren't there,' surmised Lonsdale. 'And *that's* why Dickerson's body remained undiscovered for so long – if anyone else had been doing the looking, Dickerson would've been found.'

Tears welled in Roth's eyes. 'I can't tell you how dreadful that makes me feel.'

'I can imagine,' said Lonsdale sympathetically. 'Now put down the gun and—'

'No!' The firearm trembled dangerously again. 'You don't understand what's at stake.'

'Yes, I do,' said Lonsdale, forcing himself not to cower. 'A fraud against the Natural History Museum and the British public. Your friends are Khoikhoi, not Kumu, which is why they didn't speak when Ingram was here, and why they've remained silent since I arrived, although they do know English – I heard Khade talking to you.'

There was a moment when Lonsdale thought they would deny it, but Roth sagged in defeat. 'How did you guess?' he asked weakly.

'You left a lot of clues,' explained Lonsdale, hoping Hulda would arrive before Roth decided his only option was to shoot him. He had been certain Roth would not harm him, but now he saw that his friend had more important claims on his loyalty.

'I did?' Roth looked trapped and desperate. 'What clues?'

Lonsdale began to list them. 'Saying Khoikhoi when you meant Kumu; claiming your "cannibals" liked cricket, when they arrived too late in the season to have developed a feel for it; the scent of bush tea in your house, which is a Southern African specialty; the broken Cape Colony headrest you left in your rooms—'

'None of that proves we aren't Kumu,' said Khade quietly.

'It does when it's all added together,' countered Lonsdale. 'It suggests you hail from a place familiar with British customs, which the Congo isn't.'

Roth sat heavily in a chair, although he continued to point the gun at Lonsdale. 'It was the professor's idea. It would have worked if he'd been here to see it through. But now I don't know what to do . . . it's all such an unholy muddle!'

'I can see that,' said Lonsdale. 'So how did Ingram get involved?'

'The professor introduced us to Mr Hornby,' explained Khade, 'because he's one of our sporting heroes. Gallantly, Mr Hornby said he would be at our service if there was ever anything he could do.'

'So I went to him because once the professor was dead I had no one else,' said Roth. 'Unfortunately, his brother-in-law just happened to be mounting a campaign against human zoos, and Hornby insisted that we take him into our confidence, too.'

'So Ingram agreed to help you in exchange for an exclusive interview with cannibals,' surmised Lonsdale. 'Which you can never provide. You defrauded him and his newspaper as well as the museum.'

Roth winced. 'The professor promised the museum cannibals, but then it proved impossible to get any. Rather than admit failure – Owen would've been unbearable – he hired these three, whom he found in a circus. The exhibition would've passed off with no one any the wiser, had he been here.'

'Why did Dickerson insist on exhibiting cannibals in the first place?' asked Lonsdale curiously. 'Ingram's right – human zoos are unethical. But Dickerson didn't sound like a man to exploit innocent people.'

Roth swallowed hard. 'No, he wasn't.'

Lonsdale stared at him. 'He never even tried to get real Kumu, did he? He intended from the start to use Africans who understand our culture, and who wouldn't be harmed or unsettled by the experience.'

Roth hung his head. 'He just wanted to inject a bit of variety into the displays – something other than stuffed birds and dinosaurs.

There was no harm in it. Or there shouldn't have been, until it all started to go so horribly wrong.'

'Is this why he was murdered? Because he was embroiled in a monstrous fraud?'

Roth shook his head. 'I've thought of little else since we found his body, but I believe he was killed for some other reason – something to do with the Garraway, probably. I never wanted to become a member, but he insisted, so I did it to please him. But I've never liked the place, and the only friend I have there is Burnside. I won't be going back.'

'So why not confess once everything started to fall apart?' asked Lonsdale. 'Obviously, Khade and her friends are innocent of Dickerson's murder, and if they didn't kill him, they didn't kill the others.'

'I did consider it,' said Roth hoarsely, 'but Inspector Wells told me that they'd be found guilty regardless. I couldn't let that happen. None of this is their fault.'

'No,' came a soft voice at the door. 'It's yours.'

ELEVEN

Lonsdale's first thought when he heard the voice behind him was that Hulda had brought the police at last. But the speaker was Ingram, his face as dark as thunder. Hornby was behind him, looking hurt and angry. Roth deflated as if punctured.

'I trusted you,' Ingram snarled. 'I thought you were a man of honour, but you're just a common swindler. Worse, you don't tell *me* the truth, but a reporter from a rival paper!'

'Put the gun down, Roth,' ordered Hornby. 'You can't shoot all of us.'

'I can,' blustered Roth. 'It holds six bullets.'

'Five,' spat Ingram. 'It was the weapon discharging that brought us racing back – where we heard the most disgraceful revelations.'

'I can scarce believe your audacity,' said Hornby, shaking his head slowly. 'If I had men with your nerve in my team last summer, we'd never have lost to Australia.'

'Nerve!' sneered Ingram. 'He lied to me and took my money! I'll see the lot of them in gaol for this, and I hope they rot there.'

Lonsdale became aware of other voices in the distance. This time it *was* Hulda with the police – to whom Ingram would demand that the Khoikhoi and Roth be arrested. Wells would find out and charge the Africans with murder. Lonsdale could not allow that.

'You claim to be a campaigner for human rights,' he said urgently to Ingram. 'So prove it. If the Khoikhoi are arrested today, they'll hang for a crime they didn't commit. Is that what you want Stead to write in his next editorial – that the owner of *The Illustrated London News* helped perpetrate a gross miscarriage of justice?'

Ingram gaped at him. '*I'm* the victim here! Do you expect me to overlook what they've done to me?'

The voices came closer. Lonsdale did not have much time.

'Yes, because it's the right thing to do. Circuses also abuse basic human rights, and I'm sure Khade can tell you all about the one she worked in before Dickerson hired her.'

Khade nodded quickly. 'We agreed to be part of this deception because the professor promised to get us home afterwards. The circus had trapped us, you see – we'd never have been free. And we're heart-sick, Mr Ingram. We want to go home.'

Ingram opened his mouth to refuse, but her dignified plea had touched the gallant Hornby.

'I offered you my help, ma'am, and you shall have it,' he said briskly. 'You can stay with my wife and me until passage can be arranged. I'm sure *The Illustrated London News* will settle for an exposé on circuses instead and leave the human zoos for Stead.'

Ingram hesitated still, but Hornby knew they were out of time. He grabbed Khade's hand and pulled her to the door at the back of the room, indicating that her menfolk were to follow.

'You'd better go with them, Roth,' said Ingram icily. 'No, leave the weapon. I won't have firearms near my sister. Go on – hurry.'

'What will *you* do?' asked Roth uneasily, not moving.

'Create a diversion, so that you and your fellow criminals can escape in my hansom,' replied Ingram, although there was a gleam in his eye, and Lonsdale saw he had begun to appreciate the advantages in Hornby's suggestion: circuses were indeed rich grounds for a moral crusade. 'Lonsdale will help.'

Lonsdale nodded, although he sincerely hoped Ingram's diversion would not involve anything felonious. He watched Roth disappear after the others, then heard voices in the hallway outside. Ingram pulled out a box of matches.

'I won't be complicit in setting Lord's alight,' said Lonsdale in alarm.

'I was thinking rather of lighting a cigar,' said Ingram, and sat in one of the chairs. 'Join me and follow my lead.'

They were barely seated when the first of the police burst in – a uniformed constable whose face was flushed with excitement.

'In here!' he yelled, eyes flashing around the room as he took in the obvious signs that people had been living there.

He was followed by more officers – none of whom were Peters – and Hulda.

'You're too late,' said Ingram, puffing on his cigar as though he had been lounging there for hours. 'They must've gone in the night. Lonsdale and I have been debating where they might go next.'

'Clearly, they realized it's no longer safe here,' put in Lonsdale, which was true enough. 'So they decamped while they could. I wonder if there's a similar pavilion at The Oval.'

'They're more likely to have gone to the New Forest,' said Ingram, 'a place in which they could safely vanish.'

The police clamoured questions, which Ingram proceeded to answer in a lazy drawl designed to give the fugitives longer to escape. He explained his presence there as due to a tip-off from an anonymous source, and said Lonsdale had accompanied him because he was good in a fight. All the while, Hulda's gaze was fixed unblinkingly on Lonsdale, as she tried to work out what was going on.

It was some time before Lonsdale and Ingram were permitted to leave, although the police remained to sort through the Khoikhoi's abandoned belongings in a determined quest for clues. Outside, Ingram grabbed Lonsdale's arm.

'You'd better stick to what was agreed in there – Stead gets human zoos and I get circuses.'

Lonsdale nodded and Ingram walked away without another word.

'You did *what*?' exploded Hulda, once she and Lonsdale were alone and he told her what had happened. 'Are you insane? Wells may

be a buffoon who can't tell a guilty man from an innocent one, but
he's still the police! You can't take matters into your own hands
like that. Stead and Mr Morley will be livid.'

'Mr Morley will,' conceded Lonsdale. 'But only if you tell him.
Stead will think it was the right thing to do. I'm sure the Khoikhoi
are innocent, but if they fall into Wells's hands . . . well, justice
won't be served.'

'Stead *will* be livid!' argued Hulda. 'An exposé of circuses is a
good idea – the kind of thing he loves. If he ever learns you passed
it to *The Illustrated London News* . . .'

'Quarrelling is getting us nowhere,' said Lonsdale tiredly. 'And
chasing "cannibals" has lost us most of a day. They have nothing
to do with the murders, other than knowing one of the victims.'

'The Khoikhoi might be innocent,' said Hulda angrily, 'but Roth
is a ruthless fraudster who threatened to shoot you. And you let him
go.'

'Only to Hornby's house – we can visit him there if necessary.
But never mind him. Where's Peters?'

'He couldn't come because he was busy with something he
deemed more important – the murder of Superintendent Hayes.'

'*Hayes* is dead?' blurted Lonsdale, shocked.

'I met Bradwell at Scotland Yard – he was there to drop off his
official report. He told me that the attack on Hayes was exactly the
same as the others – chopped down with a panga-type weapon, and
a blade of watcher-grass left on the body.'

'Did he know *when* Hayes was killed?'

'This morning, in the Garraway. He'd been assigned to guard the
Houses of Parliament again but told Peters that he was going to
the club for breakfast first.'

Lonsdale blinked. 'Are you saying that *Hayes* was a member of
the Garraway?'

'And a Watcher, according to Bradwell – he asked Mrs Hayes.'

Lonsdale shook his head in disbelief. 'Hayes should have told
us! He knew that the other victims were members. Why did he keep
it quiet?'

'He didn't,' replied Hulda. 'According to Peters, he informed
Commissioner Henderson *and* Inspector Wells. He didn't tell us,
because the police aren't in the habit of sharing information with
newspapers. He did everything by the book.'

'I haven't seen Bowler Hat all day,' mused Lonsdale soberly.
'And now there's been another murder . . .'

'You think it might be Maclean, like Stead does,' surmised Hulda.

'It's possible. The false-Kumu – and Roth, I suppose – can't be the culprits if they've been here the whole time. And it's a solution that suits me – I'd rather believe the killer is an escaped lunatic than a man who walks among us as though he's normal.'

'Or as though *she's* normal,' countered Lonsdale. 'Women kill, too.'

'Not with machetes,' said Hulda. 'But come back to Scotland Yard with me. Peters will want to hear what happened here.'

'Now a senior police officer has been killed, has Henderson finally seen sense and appointed a competent detective to investigate?'

'Unfortunately not. He's given the case to Wells.'

It had begun raining again, so hansoms were in short supply. Thus it took them a long time to reach Scotland Yard, as they had to walk most of the way. They arrived to find it in a state of shock. It was rare that officers were killed, especially senior ones, and the station reeled with the horror of it. Men spoke in whispers, and there was an atmosphere of numb disbelief.

Peters was in his cupboard-like office, staring at nothing. He stood when Lonsdale and Hulda entered, and Lonsdale thought the inspector looked as though he had aged ten years since he had last seen him. He closed the door so no one would hear them talking.

'Hayes was the best superintendent I ever had,' Peters said softly. 'A good and decent man. I can't believe he allowed himself to be claimed by this vile killer.'

'According to Bradwell, the first blow came from behind,' said Hulda. 'He probably didn't know he was in danger until it was too late. He was a member of the Garraway and a Watcher, so I'm sure that's why he was killed.'

'I investigated the Garraway when Tait was murdered – before Henderson took me off the case. It has about two hundred members, but the Watchers have considerably fewer. Six are now dead, so there can't be many left.'

'Seven are dead,' corrected Lonsdale. 'Robert Barkley Shaw was killed in Whitechapel last month, but it was passed off as a robbery. There may be others, too.'

Peters nodded. 'Shaw was mooted as a possible victim when I visited the club today, and I promised to look into it, but the file has disappeared. If Wells has it – and I believe he does – it means the truth about Shaw's demise is already known to him.'

'So what will you do about it?' asked Hulda.

Peters grimaced. 'I've been ordered to stay out of Wells's way, but now Hayes is a victim, I'm disinclined to oblige. Of course, this is probably why Hayes was killed – he petitioned Henderson on a daily basis, arguing that his skills lay in solving murders, not protecting the Houses of Parliament. I fear he may have pressed too hard and paid for it with his life.'

They were silent for a moment, then Lonsdale and Hulda told him all they had learned since their last meeting, including the apparent innocence of the Khoikhoi and their relocation to Monkey Hornby's house. When they had finished, Peters escorted them outside, defiantly not caring who saw him with reporters. In the street, the short winter day was fading into darkness.

'So what will you do first?' Hulda asked him.

'Speak to the victims' next of kin,' replied Peters promptly. 'You prised a good deal of information from them, but there may be more, and I shall have it. You can go to Broadmoor tomorrow, as Stead ordered. I doubt you'll learn much, but it'll save me from doing it.'

'But there's no longer any need to go,' argued Lonsdale. 'The "cannibals" are safe, and that's all Stead cared about.'

'They're not safe,' countered Peters. 'Nor will they be until we have the real culprit behind bars. Wells may be stupid, but his paymaster isn't, and he may well make the association between Africans hiding at Lord's and Monkey Hornby. And if he orders a search of Hornby's house, Wells will charge the Khoikhoi with murder.'

'But *who's* his paymaster?' asked Lonsdale in frustration. 'Henderson? Get us an interview with him – perhaps he'll let something slip and we can expose him.'

'He won't. He's not an idiot – just weak and malleable. Please go to Broadmoor. I'm not happy with Maclean's role in all this, particularly the fact that he's been seen at the sites of all the murders.'

'Gloating,' put in Hulda.

'Possibly. Regardless, I want to know more about him – whether he's also an instrument of this mysterious but influential paymaster, or is the paymaster himself. Come see me the moment you get back. And be very, very careful. Hayes won't have been an easy man to kill, so our culprit is an extremely dangerous individual.'

Hulda and Lonsdale hurried to Northumberland Street, keen to tell Stead what had happened. As they went, Lonsdale looked for Voules, wishing *The Echo* man *was* following him, because he wanted to confront him about being in Ingram's pay. But there was no sign of him, Bowler Hat or anyone else involved in the case.

'I wonder if we should warn Burnside,' said Lonsdale, as they climbed the stairs to Stead's domain. 'Perhaps *he's* a Watcher and his life is in danger. And Lord Carlingford and Fleetwood-Pelham.'

'They're suspects,' countered Hulda. 'Well, probably not Fleetwood-Pelham, as secret societies tend not to recruit gossips for obvious reasons. Regardless, I'm disinclined to seek any of them out after what happened at the Garraway last night.'

Stead was in, so they furnished him with an account of all that had happened that day. He was quietly triumphant that the Khoikhoi had been exonerated, although he reiterated Peters's concern that they would be caught eventually, at which point they would find it impossible to prove their innocence.

'There *are* answers at Broadmoor,' he declared. 'For a start, how did Maclean escape with such consummate ease when the place is supposed to be secure?'

'Then Peters should find out,' argued Lonsdale, hating to waste time when every day was precious. 'He's better than us at prising the truth from witnesses and—'

'Then this'll be good practice for you,' interrupted Stead, unmoved. 'I wish I could do it myself – I had an unpleasant encounter today, which annoyed me more than I can say, and it would be a good way to avoid another. Unfortunately, Mr Morley needs me here.'

'What unpleasant encounter?' asked Lonsdale curiously.

Stead gave one of his enigmatic smiles and declined to elaborate. 'Now go home, both of you. Rest, and be fresh for tomorrow. You look exhausted, and you'll need your wits about you if you want to thwart this sly villain. Have a roasted chestnut to help you on your way. I bought them for Audrey, but she won't mind.'

'Audrey?' asked Lonsdale, then wished he had held his tongue. Stead's wife was Emma, and no gentleman questioned another about mysterious women in his life.

'My favourite hen,' explained Stead. 'She roosts on our bedstead, although Emma finds the droppings a bit of a nuisance, especially as Audrey likes to sit directly above our heads.'

Lonsdale could not get that image out of his mind all the way home.

As Hulda always kept an overnight bag in the office, there was no need for her to return to her lodgings before moving into Cleveland Square. Lonsdale glanced at her as he led the way up the steps to his house, surprised to find himself glad she would be there. It was not just that he wanted to keep her safe, but now there was the prospect of an evening in her company, which would be balm to his soul after such a frantic and nerve-wracking day.

Inside, he helped her out of her coat, then shouted for Sybil to prepare one of the spare bedchambers, as they had a guest. It was then that Humbage stepped out of the drawing room.

'Did you say that she'll be staying overnight?' he demanded without preamble; his face was dark with angry disbelief. 'A woman?'

'Yes, Miss Friederichs is a woman,' acknowledged Lonsdale, bristling at the way he spoke as if Hulda was not there. 'She'll be in the green room, which has a nice view of the garden.'

'But you're engaged to marry my daughter!' declared Humbage hotly. 'You can't have other women sleeping here. Such behaviour is scandalous, and if my friend Lord Carlingford ever learned—'

'Stop!' snapped Lonsdale, not about to be berated in his own home, especially in front of Hulda. Thankfully, she seemed more amused than offended by Humbage's harangue. 'It's none of your business. Why are you here anyway? If it's to see Jack, he won't be home until late. There's a dinner at the club.'

'I'm here to see you,' said Humbage coldly. 'I visited Morley today, to insist you be removed from unsavoury investigations. I won't have my good name tainted by association in the vile matters you've been probing – murder, cannibals, escaped lunatics. Morley was busy, so I had to be content with that madman Stead.'

'You did *what*?' exploded Lonsdale, realizing what Stead had meant by having an unpleasant encounter. 'You have no right to interfere with my work!'

'I have every right! Family honour is at stake. Stead tried to lecture me about the plight of "poor cannibals", so I told him I don't give a damn about them, and ordered him to give you *respect-able* assignments, like horse-breeding or happenings at court.'

'What did he say?' asked Lonsdale, knowing the assistant editor would not appreciate being told what to do by someone like Humbage.

'He gave me a sweet to eat while he considered my demands, but it transpired to be a mothball,' replied Humbage stiffly. 'Then he thanked me for my "valuable insights into the mindset of my class" and said he was sending you to Broadmoor tomorrow – a prison for the criminally insane. The man is as degenerate as you are!'

'It's not a prison,' said Lonsdale. 'It's an asylum.'

'He's not degenerate either,' put in Hulda, moved to defend her mentor. 'He's—'

'I don't care what you call it,' interrupted Humbage, ignoring her and addressing Lonsdale. 'I forbid you to go. What if you catch something and pass it to my daughters?'

Lonsdale could not stop from laughing. 'I hardly think madness is contagious!'

'I disagree,' said Humbage angrily. 'Your brother was a perfect gentleman when I first met him, but ever since you moved into this house, he's grown wild.'

'Jack? *Wild?*' echoed Lonsdale in disbelief.

Humbage sniffed huffily. 'He drank a whole bottle of wine, then rebuked Emelia for telling him what she thinks of you. When I hastened to her defence, he called me a meddlesome ass.'

Lonsdale could only suppose Jack had been very drunk. Or was it that Humbage's arrogance and snobbishness had finally proved too much even for his equanimous nature?

'Here's a note for you from Anne,' said Humbage, handing over an envelope. He gave Hulda a look of disdain before turning back to Lonsdale. 'Your fiancée. She'll meet you at seven o'clock on Friday evening, when you'll have a serious discussion about your future together. I shall be there, too.'

'No, you won't,' said Lonsdale between gritted teeth. 'If we do have such a discussion, it will involve the two of us and no one else.'

'We'll see about that,' blustered Humbage. 'Now, for the last time, I *order* you to step away from these murders and leave the police to do their job. Disobey me at your peril.'

He stalked past them before Lonsdale could tell him where to put his orders, but his haughty exit was spoiled by Sybil, who contrived to drop his hat, his coat and then his umbrella before eventually opening the door to let him out. As she closed it behind him, she gave Lonsdale a conspiratorial wink that made him decide to overlook her inconvenient friendship with Voules.

'Well,' said Hulda. 'I am glad he won't be *my* father-in-law.'

TWELVE

Lonsdale was in an agony of tension when he woke the following morning. He was sure he was wasting valuable time by going to Broadmoor, and in three days it would be Christmas Eve, when the Watchers would do something terrible and his time for investigating would run out. Peters had vowed to find the killer, but he was being watched, and it was only a matter of time before he was forced to desist – or worse, suffer Hayes's fate. Thus Lonsdale needed answers to share with him fast, which he was sure would not happen with a visit to Broadmoor.

He met Hulda in the morning room for a hurried breakfast. She was ready to leave, wearing flat-heeled boots and a waterproof coat that Emelia had left behind, which Sybil had suggested would be more practical for a day in the country. Then Jack appeared and said Humbage had embarrassed him the previous night by appearing at the Oxford and Cambridge Club and making a scene.

'He wanted me to leave my dinner and come home to deal with you,' he said, still tight-lipped with anger. 'I refused. Emelia will be irked with me, but a man's club is sacrosanct. How would he feel if I arrived at *his* club and began to bellow? These Palace friends of his are a bad influence.'

'He wishes they were his friends,' said Lonsdale. 'But I suspect they find him as tiresome as we do.'

'He went on to say that important people dislike you interfering with police business,' Jack said. 'That it creates a bad precedent when newsmen meddle with the forces of law and order.'

'What "important people"?' demanded Lonsdale. 'The courtiers he fawns over? Or does he mean himself, lest he's tainted by his association with someone who wants justice for the victims of a ruthless killer?'

While they had been talking, Hulda had gone to the mantelpiece, where she looked pointedly at the clock, reminding Lonsdale that they had a train to catch. Then she saw what was lying next to it.

'Is this the dinosaur claw?' she asked, and regarded him accusingly. 'The one you promised to donate to the Natural History Museum?'

'I will,' said Lonsdale, and put it in his pocket, although he knew there would be no time to do it that day. 'The next time we pass.'

Despite Hulda agitating about the time, they were still too early for the train, so Lonsdale suggested stopping at Burnside's lodgings en route to Paddington Station. He wanted to ask the photographer about what was happening at the Garraway that necessitated Roth and Carlingford carrying guns, and was sure Burnside would help him – if he could be cornered away from the club's malign influences.

But Burnside was out, and his landlady, who answered the door, said he had not been home for several days.

'He often sleeps at his club,' she explained. 'They keep him busy there, but he doesn't mind. He's meeting people – *rich* people – whom he hopes will give him commissions in the future.'

'Does he talk about the club at all?' fished Hulda.

'All the time! He loves it, and often tells me about the wealthy and influential Liberals he encounters there. He is sure that being a member will change his life for the better.'

'Has he ever mentioned a group called the Watchers?' persisted Hulda.

Lonsdale had already asked Burnside this, and was sure he had been telling the truth when he denied any knowledge about it.

'Once,' replied the landlady, to Lonsdale's abject surprise – he could not look at Hulda, unwilling to see her gloat. 'He was elected to it at the end of last month.'

'What did he say exactly?' demanded Hulda urgently.

'That it was the proudest moment of his life, and he aims to be worthy of it.' The landlady's hands flew to her mouth in sudden horror. 'But he asked me not to tell anyone and now I've betrayed his confidence!'

'Never mind,' said Hulda carelessly. 'I'm sure he'll forgive you.'

Lonsdale was sure he would not, as the slip revealed him as a man who lied with considerable ease. The landlady could be persuaded to say no more, so they went on their way. Hulda was silent until they turned the corner, then she began to crow.

'I knew it! Burnside is a Watcher and is deeply involved in this business. I *told* you there was something odd about the way he keeps appearing. Voules was spying on us for Ingram, but Burnside has been monitoring you for his masters at the Garraway – his *Watcher* masters.'

'I'll corner him when we get back tonight,' said Lonsdale, disgusted with himself for being so easily duped.

'We both will,' determined Hulda. 'I don't care about their asinine "No Ladies" policy. Let them keep me out if they dare!'

The train was ready to depart when Lonsdale and Hulda arrived at the station. They raced towards it and leapt aboard just as it began to inch away. It gathered up speed, and Lonsdale paced in the corridor, wanting the journey to be over as quickly as possible. Ten minutes later, it stopped and sat for so long that, in an agony of exasperation, Lonsdale went to find the guard.

'Mud on the track,' replied the guard unapologetically. 'An act of God, sir.'

Lonsdale did not believe him, but there was nothing he and Hulda could do except wait and fume. They discussed the case for a while, but then two men in suits came to sit in their carriage, and they fell silent by mutual consent. The men did not look like Garraway spies, but there was no point in being careless.

The train creaked forward eventually, crawling with infuriating slowness along the Great Western main line through the suburban sprawl around Ealing. After that they came to open countryside, and the gently rolling fields west of the stinking metropolis that was London.

'I'm never travelling by train again,' vowed Lonsdale, as they alighted in Reading nearly two hours late. 'I don't believe there was mud on the track at the start of the journey or "trespassing cows" at the end – especially as that was the excuse used to explain the dismal service to Surrey on Tuesday. Either loose cattle are the official pretext of the week, or farmers have suddenly become very careless.'

They crossed to the North Downs Line, where they caught the connection to Wellington College Station on the outskirts of Crowthorne, passing through the new development of Winnersh and the historic market town of Wokingham. It was drizzling, and Lonsdale feared another long traipse through the rain, but Crowthorne was more civilized than West Wickham, and they were able to hire a pony and trap.

Once they were clattering along a long, straight road known as Duke's Ride, sure the driver could not hear them through the thick woollen scarf that was wrapped around his head, Hulda began to talk about the case.

'So who's on our list of suspects, now that the cannibals and Roth are exonerated?'

'We never had a list,' said Lonsdale tiredly. 'All we can say is that certain people are involved in whatever's unfolding at the Garraway, but we don't know how: Burnside, Lord Carlingford, Fleetwood-Pelham, others we don't know about . . .'

'Humbage,' said Hulda soberly. 'Because I'm suspicious about him constantly ordering you to abandon your enquiries. I know you don't want to hear it, but it's true.'

'Humbage is a stuffy old parvenu, but he's not a killer. Perhaps we should look more closely at Commissioner Henderson – he's the one who appointed the Metropolitan Police's least able detective to investigate the murders.'

'And then there's Maclean. Perhaps Stead was right to send us here, because the murders *did* begin shortly after his escape. So let's hope we get some answers at this place, because I'm not sure how well we'll fare at the Garraway.'

Broadmoor Criminal Lunatic Asylum was imposing and rather frightening. A giant complex encompassing fifty-three acres within its secure area, its entrance was through giant metal gates housed between two massive rectangular towers. There was a reception room at the front, where Lonsdale and Hulda were startled to hear they were expected.

'Mr Morley arranged an appointment for you with Medical Superintendent Orange, but that was for yesterday,' explained the warden, consulting a ledger with a grimy finger. 'Mr Orange is busy today, but I'll get Chaplain Ashe to have a word with you instead. We don't normally bend the rules, but seeing as it's for Mr Morley . . .'

'You know him?' asked Hulda, startled.

The man beamed. 'He said kind things about us in his report to Prime Minister Gladstone earlier in the year.'

He opened the door, and another guard came to escort them through a series of grim little rooms. Each had doors that had to be unlocked and relocked behind them, and the guard seemed to take delight in slamming them as hard as he could, so the sound reverberated unpleasantly. Lonsdale remembered how Roth had described the visit he had made with Dickerson – that the place stank of cabbage, dirty feet and despair. Roth was right.

Fortunately, the chaplain did not keep them waiting long, for which Lonsdale was grateful. Not only did he resent the loss of his time, but he hated the closed doors, the grimy grey walls, and the babble and shriek of disturbed minds. When Ashe – a small, neat man with a black moustache – arrived, Lonsdale began to ask his questions with uncharacteristic briskness.

'You were going to donate some artefacts to the Natural History Museum,' he began. 'Professor Dickerson and Timothy Roth came here to talk to you about them.'

Ashe nodded. 'But Dickerson said they already had plenty of Ashanti spears, and recommended I give mine to another museum instead. His assistant then became rather unwell, so I escorted him outside. When I got back, the professor had managed to inveigle his way into the medical superintendent's office.'

'Why?' asked Lonsdale keenly. 'What did they talk about?'

'Prisoner welfare. Afterwards, Orange said he'd found the discussion helpful.'

And had written to say so, thought Lonsdale, recalling the letter he and Hulda had found in Dickerson's home. Hulda quizzed Ashe about Dickerson a while longer, then brought the conversation around to Maclean.

'How did he escape?' she asked. 'This place seems secure.'

'It *is* secure, and we've no idea how he managed it. All we can think is that one of his visitors must've helped.'

'What visitors?'

'Ones who were concerned about his well-being – Archbishop Tait, who thought he needed spiritual guidance; a lawyer named Bowyer, who wanted to buy him the best medical treatment; and Superintendent Hayes, who stopped Maclean from being beaten by an angry mob and whom Maclean considered a friend.'

'Did Professor Dickerson ask to see him?'

'He did actually,' said Ashe. 'To compare Maclean to some Southern African regicides he'd met, although he didn't stay long.'

'And now all four are dead,' mused Lonsdale.

'Actually, there were five,' said Ashe. 'Mr Voules is still alive, as far as I know, and he's the one who came the day Maclean vanished from our care in late November. He's a reporter for *The Echo*. At least, that's what he wrote in the visitors' book.'

'Voules!' spat Hulda. 'He swore he'd never been to Broadmoor. The lying toad!'

'More weasel, I'd have said,' reflected Ashe pedantically. 'He's too thin to be likened to a toad, which I always imagine as having plump jowls and—'

'Our Voules is portly,' interrupted Lonsdale, 'with greasy dark hair, a bad complexion, and a shambling gait. His clothes are of decent quality, but he wears them badly. Is that the man?'

'No, it's not – ours was slightly built with a moustache, and his clothes were neat but cheap.'

'There's only one Voules who writes for *The Echo*,' said Lonsdale to Hulda. 'He was telling the truth for once: someone *did* use his name to gain illicit access to Maclean.'

Ashe was dismayed by the revelation. 'But we sent descriptions of all the visitors to Superintendent Hayes – he's the officer investigating the escape. His inspector, Wells, wrote back to say they all checked out!'

'*Wells* wrote back?' pounced Lonsdale.

'I felt he should have come in person, but his letter claimed that police time would be better spent hunting Maclean than travelling back and forth. It wasn't unreasonable, although I felt we deserved a more personal touch, given the significance of this particular prisoner. But if our Voules isn't your reporter, then who is he?'

'Did he wear a bowler hat?' asked Lonsdale, mind working fast.

'Yes,' replied Ashe impatiently. 'What does that have to do with anything?'

Hulda stared at Lonsdale. 'I thought Bowler Hat *was* Maclean – the description fits him like a glove. But if Bowler Hat came to help Maclean escape . . . what's going on, Lonsdale?'

Ashe was so shocked by the notion that an imposter had gained access to a secure facility with such ease that he insisted Lonsdale and Hulda speak to the medical superintendent about it in person. William Orange was a white-haired, serious man with kindly eyes, who listened gravely to what they had to say.

'I shall tell the police at once,' he said when they had finished. 'There's been no progress for weeks, now, so I'm sure Inspector Wells will be delighted to have this new intelligence.'

'He'll be too busy to act on it,' said Hulda with uncharacteristic diplomacy. 'The best man to contact is Inspector Peters. We'll do it when we return to London.'

'Excellent! Thank you. But we're conducting an investigation of our own, and I'd appreciate a written statement from you, confirming all you've said. My assistant Norris will take it down, then drive you to the station. It won't take long, and I promise he'll have you there in time to catch the next train.'

Lonsdale and Hulda nodded consent, and Norris, who would have been nondescript were it not for his large yellow moustache, took them to a miserable little cell-like room that had nothing in it except a table and two chairs, all bolted to the floor, and a bucket.

'Bear with me,' he said, indicating that they were to sit. 'I'll fetch another seat. I won't be a moment.'

He left, closing the door behind him. Then Lonsdale heard a click as a key turned in the lock. He hurried towards it, but there was no handle on the inside, and the door fitted so tightly into its frame that he could not insert so much as a fingernail into the gap.

'Perhaps he did it out of instinct,' shrugged Hulda, 'because that's what they do here – keep doors locked.'

They waited with growing unease as time ticked past. After half an hour, Hulda went to pound on the door with her fist.

'Hey!' she yelled. 'Where are you? Have you forgotten about us?'

There was no reply, and Lonsdale glanced at his pocket watch. Unless they left in five minutes, they would miss the train that Orange promised they would be on. He told Hulda, who hammered on the door even more furiously, yelling until she was hoarse. After another hour, Lonsdale did the same.

'Maybe Orange has sent for Wells,' said Hulda worriedly, after Lonsdale, too, had given up. 'He didn't seem overly concerned that the police have made no progress with recapturing Maclean – and, to be frank, he didn't seem too bothered about a would-be regicide escaping from his care either. Maybe he's in on it.'

'In on what?' asked Lonsdale.

Hulda threw up her hands in exasperation. 'Whatever's happening! The murders, Maclean's escape and his association with some of the victims, the terrible thing that the Watchers aim to do on Christmas Eve.'

'Which we won't be able to stop unless we get out of here,' said Lonsdale, kicking at the walls in the hope that one would be flimsy. But they were all solid stone, there was no window, and the only door was the one that was firmly shut.

They were silent again, waiting. Lonsdale tried not to look at his watch too often, but when the hour hand moved to six o'clock, he knew he and Hulda were in serious trouble. Would someone come in the night to kill them with a panga, and would corrupt police officers then arrange for a verdict of natural causes?

'Pity you lost your gun,' he muttered.

By eight o'clock, he was hungry and thirsty, although Hulda berated him for thinking about victuals at such a time. She battered the door again, but no one came.

'It's completely silent in here,' said Lonsdale, looking up from where he was trying to scrape the mortar from around a brick with the dinosaur claw, which was all he had that remotely resembled a weapon. He knew that, even if he succeeded in prising it out, it was unlikely to help, but he felt he had to do something. 'It was quite noisy when we were with Ashe. I could hear other people – inmates and wardens.'

'I think we might be in one of the secure interview units,'

said Hulda unsteadily. 'I read about them yesterday. They're for
when the police have to question really dangerous "residents",
and don't want them grabbing anything that might be used to do
harm.'

She dozed while Lonsdale plied his claw. He made some progress,
but not enough, and then the lights flickered out. It was so dark that
he could not see his hand in front of his face. Hulda woke in alarm,
and Lonsdale reached for her hand.

'It must be ten o'clock,' he whispered. 'That's when prisons
usually turn off the gaslights. At least now we can get some
sleep.'

'And use the bucket,' said Hulda primly, 'which neither of us
could do with the other looking on.'

'I wouldn't have looked, Friederichs,' said Lonsdale, suddenly
wondering what Anne would think if she could see him now.
They were supposed to discuss their future the following evening,
and he sincerely hoped he would be able to do it. His stomach
growled.

'Perhaps they mean to starve us to death,' remarked Hulda.

'They can't,' said Lonsdale, more firmly than he felt. 'Stead
knows we're here, and Peters is expecting us to report back to him.
When we fail to appear, they'll come looking for us.'

'Will they?' asked Hulda. 'They might just assume we're
following some lead on our own. We've done it before.'

That was true, and Lonsdale had no answer.

Lonsdale did not imagine he would sleep that night, so was
disoriented when the lights blazed on the following morning,
blinding him with brightness. Before he could do more than try to
open his eyes, the door opened, and a tray shot across the floor. He
thought he glimpsed Norris there, but the door closed again before
he could be sure. He looked at his watch.

'Eight o'clock,' he told Hulda, who looked remarkably pretty for
a woman who had just spent the night curled up on a hard stone
floor. 'Is that breakfast?'

On the tray was a bowl of watery oatmeal, two boiled eggs and
a jug of water. It did not take long to demolish them, after which
Hulda climbed to her feet, and began to hammer on the door again,
telling Lonsdale that guards changed, and one might have come to

work who did not think it was acceptable to incarcerate members of the press for no good reason. She kept it up for an hour, then sat on one of the chairs, scowling her frustration.

'Something will happen today,' she said. 'They can't keep us here indefinitely.'

But the hours slipped away as relentlessly as they had the previous day. Lonsdale scraped at the brick with the claw until he noticed Hulda sitting with her hands over her ears to block out the sound. At three in the afternoon, the door opened, and another tray was kicked in. Lonsdale launched himself forward, claw at the ready, but the guard had slammed the door shut long before he could reach it.

'Stew,' mused Hulda, although most of it had slopped out when the tray had been sent spinning across the floor. 'And a tiny glass of what may be tea. It smells like drains.'

It was barely enough for one, and while Lonsdale could have forgone the food, he was very thirsty. He paced back and forth as seven o'clock loomed. What would Anne think when he failed to appear? That he considered a future with her less important than his work? And how could he appease her with a spectacular Christmas gift when he could not get out to buy one? Worse yet, the atrocity planned for Christmas Eve – just two days hence – would swing into action, and he and Hulda would not be in a position to stop it.

Seven o'clock came and went. He tried to discuss the case with Hulda, but they ended up going over the same details and reaching the same conclusions – that although they knew the Garraway and its Watchers lay at the heart of everything, neither had any idea why someone should want to murder seven – or more – decent men in so cruel and vicious a manner.

'Maclean,' said Hulda eventually. 'He's the key. He's why we're locked in here, helpless. I know he came across as weak and imbecilic at his trial, but what if that was an act? What if he's actually a very cunning killer? He started by attempting to assassinate the Queen, so he clearly has a high opinion of his abilities.'

'You could be right,' said Lonsdale. 'And the false Voules couldn't have got him out of here on his own. Perhaps Maclean is slyly persuasive, in the way some criminals can be, and convinced gullible guards to help him.'

'Gullible guards!' spat Hulda. 'The whole asylum helped him, from that oh-so-concerned Orange to the sly Chaplain Ashe, who went scurrying to his corrupt master when he saw we were beginning to understand the truth. It makes sense now. We should've listened to Stead – he was worried about Maclean from the start. And why hasn't he rescued us? And where's Peters? He asked us to report to him – surely he missed us?'

Lonsdale had no answer.

The lights flickered out at ten o'clock, so he and Hulda lay side by side on the floor, both wondering what the next day would bring. Lonsdale's stomach was pure acid, partly from hunger and thirst, but mostly from tension.

He felt Hulda shivering – it was cold on the floor. He shifted, so she could snuggle against him, his arm around her shoulders and her head on his chest. It was not much warmer, but both gained comfort from the closeness of the other. They slept fitfully.

When the lights flared on at eight o'clock the following morning, Lonsdale staggered to his feet and stood next to the door, clutching his claw. Hulda understood at once what he aimed to do. She removed her coat and rolled it up so, at a glance, it would appear as if he was lying next to her.

Two hours passed before they heard a sound. Lonsdale braced himself. The door opened. He grabbed it and hauled with all his might. A man stumbled inwards with a cry of alarm, and Lonsdale slashed at him with the claw, which was sharp from being honed on the mortar the previous day. The man screeched in pain as the edge gashed his face. Other guards raced to his aid, and Lonsdale was battered back. Then the wounded man was hauled out, Lonsdale shoved backwards, and the door slammed shut.

'They didn't leave us anything to drink,' said Hulda in a small voice.

It was afternoon before anything else happened, by which time Lonsdale and Hulda were so parched they could think of nothing but cool, clear water. There was a soft scratch as a key turned in the lock and the door opened. It swung open to reveal Chaplain Ashe.

'Come with me,' he ordered.

THIRTEEN

I t was an effort for Lonsdale to stand, and he realized how much the spat with the guards and two days of meagre rations had sapped his strength. He supposed he would have to use words rather than muscle to convince the chaplain to let them go. Hulda had other ideas.

'You won't get away with this,' she snarled, although her voice had lost its usual vigour. 'People know where we are and questions will be asked.'

'Hush!' hissed Ashe, glancing behind him in alarm. 'It wasn't me who put you in here. *I'm* trying to help you escape, so stop bellowing or we'll all be in trouble.'

Hulda's face was full of suspicion, while Lonsdale's mind reeled, wondering what trick was in the making.

'Why would you—' he began.

'Questions later,' snapped Ashe. 'Now come with me before he realizes what's happening.'

'Who realizes?' demanded Hulda, not moving. 'Orange?'

'*Please* just come with me! We can talk all you like later.'

Lonsdale took Hulda's hand and followed Ashe out, thinking anything was better than being driven mad with thirst. There was a jug of water on a table in the corridor, and he and Hulda gulped from it while Ashe locked the door behind them. The chaplain's hands shook so badly that the operation took far longer than it should have done.

'Now follow me and pray we have more friends than enemies,' whispered Ashe, and set off along the hallway at a rapid clip. There was a door at the end, and there was another pause while he fumbled with his keys.

'You can talk while you unlock the door,' said Hulda. 'Tell us what's happening.'

'Paddy O'Brien betrayed his fellows.' Sweat beaded on Ashe's forehead as the third key he tried failed to work. 'He thought he was dying and wanted me to absolve him from his sins. I'm not

Roman Catholic, but he was too frightened to care. There was a lot of blood, you see, and his nose was all but severed.'

'The guard I tried to overpower?' asked Lonsdale, struggling to understand the disjointed explanation.

The key turned at last and Ashe bundled them through the door, after which there was another delay while he relocked it.

'I have to secure them all,' he said, seeing their exasperated expressions. 'If we leave one open, the alarm will be raised and we'll be caught for certain. We take security seriously here, particularly since Maclean's escape.'

'The wounded guard,' prompted Lonsdale tersely, itching to snatch the keys and do it himself, given that dexterity was evidently not one of Ashe's virtues. 'Will he die?'

'No, although you've destroyed his looks. But when he thought his immortal soul was in danger, he wanted to confess. He told me that Norris had you imprisoned here, and is under orders from a man who sounds very much like the false Voules. But no more talking. The next part will be the hardest.'

He opened the door to a larger room that was filled with chairs and tables. Various personal items lying around suggested it was where the hospital staff changed and took their breaks. Ashe ushered them quickly to the far end, where Lonsdale was handed a clerical hat and collar. For Hulda, there was a white scarf, which Ashe arranged to look vaguely like a religious wimple.

'Disguises,' he said, licking dry lips. 'Not very original, but it was all I could manage on the spur of the moment. It might help if you try to look a bit reverent.'

The last remark was aimed at Hulda, who was scowling her mistrust. Then they were off again, Ashe visibly frightened, which Lonsdale thought was a lot more likely to get them caught than Hulda's unconvincing impression of a nun.

'Oh, God help us!' the chaplain gulped, as they rounded a corner and saw several guards walking towards them. 'Norris's men! We're done for!'

'Keep walking!' ordered Lonsdale in a taut whisper. 'Smile. Bid them good day.'

Ashe could not have looked more terrified if he had tried, but the men barely spared him a glance. Lonsdale murmured a greeting as they passed, and most muttered back. He saw dried blood on the hands of one, and supposed their minds were on what had happened to O'Brien. They were a rough lot, and he dreaded to imagine what would happen if he and Hulda were caught.

They reached the next door, and Lonsdale braced himself for another agonizing delay, but it swung open in front of them. He stopped abruptly, wondering whether to charge forward or head back the way they had come.

'Come on, Chaplain,' whispered the guard on the other side. 'Let's get you out.'

He turned and hurried towards the next door, which he had open in a trice. Another guard was waiting to close it behind them, and when they passed a gaggle of warders in the corridor beyond, every one of them gave Ashe a conspiratorial nod or a smile. The first guard turned back the way he had come, but there was another waiting to see them through the next section, and then they were outside, in air that was fresh, clean and cold.

'Now, Father,' said the last guard urgently. 'There's a cart waiting down the road. Just walk nice and casual – you don't know who might be watching.'

'Bless you,' muttered Ashe, weak with relief. 'Bless you all!'

He led the way at a brisk pace, Lonsdale's hand on his shoulder to prevent him from breaking into a run and giving them away. They rounded a corner, and there was the horse and trap. A driver was on it, cloaked against the rain, hat pulled low. He turned as they approached, and Lonsdale stopped in alarm.

It was Medical Superintendent Orange, a hard, cold gleam in his eye.

Lonsdale took several steps backwards, stomach lurching. He considered running, but that would mean abandoning Hulda, and he could not leave her to fend for herself. And yet, if he stayed, they were doomed for certain – they would be returned to their cell and then no one would ever know what had happened to them, as at least two dozen guards could swear they had left the premises.

'Get in,' ordered Orange, taking up the reins. 'We can make the next train if we hurry.'

'The last time you said that, we were locked up for two days,' said Hulda accusingly.

'What Norris did had nothing to do with me,' averred Orange.

'And nothing to do with most of my staff either – just a few rotten apples who'll be incarcerated themselves when I get back. Now climb in, before you miss the train.'

'How did you know to be here?' asked Lonsdale suspiciously, not moving.

'One of the guards told me,' replied Orange, and gave a brief smile. 'My chaplain arranged for you to escape from the asylum, but that's as far as his plan went. Obviously, you need to be spirited a lot farther away than this lane in order to be safe.'

'Oh,' said Ashe sheepishly. 'I was going to let them walk to the station.'

'Then Norris would have recaptured them for certain,' said Orange. 'They need to be on the next train – and you and I must make sure he doesn't follow. Now, get in – all of you.'

Lonsdale scrambled aboard and held out his hand to Hulda, who took it warily. Ashe jumped in behind her, and Orange snapped the reins. The trap took off at a tremendous lick, forcing his passengers to cling on for dear life.

'How long have you known Norris?' shouted Lonsdale as they hurtled along.

'Years,' Orange replied. 'He's tipped to be my successor, but there's plenty of life in me yet, and I fear he's tired of waiting. I imagine his discontent reached the wrong ears, and he was offered a chance to speed matters along – Maclean's escape was nearly the end of me.'

'You think he was involved in that?'

Orange nodded. 'I do now. I guessed at the time that one of my senior officers helped to spirit Maclean out, although Norris was never a suspect. Then I found out what he'd done to you.'

'It makes sense now,' put in Ashe. 'His sly, whispered conferences with certain guards, his altering of rotas to put his favourites in specific areas, his murmurs that the asylum staff had grown complacent under the current regime . . .'

'But more significantly, his "accidental" leaving of a novice warden on duty the day that Maclean vanished,' said Orange. 'Then you came here asking questions and he panicked.'

'He locked you in a room we never use,' elaborated Ashe, 'although I can't imagine how he thought that would help him in the long term, given that keeping you there was a risk in itself.'

'I know exactly what he intended,' said Orange grimly. 'He goes off-duty this evening and will be gone until Tuesday – he has a young family, so I offered to cover the Christmas period in order to let him be with them. He'll have told his paymasters about you and arranged for them to come and kill you at a time when he wouldn't be on site to take the blame.'

'So if the police ever did trace two mysteriously missing reporters to our asylum,' surmised Ashe, 'he could say it happened on your watch.'

'Precisely.'

'Who are these paymasters?' asked Hulda. 'Maclean, whom we believe to be a cunning and ruthless murderer, not the poor, confused lunatic we saw at his trial?'

'I treated Maclean myself,' said Orange, flicking the reins to encourage the pony to trot even faster. 'If he *is* feigning his insanity, he's a damned genius, because I have thirty years' experience of lunacy, and he seemed genuinely ill to me.'

'But it's possible?' pressed Hulda.

Orange nodded reluctantly. 'Although Norris never went near him, so I don't see how one could have recruited the other. Perhaps the answer lies with "Voules", and the fact that the police brazenly ignored him being an imposter.'

'Wells?' asked Lonsdale of Hulda. 'Could *he* be the sly mastermind?'

She spread her hands in a shrug. 'How could a mere inspector compel the commissioner to ignore a series of murders?'

'Very easily,' replied Lonsdale soberly, 'if the culprit is as clever as we suspect.'

They reached the station, where their train sat wheezing and blowing, ready to leave. Orange jerked the cart to a standstill, and his passengers clambered out. Hulda raced for the platform, but Lonsdale turned back to Ashe and Orange.

'What happens when you get back? Norris will be waiting.'

'Don't worry about us,' said Orange. 'There are more loyal wardens than corrupt ones, and there are only so many crimes Norris will commit for the sake of his ambition. He could've killed you the moment he had you locked away, but he's a coward and he hesitated. He'll surrender when I confront him.'

* * *

Despite Orange's assurances, Lonsdale still had misgivings about leaving him and Ashe while Norris was still in a position to do them harm. He flung himself on the train just as it was pulling out of the station, Hulda howling at him to hurry, and glanced back to see another trap clattering to a standstill next to theirs. Norris and a pair of guards jumped out.

Lonsdale gripped the window hard, debating whether to leap off the train and go to their aid, but the last thing he saw before trees obscured his view was Orange felling his deputy with a punch and Norris's henchmen taking to their heels. Clearly, Orange could deal with the vipers in his midst.

'It'll be dark by the time we get home,' said Lonsdale. 'And I have no idea where to start looking for Maclean – other than the Garraway, perhaps.'

'Why would he be there?' asked Hulda sceptically.

'Because it lies at the heart of everything.'

'We'd do better going straight to Peters and telling him what we've learned. Then he can get us an interview with Commissioner Henderson, and we can confront him with what we know of his role in the affair. He'll confess and provide us with information to answer all our other questions.'

Lonsdale doubted it would be that easy, but agreed that Peters should be their first port of call. He sank down on the seat, relishing its softness after the stone floor in the asylum and the wooden sides of the trap.

'The false Voules,' said Hulda after a while. 'Slim, short, poor but neat clothes. Does that sound like anyone you know?'

'Who?' asked Lonsdale, too tired and fraught to play guessing games.

'Burnside,' replied Hulda. 'A man who's a member of the Garraway, who's a Watcher, who tells lies, who appears at unexpected moments, as if he's been following us . . .'

'He isn't . . .' began Lonsdale, and trailed off, recalling that he had bumped into the photographer more often than would normally be expected in a city of four million people – at the Natural History Museum twice, in the haberdasher's shop, and then in the Garraway. 'He saved the Queen's life.'

'Yes, from *Maclean*,' Hulda pointed out. 'And he feels slighted, because the Palace refuses to be suitably grateful. He's impoverished, bitter and angry.'

'Yes,' acknowledged Lonsdale. 'So we'll talk to him when we go to the Garraway.'

Although Lonsdale and Hulda were exhausted, neither slept on the journey home. Once on the train from Reading, they sat in the dining car drinking cups of railway tea that tasted like nectar. Lonsdale kept looking at his watch, willing the train on, but it hurried for no one, and was an hour late when it finally steamed into Paddington, stopping so abruptly that all its passengers were sent staggering forward.

Lonsdale grabbed Hulda's hand, and hurried her off the platform, aiming to reach the waiting hansoms before they were claimed by others. As they went, it occurred to him that he had held her hand a lot over the last few days, and that it had become a very natural thing to do. He wondered what Anne would make of it. Then he recalled that Anne would be angry with him for missing their appointment the previous evening. He hoped she would let him explain before making any precipitous decisions.

Traffic was heavy as their hansom eased out of the station and along Praed Street, stopping so often that Lonsdale itched to jump out and run. Only the sight of Hulda's exhausted face kept him in place, although it did nothing to prevent him from muttering under his breath at delay after delay.

'London *is* pretty,' said Hulda, staring out of the window. 'Even in the drizzle, on a dark December night. The lights and Christmas decorations . . .'

Her words only reminded him that it would be Christmas Eve the following day, at which point the Watchers' plan would swing into action.

They reached Scotland Yard eventually, where Lonsdale would have stormed inside and demanded to see Peters at once. Hulda stopped him.

'If you race in like Attila the Hun, someone is sure to notice and tell Wells or Henderson – and if one of them *did* plan to have us dispatched at Broadmoor, they may decide to do it here instead. Moreover, it'll draw attention to the fact that Peters is investigating matters he's been ordered to leave alone.'

'I imagine everyone knows that anyway,' Lonsdale pointed out impatiently. 'He made no secret of the fact that he aims to catch Hayes's killer.'

'That was three days ago,' said Hulda bleakly. 'Who knows how the situation might have changed since?'

'Then we'll demand an interview with Henderson immediately,' determined Lonsdale. 'We'll tell him we know what Wells has been—'

'We will, but only if Peters is in a position to come with us,' interrupted Hulda. 'If we do it alone, Henderson will deny everything, and then what'll we do? Call him a liar? Henderson will order us to be arrested, and that will be that.'

'So what do you suggest we do?' demanded Lonsdale tautly. 'Sit back and wait for the Watchers to strike?'

'Of course not. We'll send Peters a message that only he'll understand. Asking him to meet us at your house will be best – a place where we know there won't be unwanted ears flapping.'

Lonsdale clenched his fists, hating the notion of yet another delay, but Hulda was right. Three days *was* a long time, and if Henderson had any sense, he would have taken measures against one of his best detectives meddling in a case that might bring him down. Peters might not even be in London any longer, or he might – and the prospect sent a chill down Lonsdale's spine – have been dispatched like Hayes.

'I know what to write,' said Hulda. 'It occurred to me on the train that getting hold of Peters might be a problem, so I mulled it over all the way from Reading. Do you have a pencil and a scrap of paper?'

Lonsdale handed them over, and she went to lean on a wall to write. He read over her shoulder, marvelling at the cleverly cryptic nature of her words. She phrased the message in such a way that no one but Peters would know she was the sender, or that she wanted him to hasten to Cleveland Square at his earliest opportunity. When she had finished, she saw the admiration on his face and smiled rather smugly.

'I'm a professional writer, Lonsdale. What did you expect?'

She handed it to a uniformed constable and informed him that he would lose his post unless he handed it to the inspector personally and immediately.

'Now what?' asked Lonsdale, when the man had hurried away.

'We go to your house,' replied Hulda. 'Fun though it would be to burgle the Garraway again, it would be a mistake. They'll have taken steps to prevent it, especially now the day of their atrocity is to hand. All we can do is hope Peters comes soon.'

They took a hansom, alighting before they reached Cleveland Square, so they could make sure it was not being watched. They entered through the back door, startling Sybil, who was drinking Jack's best port next to a roaring fire.

'He's gone,' she told him accusingly and rather fearfully. 'Mr Voules, I mean. He hasn't been round since Wednesday. What did you say to him?'

Lonsdale mumbled something noncommittal, but his thoughts tumbled. Had Voules fled because Ingram no longer needed him to spy? Or was there a more sinister reason for his disappearance – such as that he was involved in whatever was unfolding at the Garraway?

He hurried to the dining room, where Jack took one look at their grey, exhausted faces, and hastened to pour them large brandies.

'I'm afraid I've bad news,' he said. 'Emelia came to tell me that Anne no longer wishes to marry you. I suspect Humbage poisoned her against you. Ever since he started hobnobbing with courtiers, he's been an unbearable snob. He'd rather she married a lord.'

'Then it's her loss,' declared Hulda stoutly. 'One day, she'll regret it bitterly.'

Lonsdale rather suspected Anne would think she had had a narrow escape. So had he, because he was not nearly as dismayed as he should have been.

FOURTEEN

Although Lonsdale paced like a caged lion while they waited for Peters, Hulda made good use of the time. She bathed and went to bed, announcing that they would need all their wits about them if they aimed to thwart the Watchers the following day. At midnight, it became clear that Peters was not coming, so Lonsdale sat at the table and wrote out all they had learned since discovering Dickerson's body in the museum. When he had finished, he slept fitfully, waking a dozen times because he thought he heard someone at the door.

Christmas Eve – a Sunday – dawned dull and grey. Lonsdale rolled out of bed, thinking how different this one was to others in his past, when he had been full of excited anticipation. All he felt that day was a sense of impending doom.

He went to the morning room, and found Hulda already there, looking neat and fresh in clothes that had been laundered by Sybil overnight – a service given in exchange for news about Voules when it became available. He sat and drank a cup of coffee that was so strong he feared for his teeth. He was not surprised to hear that Hulda had made it.

'Your brother has gone to see his fiancée,' reported Hulda. 'He's afraid Emelia will follow Anne's example, and decide she can do better for herself.'

'I'm surprised he'd do that this early, and before church,' mused Lonsdale. 'He must be very agitated.'

'Not unlike you, then,' observed Hulda dryly, as Lonsdale paced.

'Peters should have come,' he said worriedly. 'Do you think something has happened to him? What if he never appears? Do we just sit here and let the Watchers get on with it?'

Hulda opened her mouth to reply, but faltered when there was a loud, important rap on the front door – too loud and important for any normal caller. They were silent as they heard Sybil go to answer it. There was a murmur of voices, then footsteps thumped down the hall. The door was thrown open . . .

'Peters!' exclaimed Lonsdale in relief. 'Where have you been?'

'Addington Palace,' replied the inspector. 'To talk to Tait's daughter. Afterwards, I went straight home, so only received your message this morning – from a constable who spent the night in my office, too frightened to leave. More importantly, where have *you* been? I was worried.'

Hulda opened her mouth to reply, but Lonsdale cut across her. 'Has anyone tried to stop you from investigating? Or followed you?'

Peters's moustache twitched. 'Both, but not successfully. Today's shadow will be fuming on the train to Clapham as we speak.'

'What have you learned since we've been gone?' demanded Lonsdale urgently. 'Do you know the identity of the killer?'

Peters grimaced. 'No, but I sense you've been more successful. Tell me.'

Hulda did, because Lonsdale was too restless for talking. As she finished her tale of their escape, he abruptly stopped pacing. 'What about the Khoikhoi?' he interjected. 'You said last time we saw you that they weren't safe. Are they still at Monkey Hornby's house?'

'They're on a ship to the Cape with Roth,' replied Peters. 'Wells may not be the brightest star in the sky, but he's not stupid – the groundsmen saw Hornby popping in and out, and he would've made the association eventually. So I arranged for your cannibals to leave the country.'

'So you agree that they didn't kill Dickerson?'

'I only thought that before I knew there were other victims – men your Khoikhoi had no reason to harm. Wells refused to see it, though. He leaked information to *The Echo*, aiming to whip London into a frenzy of fear, so they'd be caught the moment they left their hiding place. He would've seen them hang, so I decided it was best to remove temptation from his reach.'

'Because their only real link to the murders is that they knew Dickerson and happened to leave the museum on the day he was killed,' said Lonsdale. 'We have to go to the Garraway – that's where answers lie.'

Peters stood. 'But first, we must confront Commissioner Henderson. As long as he's under the sway of this "higher authority", he'll counter our every move. We need to make him desist.'

'He'll refuse,' predicted Lonsdale. 'Or arrange for all three of us to be murdered. This is the man who looked the other way while his best officer was dispatched. Why would he listen to us?'

'Because you two are from *The Pall Mall Gazette*. I assume you've written everything down? Good! The press terrifies him – he'll crumple the moment he knows he's about to be exposed. We'll see what he has to say for himself after we deliver your report to Stead.'

'Not Stead – he doesn't work on the Sabbath. Nor Mr Morley, as he's too preoccupied with events in Ireland. It'll have to be Milner – he doesn't live too far away, thank God!'

'Then let's go,' said Peters.

There was sleet in the air as Lonsdale, Hulda and Peters hurried through a city that could think of nothing but Christmas. Despite being closed, almost every shop boasted some kind of decoration, and carol singers warbled by the dozen. It made Lonsdale feel like an outsider – he was not in the mood for celebrating.

When they arrived at 54 Claverton Street, Pimlico, they had to wait several minutes before Milner was ready to receive them – he was fastidious and refused to let himself be seen in a state of undress. Lonsdale shoved the report into his hands and asked him to make copies and lodge them with as many friends as he could – their insurance against death by panga. Sensing the urgency of the situation, Milner took it and began writing immediately, waving one hand to tell them to leave him to it.

'Will Henderson be at work today?' Lonsdale asked, as he, Hulda and Peters headed for Scotland Yard. 'A Sunday *and* Christmas Eve?'

'Probably not,' replied Peters. 'But next door to headquarters, he has an office with living quarters attached. He'll be there alone, as his wife and daughters have gone to Kent for Christmas.'

The commissioner's apartment comprised a handsome, spacious suite of rooms on the first floor, overlooking a pretty courtyard. A sergeant shot to his feet as Peters walked towards the door.

'He's not available, sir,' the sergeant said, moving to intercept him. 'He's taking the day off.'

'He'll see me,' said Peters, shoving past the man, and opening the door without knocking. While the sergeant gaped his disbelief, Peters ushered Lonsdale and Hulda inside and closed the door behind them.

The sitting room was obsessively neat and smelled of wax polish. Several beautiful uniforms hung on a rack against one wall, while a glass cupboard held Henderson's collection of antique truncheons. The commissioner himself was in front of a mirror combing his moustache. He whipped around in surprise when Peters surged in.

'How dare you burst in to my private residence!' he bellowed indignantly. 'Leave at once! I'm getting ready to go to church with the Lord Mayor.'

'Then I'll be brief,' said Peters. 'We're here about the murder of Superintendent Hayes.'

'A terrible tragedy,' said Henderson shortly, 'but Wells informs me that he'll have the cannibals locked up by the end of the day. Now kindly remove yourselves—'

'The "cannibals" have alibis for Hayes's murder,' interrupted Peters. 'If Wells charges them, he'll be making a serious mistake.'

'Nonsense! Their so-called alibi will be a lie. Regardless, it's nothing to do with you, Peters. You were reassigned.'

Peters smiled coldly. 'And who told you to do that, Commissioner? Who's so important that you're willing to ignore the murder of one of your own men to curry his favour?'

The blood drained from Henderson's face. 'Get out! And take these people with you.'

'Fine, but they're reporters. And their story will appear in all the major papers tomorrow: how you prevented your best detective – the famous Superintendent Hayes – from solving a series of vicious murders.'

'I never—'

'And when Hayes demanded to know why, you arranged for him to be dispatched, too,' Peters went on coldly. 'Your own officer, Henderson! Don't deny it – there's proof.'

Stunned, Henderson groped for a chair and sank into it, while Lonsdale wondered how he would react when he discovered that Peters was bluffing. Suspicions weren't evidence, and *The PMG* could not go to press with what they had.

'I don't know what . . .' began Henderson. 'There can't be . . .'

'You were afraid that Hayes and I would investigate anyway, so you ordered colleagues to spy on us,' Peters forged on. 'They dogged our movements day and night, when they should've been hunting the lunatic with the panga.'

'Because you couldn't be trusted to do what you were told,' bleated Henderson. 'I was right – you both disobeyed me and continued to meddle. However, I did it to *protect* you – to prevent you from swimming in dangerous waters. Can't you see this is bigger than all of us? My orders came from the very highest authority.'

'A higher authority than the law?' asked Peters archly. 'We're *police* officers, Henderson – we don't turn a blind eye to crime, no matter who asks.'

'The Queen,' blurted Henderson. 'I swore an oath to serve her.'

'The *Queen*?' echoed Peters in disbelief. 'You claim *she* told you to look the other way while her subjects are hacked to pieces?'

'Or her government and ministers,' elaborated Henderson, desperately. 'Men who have the best interests of our country at heart.'

'And how is the murder of the Archbishop of Canterbury in our country's best interests?'

'It's not my job to ask that sort of question,' blustered Henderson. 'It's—'

'You don't know, do you?' said Peters, shaking his head in disgust. 'When these orders came, you followed them dumbly, like a faithful dog. You've no idea who issued them!'

Henderson's face was ashen. 'I don't need to know, and nor do you. It came from on high, and our duty is to obey.'

'Our *duty* is to protect life and catch criminals,' said Peters, not bothering to conceal his disdain. 'Not bow to the whim of some anonymous master. He told you to look the other way while men were brutally murdered, for God's sake! Surely you questioned the ethics of it?'

'Yes, but orders are orders. It isn't my place to refuse.'

'Of course it's your place to refuse!' exploded Peters. 'You're the Commissioner of Police! If you can't draw the line at perverting the course of justice, then who can? Worse, it sounds as if you didn't even ask *why* he wanted his crimes covered up.'

'I did, but an explanation was refused,' mumbled Henderson, then looked worriedly at Lonsdale and Hulda. 'You can't publish any of this. It would upset some very powerful people and put your own lives in danger.'

'On the contrary,' countered Hulda. 'Publishing it is the only way we'll be safe. Once the story is out, no one will need to ensure our silence.'

'You have two choices,' said Peters icily. 'You can take the blame for everything this "higher authority" has done. Or you can begin to make amends for your role in his vile crimes.'

'How do I do that?' asked Henderson worriedly.

'By appointing me to investigate the murders and dismissing Wells. You can also reflect on your criminal paymaster – you must know something to identify him.'

'But I don't! I never met him – he just sent me messages via another important man.'

'What important man?' demanded Hulda.

'I don't know his name. All I can do is promise to point him out if I ever see him again.'

'I suppose that'll have to do,' said Peters in disgust. 'Now summon Wells.'

The atmosphere was tense in the commissioner's room as they waited for the inspector to arrive. Henderson had been given a serious fright, but he was a reed in the wind, and was already bending to his new circumstances. He began to negotiate – offering snippets of information in return for leaving his name out of the report. Peters ignored him and went to the window, staring moodily into the yard outside.

Lonsdale chafed at the passing minutes, wondering what was happening at the Garraway, and no longer sure it could be stopped. What if the rot went deeper than Henderson and Wells, and the "higher authority" held other senior officers under his sway? Which way would the police jump if it came to a final confrontation?

There was a knock, and the duty sergeant opened the door. His expression was carefully neutral, but Lonsdale knew he had heard every word spoken. Was *he* in the killer's pay, and news of Henderson's capitulation was already on its way? He ushered in a small, slightly built man with dark hair and a moustache, who carried a bowler hat.

'Inspector Wells,' said Henderson. 'Please come in.'

'Wells?' gasped Lonsdale. 'It's *you* who's been following us!'

Wells looked shifty. 'No, I haven't.'

He was not even a very good liar, thought Lonsdale, as a light of understanding began to gleam in the back of his mind.

'You look like Maclean,' he said, 'but that's the point, isn't it?'

Wells's expression was genuinely bewildered. 'The escaped lunatic? What're you jabbering about? We look nothing alike – I've got ten years on him, for a start.'

But Lonsdale now knew exactly why Wells had been chosen to 'investigate' the murders – and it was not just because he was unlikely to solve them.

'How long have you had that moustache?' he demanded.

'Ages,' replied Wells shiftily, glancing at Henderson. 'It suits me.'

'It appeared about a month ago,' countered Peters, also beginning to understand. 'Around the same time that you started wearing a bowler rather than your usual cap. And yes, Lonsdale, it *was* roughly when Maclean escaped from Broadmoor.'

Wells glared at Henderson. 'Tell them, sir.'

'Tell them what?' asked Henderson slyly.

Wells scowled. 'That *you* suggested the moustache and bowler. You said they made me look like a proper detective.'

'You misremember,' said Henderson flatly. 'I'd never presume to lecture my officers on their personal appearance.'

'The killer is even more cunning than we thought,' said Lonsdale to Peters and Hulda. 'He wanted "Maclean" seen around London and used Wells to achieve it. Stead's urchins reported seeing Maclean at the scenes of the murders—'

'But it was Wells,' surmised Hulda. 'Who had every right to be there, of course, because they were his cases.'

'The killer also wanted us to think it was Maclean who was dogging our footsteps,' Lonsdale went on; he glanced at Wells. 'No doubt you were ordered to do it. Were you told to burn down the mortuary as well?'

He expected Wells to deny it, but the inspector was unnerved by the fact that Henderson had declined to defend him.

'*He* said I should.' Wells nodded at the commissioner. 'He sent me to persuade the doctors who looked at Shaw, Haldane, Tait and Bowyer to revise their reports, too, but we couldn't do that with Dickerson, because too many people saw the body. He said burning it was the only way to "eliminate confusing evidence". But I waited until everyone was out.'

The way he glared at the commissioner suggested that the original order might have included disposing of anyone who had witnessed the post-mortem as well. Henderson opened his mouth to deny it, but Wells forged on.

'It wasn't me who tried to push you into the road either. Henderson said it was in our country's best interests, and that important people would be grateful, but I drew the line at murder. He sent others instead.'

Henderson leapt to his feet to deny it, and a furious row ensued. Peters let it run, listening with contempt as they accused each other.

'Enough,' he snapped eventually. 'Now tell us about the Garraway Club.'

'*He* said never to go near it,' replied Wells. 'And that if my enquiries ever pointed in its direction, I was to tell him at once.'

'And did they point in its direction?' asked Peters, cutting across Henderson's response.

'Yes – I found out that some of the victims belonged to a society called the Watchers, which met there. *He* said he'd look into it personally.'

Peters turned to Henderson. 'And what did you discover?'

Henderson licked dry lips. 'Nothing – I've been too busy to—'

'Are you a Watcher?'

Henderson blinked his astonishment at the question. 'No! I'd never even heard of the society before Wells mentioned it. But I did intend to explore the—'

'Are you aware that some of its members are planning an atrocity today?' interrupted Lonsdale. 'Almost certainly at this club you've been so careful to shield?'

The startled expressions of both men made it clear they were not.

'Right,' said Peters briskly, unwilling to waste more time. 'Here's the situation: you're both guilty of conspiracy to murder and will answer for it, but you might escape the noose if you help us catch the man who corrupted you. I want his name.'

'But I don't know it!' cried Wells, frightened.

'Then I'll settle for a description.'

'I can't do that either!' wailed Wells. 'Most of my orders came via Henderson, and the few times I did meet the other fellow, it was always dark. However, he was a military man – I could hear it in his voice. And he said he has friends at the Palace. I followed him home once. He lives on Gordon Square.'

Lonsdale felt himself go weak at the knees. 'Humbage!'

Although Lonsdale was ready to race to Gordon Square at once, Peters took him and Hulda to an empty office to talk.

'Henderson won't have risked so much for just anyone,' he began. 'Therefore, Humbage must be powerful, resourceful and dangerous.'

'What of it?' demanded Lonsdale tightly.

'It means we must be sure of ourselves before challenging him, or he'll slip off the hook, and I won't see him walk free just because we're precipitous. I want hard evidence and I want men in place, lest he tries to run – *good* men, not Henderson's rabble.'

'But he may run if we don't corner him now,' objected Lonsdale. 'That sergeant heard every word we said. For all we know, he's already warned Humbage. We must go *now!*'

Peters considered. 'You go – monitor his house until I arrive with reinforcements. I'm sure I can trust you not to burst in on your own.' He gave Lonsdale a piercing look.

'How long will you be?' asked Hulda anxiously.

'Obviously, I need to deal with Henderson and Wells first. They're just as responsible for Hayes's death as he is, and I aim to make sure they don't escape in the interim.'

Lonsdale could see the sense in it, although every moment that Humbage was free seemed a travesty of justice.

'Then please hurry,' he said. 'We'll never forgive ourselves if he escapes, and whatever he has planned for today swings into action before we can stop it.'

Peters grabbed his arm as he turned to leave. 'Are you *sure* it's Humbage? There's no one else on Gordon Square who might be the culprit?'

'It's him,' said Lonsdale tiredly. 'And our experiences at Broadmoor prove it. He was the only one, other than Stead, who knew where we were going. He sent word ahead to Norris, telling him to make sure we never came back. Moreover, he ordered me not to explore the murders – *his* murders – any number of times.'

'He did,' nodded Hulda. 'He claimed our investigation might result in a scandal that would reflect badly on him.'

'But what reason can he have for killing all those men in so brutal a manner?' asked Peters, still sceptical.

'We can ask him when he's arrested,' said Lonsdale. 'Although I imagine the answer lies at the Garraway Club. As I keep saying: it's at the heart of everything.'

'Burnside,' said Hulda grimly. 'I've never been happy with his role in this affair – his opportune appearances, the fact that he's a liar, a Watcher, and bitter over his treatment after saving the Queen . . . If Humbage is involved, then Burnside will be his helpmeet.'

'What about Humbage's friends?' asked Peters. 'The courtiers – Lord Carlingford and Fleetwood-Pelham? I understand they're the reason why Humbage joined the Garraway in the first place.'

'They're not his friends, no matter how much he might wish

otherwise,' said Lonsdale. 'They barely know he exists. But we can discuss this later, when we have him in custody,'

'Then off you go. And mind he doesn't see you first.'

The city was busy as Hulda and Lonsdale left Whitehall Place. No shops were open, but every road teemed with people, and there was a buoyant, holiday atmosphere. Families toured the bright shop-window displays and bought hot chestnuts, spiced cakes, and cups of hot apple wine from street vendors. Lonsdale took one look at the traffic and, much to Hulda's disgust, decided it would be quicker to walk the mile and a half to Gordon Square.

His stomach churned as they went. He had resigned himself – with a speed that astonished him – to losing Anne, but he hated the notion of accusing her father of terrible crimes. Despite the break, he had no wish to see her hurt.

They weaved in and out of the merrymakers, and he was glad when they left the main roads and entered the quieter streets beyond. They reached the edge of Gordon Square, where he aimed for a shrubbery in the central garden that stood almost opposite Humbage's front door and provided an excellent vantage point.

'I hope Peters doesn't take long,' muttered Hulda, wincing as a soggy branch slapped into her face. 'This is no place for a lady.'

An hour passed. Lonsdale did not feel like talking, and was grateful that Hulda sensed it and did not press him. Then Humbage's door opened.

'He's leaving!' whispered Hulda in a strangled whisper. 'Now what?'

'No, it's Lady Gertrude,' Lonsdale whispered back. 'That's odd – she doesn't usually go out alone. Humbage is embarrassed of her and keeps her on a very short leash.'

'Then Humbage can't be home,' said Hulda, 'because look at her – she's virtually dancing along the road, like a naughty child escaping the nursery.'

It was true. There was a spring in Gertrude's step, and under her cloak she wore a gown that looked almost as old as she was, revealing a shockingly low-cut bodice. Lonsdale abandoned the shrubbery and set off after her. She laughed gaily when she saw him.

'Would you fetch me a carriage, dear? I'm off to Gloucester House to see Georgie.'

'Georgie?'

'Prince George, the Duke of Cambridge. He told me to drop in any time I was passing. Of course, that was thirty years ago, but I thought he might be lonely, as his mistress died recently. That's the mistress he took *after* he married his previous mistress, who was an actress.'

'Sir Gervais,' said Lonsdale when he could get a word in. 'Is he home?'

Gertrude raised her eyebrows. 'Do you think I could embark on a pleasant adventure if that killjoy was about? He left for Birmingham an hour ago, taking Agatha and the girls with him. He dismissed all the servants except the butler, who is to close the house and follow the family north. Poor souls! What a time to be cast out with nowhere to go.'

'Birmingham?' asked Lonsdale suspiciously. 'But he hates Birmingham – I heard him call it a blot on England's green and pleasant land.'

'Really? He told me that he arranged to spend Christmas there weeks ago.'

'He's lying. You know he was supposed to spend it with Jack and me. You were coming, too.'

'*I* still shall,' declared Gertrude firmly. 'But today, I'm off to Gloucester House.'

'Come back inside,' said Lonsdale, taking her arm. 'We need to work out where Humbage has really gone, because it isn't Birmingham. He said that to mislead everyone.'

Gertrude grimaced that her jaunt was to be abandoned before it had started but did as she was asked. In the house were signs of a very hasty departure, and it was clear that the family was not intending to return. Lonsdale experienced a pang of disquiet.

'No,' said Gertrude, reading his mind. 'Whatever my son-in-law has done in his quest to be noticed by "the right people" doesn't involve Agatha or the girls. They objected strongly to being whisked away – and to leaving me behind – but he overrode them.'

'What's going on here?' came an angry voice. It was the butler, immaculate as always, with a clean white apron over his dark suit.

'Deceit and betrayal, Taylor,' explained Gertrude crisply. 'Tell them what Gervais asked you to do once you had packed the spoons away.'

'More than just the spoons,' objected Taylor stiffly. 'But he told me to catch a train to Birmingham as soon as I finished, where he'll reimburse me the fare.'

'Poor Taylor,' said Gertrude pityingly. 'You've given us nigh on three decades of loyal service, but Gervais has no intention of meeting you in Birmingham, or anywhere else.'

Despite his antipathy for the butler, Lonsdale could not bear to watch his face as Gertrude told him what had happened. He began to search for clues as to where Humbage might have gone, but moments later he heard footsteps in the hallway. He braced himself to confront the man, but it was Jack, his face ashen.

'Where's Emelia?' he demanded hoarsely and waved a letter. 'She's broken with me – says we can never marry. Where is she? I want more than this meagre excuse for an explanation.'

'Gone,' replied Gertrude, and led him to a horsehair sofa where she repeated what she had just told Taylor. Lonsdale felt his brother's anguish but had no time to comfort him. He and Hulda continued their frantic search through Humbage's papers, hoping against hope to find a clue as to where he might have gone. After hesitating uncomfortably, Taylor joined in.

'And he has Emelia and Anne?' cried Jack when Gertrude had finished. 'Then we have to rescue them! We can't leave them in the hands of a killer!'

'He'd never hurt them,' said Gertrude soothingly. 'But yes, we should prise them away from him. All we need to do is find out where they are.'

She and Jack joined the others in their increasingly desperate hunt for clues.

'Look at this,' blurted Hulda suddenly, holding up a piece of gold-painted wood. 'The nameplate from the bottom of the painting in the Garraway – Lord Carlingford was furious when he saw someone had made off with it.'

Lonsdale frowned his bemusement. 'The first time I was in the Garraway, this read simply *The Watcher*.'

'What does it say now?' asked Jack.

'*The Watcher of the Dead*,' replied Lonsdale soberly. 'Humbage must've intended to put the amended version back but didn't have time. It's proof of his guilt!'

'It's proof of something, certainly,' said Jack. 'Hah! Look! Here's a letter from his brother. Strange! He always told me that Horace was a canon in Peterborough Cathedral, but it seems he's an accountant in Woking. I bet they've gone to him. Emelia told me that he and Humbage are close.'

'Go after them,' ordered Gertrude. 'Bring my girls home.'

'I don't believe Humbage went with them,' said Hulda, standing her ground. 'Too much is at stake. I think he's still in the city, seeing what might be salvaged from the pit he's dug for himself.'

'Then he'll have gone to the Garraway,' said Lonsdale. 'The hub of everything.'

'I'll go to Woking,' said Jack. 'I don't care about Humbage – just Emelia and Anne. You can stay here and corner him.'

'Then be careful,' warned Lonsdale worriedly. 'Hulda might be wrong – Humbage might well have decided to stay with his womenfolk.'

'This came for you,' said Jack, shoving a letter at Lonsdale. 'I opened it. It's from Galton – a rambling discourse on grass.'

Lonsdale scanned it quickly, then shoved it in his pocket. 'Someone needs to stay here and tell Peters what's happened. Hulda—'

'I'm going with you,' she stated, so determined that he knew he would never change her mind. 'Perhaps Lady Gertrude—'

'I'll tell the police what's happened,' said Taylor with quiet dignity. 'Sending me to Birmingham was unkind. It'll be revenge of sorts.'

'Then I'll go with Jack to Woking,' said Gertrude. 'Georgie's been waiting thirty years. He'll manage without me for a little longer.'

Although Lonsdale thought it would be quicker to walk than wait for a hansom on the crowded streets, Hulda disagreed. They flagged one down at the junction of Woburn Place and Russell Square, and made good time for a few minutes. Then an accident slowed them to a crawl. Lonsdale wanted to jump out and run, but Hulda argued that it would be quicker to stay.

'What happens when we get there?' asked Lonsdale, feeling his head ache with tension. 'It won't be as easy to watch the club as it was Humbage's house – there are too many exits.'

'He won't stay there long,' predicted Hulda. 'His fancy friends won't want anything to do with him once they realize what he's been doing, so he'll run – not to Woking, because he's not stupid, but to somewhere he'll never be found. I doubt even his helpmeet Burnside will know where to find him. We have to tackle him *now*.'

'But Peters told us—'

'Peters will be hot on our heels – Taylor will see to that. We're here! Come on.'

'We can't—' began Lonsdale, but she was already out of the hansom and hurrying through the club's front door. He ran after her, sure the duty porter would give her short shrift.

But the lobby was deserted, and the whole building was oddly silent. He recalled the notice that had been pinned on the dining-room door – that the place had been booked for a private function, and members were asked to stay away. *Whose* private function? Was it Humbage's, and was the atrocity spinning into action as they stood there wondering what to do?

'Heavens!' Hulda breathed as she opened the dining-room door.

It was an exact replica of the one in Buckingham Palace, complete with trees hanging from the ceiling, silver and gold streamers on every wall, and stacks of gaily wrapped presents. The tables were adorned with crisp white linen, and each place was set with silver cutlery and several glasses. It looked magnificent.

'Hark!' hissed Hulda, cocking her head to one side. 'Can you hear that?'

They inched towards the sound, which was coming from the room at the far end of the hall – a vestibule, where members left their hats, coats and umbrellas. There were also rows of lockable cupboards where more valuable items could be deposited. Lonsdale glanced behind him. Where was Peters?

At the far end of the vestibule was Humbage, rummaging frantically through one of the lockers. His face was flushed, and his agitation showed in his trembling hands and the number of belongings that had dropped on the floor.

'Humbage!' shouted Hulda.

Humbage barely gave her a glance before taking to his heels.

There followed a rather bizarre chase through the club, with Humbage pounding along with all the elegance of a rhinoceros, and

Hulda flying after him like a harpy. Lonsdale followed, yelling at them both to stop.

Humbage shot through the door at the far end of the vestibule, and they heard a rattle as he tried to lock it behind him. Lonsdale reached it before he could succeed, and Humbage darted off down a dimly lit corridor. He raced into the smoking room, then realized his mistake – there was only one way in or out. Lonsdale followed cautiously, aware that their quarry might be even more dangerous when he was cornered.

'You're a murderer!' declared Hulda, shoving past Lonsdale to stand with her hands on her hips. 'You killed seven good men – all members of this club – and persuaded the police to look the other way. You're despicable! You pretend to be upright and honourable, but you're just a common felon! The lowest of the low.'

Humbage gaped at her. 'What nonsense is this? And what are you doing in here anyway? It's a *gentlemen*'s club – women aren't allowed.'

Hulda laughed harshly. 'You kill, lie and deceive, but all you can do is bristle because I enter a male-only domain?'

'Why did you do it?' asked Lonsdale, before Humbage could respond. 'Why kill Tait, Dickerson and the others?'

'I haven't killed anyone,' stated Humbage indignantly.

'Prove it,' challenged Hulda.

'Why should I?' snapped Humbage. 'You're not the police. However, as I don't want my name printed in your nasty rag, I shall oblige you. I was with Jack when Haldane was killed – *ask* him. Tell me when the others died, and I no doubt have alibis for their deaths, too.'

'You were with Jack?' asked Lonsdale uncertainly.

Humbage regarded him smugly. 'You should've checked your facts before storming in and making unfounded allegations. Now get out!'

'Jack would have told us if that were true,' argued Hulda.

'Did you tell him exactly when Haldane died?' demanded Humbage arrogantly. 'And ask where *he* was at the time? No? Then go and do it now. Then come back and apologize to me.'

Lonsdale was beginning to wonder if they had made a serious mistake – Humbage would not use Jack as an alibi unless it was true, which meant he was not the killer. Yet Humbage, like Henderson and Wells, was not entirely innocent either.

'Then why did you keep telling me not to look into the murders?' he demanded.

'Because people who matter reminded me that no respectable man wants members of his family – even ones only related by prospective marriage – dabbling in that sort of thing.'

'What "people who matter"?' asked Hulda.

'The Palace,' replied Humbage shortly. 'Not that it's any of your business, madam. But they're right – murder is for the police to explore, not reporters.'

'But the police weren't doing their job,' argued Hulda. '"People who matter" told the commissioner to appoint an inept investigator, so the murders would never be solved. What you did, *sir*, is pervert the course of justice.'

'Rubbish! The police know the murders – if indeed they *are* murders, not natural deaths – are the work of rampaging cannibals. Your sanctimonious *Pall Mall Gazette* denies it, but *The Echo* prints the truth.'

'The cannibals are innocent,' stated Lonsdale. 'Although the killer certainly wanted them blamed. You denounce me for dabbling in murky waters, but you've done the bidding of a madman with a panga!'

'You and Burnside,' put in Hulda. 'We know he's involved, too.'

'I've done nothing of the kind,' snapped Humbage. 'I know nothing of any madmen, and if by Burnside you mean that scruffy commoner, then you're insane yourselves – a man like me doesn't associate with mere photographers.'

'Then why have you sent your wife and daughters to Woking and dismissed all the servants?' pounced Lonsdale, pointing at the bags in Humbage's hands, which he imagined would contain his valuables.

'Birmingham,' corrected Humbage, although the flash of unease in his eyes betrayed him. 'But what did you expect? We can hardly join you in Cleveland Square now that Anne and Emelia have broken off their engagements. I like Birmingham, so I decided to take Agatha and the girls there until the new year.'

'You called it a blot on England's green and pleasant land,' countered Lonsdale. 'You sent them to Woking.'

Humbage glared at him. 'Very well, I did. However, I lied to prevent *you* from following them and begging Anne to reconsider. She wants nothing more to do with you.'

'And how do you explain the nameplate you stole?' persisted
Lonsdale. 'Carlingford was livid when he realized someone
had unscrewed it.'

'Lord!' gulped Humbage. 'Was he? I aimed to have it mended and
put back before anyone noticed, but with all that's happened . . .'

'Mended?' asked Hulda suspiciously.

'The title was *The Watcher*, but some degenerate came along
and added *of the Dead*. I didn't like it, so I took it home to put it
right.'

He had an answer for everything, but Lonsdale was beginning to
accept that he was more fool than criminal – one who cared more
about his reputation than justice and truth.

'None of this explains why you ran away from us,' said Hulda,
persisting anyway. 'The innocent don't do that.'

Humbage regarded her with dislike. 'I had a feeling something
peculiar was unfolding, and I didn't want to be associated with it,
even though any role I played was unwitting. It seemed sensible to
disappear for a few weeks until the dust had settled.'

Hulda was unimpressed. 'Who are "the people who matter", who
told you to stop us from investigating?'

'It was a friend,' replied Humbage stiffly. 'One who deserves my
loyalty, so ask me no more, because I shan't tell you.'

'You protect a killer?' demanded Hulda. 'What a twisted morality
you have! This person murdered the Archbishop of Canterbury, not
to mention poor Professor Dickerson and the others. They were
good men, who wanted to make the world a better place.'

'My friend didn't kill them, any more than I did,' stated Humbage
firmly. 'But this discussion is over. If you have any sense, you'll
walk out and forget any of this ever happened. I'll persuade my
friend that you meant no harm.'

'He won't believe you, and then there will be yet more victims
on his tally,' said Hulda. 'He's already ordered his minions to
dispatch us twice.'

Humbage looked as though he rather wished the minions had
succeeded. 'I repeat: let the matter drop. You can go back to dabbling
in the gutters, and I can get on with securing a royal appointment.'

'Is *that* why you've aided and abetted a killer?' breathed Hulda,
shaking her head. 'For a position at court? My God! I knew you
were ambitious, but—'

'Lord Carlingford,' interrupted Lonsdale heavily. 'The man you call your friend, even though he barely knows you exist. He's the killer and you're protecting him.'

'How dare you impugn him!' cried Humbage. 'He's a man of the utmost integrity.'

'What's going on here?' came an angry voice from the door. 'Who's talking about me? And you, Humphrey, why have you brought a woman into our domain?'

It was Carlingford, and he held his gun.

FIFTEEN

L onsdale slumped, wishing he had waited for Peters, rather than charging in to confront a killer they knew was ruthless, powerful and determined. Now he and Hulda were at his mercy, and who knew when Peters would arrive? It was no small matter to assemble a squad of men – and that was assuming all went according to plan with Henderson and Wells. There was a lot that could go wrong – Henderson seizing back control, for a start. Why had he let Hulda charge into the Garraway like a bull at a fence?

'So it *is* you,' said Hulda softly. 'It all makes sense now.'

'What's me?' demanded Carlingford, and Lonsdale saw his face redden as his temper began to erupt – the same temper that had seen him take potshots at 'burglars'. It did not bode well for a peaceful resolution to the confrontation.

'I didn't bring them here, Carlingford,' gushed Humbage.

'Who did then?' demanded Carlingford hotly.

'They must have sneaked in while you and the others were in the kitchen. I did suggest it was unwise to leave the front door unattended—'

'Then you should have used your common sense and minded it yourself, Humber,' snarled Carlingford. 'Although *you* have no business being here either. I told everyone to stay away today except Watchers. You all agreed.'

'To do what?' asked Lonsdale, forcing himself not to cringe when the gun swung towards him. 'What atrocity has your nasty sect planned?'

'Atrocity?' echoed Carlingford indignantly. 'Nasty sect? For your information, we've reserved the club to feed the poor – a sumptuous Christmas feast in luxurious surroundings that will bring joy into their miserable lives.'

'Patronizing devil!' muttered Hulda. 'And a liar, too.'

'My daughter is no longer engaged to this man, Lord Carlingford,' said Humbage with an ingratiating smile. 'His presence here has nothing to do with me. Now, perhaps you and I—'

'Quit your sycophantic babbling, you ridiculous fool,' snapped Carlingford, 'and tell me what they think I've done.'

'Murdered Tait, Dickerson and the others,' explained Humbage, manfully overlooking the insult. 'They're fools, not worthy of our time. Shall we toss them out and—'

'*What?*' cried Carlingford. 'What asinine logic led them to that conclusion?'

Lonsdale would have admitted to making a mistake in the hope of wriggling out of their predicament, but Hulda was too straight-forward for her own good.

'Because the killer is influential, persuasive and powerful,' she replied promptly. 'Someone who can sway a Commissioner of Police and the Broadmoor staff.' She sneered at Humbage, who curled his lip back at her. '*And* pathetic creatures like him – he's been scrabbling to do your bidding for weeks.'

Carlingford blinked. 'Has he? How?'

'By ordering Lonsdale not to investigate the murders,' stated Hulda with such bristling defiance that Lonsdale was sure it would see them shot there and then. 'The fool worships you and will do anything to win your favour – and the benefits it will bring.'

'I don't!' objected Humbage, then grimaced. 'I mean I admire you, of course, Lord Carlingford, but wanting your friendship has nothing to do with hoping you'll recommend me for a post at court.'

'Good – because I'd rather endorse an ape.' Carlingford swivelled back to Hulda. 'I assure you, madam, if I'd known Lonsdale was investigating these terrible murders, I'd have encouraged him to continue, not ordered him to stop. That bastard has slaughtered seven fellow Watchers, which is why I've taken to carrying a gun – to protect myself.'

'I didn't know *you* were a Watcher,' gushed Humbage. 'I'd have applied to join myself had I—'

'You would've been rejected,' said Carlingford bluntly. 'Shaw, Tait, Haldane, Dickerson, Bowyer, Gurney and Hayes were fine, generous, noble-minded men. Indeed, it was their idea to feed the poor today. Two hundred of them. We've been planning it for months, to show what the Watchers are capable of. London will never forget it and others will be inspired to follow our example.'

Lonsdale frowned at the choice of words, recalling the letter he had found in Dickerson's house – the one in different writing from those penned by Grim Death. 'Did you write all this in a letter to Dickerson?'

'I wrote it to *all* the Watchers – encouraged them to make a sacrifice of their very souls to our Great Lord.'

'What Great Lord?' asked Lonsdale uneasily.

'Why, Jesus Christ, of course,' replied Carlingford irritably. 'There is no other. He made the ultimate sacrifice to redeem the world, and we must emulate His example – not with blood, obviously, but with our money and time.'

'Do the other Watchers share your convictions?'

'Yes – all are devout men. Of course, not everyone thought the feast was the best idea. Gurney, for example, wanted to build a refuge for retired horses instead.'

Which was why he had expressed his anger about it to his secretary Olive, thought Lonsdale. And he and Hulda had misinterpreted everything – the 'great event' was not something terrible, but something Gurney considered less important than the rescue of animals.

'This is hardly an "unspeakable happening",' said Hulda sceptically, 'which is how Grimaldi d'Atte described the Watchers' Christmas celebrations in a letter to Professor Dickerson.'

'The "unspeakable happening" is tomorrow,' said Carlingford shortly. 'And refers to the birth of Jesus Christ. Perhaps "unspeakable" was the wrong word to use, but d'Atte is Italian, and his English can be eccentric.'

'It was all about Christmas?' asked Lonsdale, running through what he could recall of the letters in his mind and supposing they could be interpreted in the light of Christian symbolism. But he and Hulda had assumed the worst and it had misled them badly.

'We Watchers may be a disparate, ill-matched rabble, but we all have a deep religious faith. Why do you think we had an archbishop as our head?'

'We didn't know Tait led you,' said Lonsdale lamely.

'Well, he did, and when he was torn from us, we voted unanimously to continue his work. Of course, then we lost Bowyer, Haldane, Dickerson, Gurney and Hayes, which has left us seriously short-handed. Thank God for Burnside – he's been a marvel.'

'I'm sure Sir Algernon has been a boon, too,' gushed Humbage. 'A more worthy gentleman doesn't exist – other than yourself, of course.'

'Fleetwood-Pelham isn't a Watcher,' said Carlingford curtly. 'He wanted to join, but he didn't meet our requirements.'

'He was rejected?' blurted Lonsdale, and reached into his pocket, where he had stuffed the letter Galton had sent about the watcher-grass. In it, the great man had identified the sub-species and the region where it grew.

'Yes – in November,' replied Carlingford. 'He's a pleasant enough chap, but we don't recruit men for being nice. We want ones who are prepared to act on their moral convictions without desire for recognition or reward.'

'Then why elect Burnside?' asked Hulda doubtfully. 'He's spent the last eight months demanding favour for saving the Queen.'

'That was Shaw's doing – he got him in while I was away, assuming he acted out of loyalty to the Crown. But Burnside has redeemed himself in my eyes these last few days, by working tirelessly to decorate the hall.'

But Lonsdale was still thinking about the grass, because everything had suddenly become horribly clear.

'The killer,' he blurted. 'It's Fleetwood-Pelham!'

'Rubbish!' cried Humbage. 'He's a courtier – a Groom-in-Waiting, no less.'

'And Mr Morley's friend,' put in Hulda more quietly. 'Mr Morley wouldn't associate with a murderer.'

'Fleetwood-Pelham mentioned the friendship,' countered Lonsdale, 'Mr Morley didn't. And it was a lie, aimed to make us more favourably disposed towards him.'

'No, I agree with Humberg,' said Carlingford. 'Fleetwood-Pelham isn't a killer. He was in the army, for God's sake.'

Lonsdale waved the letter. 'The grass left on the bodies is called Watchers of the Dead. Francis Galton has identified that particular variety as endemic to Zululand – and Fleetwood-Pelham was in the Zulu war. He had other keepsakes from that region in his rooms, although most came from India and Bhutan.'

'The comb!' exclaimed Hulda. 'He bought it after the battle of Ulundi, where the Zulus were crushed.'

'But thousands of men fought at Ulundi,' Carlingford pointed out. 'Your "evidence" is flawed.'

'But thousands of men don't have an interest in horticulture and a glasshouse for growing exotic species,' countered Lonsdale, recalling how quickly Fleetwood-Pelham had drawn the curtains when Hulda had tried to look outside. 'Moreover, consider his rank and connections – I imagine *he* was the one who whispered orders in Humbage's receptive ear.'

Humbage scowled. 'Yes, he did tell me the Palace would appreciate me urging you to abandon your enquiries, but that doesn't mean that—'

'And we now know his motive,' interrupted Lonsdale. 'The victims basically told him he was a lesser man than them.'

'I was rather hoping you'd never guess,' came a soft voice from behind them. 'Now I'll have to kill you, too.'

It was Fleetwood-Pelham, and with him were the five men who had tried to push Lonsdale and Hulda under the omnibus. All were armed.

The courtier acted quickly and decisively. Carlingford was ordered to drop his weapon, then all four prisoners were made to sit in upright chairs, where they were bound with cords from the curtains. When they were immobile, Fleetwood-Pelham tucked his gun into his trouser belt, which was when Lonsdale saw the panga.

He studied the Groom-in-Waiting's face – the great domed forehead above the tiny chin, rendering him benign and vaguely comical. But there was nothing amusing about his eyes, which were cold, hard and calculating.

Hulda sat stiff and angry, frantically trying to devise a way to escape. Carlingford was full of indignant disbelief, while Humbage was frightened and bewildered. Lonsdale took a deep breath, calming himself with the knowledge that Peters was coming. Fleetwood-Pelham read his mind.

'Don't expect rescue. Peters will be on his way to Birmingham by now.'

'He won't,' countered Lonsdale. 'Humbage's butler will have told him the truth.'

'Taylor?' asked Fleetwood-Pelham smugly. 'He's been in my pay for weeks, making sure Humbage here did as he was told.'

'Taylor would never betray me,' said Humbage in a strangled voice. 'He's been with the family for years.'

Fleetwood-Pelham smiled. 'Yes, but he's weak, ambitious and greedy. Such men are easy prey. I did the same with Henderson, Wells and Norris.'

'Who's Norris?' asked Carlingford, more angry than fearful at the situation in which he found himself.

'He wants the medical superintendent's job at Broadmoor,' replied Fleetwood-Pelham. 'I offered to arrange it for him in exchange for . . . certain services.'

'Arranging Maclean's escape and, later, getting rid of us,' said Lonsdale, and glanced at Humbage. 'And it was *you* who told him we were going there.'

'Norris failed me, unfortunately,' Fleetwood-Pelham went on, while Humbage refused to meet Lonsdale's eyes. 'Just as Wells failed me when I told him to burn down the mortuary with several inconvenient witnesses and Dickerson inside it. I'll pay each a visit when I finish here.'

'Taylor would never—' repeated Humbage hoarsely.

'Well, he did,' interrupted Fleetwood-Pelham. 'For fifty pounds – the same sum I paid Wells for doing my bidding. Others, like you and Henderson, I won with promises of royal favour. But the upshot is that Peters won't be coming.'

'I can't believe this is happening to me,' said Humbage unsteadily. 'Why? What have I ever done to deserve such a fate?'

No one bothered to answer him. Fleetwood-Pelham smirked at Lonsdale and Hulda. 'I've arranged for Henderson to resume command. You'll disappear today, but his officers will make no great effort to find you – not when your removal represents a solution to all his problems.'

'Not even Henderson can overlook more murders in the Garraway,' argued Hulda hotly, 'especially now word of his dubious probity will be all over Scotland Yard.'

'Murder?' echoed Fleetwood-Pelham in mock horror. 'Who said anything about murder? In an hour, poor, silly Humbage will accidentally set his chair alight with a cigar. The whole club will burn down and your bodies will never be identified.'

'In an hour?' cried Carlingford. 'But our paupers will be here then, eating.'

Fleetwood-Pelham's smile was unsettling. 'Then what a pity the Watchers will be forever associated with that terrible tragedy. The doors will be locked and *no one* will escape, including all the remaining Watchers.'

'You will kill more than two hundred people for *spite*?' breathed Hulda, shocked. 'Because you wanted to be a Watcher and they rejected you?'

Fleetwood-Pelham's eyes flashed dangerously. 'My name was put forward at the same time as Burnside's. *Burnside* – a rogue who aimed to profit from disarming the lunatic who tried to shoot the Queen. They chose him and refused me. It was a deliberate insult to my name and honour. It couldn't be overlooked.'

'Shaw proposed Burnside,' said Lonsdale, as more answers snapped clear in his mind.

Fleetwood-Pelham sniffed. 'And he was seconded by Haldane and Bowyer. Then it was my turn, but four men had written letters of objection: Tait, Gurney, Dickerson—'

'And me,' finished Carlingford heavily. 'My God, man, you're mad! And why kill in such a violent, brutal manner? Was that really necessary?'

'I would've preferred something less messy, but it was the only way to ensure Dickerson's cannibals bore the blame,' replied Fleetwood-Pelham, and removed the panga from his belt. 'It worked, with a little help from certain newspapers. And before you ask, I killed Hayes because he was conducting an investigation on the sly.'

'But this is—' began Carlingford angrily.

'I shan't need this any more,' said Fleetwood-Pelham, and tossed the panga in a corner. 'The fire will do all I require.'

He began to pile kindling against Humbage's chair.

'They were wrong to reject you,' said Humbage quickly, watching his preparations in alarm. 'You *are* a more honourable man than

Burnside. Than all of them. I've always thought so. Let me go and I'll make sure everyone knows it.'

'His honour wasn't the issue though, was it?' asked Hulda of Carlingford. 'It was his love of gossip – the fact that Watchers' deeds would no longer be secret.'

Carlingford scowled. 'We couldn't elect a member who can't keep his mouth shut. And don't say you do, because look at what's in today's *Pall Mall Gazette* – a full report on the Queen's Christmas travel arrangements, which was highly classified information.'

'He even gave me the itinerary,' put in Hulda.

'I don't see why good deeds need to be furtive,' grumbled Fleetwood-Pelham. 'Why not take the credit for what you do?'

'Because we're *Watchers*,' snapped Carlingford. 'We *watch* silently, then *act* silently. We don't bray about what we do.'

He glanced up at the painting of the angel that hung on the wall – the silent Watcher with its hauntingly beautiful expression. Lonsdale recalled the pictures in Fleetwood-Pelham's rooms, and wondered why he had not realized sooner that *The Watcher* was his work.

'Changing the nameplate was a risk,' he remarked. 'From *The Watcher* to *The Watcher of the Dead*. If Humbage hadn't taken it home to mend . . .'

Fleetwood-Pelham laughed harshly. 'It was my little joke, as was leaving a piece of African grass behind. I knew no one was clever enough to understand its significance, and I was right.'

He turned on his heel and walked out.

Fleetwood-Pelham's men began to heap logs and coal in places where flames would leap from them to the curtains and the wood-panelled walls. Lonsdale had no doubt that the room would be an inferno within moments of a match being set to the kindling. After receiving a hefty punch apiece for trying to talk, he and Carlingford fell silent. Humbage began to weep, while Hulda sat stiff and proud, defiance in every bone.

Behind his back, Lonsdale struggled frantically with the rope, although it was so tight his hands and feet were numb. In his pocket he had the dinosaur claw, sharp from its use in Broadmoor, but he could not reach it – and nor could anyone else pull it out without the guards seeing. He glanced at Hulda, wondering if she had a plan, but when she met his gaze, he saw only angry helplessness.

Then the clock struck noon and there was a low rumble. At first, Lonsdale could not place the sound, but then he realized it was the Watchers' paupers being led along the hallway and into the dining room. The rumble quickly turned to a babble of excited voices as the guests began to avail themselves of the refreshments.

'Two hundred people!' cried Carlingford in despair. 'We *can't* let him murder innocents who came here on trust!'

One of the guards strode towards him, fist raised, but the door opened and Fleetwood-Pelham was back. The henchman let his hand drop to his side.

'They're here,' the courtier said pleasantly. 'Twice as many as you invited, because word of free victuals spread, and your Watcher friends aren't man enough to turn interlopers away. But all the better for me. The Watchers will be blamed for slaughtering *four* hundred beggars, and the name will live in infamy forever.'

'Please, no!' breathed Carlingford, ashen. 'These folk have done nothing to harm you.'

Fleetwood-Pelham turned to his men. 'I've locked all the doors, while we took care of the windows last night. We're ready. Light the fire.'

'*No!*' screamed Humbage, struggling frantically. 'You can't kill me! I did what you asked. Please let me go! I'll be your man, and I promise never to expect anything in return.'

'Tempting,' said Fleetwood-Pelham drily. 'But only a fool trusts your kind, and no one could ever accuse me of stupidity.'

He nodded to his men. Four left at once, while the last touched a taper to the kindling around Humbage's chair. Humbage struggled so violently that Lonsdale was sure his heart would burst. There was a wisp of smoke, then the kindling began to crackle. The henchman hurried out, although Fleetwood-Pelham paused to glance back.

'Inhale the smoke,' he advised. 'It will be an easier death than the flames.'

He left, and they heard the door lock behind him.

'Help me!' howled Humbage, as flames began to lick around his trousers. He leaned back and waved his legs in the air like an over-turned beetle.

'The claw!' Lonsdale yelled at Hulda, twisting so that his pocket was within her reach. 'Get the claw and give it to me.'

She understood instantly, and within seconds it was in his hand. He began to saw, heart pounding when he could not gain proper purchase and the flames around Humbage licked higher. Terrified, Humbage kicked his legs so violently that his chair tipped over backwards.

Lonsdale felt the claw slippery in his fingers, although whether from blood or sweat, he could not tell. Then the cord began to part. He pulled with all his might, and felt it snap. The rope dropped to the floor. He freed his legs, then untied Hulda. She snatched the claw.

'Get the panga and smash the door,' she ordered, going to hack through Carlingford's bonds. 'Hurry!'

Lonsdale hauled Humbage away from the flames first, then ran to where Fleetwood-Pelham had tossed his murder weapon. He grabbed it and aimed for the door, swinging at it with all his might. But the door was old, hard and thick, and the weapon made scant impact. Carlingford jostled him out of the way, and began flailing at it with a chair, although that was no more effective than the panga.

'Don't stop!' bellowed Hulda, when Lonsdale and Carlingford paused, both realizing that their efforts were futile.

'The window!' gasped Lonsdale, eyes smarting as the smoke thickened. 'We can climb through the window.'

'Nailed shut,' rasped Humbage, who had raced to examine it the moment he was free. 'Keep hitting the door. Someone will hear and come to save us.'

'They won't,' said Carlingford tautly. 'Our guests are making too much noise.'

It was true, and Lonsdale could hear the racket they were making even above the roar and crackle of flames. He looked around frantically, unwilling to stand by while innocents died, just because decent men had fallen foul of Fleetwood-Pelham's pride.

He hurried to the window, but Humbage was right – it would not budge. In frustration, he hurled a chair at it, but it had leaded panes that refused to break. He persisted though, determined not to die like Humbage, who had retrieved the gun Carlingford had dropped, and was preparing to use it on himself.

Then the door flew open with such force that Carlingford was sent staggering backwards. Peters stood there, Burnside on one side and Voules – of all people – on the other.

'The flames!' shouted Lonsdale, feeling explanations could come later. 'Douse the flames. And evacuate the building.'

'Rip down the curtains before they catch light,' Peters ordered his men. 'Voules – get water.'

The next few moments were a blur of frantic activity as everyone hastened to obey. A few guests came to see what was happening and found themselves drafted into lugging buckets of water from the kitchen; with so many willing hands, the fire was soon extinguished. Lonsdale leaned against the wall, coughing and rubbing his smarting eyes.

'You owe me, Lonsdale,' said Voules with one of his irritating smirks. 'Peters would be halfway to Birmingham by now if I hadn't stopped him.'

'It's true,' said Peters. 'We were given false information by Humbage's butler, but Voules had followed you here. He smelled a rat when a lot of beggars began to gather outside and ran to Scotland Yard. He caught us just as we were leaving for the railway station.'

'The rat wasn't the paupers,' snarled Carlingford furiously. 'It was that damned Fleetwood-Pelham. Where is he?'

Peters nodded down the corridor where the courtier was being held by two officers. He was talking to them, and Lonsdale was sure he was using his slippery tongue to bribe them into letting him go. He started to shout a warning, but Humbage still had Carlingford's gun. Everyone jumped as he aimed it and fired. Fleetwood-Pelham sagged between the officers, then fell to the floor amid a spreading stain of red.

'What did you do that for?' demanded Peters, shocked. 'He was under arrest.'

'For justice,' replied Humbage stiffly. 'He deserved it.'

EPILOGUE

Neither Lonsdale nor Hulda felt much like celebrating Christmas after the events at the Garraway Club. They were weary, battered and reeked of smoke. They went to their respective homes, where Hulda spent the rest of the day trying to scrub the stench from her hair, and Lonsdale slept for ten hours straight.

The following week was busy for them both, with Lonsdale taking over Milner's editorial duties, and Hulda doing the work of two reporters. Peters gave them permission to write up the Watchers of the Dead case, as he referred to it, but they had done no more than gather their notes before Stead came to tell them it would never appear in print.

'Why not?' Hulda demanded.

'Fleetwood-Pelham may be dead, but his reputation must remain unsullied because of his connection to the Queen,' replied the assistant editor sourly. 'The Prime Minister himself asked Mr Morley not to run the story, because of the damage it might do to the monarchy.'

'Justice!' spat Hulda in disgust. 'Perhaps Humbage was right to shoot him – he doubtless would've walked free otherwise, to kill again out of pettiness and spite.'

Lonsdale invited Hulda to see in the New Year with him and Jack – and with Lady Gertrude, who was staying with them until her old friend the Duke of Cambridge found her more appropriate accommodation. He had been delighted to renew their friendship after so many years, and she was looking forward to a far more interesting life than the one Humbage had allowed her.

The four of them sat around the dining-room table, where the staff, openly delighted that there were to be no Miss Humbages in their future, had provided a sumptuous feast.

'Hark at them!' exclaimed Gertrude, cocking her head at the sounds of merriment that emanated from the kitchen below. 'It can't all be because my granddaughters are out of the picture, so it must be because Voules has asked Sybil to marry him.'

'She hasn't accepted, has she?' breathed Lonsdale, horrified.

'Of course not! She can do a lot better than Voules, even if he did save your lives. He'll want something in return, you know. How will you repay him?'

'I already have,' said Lonsdale. 'He was dismissed from *The Echo* because he spied for a rival paper, so I persuaded Ingram to take him on the staff of *The Illustrated London News*. Ingram won't know what's hit him!'

'Have you heard from your family at all, Lady Gertrude?' fished Hulda.

'Only to say they won't be returning to the city for the foreseeable future. Agatha and the girls will stay in Woking, while Gervais has taken a post with the 24th Punjabi Infantry Regiment, which will keep him looking over his shoulder in a very unsettled Kandahar. I don't anticipate meeting him again. He's lucky Inspector Peters looked the other way while he boarded a ship, because he did shoot a man in cold blood.'

'And he aided and abetted a killer,' said Lonsdale. 'Maybe not knowingly, but he should've asked why Fleetwood-Pelham wanted a murder enquiry suppressed.'

'That would have required original thought,' said Gertrude smugly. 'And Gervais isn't very good at that.'

'Poor Em,' sighed Jack, who had recovered even more quickly than Lonsdale from his broken engagement and had already noticed that one of his legal colleagues had a very pretty daughter. 'She must be devastated. Anne, too. They looked up to Humbage.'

Hulda grinned wickedly. 'At least they dropped you *before* Christmas, which spared you from the need to provide them with expensive gifts.'

'Lord!' muttered Lonsdale. 'I'd forgotten all about that. I got *you* something, though.'

The box of pens was produced and admired, and Lonsdale found himself thinking that perhaps Anne was no great loss after all. Next to Hulda, she was staid and colourless, and although Hulda could be exasperating and irritating, she was never dull. Eventually, the discussion turned back to the Watchers.

'It was not some dark and dangerous plot after all,' said Hulda.

'Just one man irked that he was rejected from a secret society while someone he deemed inferior was elected. It was all rather banal.'

'Fleetwood-Pelham murdered seven good men,' said Jack soberly. 'London will be the poorer without them, although Carlingford and Burnside have vowed to continue what they started.'

'Dear old Carly,' said Gertrude. 'He's a curmudgeonly old devil, but there's a heart of gold under all that angry bluster. And I like young Burnside, although I hope he realizes that his heroics at the Garraway still won't win him a royal commission. Carly never rewards anyone for doing what he considers to be his duty.'

Hulda winced. 'I misjudged Burnside. And Roth.'

Lonsdale agreed. 'I had a letter from Roth yesterday, sent from Southampton before they sailed. His Khoikhoi friends are delighted to be going home. Ingram is storing Dickerson's collections until Roth comes back – he looked inside some of the boxes and tells me that the Natural History Museum will inherit many fabulous artefacts.'

'Speaking of the museum, did you ever hand over that claw?' asked Hulda.

Lonsdale nodded. 'It'll go on display in the spring, as part of a massive new dinosaur exhibition. Owen says dead dinosaurs are a lot safer than live cannibals.'

'Not according to *The Echo*,' chuckled Jack. 'Voules's final story was that the museum released a herd of Megalosaurus on Hampstead Heath.'

'*The Echo*!' spat Hulda in distaste. 'It created panic about Maclean's escape and blamed innocent Khoikhoi for the murders. It's an irresponsible rag and should be closed down.'

'Fleetwood-Pelham arranged for all that to be published,' said Lonsdale, 'to draw attention away from his own crimes. And Maclean never did escape, of course.'

'He didn't?' asked Jack, startled.

'He was safely in Broadmoor the whole time,' explained Lonsdale. 'Peters told us. Fleetwood-Pelham promised to give Orange's job to Norris if Maclean "escaped". So Norris put Maclean in a solitary-confinement cell, minded by guards in his pay, and told the world that he was on the loose.'

'Eventually, Norris planned to "catch" Maclean himself – the final nail in Orange's coffin,' finished Hulda. 'Instead, he'll be charged with kidnapping and perverting the course of justice. I don't know if he'll go to prison, but he'll certainly never run one.'

'And there was nothing suspicious in the fact that Tait and Dickerson went to Broadmoor shortly before Maclean's escape,' said Lonsdale. 'Mr Morley was right – Tait went because he had an interest in prison reform, while Dickerson went to assess Ashe's Ashanti spears – and took the opportunity to make helpful suggestions to Orange while he was there.'

'There *was* something suspicious in the fact that Voules went there, though,' said Hulda. 'It was actually Wells, visiting to connive with Norris.'

'So there we are,' said Gertrude, sitting back in her chair. 'Fleetwood-Pelham is dead, and all those who helped him are punished in one way or another, whether by gaol, disgrace or banishment. And the time is one minute to midnight. It's nearly eighteen eighty-three.'

'I wonder what the new year will bring,' mused Hulda, and smiled at Lonsdale. 'Something good, I hope.'

Lonsdale reached out to take her hand in his. 'I'm sure of it.'

HISTORICAL NOTE

In 1882, *The Pall Mall Gazette* was a small but influential London newspaper. Its editor was John Morley (1838–1923), a much-respected intellectual and political commentator, called 'the last of the great nineteenth-century Liberals'. Morley left *The PMG* in 1883 after being elected to Parliament. He later served twice in the Cabinet as Chief Secretary for Ireland, having drily informed Prime Minister Gladstone that if he could manage Stead, then he could manage Ireland; he was also twice Secretary of State for India, and was created Viscount Morley in 1908, after which he became Lord President of the Council.

One of Morley's first moves as editor had been to hire the Liberal firebrand W.T. Stead (1849–1912), from *The Northern Echo* of Darlington, to serve as his assistant editor. Stead later succeeded Morley as editor. Over the next seven years his 'New Journalism' introduced many innovations and demonstrated how the press could be used to influence government policy in the creation of child welfare and social legislation – what Stead called 'Government by Journalism'. In 1890, he founded and became editor of the monthly *Review of Reviews*, a position he held until his death; he was one of those who went down on *Titanic* in 1912.

Under Morley and Stead, the staff of *The PMG* was one of the most remarkable in the history of the press. Alfred Milner (1854–1925) served as a reporter and then assistant editor, before turning to a career as a politician and colonial administrator. He was High Commissioner for South Africa and Governor of the Cape Colony, a member of the War Cabinet during World War I, Secretary of State for War, and Secretary of State for the Colonies. He was knighted in 1895 and created Viscount Milner in 1902.

Hulda Friederichs (1856–1927) initially joined *The PMG* as Stead's personal assistant, but then became the first woman journalist in London to be engaged on exactly the same terms as male members of staff. In 1896, she became editor of the *Westminster Budget*. She later wrote biographies of several important British figures of the time.

The PMG continued publication until 1923, when it was absorbed into the *Evening Standard*. *The Echo*, which existed from 1868 to 1905, was London's first halfpenny evening newspaper; although not considered one of the 'quality' newspapers, it was not the sensational rag presented in *Watchers of the Dead*.

The Illustrated London News, the world's first illustrated news magazine, was founded by Herbert Ingram in 1842. His son William (1847–1924) later took control. It appeared weekly until 1971. William Ingram's sister was named Ada. She married Albert 'Monkey' Hornby (1847–1925), one of only two men ever to captain England at both cricket and rugby. Unfortunately, in August 1882, his cricket team had suffered a shocking defeat to Australia, a match that, due to an 'obituary' for English cricket published in the *Sporting Times*, gave birth to what is today known as The Ashes.

Many of the events mentioned in *Watchers of the Dead* actually occurred. On 2 March 1882, Roderick Maclean attempted to shoot Queen Victoria. On 19 April that year, a jury found him 'not guilty, but insane' after only five minutes deliberation. He was sent to Broadmoor Criminal Lunatic Asylum, where he remained until his death in 1921. The verdict prompted Queen Victoria to demand a change in the law so that similar cases could be adjudged 'guilty, but insane'. The act allowing this was passed the following year.

Contemporary drawings show Maclean as a slight, bowler-hatted man. He really did believe that the colour blue had been created for him and that he had a special relationship with God. It later emerged that he had been deeply offended when the Queen had neglected to show due admiration for a poem he had written for her.

James Burnside was a photographer who helped disarm Maclean, while two Eton boys flailed at the would-be assassin with their umbrellas. Maclean was arrested by Superintendent Hayes of the Windsor Police. Burnside spent the rest of his life demanding recognition for what he had done and grew bitterly resentful when the Palace declined to help his failing business.

The Queen did open the Royal Courts of Justice on 4 December 1882. However, there was no formal ceremony at the Natural History Museum, then known as the British Museum (Natural History) – the doors were just thrown wide and the public walked in. This, though, was in April 1882, not December 1882. The first superintendent of the museum was Richard Owen (1804–92), called 'director' in *Watchers of the Dead* to avoid confusion with other characters who had the title of superintendent. In 1884 Owen was succeeded by Dr (later Sir) William Henry Flower (1831–99).

Gilbert and Sullivan's *Iolanthe* opened on 25 November 1882, as the first work to premier at the Savoy Theatre. Alice Barnett (1846–1901) was the Queen of the Fairies.

Francis Galton (1822–1911) was one of the great gentleman-scientists of his generation. He had travelled in Africa and later achieved prominence for his investigations into heredity and genetics. The originator of the concept of eugenics, he also founded psychometrics and was one of the fathers of fingerprinting.

He and the famed explorer Henry Morton Stanley (1841–1904) despised each other and had a long-running feud that began after Stanley famously 'found' David Livingstone. The British geographical establishment objected to Stanley who, in Galton's words, was 'a journalist aiming at producing sensational articles'. Key members of the Royal Geographical Society portrayed Stanley negatively for decades thereafter.

Most of the murder victims were significant individuals in real life. Archibald Campbell Tait, the Archbishop of Canterbury, did die on 3 December 1882 at Addington Palace, although there was no sign of foul play. The barrister and Evangelical newspaper proprietor Alexander Haldane died of natural causes that same year. Sir George Bowyer, the foreman of the grand jury that brought the murder charge against Maclean, was a Member of Parliament, who died peacefully on 7 June 1883, in his bed at King's Bench Walk. Samuel Gurney (1816–82) was a member of a family of bankers and philanthropists. And Robert Barkley Shaw (1839–79) not only explored the mountainous regions of Central Asia but also served as a British diplomat. Only Dickerson is fictional.

Chichester Parkinson-Fortescue, Baron Carlingford (1823–98), was at the height of his political career in the 1880s, serving as Lord Privy Seal (1881–85), Lord President of the Council (1883–85), and Lord Lieutenant of Essex (1873–92). However, his wife had died in 1879 and, with no children, his titles became extinct upon his death.

Lieutenant-Colonel Sir Edmund Henderson (1821–96) had been Commissioner of Police of the Metropolis since 1869, but by this time his inefficiency meant that he had lost control of his force. He resigned in 1886 after mishandling the infamous Trafalgar Square Riot.

The medical superintendent of Broadmoor was William Orange, who was in charge from 1870 until 1886. The facility's chaplain in the mid-1880s was Thomas Ashe.

The businesses mentioned – the Aerated Bread Company, Garrard, Liberty, Harrods and John Lewis – were all successful at the time. There was no Garraway Club, but its place on what was then known as Exchange Alley is the same as that of the old Garraway's Coffee House, which was first opened in the seventeenth century. The houses where Lonsdale, Galton, Stanley, and Milner lived still exist, although Galton's is much changed after being damaged by a bomb in World War II.